I0676470

The Z Chronicles

WINDRIFT BOOKS

Subscribe to *The Future Chronicles* newsletter for news of upcoming titles in this series, and to be eligible for draws for paperbacks, e-books and more – *http://smarturl.it/chronicles-news*

THE Z CHRONICLES

Edited by Ellen Campbell
(http://ellencampbell.thirdscribe.com)

Cover art and design by Faustino Leonidas Gaitan
(www.fausga.com)

Print and ebook formatting by David Adams
(www.lacunaverse.com)

The Z Chronicles is part of *The Future Chronicles* series produced by Samuel Peralta (www.samuelperalta.com).

978-0-9939832-2-1

THE Z CHRONICLES

STORY SYNOPSES

Vindica (*Ann Christy*)
Vindica is a doomsday shelter built for those who can afford the very best. It represents luxury, as well as safety, for the end of the world. Gordon made it inside when the alarm sounded, with only hours to spare, thinking he would be safe. Outside, the world died, afflicted by its worst nightmares. But inside Vindica's promised paradise, a different sort of nightmare begins.

Six Days (*Theresa Kay*)
The longest anyone has survived a zombie bite before succumbing to the madness is six days. If she's lucky, Sarah has four more days before she goes full-on flesh eater and she needs every single one of them. The life of her infant son depends on her finding an uninfected person willing to take him before she loses her mind. Her husband is dead, her child is depending on her, and the countdown is on.

Kamika-Z (*Christopher Boore*)
Florida summers are hotter than hell. One broken family must face the heat, as sinister objects in the sky begin to fall.

The Fall of the *Percedus* (*Jennifer Foehner Wells*)
Tarn is a sectilian research and development engineer in the field of robotics, dedicated to the design of machines to work on molecular scales. His life's work is to combat the Swarm, his race's implacable enemy. When his sister Pyona comes to him for help he must move from theoretical to practical applications of his work. The outcome may not be the one he expects.

Z Ball (*Will Swardstron*)
The zombie outbreak is in the past. Society is regrouping and getting back to normal, but the sports that once held the public's consciousness are too tame. Enter Z Ball. Vince Lager, star quarterback, is on his way to the Brain Bowl when the truth of Z Ball threatens everything.

Gloria (*Hugh Howey*)
All those fingernails gouging and scrambling against the bark of the tree. Mother and daughter sat above, quietly crying and whispering false hopes, cornered like cats by a pack of dogs. Gloria jostled with the pack beneath the limb. There was no escape, Gloria saw...Not for any of them.

Her (*David Adams*)
Diane, when she was alive, used to wonder: can a ghost and a zombie come from the same person? A zombie was the reanimation of flesh without a soul in it; a ghost was a soul without flesh. It turns out that zombies are real; but ghosts are not, because when you're bitten and turn into a zombie, your consciousness is still in there. But what about the person you were?

The Soulless (*Lesley Smith*)
Monsters exist in all cultures but the *zombie*—a Terran designation referring to re-animated corpses popularised in local media towards the end of the pre-Contact period—is a prevalent one. The Union has its monsters and medical science is often to blame, as is the case with the Soulless.

Hybrid (*Geoffrey Wakeling*)
Attempting to cure the diseased is next to impossible, especially when you're only seventeen. Freya, plunged into a horror-filled world, has the weight of her community's hopes on her shoulders. Infection is spreading. To survive, she'll do whatever it takes.

Free Fall (*Peter Cawdron*)
Jackson is an astronaut conducting a test run in deep space. When he returns home, there's no one to greet him. Earth has fallen silent. Now he must decide—stay in orbit, watching a dead planet roll slowly by beneath his window, or land and fight for life?

Girl, Running (*Kris Holt*)
An athlete and her former lover face a footrace against time as the hordes close in. Can they learn to work together again, or will they perish at the hands of their relentless foes?

The Sin Eater (*Stacy Ericson*)
Continuing an ancient tradition among cottonwoods and picket fences, a young girl consumes sin with cornbread over the flesh of the dead.

The World After (*Angela Cavanaugh*)
Ella and Mark spent their lives working for the Center for Zombie Control. But when Mark is infected, Ella finds that her life hangs in the balance. Now she must escape the CZC and the city, and seek help from an unlikely source. But what she discovers in her search for the cure could change everything.

Curing Khang Yeo (*Deirdre Gould*)
A terrible plague has devastated the human population of the Earth, turning those infected violent and cannibalistic, even toward those they love. At the brink of extinction, a Cure was found. This is one man's story of waking up to realize what he has done.

CONTENTS

Foreword
by Samuel Peralta

"We make up horrors to help us cope with the real ones."

– Stephen King

My brain. There it was, dissected and laid out in horizontal slices.

The screen-saver ran on my computer in a macabre slideshow, a periscope into my translucent skull. Starting from the top, and working its way down just before the spine, the images flickered, one fissured layer after another, like an animation rotoscoped from life.

Weeks before, I'd driven to my appointment with the Magnetic Resonance Imaging unit of a University Avenue hospital. It was early morning, and the multi-level parking lot behind the hospital was empty, quiet – so quiet I could hear my breath. I remember parking the car across from a black Volvo station wagon. As I made my way toward the second-floor exit, the sound of my shoes echoed from the concrete walls.

Later at the MRI unit, shoes off, I let myself lie back on the narrow, sliding bed of the machine that was about to engulf me in its coiled Helmholtz embrace. I closed my eyes and tried to quell my fear, that fear that had trailed me from my home when I'd left that morning, from my office the day before, from the clinic where my doctor had read through the results of my first tomographic scan.

"We don't know," he'd said. "We have to make sure."

Such simple words, so piercing. So there I was – bereft of metal, any armour – under the thin drapery of a hospital gown, wrapped in wool blankets, and injected with a tracer that slowly coursed its way through my blood like an insidious, multi-headed snake. The bed slid forward, and I was in the maw of the beast.

Fear is the zombie that pursues you, mindless, unrelenting, hungry.

It waits for you in the shadows of an empty parking lot as you turn the corner of the stair. It appears when a car careens across the intersection, and you jab your foot at the brake pedal, slipping at its edge. It stalks you in the face of crowds after a lost football game. It grips you when you turn around at the supermarket and suddenly realize your little girl isn't there beside you, and those aisles of canned spaghetti and bathroom tissues and pet food loom like a monstrous labyrinth, where you run and scream her name.

With every *click, click, click, click, whir* the machine devoured my brain, spitting it out into electrons – cortex, cerebellum, medulla oblongata. I would bring it home under my arm, a digital copy captured on disc, to play and re-play at home until I knew by heart that blossoming by the intracranial section near the left cochlear nerve, that intimate shadow of something the physicians hesitated to call by name. A tumor.

And so we invent our monsters – fictions about zombies and the undead, eaters of flesh and soul – in part so we can close the book at night on them, stifle a nervous laugh, and reassure ourselves they are not real. We face our fears by imagining those we can defeat, because in real life we cannot close the book. We cannot defeat all the monsters.

We hope that every time we will come out, whistling, from that parking lot. We hope the brakes slow down the car in time; that the boisterous crowds go home; that our little girl comes running from the other aisle and wraps her arms around us, crying, never again to stray. And we hope we will be set down by the doctor, and that he will nod, point to the shadow on the screen, and say, "Don't worry, we'll beat this."

But fear is the monster, hungry, relentless. And no, we cannot defeat them all.

_____

Samuel Peralta is a physicist and storyteller. As well as his own work, he is the creator and driving force behind the Chronicles *short story anthologies, including the speculative fiction series* The Future Chronicles.

www.amazon.com/author/samuelperalta

Vindica
by Ann Christy

CHAPTER ONE

GORDON PUSHED THE BROOM down the hallway, the debris from last night's party wedging itself into the growing pile in front of him. Another survival party, this one celebrating sixty days since the doors to the shelter closed. Another party he wasn't invited to or allowed to show up at. Another party he was expected to clean up after while the others slept through their fuzzy-headed dreams.

A sequin from someone's dress clung stubbornly to the floor tiles, resisting the angry pushes of his broom. He bent and scraped it up with a fingernail, flicking the silvery disk into the pile of who-knows-what he'd already swept. Given that the shelter was a sealed environment, it was a mystery as to where all this debris came from. However it got here, it collected with alarming rapidity along the corridor edges and it was his job to sweep it each morning.

The hallway was dim and quiet, the lights at half-brightness because of the extra energy used the night before during the festivities. The only ones not sleeping were those who had no right to complain of the poor lighting that made work more difficult than it had to be. People like Gordon.

All because of twenty thousand bucks. Out of two hundred thousand.

"Frigging ten percent short," he complained to no one, his voice gruff and sounding louder than it should in the quiet hallway.

Nothing save the strange breathing sounds of the ventilation responded to his words, not that he expected an answer. He was alone in this passageway. The other "Shorties" — the pejorative given to those like him who had come up short on the price by the time the shelter was needed — were all at work in other parts of the facility. Ramon was probably in the kitchens. Larry and Lewis were trying to do maintenance on the off-cycle air filtration system. And Violet, that bull of a woman, was probably preparing for her run outside the facility to check the solar panels and wind systems.

The other one hundred and twenty-two residents were probably still in their beds or lounging the morning away. Not that morning really mattered anymore except in what choices they were able to order from on the menu of freeze-dried foods.

"Gordon, do you read me?" a scratchy voice asked from the general vicinity of his waist.

He unclipped the radio from his belt and sighed, swallowing down the sudden flood of bitterness that washed up from his stomach and twisted his mouth. "Gordon here."

"Need a clean-up in the Gathering Hall restroom. The ladies," the voice said.

Again Gordon swallowed, this time holding back the angry retort trying to make its way up and out of his mouth. Instead of telling the voice — one that belonged to Paul Crabtree, the organizer of this whole shebang — to stuff it up his ass or clean it himself, he said, "Roger. I'll be done in the Gold passageway in about fifteen minutes."

"No good. I want this cleaned up before anyone gets up. Somebody threw up everywhere," Paul said.

Gordon gripped the radio so tightly that his knuckles went white against the plastic, contrasting sharply with his otherwise work-reddened hands. There was so much information conveyed through that simple answer. It said that Gordon's schedule didn't matter, that his work day would never end, so Paul didn't need to consider it. It said volumes about who mattered and who didn't. And Shorties didn't matter when compared to the puking needs of those that had finished paying off their berth inside Vindica.

"Roger," Gordon said, his voice betraying no hint of the fury and frustration inside.

Slipping the radio back into the clip, Gordon eyed the pile of dirt on the floor in front of him, then looked down the hallway at the dust bunnies drifting along the edges of the corridor as the ventilation kicked on again. He scooped up what he could into the dustpan, knowing that anyone who happened to walk down this passage wouldn't think twice about scattering it again with their careless tread.

A low laugh—the kind a woman makes when a man surprises her in just the right way as she wakes—bled through one of the Gold Pod doors near the spot where Gordon crouched. He winced at the sound. His girlfriend, a more patient soul than he had ever deserved, wasn't here with him. That sleep-deepened laugh reminded him of hers.

He'd never even considered buying a slot for her. He regretted it now, his lack of caring and foresight. If he hadn't finished paying off his slot, he certainly wouldn't have finished paying for two of them, but at least he wouldn't be alone right now. Even working eighteen hours a day left six hours for him to sleep next to her, dreaming of a day when all of this would be over and they could go into the sunshine above once more.

He missed her warmth, the way she was like a furnace when she slept, making him sweat and kick off the covers even in the depths of winter. He missed her crazy smiles and that scar on her lip from some childhood accident he could never remember the details of. He missed the bright white line of it as her lips stretched wide in a grin. He missed the way she smoothed back his hair while they watched TV at night and that she never teased him when he cried during a movie.

He missed all of her.

Sarah.

Sarah who had already barricaded herself into her office when he'd spoken with her on the phone, before the phone finally went silent. And before that final click, the keening screams of the revived dead had grown in volume as the sound of a splintering door sounded out. And her screams.

Sarah, who was probably dead along with a billion others.

Gordon shook his head, pushing those thoughts away because they didn't do any good. They never did any good. After sixty-one days down here below the rocky soil of Kentucky, very little about his old life did him any good to remember anymore. Not his memories of life above, not his degree in chemistry, not the job he'd been so excited to get at ChemGo, and definitely not Sarah.

An image of Sarah's hand on his leg flashed through his memory. Her hand, freckled like the rest of her, patting his leg in time with the music as they drove to the lake that last week before the nanites swept everything else aside. The fleeting sensation of that day overcame him for a moment as he made his way through Gold Level toward the central Atrium. His breath hitched in his chest and the air wheezed weakly past his tightening throat.

A panic attack. He could feel it coming. It wasn't the first.

He sank into one of the deep chairs in the Atrium, lowered his head between his knees, and fumbled for the little packet of pills in his pocket. Pills were the one thing they had plenty of in this shelter that he could also have his fair share of. It wouldn't do for anyone here to succumb to panic, and it was bound to crop up now and then, given their situation. He swallowed the tablet dry, working up a measly slug of spit to help ease it down.

After a few minutes, his breathing began to even out and the shakes subsided enough that he thought he might be able to stand without falling straight over again. His face was wet with sweat and his coveralls stuck to him like he'd put them on without drying off after a shower. What he really needed was to lie down and get a grip, maybe take an hour to let his feelings sort themselves out. But time was another one of the things he wasn't permitted anymore.

Levering himself up from the deep leather took effort, real arm-shaking effort. At the railing surrounding the stairwell, he leaned over the gap and faced the darkness below, letting the breeze that funneled up from the levels cool the sweat on his face and tease loose the last, lingering filaments of anxiety threading through him.

He knew Paul would be radioing him again any minute if he didn't show up, so he pushed away from the railing. The elevator was strictly for emergencies, even for the fully paid up members of the shelter, so he took the stairs, winding upward to the Main Level and the Gathering Hall there.

As he rounded the second spiral, a Bronze Level couple sauntered through the Atrium, heading for the stairs. Both were dressed in swimsuits, the woman wearing a fringed wrap around her hips that swayed as she walked. They were probably headed for the gym and the tiny pool down below the Platinum level.

He hurried his steps, wanting to avoid them if possible. He was meant to have been a Bronze Level resident himself, and he'd met these two during the walk-through tour all residents were permitted. It was supposed to be an annual event, a time when residents could see for themselves that their investment was being maintained and get a feel for where their hefty dues were going. It turned out that they'd only had two such events.

If only the nanites had waited another year, or rather, if only those who created the nanites had waited another year. Just one more year and Gordon would have been paid up in full. Maybe by then he would have seen the light and started paying for a berth for Sarah, if there were any available or for sale by owners that had lost interest. Or maybe he might have seen a different kind of light and started looking for a different group, or even decided to invest in a piece of property for a shelter of his own. Another year and it might be him sauntering across the Atrium without a care in the world except for the desire for a swim to clear his head.

But life hadn't waited that extra year.

"Gordon, where are you? I haven't got all day," Paul said over the radio, his voice quick with impatience.

He clicked the button on the radio without unclipping it, leaning over a little so that his voice would carry toward the microphone, and said, "One level away."

There was no answer. That alone smacked of rebuke or correction.

At the Main Level, the logo of the shelter gleamed under the glow of recessed lights around the perimeter of the room. Inlaid into the shiny brass—brass he and Violet had polished just the other day—the tagline of the project ran in slanted letters that bespoke motion and movement.

Somehow the irony of a dynamic looking script being used for a shelter meant to keep people safe by burying them under the ground had been lost on him before. He'd noticed it only after he struck the bargain that would save his life, but only at the cost of his freedom.

Vindica
Shelter in Style
Luxury at the End of the World

Across the Gathering Hall, past the precisely placed leather couches and chairs that created a deceptively open and casual air, lay the dim hallway that led to the restrooms and the service areas beyond. Paul stood with his back to Gordon looking up at a vast stylized diagram of the Vindica shelter. His posture was that of a person who has gotten what he wants out of life and expects to keep on getting it.

At the squeak of Gordon's work boots on the shiny, marble-tiled floor, Paul turned around. He was wearing clothes more suited to a day at a tennis club than an underground shelter where the sun never reached, but unless he was dressed in a tuxedo, he always looked this way. He seemed to have shirts in an endless array of candy and pastel colors.

Paul's frown as Gordon approached was overdone. His expression was far different from the oily, overly friendly smiles he'd worn while he was selling the units inside Vindica. Even a Bronze Level accommodation—a shared room with four bunks—had cost as much as a house would in some parts of the country, and Paul had worked hard to sell each one. Now, the salesman smiles were gone and it was the frown of an overseer he wore.

"Took you long enough," Paul said, arms crossed and his mouth drawn down, lips thinned in displeasure.

It was too much, that frown. "You keep pulling your face down like that and you'll get wrinkles," Gordon snapped.

And *that* was too much as well.

Paul's immediate look of affront was quickly replaced by a sort of satisfied smile. "If you don't like it down here, you can always leave."

And that was the key to all of this, wasn't it?

Gordon wouldn't leave and both men knew it. He couldn't leave. The world outside these walls was dying and doing it quickly, making a great deal of mess in the process. If he left, he would die just like everyone else. Either that or turn into a monster like everyone who didn't stay dead.

As it was, Gordon had made it to Vindica with only hours to spare before the shelter closed its doors on the last couple of dozen members. And all of those left out had been fully paid up members, too. Paid up status didn't matter once the deadline for closing the big door was past. You got to Vindica in time or you got left outside.

If he'd ever been tempted to call Paul on his bluff and walk out of that airlock, watching the couple that showed up on day fifteen had put that temptation entirely to rest. They had banged ineffectually on the blast doors for hours, yelling and screaming into the camera placed high on the outside structure. They'd banged long enough for the noise to draw some of the afflicted.

And once those revived dead people had shown up, it was all over but the blood and screaming. The man—Gordon couldn't remember his name and didn't want to look it up later—had emptied his gun into the first two. One of those two had gone down with that bizarre, stuttering jerkiness while the nanites inside worked to fix their host's body, but the others had plunged onward toward their prey. And after a few minutes, long before the others had finished their meal of the two Vindica members, the downed one had stopped jerking, sat up, and made it to the pile of bloody bits in time for dessert.

They had been Gold Level members.

Gordon saw it all from his watch station at the security monitors. It had been a horror played out in vivid color. What had been worse was the clinical way Paul examined the pair through the monitors, the glow of the screens picking out the glints of intellectual curiosity in his eyes. Interest he'd had plenty of, but of concern or compassion there had been not the slightest hint.

So, no, Gordon wouldn't be walking out and Paul knew it.

"What happened to every member contributing to the operation of the shelter, Paul?" Gordon asked. It was a serious question. He held up his work-roughened hands. Bright red cracks seamed his palms and fingers from too much time spent wet and cold as he scrubbed, washed, and shined the vast facility. "Was this your plan all along?"

Paul didn't so much as bat an eyelash at the first question, but the second one stiffened his spine. He apparently didn't mind using people as slaves, but he certainly did mind anyone thinking he *planned* to use them that way.

"It's not my fault you didn't pay off your berth. Everyone else did. Should they pay for you as well? As I see it, you owe them your keep here," Paul said.

"Really? This place was supposed to take a few hours of work each day from every resident to operate. How exactly is it that five people now do the work of one hundred and fifty?"

Paul snorted. "Don't exaggerate. The work requirements were simply a contract number, a just-in-case agreement. It doesn't take nearly that much labor to run this place or *you* couldn't do it. And, if your work is good, eventually you'll be paid up. Try to think of it that way and you'll be less unhappy."

Gordon examined Paul's face, looking for that hint of something that would tell him the other man knew what he was saying was complete crap, but it wasn't there. Paul actually believed his own hype. That chilled Gordon right down to his bones.

It also made him very sure that what he planned to do was the right thing to do.

"Besides," Paul continued, warming to the subject, "others do help out. It's not just the five of you. That's another exaggeration and it makes it very hard to take any complaints seriously."

Gordon nodded, not in agreement, but because he understood that Paul was guarding his carefully constructed mental justification for what amounted to enslavement of five paying—though not completely paid up—members of the shelter. He would have had to build that construct to sleep at night, Gordon supposed.

"You've got Steel Level members taking a turn on the security monitors and taking readings on the systems up top. When is the last time anyone else picked up a broom or a mop besides a Shortie?" Gordon asked, but he could tell his words weren't even sinking in. That glazed look of disinterest had fallen over Paul's features and he glanced down at his watch as if he had some important meeting to go to.

"Like I said, you can leave," Paul said and waved a hand down the hallway toward the bathroom where some drunken woman's puke needed cleaning up.

Gordon stepped past Paul, reached for the knob on the supply closet door, and said, "Yes, you did say that."

Paul didn't see the little smile on Gordon's face as he walked away.

CHAPTER TWO

"Are you sure?" Gordon asked again as he adjusted and checked the biohazard suit encasing Violet's enormous frame.

She turned around at the pat on her shoulder so that Gordon could check the front once more, and he saw her deadpan expression though the plastic face shield.

"I'm sure," she said, her voice sounding a little muffled and far away inside her protective cocoon of plastic.

Gordon looked closely at her face while he checked the seal around her face shield, making sure the tape around her air supply was perfect. She didn't seem even the slightest bit nervous or hesitant. Violet acted like she was going outside for nothing more dangerous than a trip to the corner market for a carton of milk on a normal Sunday morning.

She caught him looking and seemed to recognize that he needed something more. Violet's gloved hand came up and rested on his forearm, pulling his hand away from her hood as she did. "I'm sure. What's going on here isn't right and leaving won't change a thing. It'll just be someone else who takes our place, probably someone from Steel."

He nodded, knowing she was right. Steel Level, the least expensive of the accommodations offered here in Vindica, had members housed in two large open bay rooms, one for men and the other for women. While very nicely appointed, there was no escaping the fact that they were in a different class than the Platinum, Gold or Silver Levels. Even the rooms in Bronze came with perks not enjoyed by the Steel residents. Steelie food was served lunch-room style, with no menu of choices they could select from, and while hearty and wholesome, it wasn't fancy.

And yet, Steelies treated the Shorties no different than anyone else. Some of them were worse. Gordon thought it might be because they were so low on the ladder, so low that they needed to artificially extend the distance between the Shorties and themselves.

Anyone who could justify what had been done to the Shorties would have very little trouble justifying one more step in that direction and take a few Steelies for the hard labor if there were no Shorties.

It was already moving that direction, really. There had never been any intention to have room service or housekeeping inside Vindica. That had been right up front during the sales pitches. Everyone would have to maintain their quarters in a livable condition. It hadn't taken long for that to change once they had Shorties.

First it was the Platinum Level, then after a few weeks, the Gold Level got that same privilege on a weekly basis. When the burden simply became too much for the five Shorties, Steelies had been put onto the roster for security monitoring and technical rounds. How much longer before even that pretense fell away and they became nothing more than Shorties that slept on another level?

Violet squeezed his forearm, bringing his eyes back up to her face and disrupting his reverie. She smiled at him and squeezed again, letting him know with that small gesture that she understood and that they were in agreement. As always, the change in her face that simple expression made startled Gordon and made him unable to look away or do anything other than return her smile.

When Violet smiled, it transformed her face entirely. She was still six inches taller than he and had shoulders as wide as a pro football player's, but when she smiled, she was breathtaking. Her curiously delicate nose, sharp cheekbones, and large, dark eyes with lashes so long they looked false, were matched by lips as generously proportioned as her biceps. She reminded Gordon of Sophia Loren during her prime. Only taller. A lot taller.

Lowering his arm and breaking contact, he gave a small head shake, and asked, "You remember where they were? The targets?"

"Precisely. Approximately one hundred and fifty yards southwest of the solar array, near the gully," Violet answered.

"Exactly," Gordon confirmed and picked up her tool box. Made of plastic so that it would survive the decontamination process without rusting, he opened it and showed her the bag folded neatly inside. Next to it lay a folding saw, a funnel, and the small hatchet he'd added to the assorted tools. And finally, several pint-sized plastic bottles with lids. "And the box is bigger so that the…uh…"

"Objects?" Violet offered as his voice faltered and he couldn't find the word.

"Yeah, objects," Gordon answered. He could feel himself going pale and a vague lightheadedness came on at the mere thought of the "objects".

"And the sealant?" Violet asked, poking the box with fingers made awkward by the thick plastic of her gloves and the three pairs of nitrile gloves beneath.

Gordon plucked up a tube from the open box and said, "Here. I took the cap off already and just plugged it with some silicon. You don't need to unscrew it, just yank the plug right off." He put the tube back and pulled out a small bottle. "And spray this all over the bag once you've got it sealed. This stuff will kill anything and creates static. That should deactivate any nanites."

Violet nodded, making her suit crinkle and crackle. Then she looked up at the clock in the ready room and said, "Time to go. You know they're watching. Let's not give them any reason to wonder what we're up to."

"Don't worry. So far we haven't done anything we haven't done before," he answered, careful not to obey the impulse to look behind him at the camera mounted on the wall.

Violet took the toolbox from his hand and gave him a wink. "Then we're good. Ready?"

"Ready," Gordon answered and opened the airlock for her to enter. He sealed the door behind her, then turned around to the camera and gave it a thumbs-up. There was a microphone, but Gordon had done his part and made sure it was broken before today's events. They couldn't hear anything said inside the ready room or airlock up at the security monitoring station.

The speaker worked fine, even if the microphone didn't, and Gordon could hear Paul talking in the background as Ramon spoke. "Door seal confirmed. Outside is clear. Go ahead."

Gordon slapped the big button and a red light immediately began flashing over the door, the *thunk* of the locks reverberating loudly in the entry room. He couldn't open the door now even if he wanted to. Vindica was designed for safety, of that there was no doubt.

He watched the airlock brightening as the outer door opened. Sunlight streamed in as the door retracted in a widening rectangle of beautiful, yellow light. For a moment, Gordon wanted that light badly and his fingers tightened on the door's wheel, the temptation to spin it strong. It wouldn't have budged because of the locks, but the temptation was there all the same.

Violet stepped over the sill and he saw her glance down and to her left, no doubt looking at the scattered remains of the couple that had banged on the door for so long before being torn apart and eaten. He'd watched their rapid dissolution on the security monitors, the animals taking whatever meat was left. And the heads, with their clacking jaws and moving eyes. He'd watched them, too.

He'd wanted to move them, maybe smash the heads so that the people could go to their rest, but Paul had vetoed the idea, saying they provided a deterrent to anyone who might find their shelter. As disgusting as that statement was, Gordon knew it was true.

But he also understood that it was meant to be a deterrent against any of the Shorties leaving, as well. After all, it had been made clear they wouldn't be leaving with a biohazard suit or weapons, only the clothes they came in with or had stored in the facility. Nothing else. They would have to step over the contaminated bodies if they wanted to leave. They would have to make their way out of the Kentucky woods in their street clothes and weaponless. That would be death and everyone knew it.

Violet was out of sight — a final flash of moving blue plastic — in less than a minute. Gordon turned to hold up his thumb for the camera again.

"Personnel clear. Closing outer door," Ramon called through the speaker.

She would be gone for an hour or so. Every month the maintenance and checks on the solar and wind systems had to be done. Cameras gave them the ability to see if anything obvious happened, but cameras couldn't replace good old-fashioned labor with a wrench and a broom.

Gordon turned away from the door and began to prepare for her return. He didn't need the same gear she wore, but he needed a biohazard suit for the second part of her decontamination. He took his time, avoiding the buildup of heat and sweat inside the plastic suit by delaying the donning of it. Instead, he arranged his brushes, sponges and all the other gear he would need, and tried not to think about what she was doing outside.

Ramon knew his part in this. He would need to make sure Paul found little of interest inside the security room and wandered off while Violet was outside. He would also need to give Violet the signal through her suit radio, and be sure that no one saw her wander off course or leave the equipment array. There were a lot of pieces to keep shuffled, but their plan was doable.

Violet was a military engineer and Ramon a security expert, or rather, that's what they were before the nanites. Like Gordon, they were now janitors and errand boys, but it was always a mistake to underestimate people, and Paul had done precisely that. As had the others who formed the power-clique inside Vindica.

Once they'd begun to treat the Shorties as servants, they'd begun to see them that way as well.

Ramon's voice startled him when it came through. "We're clear."

Gordon let out a breath he hadn't realized he'd been holding, his heart thudding and a wave of heat rushing through his belly.

Oh, god, what have I started?

Time dragged, but also seemed to move too quickly. By the time Ramon called out that Violet was a hundred meters from the airlock, Gordon was dripping with anxiety sweat inside his biohazard suit and his face shield was fogging up around the edges.

He pressed his shielded face to the thick pane of glass set into the inner airlock door and watched her take those last few steps. Was it his imagination or did the toolbox seem more weighty, her shoulder just a little lower on that side? It had to be imagination. She was as strong as an ox and it would be what...maybe eight pounds of extra weight? Ten? Certainly, it could be no more than ten pounds of weight.

It was hard to process her back into the shelter as if everything were normal. It took almost all his willpower not to shrink away from the toolbox she handed him, still dripping from the antiseptic shower she took during first-stage decontamination. As he scrubbed first her suit, then the toolbox, his anxiety grew. He could feel that tightening in his chest that signaled the rise of another panic attack.

She must have sensed it too, because she took the scrub brush gently from his hand and surreptitiously squeezed his fingers in reassurance as she did. Gordon closed his eyes for a moment and when he opened them, she smiled at him in sympathy through the drops of moisture on her face shield. He felt better for it. She'd already done the hardest part. He just needed to keep it together for a little while longer.

He opened the toolbox and dunked everything inside the box into the bucket of solution, including the large bag, now sealed and bulging with its contents. He tried not to flinch at the squishy feeling of the bag and the intermittent rounded edges of the bottles that he felt as he rolled the bag in the bucket of solution. Violet pressed a plastic-covered leg lightly into his back as she blocked the camera's view for that critical moment.

Once inside the entry room, they processed just as they normally would, each of them stripping down and showering one more time, bathing in the UV light and storing the biohazard suits just as they had done for the walk on day thirty-one when it had been Gordon who went outside.

When Ramon's voice gave them the all clear, Violet grabbed the bag from the toolbox and tucked it under the spare clothing she had brought for just this purpose.

Paul was waiting for them when they exited into the Entry Level, where each resident had processed in that first day. Since then, it was only the Shorties and Paul that visited this utilitarian level. Here there were no marble floors or deep sofas, just easily decontaminated tiles and lots of plastic.

"What took you so long?" Paul asked straight away. There was no thank you or any other nicety, only the demands of an owner toward the ones that were owned.

Violet didn't so much as blink at his tone. She simply shifted her hoodie and sweatshirt a little in her arms, pushed back her sweat dampened hair, and said, "Mud. The rains made the ground soft and I had to be careful. Plus, there was a lot of dirt on the lower panels."

There was no suspicion in Paul's expression, only annoyance. Maybe he'd missed a card game.

"Fine, fine. Carry on," he said, turning to leave.

At the stairwell, Paul stopped and turned back to them, his eyes in shadow so that Gordon could see only deep pits where they should be. He repressed a shudder, but only with effort.

"Someone reported a rattle in one of the ventilation fans on Silver. Near pod S4. It's keeping them awake. See to it first thing," Paul said, then turned back to the stairs. When no reply came, he paused again, looking back.

"I'll see to the ventilation," Violet said and Gordon felt a hysterical laugh beginning deep in his belly. His fists bunched inside the pockets of his coveralls as he tried to hold the laugh inside.

With a grunt, Paul continued down the stairs, his head finally lowering out of sight. Violet waited a tick after he disappeared, then softly said, "Oh, I'll take care of the ventilation all right."

Gordon looked at her, the second and third and fourth thoughts that had been plaguing him making him want to snatch the bag out from under the clothes and run screaming for the airlock to toss it out. Then the radio on his belt squawked and Paul's voice called for Ramon to turn over the security monitor watch to a Steelie and report to Platinum for housekeeping duties.

All those second thoughts faded immediately and Gordon looked up at Violet's beautiful, but hard, face.

"No time like the present," she said.

CHAPTER THREE

That evening the residents of Platinum, Gold, and Silver celebrated Paul's birthday. Baby lettuce grown under the grow lights in the atriums peeked out from beneath an array of brightly colored baby vegetables Ramon had harvested. Tiny radishes, beets, and carrots that would have provided fresh food when full-sized decorated the salad plates like little gems.

And over it all, a very special salad dressing made by Violet containing a very special ingredient.

Gordon tried not to flinch when he set the plates down at the table in the Precious Metals dining hall. He had to try harder not to flinch when he saw someone take a bite.

The special ingredient made it into most of the meal that evening. Only the cake was spared, since none of the Shorties could figure out how to hide the taste of old blood in such a sugary confection. Gordon didn't even want to think about the roast with its tiny nuggets of spiced "pork."

As they washed dishes after the meal was concluded, hearing the last lingering traces of satisfied laughter leave the dining room for a bit of dancing in the Gathering Hall, Violet seemed utterly at ease. Inside, Gordon felt like his guts were twisting into knots.

"Well?" he finally asked, accepting a thoroughly scrubbed roasting pan from her hands to dry.

"Well, what?" she returned, reaching for the next dirty pan to wash.

"Do they all have nanites inside them now?" he asked.

For a moment she didn't answer him, only continued scrubbing. When Gordon didn't turn away, she sighed, turned on the water, and then bent down toward him. She said, "Most of those people already have nanites, I'd bet. That's what rich people do. The ones for heart attacks, cleaning arteries, or whatever else could be gotten on the black market pretty easily. You know they got them. I was even thinking of ordering some of the knock-offs from China."

"Wait," Gordon interrupted. "Then why didn't you say that before? If we didn't need to do this, then why did we?"

Violet winked at him and said, "Just in case some of them didn't have nanites. And, who knows if you need certain kinds, or maybe you need a bunch of different ones inside to make it happen. Who knows? The more we stack the deck the better. Am I right?"

Gordon looked at Violet's cold smile, so utterly devoid of guilt at what they had just done, and he shuddered. She laughed and returned to her scrubbing.

"How long do we wait?" he asked.

"Let's give it a week. We'll just see if there's anyone worth saving in the meantime. Okay?"

All Gordon could do was nod and accept the skillet she handed him.

CHAPTER FOUR

"You got enough water?" Larry asked Ramon for the tenth time.

"Yes!" Ramon hissed into the dim light of the Supply Level corridor. "There's enough for three days, easy. Stop fussing. Just make sure you get your packs and we'll be fine."

Larry's flashlight flared to life, making the others squint in the sudden light, and then swept across the row of packs in the corridor, hesitating over the two labeled with his name and the biohazard suit bagged in front of it.

"Put out that light! You're ruining my night vision," Violet hissed and smacked his wrist down.

"Lewis, you and Ramon go ahead and get to security. Relieve the Steelie on duty and wait for us," Gordon said, trying to get them back on track.

Lewis reached for his pack, but Violet stopped him with a restraining hand. "No, we'll bring them. The security cameras."

"Right, sorry," Lewis said, his face gleaming and pale in the dim light.

Violet tapped her watch as they departed and said, "We've got fifteen minutes. Get me suited up."

Gordon handed the tape to Larry, more to keep him busy than because he needed a helper, and held open the suit for Violet to step into. As he tugged it up her muscular frame, she rested a hand on his shoulder until it was time to put her arms into the sleeves. As much as Gordon loved Sarah — even now, knowing she was gone — his heart gave a lurch as Violet's hand lifted from his shoulder. He wondered if she would ever touch him, or anyone else, ever again. Would they die or would they make it?

Violet was going to be wearing two suits, the first layer the same as the ones Gordon and the others would don. Lighter and not as protective, it could be worn for as long as the person inside could tolerate it or the batteries inside that ran the air filter lasted. Over that, she would wear the suit she'd worn outside earlier, with its bottled air and thick plastic. It was more than a little difficult to slide the second suit over the first, the squeak of plastic on plastic loud in the room. But they managed.

Once Larry started applying the tape around each seam in the top suit, he seemed to calm down, his hands sure and quick at his work. Both men then checked Violet's suit while she closed her eyes against the glare of their flashlights.

"You're good," Gordon said and clicked off the light. He looked at the watch Violet had removed from her wrist and said, "Fourteen minutes gone."

She nodded inside her crackling suits and said, "Grab the gear and go. I'll wait ten minutes."

Larry's gulp was loud in the passageway, but his hands were steady as he loaded the packs onto the janitorial cart emptied just for this occasion. Inside the service elevator, Gordon looked back as the doors slid closed and saw Violet swathed in her plastic suit, her face nothing more than a glare behind her plastic face shield. She stood there alone, her hand raised in a wave and a lumpy bag at her feet, the door to the ventilation machine room door standing open behind her. Then the doors closed and they were on their way.

CHAPTER FIVE

Lewis and Ramon met them at the entry room door and each of them donned their bio-hazard suits quickly. These weren't suits like Violet's, but rather the lesser suits stashed in each of the pods within Vindica, meant to be donned quickly in case of a temporary breach. They were the same as Violet's inner suit. Not the best, but good enough. The suits would keep the smell of their human bodies inside so as to not attract the monsters, and keep any nanites outside of their bodies if they were airborne. Gordon hoped they would, anyway.

The tiny air filters and fans inside the hoods clicked on one after the other, disrupting their ability to hear each other and leaving each in their own world of white noise. They would have to speak loudly to hear each other, and Gordon was reluctant to do so.

Without the need for tape or heavy racks for air supply bottles, they were finished quickly and then helped each other to hoist the heavy packs, also wrapped in plastic, onto their backs. It was the work of a minute to hang the add-on packs to the various clips until each of them looked like some odd misshapen apparition or bizarre, humpbacked animal colored an improbable bio-hazard blue.

The digital clock on the wall seemed to blink more slowly than normal, the shift from one number to the next happening with far less frequency than it should. Gordon waited and watched each blink of the red lights as if they might suddenly change rhythm and shoot forward in time.

At last, the entry room door swung open and Violet stepped inside, another bulky apparition to join the crowd. But unlike the rest of them, she was no longer entirely blue. Wide smears of deep red crisscrossed her belly and chest, and her arms were covered with more red streaks all the way to her elbows.

Gordon stared at the vivid red color in the dim light of a single LED light on the wall. The others must have been just as captured by the sight, because all four of the other men had gone utterly still. Violet looked down at herself at their glances, but rather than be horrified at her appearance, she merely shrugged.

"Those livers and spleens were slippery bastards," she said, her voice betraying a hint of humor not at all in keeping with their situation.

"Oh my god," Larry croaked. Even over the fan in his hood Gordon could hear the retching noises.

"Don't puke, for heaven's sake!" Violet demanded, and pushed through them to get to the airlock door. Without further ado, she entered the open airlock door. When no one followed her, she beckoned them forward with an impatient gesture.

Ramon recovered first. He grabbed Violet's pack and pushed Larry forward into the airlock. Gordon gave Lewis a similar little shove and entered last, squeezing in with difficulty as they all shifted to accommodate five people bulked up with packs in the small space.

It took a bit of further shoving and squeezing for Violet to get her hand up to the emergency release box. Once she pulled that cover off and hit the lever, all hell would break loose. Sirens and red lights would wake the entire population of Vindica immediately. They would need to hurry and there was no going back once she hit that button.

Of course, there really was no going back *now*. It was already too late. They couldn't remove their suits and pretend none of this had happened anyway. Yes, it was far, far too late for second thoughts. Even now, while the people inside Vindica slept, red mist filled with nanites was spewing forth from the ventilation, covering them in their beds. And very soon, no more than ten minutes from now, that same ventilation would shut down forever in an explosion just big enough to destroy the big fans. No one in the airlock could possibly get down there fast enough to stop what they had started.

And then?

And then someone would die and it would begin inside Vindica just as it began all over the world. And there would be more death. Some would escape it, but not many.

Violet's hand paused over the cover, perhaps waiting for anyone to object, or maybe just so that she could suck a deep breath to steel herself for what would come next. In one quick move she ripped the cover down and palmed the big red button beneath.

As expected, red lights and sirens split the quiet, no doubt ripping everyone from their sleep and directly into panic. The door slid open, but it seemed to move so very slowly to Gordon, even though he knew it opened at the same speed as it had last time.

Violet was nearly pushed out of the airlock, stumbling a little over the sill at the pressure of the bodies behind her. She recovered and had the presence of mind to turn and hold out a hand to help the next person out. Ramon hoisted her pack as if to help her don it once they were all out, but she held up a hand for him to wait and stepped over toward the decaying body parts lying in a tangle near the door.

She hoisted one of the heads up in one big fist, the parts of the body that were still attached falling away and hitting the ground with wet slaps as she did. Then she bent for the other. Both of these she threw into the airlock with two underhand tosses that looked deceptively easy to Gordon's eyes. Slime splattered the walls of the airlock and Gordon almost lost his dinner.

He looked to Violet, the question of why on his lips. She had to know that once they closed the airlock door, the decontamination would commence and all that infected fluid would drain away in a sea of antiseptic solution.

She must have read the question there, because she smiled. It was a smile that looked ominous and very satisfied at the same time. "They won't open that airlock until they have absolutely no choice. You can bet on that. No one will come after us for a while," she said.

He realized she was right. She hadn't just bought them time, she'd bought them a clean escape with that simple toss of two rotten heads. This was particularly true since both of those heads were swimming with the nanites that were still killing the world. And especially so since both heads were even now blinking owlishly and clacking their teeth as their jaws rhythmically opened and closed.

A sudden noise from beyond the airlock drew Gordon's eyes. Paul's panicked face was framed in the circular window. How he'd gotten up here so quickly, Gordon couldn't guess, but it didn't matter. Paul's wide, round eyes darted from the decayed heads in the airlock to the people outside so rapidly it was almost funny.

And as Paul pressed his face to the window, he left a light red smear. The red mist had gotten to him already, the nanite-filled blood sprayed for good measure. Their former overseer banged on the thick window with his fists, screaming words none of them could hear and wouldn't have listened to anyway.

Gordon would have liked to think of something pithy or cutting to say, but really, all he could think about was how deeply Paul was breathing and what was now circulating in the air inside Vindica. It was Violet—of course it was—who rallied. She raised her gloved hands and extended both her middle fingers. Even as she sent back that one, eloquent response, the airlock timer ran out and the door slid shut with a subdued *thud*, marking their passage from protected to unprotected.

"That's that, then," Ramon said over the sound of the fans.

"Yeah, let's move. Let's get her out of that suit and get some distance between us and this place. Just in case," Lewis said.

No one argued and they set to work, carefully removing the outer suit from Violet's body and inspecting the inner suit to be sure it maintained its integrity. All of them were particularly careful to fold down the chest and arms of the outer suit so that no one came into contact with the infected fluids and blood smeared all over her. They bagged the suit and dragged it along behind them.

Through the single face shield, Gordon could now see Violet much better. She was red with exertion and sweat streaked her face from the heavy suits. "You okay?" he asked.

She gave him a thumbs-up and hoisted her pack to her back now that she was free of the oxygen bottle and rack.

"Lights?" Gordon asked. Their original plan called for red lights only, but that had been made under the assumption that someone from inside might actually come after them. That wasn't at all likely now.

Violet answered him from just a few feet away, her bulk a surprising comfort to Gordon. He was glad she was staying close. "No lights except the red lamps. No need to advertise our location. There could be some of those zombie things around."

That settled, they set off, walking the rough dirt road with cautious steps under their heavy packs and hot suits. The summer night wasn't overly warm, but it didn't have to be. Gordon knew he wouldn't last long in the suit. Eventually, he would have to shrug it off and take his chances, staying clear of any person except the people he was with, hoping to keep free of the nanites. He didn't want to die, but if he did, he didn't want to come back as a monster either.

When they reached the path that branched off to the solar panels and wind turbines, Lewis asked, "Should we disconnect their power?"

Gordon hadn't ever considered that, and his first reaction was a sort of vengeful glee, but then he thought twice and said, "No. We don't want to make it so they have to come out, and that would definitely do the trick. They might not notice the ventilation for a while, but they will notice if the lights go out."

Ramon trudged on ahead, tossing back the words, "Too bad. That would have been fun," over his shoulder as he did.

A little further up the road — now no more than a kilometer from the main highway that ran through this region of defunct towns, shuttered factories, and some of the most beautiful country the nation had to offer—Gordon couldn't stop himself from shining his flashlight down an incline to the little clearing he had seen on his first trip out.

Just as before, he saw the two tents, one of them now half collapsed and both shredded from the elements or animals. He saw the scattered supplies and the bright reflection of a hot-pink bike frame lying on its side with a trailer still upright behind it.

Of the bodies, he saw nothing.

"Turn the light off," Violet said.

He did, and realized he was now completely blind in the darkness. The red lights had seemed bright until he ruined it with his flashlight. "Sorry. I can't see for shit now."

"No one can," Ramon said dryly.

"Is this where we're going to ditch the weapons?" Larry asked. He back was bowing under the weight of all the extra bags added to it.

"Yeah, right down there. We need to throw them as close to those tents as we can," Gordon said, tapping Lewis on the shoulder. When the other man turned around, Gordon began fumbling for the clips, but couldn't see.

"I think we're going to have to turn on the lights again to do this," he said.

"Dammit," Ramon muttered, but his flashlight came to life anyway. He pointed it at the ground, but even so, Gordon felt highlighted and exposed.

They all took turns unclipping the bags from each other's packs, ending up with a pile at their feet. Violet hefted the first of them and gave it an impressive throw, arcing the bag over the sloping ground to land mere feet from one of the tents with a loud clatter.

There was no way she could see their faces through the glare of light on the plastic face shields, but their still and awed stances must have been apparent, because she laughed. "It's only guns, guys."

Ramon whistled his appreciation at her muscle and handed her another sack.

When the last of the sacks was gone, they all stood and looked at the scattered blue bags. Lewis said, "We got all the guns except for the ones we left in Steel. We left them three guns and one box of ammo."

Larry laughed, but it was a bitter laugh.

"What?" Gordon asked.

"Well, think about it. After all of that, the only people left in Vindica that have any way to defend themselves are the lowest ones left on their social ladder. That's going to be interesting," he said.

Gordon supposed it would be interesting, assuming there was enough time left for the occupants of Vindica for things to get interesting at all. Once the ventilation went off, how quickly would the oxygen deplete? Would those who paid the most and whose pods were at the lowest levels of the shelter run out of air first? Would they even figure out the ventilation was off before it was too late to leave?

The flashlight clicked off, and once more Gordon found himself completely blind in the darkness.

"Take a minute to get your night vision back," Violet said, then trudged back to stand near Gordon. She leaned down a little to peer into his face and asked, "You okay?"

"What did you do with the bodies?" he asked. He didn't think he would be able to let that question go until he knew the answer. He had to know. It wasn't as if he knew the people, because he didn't. But what he started with his idea and what Violet had finished with her bloody gloves was brutal in so many ways that it needed an accounting for in his heart, if nowhere else.

He didn't so much hear her sigh as feel it through their face shields when she leaned over and touched hers to his. "I put them inside the tent, the bigger one, so they could be together." She paused a moment, then added, as if embarrassed, "And I said a prayer for them."

Gordon nodded. He wasn't a religious man and he hadn't known that Violet was religious either, but he appreciated the gesture. He cleared his throat and asked, "And you took all four sets?"

This time he did hear her sigh, but he also heard the sadness in that simple human sound.

"No," she said. "I only took from the two adults. You were right about them. They had tied themselves to trees so they couldn't go anywhere when they came back. I just smashed in their heads and it was done. Besides, two sets of organs were enough.

The kids, well, they hadn't come back. Not infected. I just laid them out together in the tent and left them be."

Again, he nodded, thinking back to the lumpy bag that felt so squishy to the touch. Would the dosing of their food with the blood and organs ensure they were infected? Had they really just killed all of those people?

Gordon hoped so.

Anyone whose first act at the end of the world was to enslave another survivor deserved nothing less.

He reached out and squeezed Violet's glove with his own, letting her know he was ready. They both turned back to the road and the others started walking again as well.

"So, South Carolina. You sure it's safe there?" Larry asked.

Violet, a military engineer with contacts seemingly everywhere, said, "Yep. I heard the base was open for military to shelter in right before the call for Vindica members came. I was going to go there if Vindica didn't get its act together. All we have to do is get there."

Ramon grunted from up ahead, "But South Carolina? Why there? There are bases everywhere."

"It's not really a shelter so much as a safe zone, I think. Something to do with the military hospital there. They made the nanites there. Plus, the ocean is close by and that's the best barrier there is. Lots of people were going there. All we have to do is get there and stay nanite free and alive until we do. And if no one is there, we go on to the coast, find a boat, maybe go to one of the islands."

Gordon had his doubts, but really, what else was there to do? They could hole up, wait this thing out, but their odds weren't good given how bad things had gotten so quickly. South Carolina. He'd never been before.

He wondered what the beaches there were like this time of year. He hoped they were warm and sunny.

And he hoped zombies couldn't swim.

A Word from Ann Christy

"Vindica" takes place in the *Between Life and Death* world, but it's a stand-alone story. I love zombie stuff — TV, books, movies, you name it — but I do get tired of it always being a virus that spreads too fast for reality. In the *Between* world, I decided to take what I know of physics, epidemiology, and nano-tech and try to create a sort-of-zombie situation in which the boundaries of reality weren't strained beyond belief. I used nanites because, let's face it, they're cool. As a bonus, they are also ripe for this sort of thing if we're not careful in the near future. I hope you enjoyed the story.

Ann Christy is a recently retired navy commander and secret science fiction writer. She lives by the sea under the benevolent rule of her canine overlords and assorted unruly family members.

She's the author of the popular Silo 49 *series set in the* WOOL *universe, assorted novels and a slew of stories. Her latest work, the* Between Life and Death *series, is a new and entirely novel take on the zombie genre that is turning out to be equally popular with teens and adults. It includes* The In-Betweener, Forever Between, *and the exciting – and very satisfying – conclusion,* Between Life and Death.

You can find out more about Ann Christy and read extended sneak peeks of her books at http://www.annchristy.com.

Six Days
by Theresa Kay

THERE ISN'T MUCH LEFT OF ME. I'm not talking about my body, the outer shell that sloughs off a little more each day, but my actual self. My mind. What makes me…well, me. There isn't much of that left. Little by little I'm fading away and soon there will be nothing left to propel my rotting corpse but blind instinct and hunger.

They call it the Zombie virus. It's a slow moving one, but it was enough to knock out half the world's population before people stopped trying to cure it and instead holed up to avoid it. Some cower behind tall walls in city strongholds and some, like me, chose the more rural life. If you're cautious and make smart choices, the infected are easy to avoid. But all it takes is one stupid decision, one misstep and one single bite…

From the time you're first infected with the virus, you have two, maybe three, days until the symptoms begin. Your body temperature drops. Your eyes turn completely red and become increasingly light sensitive. Your skin pigment fades and you're left a pasty white color and, in the later stages, layers of your skin actually peel off. The joints in your already stiff limbs start to freeze up, so all you can manage by the end is a slow shuffle walk. And those are just the physical symptoms.

The mental symptoms, in my opinion, are even worse. Your mind sticks in there for a while as your body deteriorates around it. Then comes confusion, blackouts, and strange urges. Urges to kill. Urges to eat. Eventually, the mind loses the battle against the baser instincts of the body and checks out while what's left of you gorges itself on human flesh — at least, I hope the mind checks out by that time.

The longest I've heard of anyone staying...coherent... from the day you begin the process of transitioning into a cold, pale, red-eyed monster is six days. I'm on day two and, for now, I'm in control.

At least I think I am.

I have to be.

My eight-month-old son's life depends on it.

DAY TWO

I squint against the sunlight that has slithered its way between the boards over the window and roll to the side. Time to get up. Benjamin's hungry. His cries play in my ears while I fumble around trying to rise from the dingy mattress. It takes much longer than yesterday.

Once I'm on my feet, I massage my right elbow for a moment then grit my teeth and force it to bend. I repeat the process with my left. Not too bad this morning. I got them almost to ninety degrees, much better than the pathetic range of motion in my knees and hips. Next come my shoulders. They've gotten worse. I can't get my arms parallel to the floor, and my left one barely gets a foot from my side. I guess any overhead movement is out. Maybe I should try to sleep with my arms extended? Though, I don't know that it'd be much more help-ful for my shoulders to freeze in that position.

I shuffle toward the corner where Benjamin's standing and gripping the edge of the playpen with his chubby little fingers. He's still crying, but when he sees me coming he gives me a near toothless smile and lifts his arms up.

Picking him up has become an awkward ma-neuver, with me bending my knees slightly and slipping my hands under his arms and then kind of tilting him to the side so I can use my shoulder to steady him as I lift. Thank goodness I wasn't infect-ed when he was any younger, before he could at least stand up on his own, or there'd be no way I'd be able to get him out of the playpen.

He giggles as I sit him on the edge of a table. I steady him with one hand and use the other to pull a section of ripped up bed sheet closer. Then, with one hand behind his head, I lower him to lie on his back. Somehow, I get his makeshift diaper changed and then hoist him back up into my arms.

Babbling and cooing, he keeps trying to shove his fingers in my mouth as I carry him across the room. I keep my lips pressed tightly together and turn my face away. The virus is spread through saliva and I'm not taking any chances. He makes that sputtering about to cry noise and grabs for my hair instead. God, I hope another chunk doesn't fall out in his hand like it did yesterday. Ugh.

At this point, I don't understand how he still looks at me with nothing but adoration in his eyes. Yes, I'm still his mom, but I've caught my reflection a few times lately and it scares *me*.

I feed him some watered down baby food and choke down a protein bar myself. The food's getting low and, besides that, no one's come through here for a few days now. I can't leave my son with just anyone, but I have to leave him with *someone*. Looks like today is the day we head toward the city, something I've been hoping to avoid, though the voice in the back of my head is cursing me for not doing it sooner.

There's a good reason Devin and I settled out here instead of in one of the city strongholds. They're rife with crime and who knows what else goes on in there, but I have no other choice. There'll be plenty of healthy people there and I'm sure one of them will be willing to take Benjamin.

It'll be bittersweet leaving this tiny cottage—no, on second thought, it'll just be bitter. Tucked back in the woods and with the extremely useful amenity of a hand pump for the well, this has been my home for the past two years. My son was born here. And this was the last place I shared with Devin—*miss him, want him, need him* — my husband and Benjamin's father.

It was such a stupid, stupid idea to go out there in search of real diapers for Benjamin and Devin paid the price for it. Well, I guess I've been paying the price too…and maybe have it worse. My husband was ripped apart before my eyes, but at least it was a quick death. This one isn't even really death as much as a transformation into something I desperately don't want to be…a thing that would eat my infant son just as soon as look at him.

My stomach twists at the thought and I turn my head away. The protein bar comes back up. I didn't expect it to stay down anyway. My appetite begs for meat and I haven't been able to keep anything but beef jerky down for the past two days. I keep trying though, because, for those few minutes my stomach feels somewhat full, I can forget the other hunger.

I put Benjamin back in the playpen and then shamble around gathering the things I think we'll need. At my speed, it takes a while for me to load up a backpack with enough supplies to last us…until. Until what, I have no clue. I have maybe four good days left and I have to make sure he's safe before then.

The infected are killed on sight, so next up is something to help me blend in. I've always been fair and, with my blond hair, I might be able to get away with being as pale as I am, but there's no hiding the eyes. I dig through the clothes pile to find a hoodie big enough to hide my face, then slide one arm in and hunch down so I can pull it over my head. It was Devin's and it still smells like him. My stomach growls.

I get sick again.

Benjamin laughs. It's probably best he thinks mommy's trying to be funny with the horrible retching noise.

Another bed sheet becomes a sling so I can have my arms free. Then, I carefully pull the straps of the backpack onto my shoulders and move to the play-pen to pick Benjamin up. It's awkward as hell getting him situated, but eventually he's snuggled against my chest.

I squeeze my eyes shut. *He absolutely does* not *smell appetizing. Not one single bit.*

We exit through the side door into the garage and the waiting ATV. This is going to be interesting. I manage to slide the garage door up with little trouble, but it takes three tries for me to swing one leg up and over the ATV and then wiggle into a semi-comfortable position that allows me to drive without squishing Benjamin against the handlebars. The thing's been kept in good repair, so it starts up easily and we putter down the steep driveway to the road.

I drive relatively slowly, but the miles pass by and Benjamin is eventually lulled to sleep by the steady movement and noise. By the time he starts to get fussy again, dusk is falling. I pull the ATV over and drive it into the woods a little way. Yeah, I haven't seen any other people around, but sleeping right by the side of the road is not a risk I'm willing to take.

Dinner is another jar of watered down baby food for Benjamin and me choking down a protein bar and then devouring the rest of the beef jerky. I'd meant to ration it, but, once I caught whiff of the smell of the dried meat, I couldn't stop. And I hate myself for it.

After the protein bar is ejected from my stomach, I settle my back against the tree with Benjamin curled up on my chest. He pops his thumb in his mouth and then slowly drifts off while playing with a strand of my hair. Thankfully, he's asleep by the time his chubby fist pulls that lock of hair lose. I shudder and remove it from his hand, then join him in sleep.

DAY THREE

Another morning, another session of self-imposed physical therapy. Not too much worse than yesterday, but now my joints ache on top of the stiffness. That probably has more to do with the night spent on the ground than worsening symptoms. I shake my head. Yeah right, I can't even make myself believe that.

More baby food and a diaper change for Benjamin and another nauseating protein bar for me. Strangely, I used to enjoy the damn things. Before the Zombie virus, when the world was normal, I'd eat at least one a day, especially the chocolate ones. Now, they all taste like cardboard.

My stomach growls and I find myself scrambling to find the empty beef jerky bag and then licking the inside of it with long strokes of my tongue. My mouth waters at that hint of salty meat and — Jesus. What is wrong with me? Has it really come down to this?

I drop the bag and wipe my mouth with my arm. Shoving the plastic further away with my foot, I close my eyes and curl my fingers into my palms. *Get a grip, Sarah.* A tear leaks from the corner of my eye and trails down my cheek. How much longer do I have?

Awkwardly swiping at my eyes with the back of my hand, my gaze goes to my son. He's sitting there babbling happily to himself and playing with a stick. He has no clue about the turmoil twisting my stomach and slowly warping my mind. He'll probably have no memory of me when he's older. He won't know what I went through to keep him safe. He won't know how much I loved him.

Another tear escapes and I wipe it away. There's not enough time for me to waste it mourning all the things my son will never know. If I don't get moving he may never grow up at all.

Loading up takes longer today, self-hatred making me question every thought and every movement. Should I carry Benjamin that close to my face today? How much do I trust myself? What if the proximity — No. There isn't any other choice. I finally get everything situated and get back on the ATV.

The miles flow away under the wheels as I let my mind wander. It's day three now. If everything goes right, if my immune system fights it off, I have until day six. At best.

My stomach churns and growls. I tried to eat another protein bar at lunch and I couldn't even swallow it. This new hunger worries me. What if I'm entering the final stages? What if today is my last clear day? What if I wake up tomorrow as...not me?

The endless cycle of worries has no room for more, so, when I see the two forms walking along the side of the road ahead, I continue driving. I should stop. I should see what kind of people they are. I should be doing everything in my power to find a safe place for Benjamin sooner rather than later. But I'm not. For the same reason it took me two days to leave the cottage, I drive on by the decent-looking couple with barely a wave. I might have a few more days left to spend with my son and I'm not ready to let go of him yet.

As the sun drops lower in the sky, I begin looking for a good spot to pull off the road for the night. The road's wider here with open spaces on either side. Not too many places that look promising. It's been quiet today and the only people I've seen were the two I drove past, but I don't want to take any risks. I keep going until I spot a stand of trees and then drive the ATV over the open field toward it.

It's big enough to give us some cover so I guess it'll have to do.

I've almost got the whole changing, feeding, settling ritual down, even with my limitations. It goes much quicker tonight than it did last night and Benjamin is snuggled against my chest fast asleep before the sun has fully set.

I'm staring at an unwrapped protein bar, trying to talk myself into eating it. My stomach's been twisting and my hunger is becoming a deep seated ache. I can't bring myself to lift the damn thing to my mouth. As soon as I get a whiff of it, I'll be sick. I know it. I should try anyway.

Since my elbow won't bend enough to allow me to pinch my nostrils shut, I move one arm across my face to cover my nose. I close my eyes. I can do this. I need to do this. The protein bar hits my tongue and I gag. Dammit! I'm getting too weak and I need to eat something. I'll just have to hope I can hold out. I kinda wish I'd kept the beef jerky bag.

Bang!

At the sound, I jerk and my heart rate picks up. Someone's close. Too close. And they have a gun. I use the tree behind me to leverage myself into a standing position, one arm wrapped around Benjamin, praying he won't wake up. I'm slow, but I can still get out of here. I simply have to move faster.

I half stumble toward the ATV, my knees screaming in pain from the rapid movement. I get my leg over the seat on the first try — *score me!* — and adjust the sling with the still snoozing baby so he sits comfortably against my chest. I turn the key. It starts up…and I forgot the goddamn backpack.

My leg smacks into the handlebar as I try to dismount and it turns sideways, the rubber grip nudging not-so-gently into Benjamin's side. He sniffles. I grit my teeth to hold back a curse, both at my luck and at the new fiery pain raging on the side of my leg. His eyes crack open and his lower lip wobbles. A few seconds pass and then Benjamin's cry breaks through the night air. I cringe.

Something comes crashing through the brush on my left and I slide back against the tree. Maybe the shadows will cover me. Maybe they won't see. Maybe I can be safe. Benjamin's still crying, though. A form steps in front of me, silhouetted against the moon, and points a rifle at me.

My budding new instincts scream at me to growl and snarl, not only to protect my son but because I am so damn hungry and the person in front of me smells absolutely delicious. I can't. I can't. I can't. I push down the urge to gnash my teeth and squeeze the small bundle closer. "Please don't hurt him," I whisper.

"Lee!" A woman's voice. The barrel of the rifle lowers.

More crashing noises to the left and another shape rushes between the trees and sweeps the woman into a tight hug. "Jesus Christ, Jenna. What the hell were you thinking? You can't just go running off like that."

"I'm perfectly fine. I know how to tell the differ-
ence between a baby's cry and one of the infected."
She pats his back and tilts her head in my direction.
"It's that woman with the ATV from earlier."

The man—Lee—turns to me. "What are you doing out here? Why are you alone? What are—"

"Lee. Stop it. Can't you see she's terrified." She
steps closer and holds a hand out. "I'm Jenna and
this is my husband. If you're okay with it, we'd like
to share your campsite."

I nod my assent.

* * *

That gunshot? It was Lee killing a rabbit. The same
one whose skin his knife is now splitting. My mouth
waters. *Meat. Want... No!* I look away and close my
eyes. I can't close my nose though and the scent of
fresh blood creeps into my nostrils. My stomach
growls.

"Squeamish?" Lee asks.

A chuckle escapes my mouth. If only he knew
that it was taking all my self-control not to snatch
that—*juicy, bloody, tasty*—rabbit from his hands and
eat it raw. He might be the squeamish one then.

Lee sets the rabbit on a stick over the fire and
leans back with his hands intertwined behind his
head.

I dole out a few of the protein bars I have left
and wave Jenna away when she tries to offer me an
apple. The thought of biting into something tart and

crisp nearly makes me gag. My mind, eyes, and stomach are all concentrated on the scrawny rabbit roasting over the fire.

Benjamin's still awake, his thumb in his mouth and his fingers in my hair. I glance down at him and he gives me a gleeful smile, the one reserved only for me, and I smile too while blinking back tears. How can I possibly give him up?

"Huh?" I bring my head up to face Jenna.

"I asked how old he is," she says.

"Oh, um, eight months." My head tilts down as I go along with my son's pulling fingers. It's dark enough and my hoodie provides enough cover that they have no idea I'm infected, but I doubt I could explain away a chunk of my scalp falling off. As it is, the side of my leg that had hit the handle bar of the ATV is...squishy. I think the skin may be coming off, but I haven't dared trying to lift my pant leg to see.

"Where's, uh," she stammers.

"His father?"

"Yeah."

"Dead." Even in the dark I can see her flinch. "We ran into a pack of infected and...yeah."

"How'd you escape?" Lee asks from his position across from us. The question is quiet, but it's laced with suspicion.

Alarm bells ring in my head. They can't know. If they find out I'm infected — "What?"

"You said *we* ran into a pack of infected. I'm asking how *you* got away."

"I...I ran." I swallow back the lump in my throat. Devin had told me to run and I'd started to, but I wasn't able to leave him there. If I hadn't gone back, I probably wouldn't be in this situation. "I wanted some real diapers for Benjamin and there hadn't been any reports of infected in the area for quite a while, so we decided a quick trip to that big box store down on 17 would be okay. There were so many. I think they'd gone inside to escape the light. Devin didn't have a chance."

Lee makes a tutting noise in the back of his throat and Jenna reaches out to touch my arm. "I'm so sorry."

"It only happened about a week ago," I say softly. I swipe at my eyes with the back of my hand. Carefully. My nose isn't feeling too sturdy these days and the last thing I need right now is to scare them off. Maybe they could be the ones.

"So you're headed to the city for protection?" asks Lee.

"Yes," I say. "I needed to find some place safe for Benjamin."

Jenna smiles. "Us too. Well, our little one's not here yet." She rubs a hand over her stomach. "About six more months and she will be. Lee thought it best that we head someplace where there's some semblance of security. I know there aren't too many infected around anymore, but..."

"Better safe than sorry." I run my fingers through the dirt. "All it takes is one."

She smiles again.

"I think it's ready," says Lee as he lifts the stick holding the rabbit out of the fire.

My mouth waters and my stomach growls. I don't want to ask. They don't have to share with me, but...I sigh, but it sounds more like a groan. *Need it. Soooo hungry.* Benjamin shifts in my lap and my face jerks toward him, nose twitching. *Oh God. Oh God. Oh God.* More hunger pains stab into my stomach and I hunch over. *Not now. Not yet.*

"You all right?" Jenna reaches out to touch my arm. It takes every ounce of willpower I have to turn my face away and not chomp down on one of her fingers.

"Yeah," I croak out. Another rumble from my stomach. "Can I—Would you mind sharing a little of that? It's just I haven't had meat in so long and I—"

Lee shuts me up by handing a hunk of the freshly cooked meat to me. "Here."

"Thank you." My shoulders relax and I take a deep breath inhaling the scent of it—*fresh, hot, meatmeatmeat*—something in my chest rumbles and this noise is almost a growl. I shove it into my mouth without bothering to let it cool. It's the most wonderful thing I've ever tasted and the *feeling* of it slipping down my throat...I...I...I...

A bone cracks between my teeth and a jagged fragment burrows into the inside of my cheek and through the other side. The pain draws me back as horror washes over me. That was close. Too close. I clap my hand over my punctured cheek and pull the hood lower over my face.

My body screams for more food, twisting my stomach and pulling at my willpower. I squeeze my eyes shut and take a few deep breaths through my mouth. That's better. I can do this. I have to hold on a little while longer. I open my eyes and look down at Benjamin. I can do this for him.

"I'll take first watch," says Lee.

Jenna rubs a hand down his arm. "You remember to wake me up for my turn tonight though. Promise?"

He turns a brilliant smile to his wife. "Promise."

The exchange gives me hope. They might be exactly who I need.

Pulling my son closer, I rest back against the tree. I'll make it to morning and I'll make it through tomorrow. I'll make it long enough to decide if Lee and Jenna are the substitute parents I need for him.

DAY FOUR

"Lee, that's enough!" Jenna's voice snaps to my right.

I open my eyes. They're both standing over me in the pale dawn light and Lee has a gun held down at his side in a white knuckled grip. Jenna inhales sharply and takes a step back, before offering me a weak smile. Lee simply scowls.

"Why didn't you tell us you were infected?" snaps Lee.

My gaze goes to the gun in his hand and I pull Benjamin in closer to my body. I hiss and curl over my son. *Hissing? I'm hissing now?* I give my head a brisk shake and force my limbs to relax. "Sorry…I…What does it matter anyway? I told you the truth. I'm just—" My stomach growls. Lee flinches and slides to the side so Jenna is behind him. "I'm just trying to find a safe place for Benjamin before…before…well, I'm sure you realize what's going to happen to me soon. I have to find a way to protect him. He has to make it out of this."

Pity, or maybe empathy, softens Jenna's face. She walks around her husband and crouches down across from me, her eyes boring into mine. "It's what any mother would do." She turns to look up at Lee. "Put that damn thing away. If she wanted to hurt us, she could have easily done it last night."

He grumbles, but complies with her command.

"How far into the process are you?" Jenna asks softly.

It takes a moment to pull the number from my head. The days are all running together now. "Day four," I say.

"Not much time then."

I shake my head. "Maybe two days. If I'm lucky."

She stands and absently rubs her belly. As she bites her lower lips her eyes travel to Lee and then back to me. "We'll take him," she says. Lee opens his mouth as if he's about to protest, but she silences him with a hand on his arm. "It's what I'd hope for if anything ever happened to me...someone to watch over my child."

Despite Lee's obvious reservations, relief takes over my body. I release a sigh and relax my muscles. "Thank you."

"Yeah, don't thank us yet," says Lee. "We still have to get to the city without running into any more infected."

I push a hand against the tree behind me and use it to slide up into a standing position. My time is getting shorter. I can feel it in the...wrongness...that's crawling into my limbs and creeping into my mind. Lee and Jenna will have to do. "You can take the ATV. Just leave me a gun," I say.

Jenna's brow furrows and she tilts her head to the side. But Lee gets it. He meets my eyes and gives me a slight nod. Then, he wraps one arm around his wife's shoulder and leans down to speak directly into her ear.

Her mouth turns downward and she shakes her head. "We can't...that's not..." The words trail off as she meets my eyes.

I'm opening my mouth to reply when I hear it: a sort of snuffling, snarling noise in the direction of the road.

Lee jumps into action, ushering Jenna over to a tree with low hanging branches. She grabs one and starts climbing. His eyes dart around frantically and then finally land on me. Still leaning against the tree. "What are you waiting for?"

I shake my head. "I can barely walk right now. I don't think I'll be climbing any trees." I hug Benjamin to my chest and place a kiss on the top of his head, careful to keep any saliva from touching his skin and ignoring the sudden urge to chomp down on his ear. "Take him and get out of here. They haven't sniffed us out yet and they won't be able to keep up with the ATV."

Jenna slowly lowers herself from the tree and strides over to me. She grabs my hands. "Are you sure? Maybe we can—"

"There's no cure. The longer I'm around, the more dangerous it gets. I could snap at any moment." I pull my hands away and start unwrapping the makeshift baby sling. The wind shifts and the scent of blood wafts past my nose. I can't move worth a shit, but I damn sure can smell. They've already taken down some other prey. I simultaneously shudder and salivate.

Jenna makes a small sound of protest.

"Go!" I say as I hand Benjamin to her. My face is turned away and my eyes are squeezed shut. Then another gust of wind, another whiff of...*meat. Fresh and tasty. Slippery Slidy.* I push down the urges and curl my nails into my palms, practically *through* my palms as the skin sloughs away. "Go now!"

The ATV starts up as another smell drifts in on the breeze, this one ripe with decay and rot. Another infected, heading in this direction. They must have finished their meal and are on the hunt for more. Disappointment and longing fills my body — *none for me? Greedy greedy* — and my stomach rumbles.

Pain rips through me, doubling me over. It's an all-consuming hunger that can no longer be denied. I'm so fucking hungry. So hungry. Hungry. Hungry. Hungry.

I move, quicker now that I've given in to it and let the *need* take over. Still not quick enough to grab at the...the...the...loud thing carrying my meal away. I groan and gnash my teeth in rage as my empty stomach twists.

My thoughts are fleeting, jagged things that my scrabbling mind can't grasp. But a subtle sense of relief still registers.

Looks like I don't have to worry about making it to day six after all.

DAY ???

Hungry.
Hungry.
Hungry.
So hungry.
There. Meat. Fresh. Fresh fresh fresh meeeeat.
Snarl, growl, and push my way to the front. This one's almost picked clean.
A sound, the snapping of a twig. The others too involved with the meager feast to hear. But I do. My

head comes up. Swivels with my body toward the woods.

Creeping. Sloooooowly.

Brown hair. Smells so goooood. The noises of the others hold its attention. It doesn't see me.

It takes a step back, turns, prepares to run. But I am already there and in its path.

I grunt and grin, imagining the slip slide of the hot fresh meat in my hands, in my mouth, and down my throat.

Eyes widen. "Sarah?"

It's so familiar, that name... *my* name. I shake my head. *Nonono.* My gaze flies in the direction of the other body. *Is that...? Who is...? How could...? Where is...?*

"Ben...ja...min?" My voice a rusty croak.

Its hands are up. It...he... *Lee* backs away. "He's safe, Sarah. In the stronghold. With Jenna."

"Saaaafe?" That word is good.

He nods.

"Safe."

"Yes, safe. Benjamin's safe." One hand rises slowly, holding tightly to black metal.

I've seen things like that. They're bad. I growl and swing an arm out to smack it away. But too slow.

"I'm sorry," he says.

A crack. A flash. A force that knocks me backward and to the ground. Yes...a gun that thing was. And this is death. The true release I'd forgotten I craved.

"Thank…you…" I stutter.

A Word from Theresa Kay

Horror has always been one of my favorite genres. I read my first Stephen King book when I was eleven and devoured everything else he'd written over the next few years. One of my favorite things about his books was how he takes ordinary people and puts them into extraordinary situations that, more often than not, scared the crap out of me.

My early attempts at writing were mostly about monsters, ghosts, and other things that go bump in the night— including zombies. I haven't had much of an opportunity to write horror now that I'm an adult, so when Samuel Peralta announced the theme of this edition of *The Future Chronicles* I was ecstatic and I hope you've enjoyed my take on zombies.

You can find more of my writing on Amazon in the form of *Broken Skies*, a YA post-apocalyptic sci-fi novel with aliens, and *Bright Beyond*, a space opera novella serial with a free prequel short story (*Dark Expanse*).

I love chatting with readers and I'm fairly active on social media. You can connect with me on Facebook, Twitter, Instagram and Goodreads. Even if it's not about my books, I like chatting about my (many) fandoms, books and reading in general, or just about anything really.

www.theresakay.com

Kamika-Z
by Christopher Boore

There was only one wave. One highly effective attack. It was all that was needed to topple an arrogant giant, ignorantly blind to the outside world. No one saw it coming. Eyes focused inward. On June 7th, 2015, the clear, blue skies over the land of the free bled black. There had been countless escalating conflicts between the US and China over the years, but none came close to this. Cyber-attacks, petty attempts to knock out each other's knees, were common leading up to the day of silence.

China struck hard; we couldn't recover.

We securely hold the East, West and Southern fronts as of 2025. The North is lost. Everything has changed. What's left of America cowers in the ruins of the once great empire. There is one thing common to all, it crosses every survivors mind in every waking hour, violates their tormented sleep– Will they attack again, and when?

- Jackson C. Phillips, Field Commander, Southern Defense.

LUNCH

"HONEY, YOUR LUNCH IS ON THE TABLE." I hear her loud and clear, but I don't budge. I just keep scrolling through my Instagram explore feed. He's out there, I can hear him. Big Dave, the reason I don't feel like leaving the safety of my bat-cave. In his gross, flirty deep voice he's hitting on Mom again. Hard. It's getting more and more annoying every day. I feel my stomach retch, breakfast trying to exit through my throat. If I stay in my room just a little longer, he'll head outside and gear up to cut the grass.

I hope.

Again, "Honey, move it, your food's going to get cold." I don't hear Dave anymore, but I didn't hear the much anticipated closing slam of the door to the garage either. Maybe he went to the bathroom. A king on his throne. I'm beginning to think he lives in there surrounded by the "rose-like" smell of his nasty business. Heavy footsteps echo down the hallway. Boots, not mom's flip-flops slapping against the tile. Crap. I launch my phone to the desk across the room hoping it'll stop and settle in its little cubby under the built in bookshelf. My Jedi powers fail me. Epically. The phone makes contact perfectly with the edge of the desktop, and it bounces to the floor with a thud. I couldn't have done that if I'd tried.

Shit. I pick up a Deadpool comic and try to act innocent. I'm a terrible actor. A faded brown steel-toed boot comes around the corner. It's showtime, baby.

I mentally prepare to endure the verbal slaughter about to rain down on me. "What the hell? Your Mother's been calling you for half-an-hour. What are you...?" Oh man, he looks down and sees the phone lying on the floor. I forgot to hit the off button to send it to sleep. Alicia Moss, a vision of perfection, is looking up at him over her shoulder all sexy-like in a blue thong bikini bottom and nothing else. Traitor. There's no way I'm getting out of this. Death of a fourteen-year-old, incoming. I'm sure to wind up in the obituary section of the local paper this time. Dave's face is intent. His eyes squint and lock in on my destruction. His face turns deep red. One purple vein bulging in his forehead threatens to burst.

Here we go.

"Get out to the table NOW! On that damn phone again. I've a good mind to give it a bath. How many times..." My eyes glaze over. Listening to the same spiel over and over again loses its oomph. I zone out, which just makes him more upset. I can't stand it when he gets pissed off at me for stupid stuff. I know I've been told a million times, but what's the big deal? It's just a phone, and I'm destined to sit on it all day. I'm a teenager damn it. Dave should just give in, it'd be easier for both of us. The evil part of me wishes I could sprout claws, like the poster of Wolverine beside my bed, and stick them deep into his fleshy face. Slowly of course, no rush. Feel some of my pain, Dave, you POS. It's like he's always hiding right around the corner waiting for the chance, daily, to light me up.

I miss Dad, bad, especially right now. He never pulled this macho, I'm better than you 'cause I'm a man and you're just a pantywaist-kid attitude. This douche slid into the hot spot the second they lowered Dad into the ground and threw dirt over his casket two years ago. Dad was part of the US Army's cleanup crew in Afghanistan. Stuck over there training security forces and establishing a safer way of life for them. Until the country's ungrateful natives decided to destroy his convoy with a roadside bomb. A hometown tragedy. He was shipped back to the states in pieces. Mom was devastated. She didn't even get to see him one last time. The service was closed casket for good reason. Pieces.

Out of nowhere the charming and dashing Dave popped up. The old high school friend, along with his chubby in his pants, moved right in on her during her weakest moment. I'd never even heard of the guy until he showed up at the funeral. Soon after her very short-lived grieving span, he slid in there like swimwear and has been up my ass ever since. I can't even breathe without him questioning my every move. I put my comic down and push past him, making my way to the kitchen. Not making eye contact fuels the rage. I can feel the heat of his anger behind me ready to let loose and rip me a new asshole.

"I'm not done with you." Mom's coming towards me to intervene. She always knows what to say to calm him down. I look at her, my eyes heavy with apology.

"Get back here, you little punk."

"Dave, calm down. Cut him a break." She puts a hand on his chest.

"He doesn't listen..." His anger fades with her touch. I'm sitting at the table watching the whole freak show. Bile threatening to rise again. I burp to relieve the buildup. She turns on her magical anti-dick-Dave superpowers, and he begins to melt. I have no clue what she mumbles to him. Probably better not knowing. I'm purposely intent on my tuna melt, now cold because of my unsuccessful standoff.

"Are you going to eat something?" she asks him.

Hurricane Dave's calm for now. "No, thanks. Grass ain't gonna cut itself. I've got to get out there. Sky's supposed to open up this afternoon." I hear the slap of his hand on her backside and her playful yelp as he walks around her to the laundry room then on to the garage. SLAM. Good riddance. Gross. I push my sandwich away. I'm not even hungry anymore. He's such a frigging perv. Hopefully the mower flips, crushing him. Ending my torment.

I put my baseball hat on backwards, far cooler that way, and tie my DCs to my feet. Grabbing my Alien Workshop deck by a truck, I head off to the garage. My escape is close. Freedom. I just have to get past Dave.

Mom cuts me off.

"Please take the garbage out with you, and don't go far." Ugh. Worry wart.

"K, mom." I take the plastic bag from her hand. She holds on to it, not letting go right away, looks me in the eyes, "Be careful." Her look is serious. It's been a year since I broke my wrist after a horrible attempt at riding a rail in the infamous Sunshine Bank parking lot, but she's not letting go. Her baby got a boo-boo.

"I'm good mom, let it go." She releases the bag letting me take it, a tear in her eye. I feel a bad about arguing with Dave. Not so much because of Dave but because it upsets her every time. He's not the worst; he's just not my dad. I kind of get why mom got together with him after dad was killed. There's no way she could do this all alone. Despite the settlement she gets from the government, she still has to pull a full-time job to make ends meet. Dave is a necessary evil. If not this Dave, then it'd be another.

I put my skateboard down at the door to the garage and pop in my earbuds, reach into my pocket, pull out my iPod, and thumb some good old punk rock to life. NOFX is blaring hard and fast, lyrics about our failing government. Drums are slapping, strings are howling. The music's tight, but the words don't mean too much to me. Who gives a crap about government at fourteen? Time to forget. Picking up the board, I turn the knob to the garage and head out to the danger zone.

I see Dave's blue jean covered legs sticking out from under the red ride-on Toro. I smile. It's a glimpse of my wish, kind of. Man, I'm messed up. Thanks Dad, for bailing and leaving me all screwed in the head. I don't want to have to deal with the man-of-the-house again so I beeline for the garbage can sitting just outside the rolled up door. I flip the lid to the can and toss the garbage inside. With half an effort, I kick up the lid with my foot, catch it in my hand and put it back on, where it belongs. I can hear Dave calling me through my tunes but I ignore it, launch my board wheel side down at the drive-way and hop on. Pushing off hard with one leg I'm rolling, fast, faster. Gravity's my best friend, drag-ging me down the driveway. I slap the blazing hot hoods of the cars with my hand as I pass by and take a wide turn into the street.

FREE!!

I'm not the best at skateboarding. This is my first deck, and I only got it about a year and a half ago. Right before the wrist crack-a-lack-in. Zero kids live in the neighborhood so I have no one to play with. Mom and Dave never let me go anywhere anyways on my own, especially now. When I broke my wrist at the bank, I'd snuck out and met some of my friends from school. It was a blast, the most fun I'd had in a while until the snap heard round the world. I'll never forget. Mom was so pissed. Dave lost it. Another day, I thought I was a goner. They've cracked down on me and I haven't been allowed far from home since. Sucks big fat balls. I practice some low to the ground ollies and try my hand at a few unsuccessful kick-flips. My confidence is still in the pooper from the wrist incident. It hurt like a mofo. Sometimes I can twist it and it clicks. It drives mom nuts. She calls it a nervous habit. I have no clue what she means.

It's insanely hot out. Every day the same. Florida in the summer is a pit from hell. Sweat pours off my face, and my t-shirt sticks to my back. It's like running face first into a constant wall of wet air.

I look back at the yard as I turn in the street, picking up momentum for another ollie. It looks like a scene from Avatar. Everything is green and the weeds look like stringy alien overlords glaring down on the thick grass from above. The palm trees and bushes have grown out of control like they've become one with the house. Dave's whipping around in a haze of dust and clippings. No mask on his face. We'll all be sneezing for days. I stop the board and pull out the iPod; the music keeps cutting out. It's getting annoying. Can't find my groove. We've got decent Wi-Fi in the house and it usually reaches out here. Maybe it's the weather Dave was talking about heading in. I look up and see nothing but white, thin clouds. Weird.

BEEP BEEP.

I jump, looking for the noise and just about crap my pants. The Dixons, from two houses down, are staring at me from behind their windshield. I didn't see the silver SUV pull up, too busy looking at the sky. I back up, rolling my board with me, and mouth, "I'm sorry." Another screw-up I'll be forced to eat. My apology receives dirty looks. Still no music, but now a bunch of static is screaming painfully in my ear buds, making me pull them out. I look at the sky again, what gives? I try to switch to my Amazon music. It's usually a sure fire fix when Pandora's hopping around. No better. I thumb Safari. Nothing. I wonder if mom forgot to pay the bill. From the open gate I hear yelling and see Dave on the mower swinging his arms in the air like a deranged monkey and pointing at me then the house, over and over again. He's screaming for me to get inside. He looks up. I follow his eyes. There's a black spot in the almost clear sky and he's looking right at it. I keep my eyes on it even as he's yelling at me again, ignoring his orders. I don't see what he's so nuts about, it's gotta be a bird. A vulture, a hawk. We get all kinds of —

The emergency broadcast speakers dotting the coastline of Florida start raging with a high-pitched squeal. I cover my ears; it doesn't help much. I look up again. The shape is getting bigger; it's moving pretty damn fast. It looks like a huge black missile. Closer now. Mom's screaming my name.

Closer.

Whatever the hell it is, it's heading right for the backyard. The speakers are still blaring.

Closer.

I see red marks on the side of the missile, too far to read or make out. Shit, it's going to hit. I see Dave getting off the mower. Too late. Mom's shaky hand on my shoulder. Her face red, scared. Tears streaming down her cheeks. She's yanking on me, her face tight, eyes pinched in pain; I'm guessing from not cupping her ears from the speaker's constant noise. I follow her, yell at her to cover her ears. She does now that I'm being cooperative. We run towards the front door right as the oversized bullet smashes into the ground, feet away from Dave, sending him and the mower flying in two different directions.

Inside, mom bolts the front door then runs to the garage and hits the button to close the roll-up door. I hear it clank and grind to life. She runs past me again, no explanation from her, just determination on keeping her nest safe from whatever is happening. I look around. The noise from outside dulled now from CBS walls, but still out there. Every device in the house that's normally on still has power, but nothing else. The house is filled with white noise. I run to the patio doors to see Dave's fate. Concern climbing to the top of my feelings.

The dirt shower is just starting to settle from the impact of the big black missile. Dave's on his feet, the crotch of his pants dark with wetness. The lawnmower is on its back, dual blades spinning slowly to a stop. The safety feature sure paid off. I hear mom rustling around somewhere deep inside her bedroom, followed by a repetitive clicking sound. Metal on metal.

I FOUGHT THE LAWN...

Man, he really pisses me off, I think to myself as I watch the little runt cruise off down the driveway on his skateboard. He'll never see me as anything other than Dave, the guy who snuck in and snatched up his mom after his dad got shot and killed over in Arab land. He doesn't see how well I take care of him and his mom. Doesn't care about my side of the story. I try so damn hard to be patient. Losing your old man has to be rough, especially at a fragile age. I tell myself this is a marathon, not a sprint, and just hope he'll come around one day. Sliding out from under the mower I look at my work and assess the task with pride, wipe my greasy hands on my jeans, and saddle up. I turn the key, giving my baby life, and listen to her purr. I pull the iPod out of my pocket, thread the headphone cord through my t-shirt and click it in the auxiliary jack. Headphones in and ear protection over them I thumb Pandora to my Kansas station and smile as Carry on My Wayward Son kicks in, taking me back to a younger time. Perfect choice. Backing out of the garage, I switch gears, sending the Toro lurching forward. Onward to battle. The lawn is the bane of my existence.

I see the kid in the street riding his skateboard and remember last year when he snapped his wrist. Another unnecessary aggravation where he just didn't listen and went and disobeyed us just to push the envelope. I get so sick of his bullshit. I round the corner to the backyard, grab the lighter from the cup-holder, and pull the joint from behind my ear. With a click and a toke, it's lit, and the kid's crap is rapidly disappearing from my mind.

Son of a bitch, it's hot. Everything about summer in Florida is slapping me across the face, a reminder of why I hate this hellhole. I've worked every day for the last ten years in this furnace. Sweating a pool by 7:30 in the morning, two weeks of cool relief every year, then back to hell again is not my idea of a good time. I watch clouds of decimated weeds and grass puff up into the air. I sneeze and rub grit into my eyes. Maddie's consistent nagging to wear a respirator falls short, once again. I should listen next time. Maybe next time. My tunes keep cutting out and it's starting to grate my nerves, stealing my high. I only ask for one thing, just let me jam while I become the destroyer of the ever-growing grass. Looks like someone or something wants to take every tiny bit of my joy and flush it down the toilet.

They said it'd rain this afternoon. Thunderstorms likely. Thirty percent chance of precipitation. The daily south Florida recipe for unpredictable summer weather. A cover our ass forecast. The sky looks clear now, though. Cloud cover is slim. I see a hawk, far away up in the sky. At least I think it's a hawk. It's moving closer, but it looks like it's coming straight at me. My iPod screeches ear piercing static, then nothing. The Wi-Fi logo doesn't even switch to 4G. It's gone. Blank. I try other apps, but everything using a signal is down. Strange. I look up again. That's no hawk up there. It's earthbound, whatever it is, and it's sure going to hit somewhere near. Too close for comfort. Maybe it's a plane. No sound coming from it though. I look for the kid. There. Waving my arms and shouting, I tell him to go inside. He's not listening. Why would he change his ways now? He's staring up at the—whatever the fuck it is—falling from the sky, too. A deafening wail blares from the emergency speakers high up on their pole down by the street corner. I cover my ears. It's not letting up like normal. No test warning. What in the hell? I look up again. Shit! It's closer. A missile the size of a bus headed right for me.

Run you idiot!

Too late.

Boom...

I open my eyes. My brain's ringing. Where am I? I remember. The missile—shit—I'm up on my feet amid a shower of falling dirt. The mower, upside down, blades slowly stopping. I grab the hatchet I keep strapped to the side of the Toro for rogue pepper tree limbs invading along the fence line. My crotch is warm and wet. Shit. I look at the projectile.

Sleek black with red lettering covering the side like those Chinese tattoos everyone gets. The ones that don't mean what they think they do. What is this? Whatever it is, it's no good. I see the kid through the porch door. He's terrified. I completely understand why. Where's Maddie? No time.

A hiss, barely audible over the still wailing speakers.

A puff of air. A door slides open.

Something out of one of the kid's war games comes barreling out. Staggering like a drunk after too much free booze at happy hour. A god damn half-robot half-human. LED lights flashing across circuit boards strapped to its robot half are twitching on-and-off. Its human eyes are wet, dripping. It looks infected, like it's battling a severe case of the flu.

Argh. This noise. I need a hand on the hatchet, so I sacrifice one for an ear. My brain feels like it's melting. The thing is sweaty, pale eyes wide and crazy. The human and robot sides move as if they are in disagreement. The non-human side wins, dragging it towards me.

Shit.

I back up, almost tripping over the mower. I swing hard, off balance, but biting deep into its shoulder. Black blood shoots out. It doesn't flinch. My hatchet is stuck. It's on me. Metallic hands grab my arms, pushing me down. I look for a weapon. Nothing but grass and clippings. I look to the house, still no Maddie. The kid's opening the door. I shake my head frantically, "NO!" He sees and stops.

Crunch...

I feel a sharp pain then syrupy heat pours from my neck.

The screaming fucking speaker!

Stop!

It's in my face, teeth oozing with green foam, snapping, chomping.

POP POP.

A gunshot. Maddie. I start to cry. She hits, pissing the thing off and grabbing its attention. My mouth gurgles a warning, one never making it past my lips. As it turns, I see its feverish eyes. Sad. Apologetic.

It climbs off me. Behind it I see another emerge, then another. My insides are on fire with a boiling heat, moving from my neck down deep into my body. I try to understand one last time, but my brain doesn't let me, leaving me in confusion as the sunny day fades to black.

SURE SHOT

POP POP.

I push Jake away hard as I send two bullets soaring at the monster, shattering the porch door in the process. The shots hit home. The training's paid off. Nothing. I just made it mad.

Oh, hell no!

Whatever it is, it has the flesh of Dave's neck dripping from its chin. Dave's not moving. He's dead. It's looking right at us as another emerges.

I yell "NOOO" in frustration. I stop myself. I have to be strong. Jake's terrified. He's shaking. Our flimsy barrier is destroyed. No time to think. "Jake, the car. NOW." He's in shock, not moving, just standing there with a death grip on his skateboard. The monster's getting close. POP. I shoot its human leg. It goes down. Yes. The other, close behind, gets the same treatment. POP. Down. I see Dave move, flail. Alive? He's seizing, a black mist spraying from his mouth. I turn back to Jake. Sorry, honey. I slap him hard across his face. Tears well up, but he's back. "Go. Now. Car." I risk a quick glance back. They're both up again, the machine part pulling the bleeding leg along behind it. Another appears in the missile's doorway. It's different. More machine with an awareness in its eyes. I push Jake. We run to the front door, unlocking it. We plunge outside. Shit, keys. I turn, reaching around the doorframe for the keys on the hook just inside. Grabbing blindly they snag on the hook.

"COME ON!"

An infected cyborg, the only practical thing to call them, is through the shattered patio door and coming at me quick. Far too close. I get the keys free and slam the door. It doesn't close, making contact with the machine hand wrapped around the jamb. I slam it over and over. Crunch, crunch, crunch. The fingers fall to the ground and the door slams home. I put my shoulder to the door.

"JAKE."

My hand holds out the keys. "Lock it. Quick, quick." He grabs the keys and locks the door. Two seconds to breathe. I see the robot fingers twitching on the floor and the splintering door reminds me to pick up the pace. We run to the car. The street is empty. Where the hell are all the neighbors? Waging individual zombie wars in their own back yards? Jake reaches out to hand me the keys, skateboard still clutched in his hand. Something to redirect his fear. A security blanket. I smile despite the nightmare. The speakers are still blaring across the sky. I barely notice them now that other issues are taking the lead. A bang comes from the direction of the front door. "Jake, keys." I reach out an unstable hand.

"MOM."

THE BLACK

I see the thing coming quick. Where are the neighbors? It's much faster than the others.

"MOM."

Too late. She lifts the gun and the cyborg zombie backhands it away, raking the back of its hand across her face, slicing the skin deep. She hits the ground. Booming from the door persists. Earsplitting speakers. Too much. I swing my skateboard up at the freak's face. I hit so hard, the board sends chunks of wood and metal parts flying. It falls back, tiny sparks of lightning dancing over its head and blue smoke pouring out of its eyes.

Bang. Snap. Door.

Screams from somewhere in the area. Not close. Another attack?

"MOM." I tap her bloody face gently. "Wake up. Please." I'm so scared. Tears burning my eyes. "Jake." She's awake but not there. I help her up, take the gun from her hand, get her to the car, and put her in the back seat.

The two zombies come, one after another, shuffling around the corner towards the car. Human faces in pain. Wake up Jake, I tell myself. I pull the unlocked door open and rush behind the wheel. My shaky hands help the key find its home, and I give life to the Honda. A screeching and shake of the car makes me look up. A cyborg zombie hand, finger deep, is clawing the hood, tearing back metal. It's going for the engine. The other, coming straight for me.

I glance in the rearview. Mom's out again. No help from the backseat. Shit, I've never driven a real car, just in video games. I pop the stick into reverse and hit the gas harder than I should, dragging the zombie stuck to the hood. Jerking all over the place, I end up half in the street, half across in the neighbor's front yard. Still no neighbors. Still the constant insanity of the speaker's shrieking. Shifting to "D", my foot slams the pedal as far as it can go. I surge forward and hear a thud, then metal grinding. The cyborg hood ornament is gone. The Honda swerves all over the road, but I gain control. Looking in the rearview, I see the zombie roadkill clawing its way after me, half of its body left behind, a black smear stretching down the street.

I have no friggin clue where to go. Never paid much attention to where anyone important lives. No other family. I know one thing; I'm sure as shit not staying here.

I look out through the windshield and see more dark spots appearing. Thousands and thousands, multiplying every second like black stars in the summer sky. I find the switch and turn on the head-lights as the long, horrific day quickly turns to an artificial night.

The missiles are falling left and right, I can hear the distant thuds over the screeching emergency speakers and Dave's crappy CD playing low on the SUV's stereo. Classic rock, ugh. Led Zeppelin. Not bad, but not great either. CDs? Who would've thought they'd make a comeback. Other cars are on the move. I'll follow them. They're all headed the same way and in a hurry. I hit the gas to keep up. The driving is easy, as long as it stays like this. A small distraction from the heap of WTF currently crashing down around us. Invasion USA.

A bump then a groan from the back seat jerks my eyes to the rear-view. Nothing. I risk a glance over my shoulder.

She's moving.

"Mom." No answer.

The car swerves to the right. The passenger tires bump over and over. I snap my head back and yank the wheel to the left. Corrected. Fewer cars on the road now, probably best with my skills. Thick drops of rain slap against the windshield. Great, what else?

I peek at Mom again.

Rearview.

Shit.

Foamy black ick is oozing out of the cuts on her face. Her eyes are white, pupils wide and milky.

"No, MOM!"

Her entire body spasms, she's moaning, screaming.

The road.

"MOM."

Arms swinging she hits me hard on my shoulder.

Shit, it's burning. I look, blood.

The SUV's all over the road, I hold the wheel steady despite the thrashing in the back. Like Dave. "NO, NO, NO." I grab the gun in my lap. Tears roll down my cheek, dripping on my hand. I point it behind, to the back seat. She bumps it. I hold it steady.

Rearview.

BANG.

"FUCK."

Runny vision, like under water in a pool; my eyes burn. I try to hold them back but my eyes open, wide. Tears, far from soothing. Pain, all over. I hurt more inside. I want to puke. "Mom." Stillness in the backseat.

Eyes on the road, don't look back there.

I look at my shoulder. It's bubbling and bleeding. I fiddle with the gun in my hand, both resting in my lap. The road keeps coming at me. Over and over. Feels like I'm driving on a never-ending treadmill. The world seems too slow. Rain spatters the windshield. Overcast sky, missiles soaring across the horizon as far as I can see. How many more?

Tears still drop, free. I'm numb. I think about Dad, he was brave. I turn up the stereo, loud, to drown out my mind. The red LEDs on the stereo flash Led Zeppelin: Immigrant Song. Not bad. I chuckle, then swallow as the tears come again. I lift the gun, warm barrel to my temple. One hand on the wheel. "I'm coming Dad." I look at the rearview. Red, wet, tired eyes. My finger squeezes against the trigger. The metal resists, I scream…

…BANG.

A Word from Christopher Boore

When Samuel Peralta came to me and asked me to write a story for *The Z Chronicles*, I just about crapped my pants. I was terrified. I'm far from a connoisseur of this genre by any means. Don't misunderstand me, I watch *The Walking Dead.* I'm current with that mainstream zombie show, but that's about it. I've never really watched any other zombie show. I'm definitely not staying up Sunday night until 9 p.m. to watch it when it airs either. I like my sleep. You won't see me spewing spoilers all over Facebook the next day. I watch it maybe three months later to fill a void when there's nothing else on. The scenes are so slow and too boring for me most of the time, but when you get to the action...man, it's worth it. I love action.

When this project came along, I had no idea what to write or where to begin. It scared me to the core and made me realize how little I knew outside my comfort zone, let alone zombies. I'll tell you this though: This, for me, was a challenge of epic proportions. I am so glad that I accepted because it made me think far outside of my personal box of tricks. I really think I've scored a hit. I wanted to write something that hadn't been done before in, what I believe to be, an over-saturated genre. Zombie fiction, movies, TV has been done, and done, and done. Then it has been picked up, bits of flesh shaken off, and done all over again. I didn't know if I could come up with something unique and original.

Then, as I was clicking the refresh button on my Facebook feed on my phone, I thought, "What if everything turned off, and an age-old political enemy chose that moment to attack? Then I re-watched the *Terminator* movies. What better way than with cyborg-zombies? A plague that wouldn't end because the machines would never stop. What if it happened during a cyber-attack of epic proportions to cover up the incoming invasion? Take it off radar."

My biggest real life apocalyptic fear has always been digital silence. Communication breakdown.

No phones.

No Internet.

No TV.

No way to access your bank.

The world would erupt in chaos like we've never seen. It could happen at any time! Add a contagious rabies-like virus to the mix, terrifying. I have faith that in reading "Kamika-Z", you'll taste my fear.

Hopefully you enjoyed this short as much as I enjoyed writing it and please keep an eye out for my future work. With any luck the premise in "Kamika-Z" should never come to pass but hey, at least if it does, I may have given you a battle plan.

You can visit me on my website, http://caboore.thirdscribe.com/ -- stop by and subscribe to

my newsletter. I'm also on Facebook, at
https://www.facebook.com/cboore1

Also, swing on by my Amazon page and check out my
other stories,
http://www.amazon.com/Christopher-
Boore/e/B00ELG5TT6

The Fall of the Percedus
by Jennifer Foehner Wells

TARN DIDN'T TAKE HIS EYES from the hologram of the newest squillae template that hovered over his desk. He kept his voice flat—it wouldn't do to raise Pyona's ire further. "I told you it's not ready."

He heard Pyona inhale deeply, and then her words came out like a raging storm. "In the name of the Cunabula, I swear that if you say the words 'it's not ready' *one more time* I'll be forced to do violence upon you, Tarn."

Tarn let a moment go by. Then he said, "It's not ready."

Pyona yanked Tarn's seat backward and whirled him around. Her face snarled into his. "Look at me, Tarn. People are going to die—maybe all of our people. It'll never be ready—not like you want it to be. I know that you want it to be perfect, but the time is gone. We have no options left. We must use your weapon."

"And I have just lost valuable work-time to your wasted expenditure of anger. Every distraction is a delay. Remember the precepts taught to us in the schoolroom. They still hold true, Pyona. 'Desperation reaps a tainted harvest.'"

Pyona seemed to vibrate with the effort of containing her temper. Violence was in her. He hoped she wouldn't actually strike him in front of his subordinates. They weren't children anymore.

There was a blaze in her eyes. He was her brother, her only sibling. Right now she did not see him as a genetic tether, but as a source of tremendous frustration. This morning all patience seemed to have deserted her.

She did not strike him. She tapped at the tablet in her hand and shoved it at him. He glanced down at it.

"There is a pod of the Swarm gathering to feed on SetaNu Four. We will..."

He was on his feet, the chair tipping backward and crashing behind him unheeded, shock and confusion roaring through him. He grabbed the tablet from her. "What?"

On the screen was a live feed of an endless stream of dim shapes that barely reflected enough starlight to be visible at all, like a dull, grainy river of corruption flowing through the vacuum of space. It was a migratory pod of giant Swarm beetles.

He choked on his own spittle and staggered a little. He tapped the image and the coordinates came up. The monsters were indeed en route to SetaNu Four.

Pyona's brows drew together. Her voice was sharp. "You didn't know about this?"

Tarn set down the tablet absently. This changed everything. Now he understood her intensity. This wasn't about sibling rivalry. She had come to him for help.

He was her only hope to save their people.

Tarn slipped off his haptic mitts and carefully set them on his desk, the motion warping the floating magnified image of the minute machine he'd been working on refining. "Sister, I know nothing beyond the walls of this laboratory," he said slowly.

Dismayed, he looked at his beloved semi-circular desk, arranged very nearly like a bird's nest. It was stacked with books, erratically piled sheaves of writeflat, and data sticks scattered around the computer console at its core.

Then his eyes moved to the floor-to-ceiling window behind the desk. Just outside, green and blue mottled foliage spread across the warm turquoise sky, throwing shade over the hot pink flowers he prized so much as they pressed against the glass.

The lush beauty of O'Sep. He would have to leave it, at least for a while. That would be hard.

He turned to take in the silent activity of his team in the expanse of the room behind him. Some of them sat at computer stations refining software. Mili, a leading specialist in the order Coleoptera, was hunched over and had her arms deep in the decaying carcass of a giant Swarm beetle. A few of her best students were at the vivaria, taking data from various ongoing beetle experiments. All were working diligently.

His mind started to race. Not only would all of this research be disrupted, he and his staff would be uprooted and forced to race against the clock to prepare. The sheer scope of it was overwhelming.

He mumbled, "I'll need time to relocate the lab to a ship."

Pyona lifted her chin. "I've already assigned fifty people to pack your lab and transport it up to the *Percedus*. They will stay to supplement your staff onboard. Get them up to speed quickly."

He looked at her blankly and nodded. She'd already arranged it all. Of course she had.

She sighed and her expression softened. She glanced around, found a seat within reach, and drew it up, gesturing toward his fallen seat where it lay. "Sit down, Tarn. It's time to stop yelling and listen to each other."

Tarn stood on the bridge of the *Percedus*, watching SetaNu Four slowly darken. The planet took on a flickering, swirling, writhing appearance as the Swarm-pod slowly spread out into a single layer in the planet's upper atmosphere. He'd been staring at the viewscreen so long that when he closed his eyes a reverse image had burned itself into his retinas.

There was no sentient life on SetaNu Four. The biosphere was limited to small pockets of flora and fauna between vast wastelands. The few sheltered valleys and moist hollows wouldn't occupy this pod of the Swarm for long.

How easily this plague could fall on their own home. How quickly it probably would, if his sister's plan didn't work, if his own life's work failed. The seventh, youngest, and most far-flung sectilian colony world, Olonus Septua, affectionately called O'Sep, was lush and brimming with life from pole to pole. It would nourish the Swarm for decades.

O'Sep was the nearest habitable planet, its star just over half a light year away. If the Swarm chose to move in that direction, it would probably take this pod only a year, maybe two, to migrate to O'Sep from here.

A chill skittered down his spine. It was too easy to imagine.

It was unfair that the Swarm was pushing him into this before he was ready. He needed at least a decade more of research. If only he had recruited more entomologists or software specialists sooner. It had been astonishing that his peers had found his ideas exciting, had so readily seen their potential, but so few had had any interest in actually moving to a remote colony to pursue the work.

If they only knew how beautiful O'Sep was. How pristine. How untouched. How absolutely full to the brim with diverse life in a variety of ecosystems. The Cunabula, the wise race that had long ago seeded sentience across the galaxy, had valued genetic diversity above all else; O'Sep was the epitome of the Cunabulist ideal.

Tarn couldn't understand why people would choose to live on planets plagued with severe weather, volcanic activity, water shortages—and nepatrox!—when one of their own colonies was a planet like O'Sep. By comparison to the sectilian home worlds, O'Sep was paradise.

He should have taken Pyona's suggestion and presented it as if it was a vacation opportunity. He had argued that the scientific opportunity would be enough. For him, it would have been enough. *Why did she have to be right?* he thought. Regret wracked him.

He was but one man. One man against a hive of monstrous insects that devoured civilizations without compunction.

One man with an idea.

He reminded himself again that the black-blood beetle trials had been more than promising. Close cousins to the giant Swarm beetles genetically, the far smaller terrestrial beetles from LoMia Five shared ninety-seven-point-six percent of the same DNA.

Oddly, sectilians themselves shared eighty-five percent of their DNA with the Swarm. Large portions of DNA were often shared among a variety of species—even when those species were the fruit of entirely separate evolutionary trees separated by thousands of light years. It was a byproduct of the Cunabula's work combined with strange mathematical confluences. Planets with similar ecosystems evolved life along predictable lines from single-celled organisms, and often, but not always, produced analogous species. It was a fascinating line of science, categorizing and comparing genetic variance.

Sectilians shared the most DNA with other bipedal ape-derived hominids from various worlds — often as much as ninety-eight or ninety-nine percent. They shared upwards of seventy percent with various star-scattered rodents. With the innumerable examples of the bovine form, they shared as much as eighty percent or more.

Tarn looked down at his own muscular hand, as different from a paw or pincer or hoof as it could possibly be. Outwardly, none of these species resembled each other, but there was almost a mysticism in the expression of intron and exon, not to mention epigenetics. It made research unpredictable.

Regardless, the results from the beetles of LoMia Five *should* translate. The Swarm should be weakened enough to give the battleships that had been summoned from Sectilius a fighting chance to defend O'Sep.

A hand tugged at his elbow, abruptly pulling him from his musing. He turned to see that the attention of the entire staff of the bridge was concentrated on him.

Pyona's gaze was heavy with purpose from the central command seat. "Strap in, Tarn. It's beginning."

He retreated to his designated seat, out of the way. When he had secured himself with the unfamiliar restraints and looked up, the surface of Seta-Nu Four was appreciably lighter in color than it had been. This was expected. The feeding behavior of the Swarm was well documented. The adults had begun to descend to the surface to hunt, leaving mostly juveniles in high orbit until any large predators on the surface were dealt with. Then the juveniles would join them to feed. This made timing critical.

The bridge was silent except for the tapping and clicking of consoles. Outwardly it appeared that each person on the bridge worked utterly oblivious to the others, with only the occasional absent mumble, when in fact Tarn was the only individual *not* immersed in a sea of constant communication, the only one who needed to be spoken to aloud.

He wasn't linked into the mental Anipraxic network that the kuboderan navigator created for instantaneous communication between officers. Pyona had offered to introduce him to Anipraxia, to help him navigate it, but he had declined; he hadn't wanted to distract her from her other duties. That decision, like so many others, might have been a mistake.

Before Pyona had become the Gistraedor Dux of O'Sep, she had commanded a ship like this for six decades. She had told him that it felt good to be back on the bridge. She had missed the ever-present company of a kuboderan in her mind, and she liked the one installed on this ship. She'd said she was contemplating stepping down as Gis'dux and appointing herself as permanent Qua'dux of the *Percedus*.

He imagined he felt the ship surge forward, but he knew it was probably a simple visual illusion as the *Percedus* slipped out of its hiding place behind the tiny moon and rocketed toward SetaNu Four.

The ship had been retrofitted with dozens of additional thrusters for both speed and braking, as well as inertial dampeners in order to make this sort of operation plausible and not a suicide mission. They would have to get in and out quickly if they were going to survive this encounter and successfully carry out the experiment.

Tarn felt a swelling of affection for Pyona. Her angular face radiated power and ferocity. Her limbs were taut with tension. Her hand-picked bridge crew of twenty four all shared the same intense, determined look. He began to believe that perhaps Pyona could make this mission succeed just by force of will.

The planet grew in size until he began to make out individual motes in the dark churning fog of black bodies that surrounded it. Reflected light glinted faintly on their hard carapaces. His skin crawled. These beasts were so unnatural. No other known species had adapted to all three realms of air, sea, and vacuum. They were the most successful species in galactic history. And the most deadly.

If the people of O'Sep could have run, they would have. The cataclysm, if it came to pass, would be a year away at minimum. But there was no way to transport every O'Septan to a system beyond the Swarm's reach in time. There weren't enough ships in this sparsely inhabited part of the galaxy to carry them all. This was the only way.

It was time to take a stand. This would be the most ambitious preemptive strike ever attempted to protect a world's inhabitants. If it worked, Tarn's name would be immortal.

The *Percedus* took up orbit and began scanning the population for the best subjects for the experiment. Tarn's station lit up with multicolored infofeeds within moments.

The pestilent roil slid by below them. So far they were passing just above them, unnoticed— apparently not perceived as a threat by the insects. In past encounters, sectilian ships had usually been ignored unless they committed an aggression against an individual insect.

Tarn began to sweat. Everything hinged on the next few hours.

New data spilled onto his console. He forgot his anxiety as he pored over the information about the juveniles in orbit below. He had to work quickly. He identified thirty specimens that were ideal in the sector they were scanning. When he looked up, the main viewscreen had highlighted those individuals and either the kuboderan or the ship's computer had mapped out several alternate intercept routes between them. Pyona must have selected one of the routes, because all but one disappeared and the ship changed course.

Time crawled by. The ship glided just above the plane that the insects occupied.

Shuttles were deployed to herd the selected juvenile podlings into open cargo bays on one side of the ship. They moved in and among the insects with incredible grace. Tarn had expected to see violence and injured insects thrown into the cargo bay in haste. Instead, he watched as the juveniles barely twitched in response to the gentle taps of the shuttles. These pilots were incredibly well trained. His respect for Pyona and her crew grew by another level.

None of the insects appeared to be alarmed by what was happening. Of course sound wouldn't travel in vacuum, but if the podlings were signaling in some way for help from the adults, they weren't doing so until after the cargo bay doors had closed on them.

A voice spoke into the hushed silence, startling Tarn out of his stunned reverie. "Choose a few more in the immediate vicinity, Tarn. We need to go. Some of the adults are getting curious and heading this way."

He looked down at the data and selected five more podlings that were nearby. These were bigger than he'd hoped to get under ideal conditions, but he wasn't going to second-guess his sister at this point.

When he'd finished he looked up to see one of the larger insects closing in on them. Every child in the galaxy knew this bogeyman, but few actually saw it with this kind of detail and lived to tell about it. This species inspired a kind of primal fear unlike any other, and Tarn was grateful that he managed to keep his pants unsullied as the adult—a female, he saw—filled the viewscreen, her mandibles twitching and her compound eyes reflecting the ship in a million mirrors.

Pyona barked, probably for Tarn's benefit, "No time for more. Recall the shuttles. We're done. We've got nine. That'll have to be enough."

There was a flurry of silent activity as the crew carried out her orders. The shuttles looped out of view. Once the final shuttle was aboard, the *Percedus* changed attitude and increased thrust to achieve escape velocity.

Tarn's heart pounded in his chest as he waited to see if any of the insects would follow. The female that had just been curiously examining them had glanced off the hull as the ship moved off, but it didn't pursue them. The *Percedus* was accelerating away from the planet at full power.

They had put several vastuumet between the ship and SetaNu Four before Tarn was able to breathe more easily. They took up orbit in the cold distant fringe of the SetaNu system.

Tarn stood and made eye contact with Pyona. She nodded. Phase One was complete. He left the bridge for his lab near the cargo bays.

His team awaited him there. Immediately they removed the barriers between the cargo bays and lured seven of the nine podlings into one section with a heap of vegetation. Then they closed off the sections again so that the test group of seven was confined to a single space, separate from the two control individuals.

It was important to keep them relatively calm. Even juveniles could do damage to the ship and each other if they started spewing star-hot plasma around. Tarn and his assistants were prepared to prod them into place if necessary, armed with poles hastily made from deck-tubing, but, *praise the genius of the Cunabula,* the creatures docilely performed as they'd hoped.

Bile rose in Tarn's throat as he observed the test group on the monitors in his lab. They were crawling over each other as well as the walls, floors, and ceiling. They were so *unnatural.* Insects shouldn't be able to get that large. Even the smallest of these podlings was easily larger than a heavy-set sectilian.

Normally with insects the weight of the exoskeleton was a limiting factor for size, but this species had evolved with a honeycomb chitin structure which allowed its exoskeleton to be lightweight and extremely durable no matter the size of the individual.

They scanned the podlings for hours to set down a baseline before they began the experiment. It was tedious, but necessary. If the squillae didn't perform as he hoped they would, he would need as much data as possible to determine why — so that they could quickly amend the code and try again.

Before the Swarm hovered above O'Sep's gem-like skies.

Tarn grimaced and turned to his assistant, Mili. "Inoculate them."

"Yes, Master Tarn." Mili tapped at the control that had already been set and ready on her tablet.

On the screens, nozzles emerged from three of the four walls. They emitted a short blast of a sticky gel containing a concentrated suspension of Tarn's tiny machines. It coated the entire chamber, including the podlings.

He had named the microscopic machines "squillae" a long time before, when he was a younger man and in a lighthearted mood. He should have named them something that sounded stronger, more powerful.

They were powerful. And other civilizations used them to great effect. It was a benefit of the prosperity of the sectilian race that they were finally able to turn their engineering sights to the micro rather than the macro, to learn to solve problems in new ways.

Naming the squillae after his favorite minuscule seafood perhaps hadn't been his best idea. Maybe he would have been taken more seriously. These had seemed such small sins at the time. Now every one of his sins loomed large.

Not only would the squillae rewrite portions of the podlings' DNA, a small subset were tasked with monitoring the life signs of the subjects. Still others would track and relay the podlings' locations once they were released again on SetaNu Four.

He wanted his self-replicating machines to spread throughout not only this pod, but *every* pod that these individuals came in physical contact with. To achieve this dissemination, he couldn't do more to any single individual than slightly handicap it. So the squillae were designed to neuter each individual, to cap and then reverse population growth.

In addition, a secondary mechanism would work to slow their metabolism, so that they wouldn't feed nearly as much and their response times would be more sluggish. The squillae's code instructed the machines to transfer to new individuals with only the slightest tactile brush between Swarm beetle individuals. The squillae should spread through the pod like wildfire.

The immediate effects would be small. In the long term, if the squillae performed as desired, it would eradicate the galactic Swarm threat within three decades, and would make the infected much easier to fight with conventional weapons almost immediately.

He would not be the only hero in this fight.

In his most recent trials with the common black blood beetles, the squillae had successfully slowed metabolic rates by an average of forty-seven percent. They had effectively chemically neutered sixty-four percent of the beetles by altering gene expression of gonadotropins. Adult beetles had become sluggish. Larvae, pupae, and podlings had been distinctly underweight. The test colony had shrunk significantly in size over a span of ninety days, despite an abundant food supply that should have driven exponential growth.

But would it have the same effect on *Confluos giganus*?

They would know very soon. The squillae acted swiftly.

The genius of using machines instead of a bio-engineered virus was that if the Swarm beetles adapted, or if the effects weren't strong enough, he would only need to modify the software to instantly change the squillae behavior. Ships or probes could simply broadcast the update. He could target different organs, the circulatory system, or the brain. The possibilities were limitless.

The lab hummed with the quiet tension of work. The room was a maze of computer stations. Every scientist was tasked with monitoring some aspect of Swarm physiology at the most minute levels.

It wouldn't be long now. Couldn't be long, if this would work at all…

Someone—it was Mili—called out, "Confirmed! Overall respiration rate down seven percent as compared to controls!"

Soon similar exclamations were sent up from around the room and nearly every station. Each shout sounded more giddy and elated than the last.

"Group heart rate averaging nineteen percent below controls."

"Pheromone levels reduced by thirty-seven percent versus control levels."

"Caloric expenditures are now down forty percent and still trending downward!"

Tarn sagged a little in his seat and closed his eyes. It was working. All the worry had been for nothing.

When he opened his eyes, Mili stood before him, a small smile tugging at the corners of her mouth and her eyes shining. She handed him a tablet with compiled results already in the form of a report. "With your permission, Engineering Master Tarn Elocus Hator?"

With the touch of his fingertip, this first official report would be signed and encoded into a final format, ready for submission. He saw that Mili had already placed her seal. This data would soon be entered into the scientific community on every sectilian world—to be further scrutinized by his peers and, most importantly, *replicated*.

Tarn put his finger to the tablet to seal the file. He raised his beaming face to the camera that he knew was conveying their images to the bridge. Were they celebrating there, as his lab assistants were beginning to do here? Or were they still all serious, locked in their Anipraxic gestalt? "We did it, Pyona!" he said, hearing the hoarse exultation in his own voice. "Phase Two, complete!"

Someone was pressing a cup of liquid into his hand.

The room buzzed with laughter and animated conversation. He expected *some* kind of reply from Pyona, but when it didn't come, he excused himself to head back to the bridge to get the praise he so richly deserved.

The atmosphere on the bridge was not at all what he expected. The smile withered on his lips as he entered.

The mandibles of a Swarm beetle filled the viewscreen.

Tarn took an involuntary step back. When he recovered his composure he silently moved to his station and waited to see if he would be able to help in some way.

He watched in awe as the bridge crew worked together, silently communicating, almost like a hive mind themselves. He looked down at his console and entered a search for all of Pyona's most recent commands.

She had issued a fast series of them, only moments before. The ship was no longer at rest. It was hurtling deep into the SetaNu system at high velocity.

He searched farther. It seemed that the female that had inspected them while they were in orbit around the planet had followed them out to where they had hidden at the dim edge of the system and then had quietly landed on the ship.

He shook his head with disbelief and stared with awe at the large viewscreen that dominated the bridge. It was possible. In three to four hours at top speeds a Swarm beetle could traverse that distance.

But...the female had found them. *That* didn't seem possible at all.

They were now returning to the planet with a giant Swarm beetle along for the ride. The acceleration hadn't torn the beetle loose, hadn't even jostled it. The inertial dampeners that cradled the whole ship had cushioned the monster along with everything else.

A red light flashed on his console. A message had been relayed from his lab, with a video attachment. Tarn frowned and leaned forward. Something had gone awry?

The podlings' metabolism had continued to decrease, going as low as forty-eight percent of control, but at that point they'd gone into a feeding frenzy — except that they'd ignored the vegetation that'd been left for them. They had turned on each other.

Only the three largest of the seven test subjects were still alive, and when they weren't trying to kill each other they were expending a lot of energy trying to escape the confines of their cell. Their dead cellmates lay in pieces strewn about the cell, the contents of their broken shells partially pulled out and devoured. Their metabolism was significantly decreased, but aggression seemed to be proportionally increased.

Tarn wanted to fill the silence of the bridge with screams of frustration. Juveniles didn't behave like this. Compared to adults they were almost docile. And he had never read anything in the literature that mentioned any known instances of Swarm beetle cannibalism. Was this an unintended consequence of tampering with their metabolism? Or was the presence of the adult female on the hull of the ship somehow affecting the juveniles in ways he couldn't understand?

He brought the command log back up. They were nearly back to SetaNu Four. Just a little bit longer and they'd be able to release the juveniles and retreat to a safe distance to watch the results of their experiment unfold.

The squillae were clearly successfully manipulating Swarm physiology. That was all they needed. Once the squillae were in place, they'd have time to fix anything else.

Another message from his lab.

The podlings had breached containment by injecting super-heated plasma into the walls between the cargo bays. His people were working to cut them off and herd them back into their original enclosure. Tarn clutched the console. He broke out into a sweat and waited to hear word of their success. He would need to update Pyona about the status of the experiment soon.

Moments later, another message came. The three Swarm beetle juveniles had found and killed the two control podlings. A soundless video showed them tearing the control insects apart and consuming pieces of the scattered carcasses before resuming their attack on the partitions. A white flare overloaded the video momentarily. Plasma. At least one of the podlings hadn't depleted its plasma bladder yet.

Tarn stared at the console in disbelief. Before he could finish reading that message, there was already another message waiting.

Three of his team were dead.

Tarn stood involuntarily. He looked at Pyona, intently overseeing her domain. How could he tell her this?

Someone on the bridge let out a guttural cry of surprise. *They already know*, Tarn thought. He turned toward the officer who had cried out…and he saw the main viewscreen.

Partially obscured by the black, chitinous leg of the female Swarm beetle on the hull, SetaNu Four hovered in the distance, significantly lighter in color. And between that planet and the *Percedus* streamed a dark glinting river of monsters. Tarn leaned against his seat, mouth hanging open, and felt the blood drain from his head.

The source of the viewscreen's feed switched to another camera and Tarn realized the *Percedus* was already into the thick of it. This view originated aft, displaying most of one side of the ship. There were three Swarm beetles attached to the ship there.

Tarn looked at Pyona. Her lips were pursed. Her jaw was set. She was determined to finish the experiment. But how?

The image displayed on the viewscreen careened and Tarn realized that, even though he felt no change, the ship was taking evasive maneuvers.

Then he saw why. A Swarm beetle had been moving alongside, matching their velocity even as the ship swung wildly to avoid it. Then the beast simply latched on. The deck vibrated ever so slightly under Tarn's feet but the inertial dampeners did their work. The Percedus continued on.

It was the stuff of nightmares...childhood nightmares of being trapped in inky space by inky claws that catch...

He'd underestimated them. They must communicate in some way...over distances...in a vacuum...he couldn't even imagine how. He sat back down to collect his thoughts. He had to record these findings for future scientists. They had to know what had happened here.

He bent to his console, nostrils flaring, heart palpitating in his chest. Around him the bridge was a different kind of silent, every figure consumed in a struggle that he could not see or hear.

He took the sealed report that Mili had written and added every thought he could quickly type, all the messages from Mili, video clips from the lab and the hull of the ship, everything he could hastily put together. But how would he get that information back to Sectilius? Even O'Sep was too far away for radio communication now.

A shipwide message flashed on his console. Everyone knew now. Nine more of his team dead. People from all over the ship were flooding that deck to help regain control.

He broke the desperate silence. "Pyona, is there a way to leave behind some kind of information capsule?"

Her head turned jerkily toward him. Her eyes were wide. He could see the whites of her eyes from here. She was terrified, but she held fast at the helm. "Yes, we can leave behind a buoy. Send me what you want to leave behind."

They both said the words as if they didn't mean so much more.

He sent his packet of information to her console. She nodded that she'd received it.

He sent Mili a message, demanding an update.

He glanced at the viewscreen, now rotating between various cameras on the exterior of the ship, most of which were blackened by enormous Swarm beetle bodies. A white flash of plasma lit the bridge before the filters autodulled it and then the camera view cycled again.

Tarn felt cold.

No reply from Mili. That was unlike her. She needed him.

There was no way he could help from the bridge. He got up on legs that felt strange and wobbly and left.

He could think of only one thing. He had to get the podlings off the ship. Immediately. He would think about the consequences later. If he could just release them, perhaps the adults would be appeased and leave them alone. At the very least the squillae could begin to do their work. Perhaps they could escape…

He took the deck-to-deck transport to the level where his people were fighting to contain the rampaging juvenile podlings.

When the door opened he wasn't prepared for what he saw.

A wet metallic smell struck him in the face. Animalistic screams echoed through the corridors. Everywhere the ubiquitous green surfaces were smeared with black — walls, floors, ceilings. It took him a moment to see that the black wasn't really black. It was red blood, everywhere.

What had happened here? Could all of this possibly be the work of three maddened insects?

The ship rocked under his feet. That shouldn't be possible, and yet it had happened. The Swarm beetles must have damaged the inertial dampeners.

He stumbled out of the transport, uncertain where to turn to offer help since conditions might have changed since he had left the bridge. Only a few of the lights were functional. One flickered at his feet.

At the end of the corridor the silhouette of a short, stocky person stumbled backwards into view.

Tarn began to call out, but something unnatural in the person's stance checked his words in his throat. The light flickered again. It was a woman. Was she wounded? She seemed to be struggling.

Abruptly he realized that this blood-drenched woman wasn't a stranger. It was Mili. Several of the corridor lights flickered back on. Mili had turned slightly, and he could see that she was impaled on a sharp, black foreleg.

Tarn was rooted where he stood. He wanted to turn away, to run away, but he couldn't move. With sickening clarity he knew that there was nothing he could do for her. She was barely alive now. And he had no weapon.

Her name formed silently on his lips.

The Swarm beetle scuttled around the corner on it's remaining appendages. The pair clung to each other in a deadly dance. They swayed and pitched along with the ship. Suddenly the insect lunged forward and tore Mili's throat out with its mandibles. Blood gushed from the wound, showering the beetle.

As Mili sank slowly to the floor, the podling eagerly sank with her, slurping the blood spewing from her neck and then tearing at her savagely, throwing gobbets of her flesh in a dark circle of gore.

Mili's body was short, stocky, with corded musculature—the atellan body type—just like his own. He shook his head and shuddered.

Tarn fully woke to the fact that he had no way to protect himself. He was just a peaceful man. A scientist. As Mili had been.

The universe had gone mad.

He needed to find a weapon. If he could just get to the lab. The insect's attention was consumed with its prey. Perhaps he could sneak down the corridor the other way. Tarn slowly slid sideways down the wall behind him and peeked around the corner.

There were at least a dozen bodies strewn along that corridor. And to his horror he saw that there was another podling consuming another one of his team members, its head buried in the man's gaping chest.

He must have made some small sound. He hadn't meant to.

It looked up, its head lifting the body like a dangling puppet. It made eye contact. Oh…no.

Tarn stumbled back blindly. He had to get to the lab. He needed to find a solution. He couldn't think there, surrounded by the carnage of his team and the *Percedus* crew. He had to escape and fix this before anyone else perished.

He was beginning to feel separated from reality. This couldn't be happening. It had to be a terrible dream. He seemed to be moving slowly, as though underwater.

The ship rumbled and rocked. Tarn lost his footing and backed into someone.

As he turned, he automatically muttered a hasty apology before he realized that it was the podling that had been devouring Mili only moments before.

The insect was slightly bigger than Tarn. It lumbered unsteadily over the shifting decking.

Tarn froze. Every hair on his body stood on end.

Blood dripped from the podling's mandibles. There was a cold insatiable hunger in its gaze that made Tarn's blood curdle.

He was nothing but meat to this monster.

Tarn shoved the beast away, his hands slipping in Mili's blood, and braced himself to fight, his hands up, every nerve on alert, every muscle taut.

There was a horrible sound of rending metal so loud that Tarn bent at the waist against the wall and covered his ears.

The other podling came around the corner from the adjacent corridor, scuttling toward him. It had dumped its burden.

He would never make it to the lab now.

He shuffled along the wall to the deck-to-deck transport as the floor seemed to sway under his feet. It was the only route to escape. He would tell Pyona to seal off this deck. He could rewrite the code for the squillae, or deactivate them. He just had to get out.

They were closing on him. He felt the prickly brush of a tarsal claw…

The ship shuddered and groaned. His ears felt painfully full. The air was a hurricane. Tarn grabbed at something, anything. His fingers locked on the edge of the transport door.

He felt the podling lose its grip on his clothing. Tarn watched as the monster helplessly scrabbled across the deck plates and was swept away.

And then the wind was gone. There was an abrupt silence. A ghastly pull was filling his eyes with tears, stabbing his ears, dragging every wisp of air from his lungs.

Using every ounce of strength he had, he pulled himself into the deck-to-deck transport and slapped the symbol to close the door.

His saliva boiled away on his tongue. His vision began to narrow. He watched the other Swarm beetle lumber toward the transport.

The door closed. Air instantly hissed into the chamber. He gulped lungfuls of air and collapsed in a corner, spent.

His heart hammered against his ribcage. His breath dragged over a raw throat. He reached up and keyed the transport to take him back to the bridge.

The doors opened.

His heart thudded dully. He was safe. He'd escaped.

Tarn shoved his feet under himself and pushed himself up with difficulty. He yawned and swayed. He couldn't seem to get enough air.

Exhaustion from his ordeal fell on him like a heavy, spongy blanket. Lethargy dragged at his limbs. He must be in shock.

He needed to tell Pyona what was happening down there as soon as possible. He moved unsteadily toward the bridge. Walking felt like a monumental task.

He felt lightheaded. He had to stop partway there to rest. His breathing was labored and slow. He began to worry that the atmospheric pressure was low because of the decompression on the other deck. He would ask Pyona.

Finally he made it to the bridge and keyed the door symbol.

The ship lurched, hurling him to the floor in the middle of the room, but he righted himself and tried to reclaim some dignity as he straightened, but no one looked up.

He shambled to his station and slumped in the seat. Sweat poured from him. Why was his body moving this way? It wasn't responding as it should.

He looked down at himself. Had he been injured but didn't realize it?

Did the ship pitch and roll again? Or only for him?

He was dizzy. His thoughts were muddy, as sluggish as his body.

He panted in slow rasping gasps, verging on sobbing, trying to regain control of himself, but something was opposing him.

He mewled like an infant. He knew there was a horrible truth that he didn't want to contemplate, hovering just beyond the grasp of his conscious mind.

His thoughts were blurred and slow. He hung his head. His eyes filled with tears.

He had failed in the most horrific way.

Others would learn from his mistakes. This was the way of science. Of progress.

There was a disquieting feeling in the pit of his belly. And it was growing. It seemed to radiate outwards from his core like a flame.

He needed to tell Pyona.

His ears rang, but the bridge was silent. He stood, swaying, and shuffled to her command chair.

She was oblivious to him. There was another world behind her eyes, inside her head, that he would never see. Her skin was sheened with sweat. Her brow furrowed as she listened to some silent voice from the ether, on the verge of making a demand, issuing an order, coopting another life.

He felt a wave of respect and affection.

Then the emotion distorted like a distending bubble.

His entire body began to tremble. His filial feelings fell away, replaced by something unspeakable.

He leaned in close, opened his mouth.

It felt like hunger. It burned like rage.

A Word from Jennifer Foehner Wells

Nanites fascinate me. They were an important element in my first novel, *Fluency*. I had a lot of fun imagining all the practical applications that a race farther along than us on the technological timeline would use them for.

Readers frequently ask me for backstory about the Sectilius people or for stories that would feature sectilian protagonists. With this story, I decided to honor both requests.

In *Fluency*, Jane asks Ei'Brai why he hadn't used nanites (called "*squillae*" by the Sectilius, which has a meaning akin to shrimp) to destroy the nepatrox in their larval stage. He replies, "Under Sectilius law, squillae are confined to inorganic repair except under rare, tightly controlled circumstances. Technology serves life. It does not destroy it. These lessons are rooted in the very foundations of Sectilius culture and law, without deviation, under threat of penalty of strictest nature. The slug population must be dealt with, but the squillae will not perform that duty."

I decided to disclose the reasons behind this prohibition by revealing a moment in the distant past of sectilian history. It's a cautionary tale, to remind us that just because we can do something doesn't mean we should, and that rushing the scientific process can lead to disaster, no matter how good our intentions might be.

You can find out more about me, my work, and upcoming releases on my website: www.jenthulhu.com. I'm also extremely active on Twitter where you can find me as: @Jenthulhu

Z Ball
by Will Swardstrom

THE SECONDS CLICKED OFF the massive score-board in the middle of the stadium. 44...43...42...41... Each second that went by meant another endgame scenario I ticked off in my head. I had to make the call. It was all on me, but the number of seconds left in the game was hardly the number I was most concerned about.

"Hut!"

The ball popped into my hands, and I took a standard seven-step drop to get a look downfield. The pass rush was an onslaught of terror, one after another, pouring through the offensive line, grunting, running, and chasing me. Arms flailing around as if the defenders had never played football before. Most likely, they hadn't. Even so, they would pursue me unrelentingly.

With just seconds before they reached me, I swung my arm around and the blades tucked inside my arm pads sprung out and slashed deeply into the throats of the two closest to me.

Of course, this wasn't really football. And they weren't really pass rushers.

It was Z Ball.

And I'd just decapitated two zombies.

127

No rest for the weary. At least nine other threats patrolled the field. Just like football, there was an even amount on both sides — eleven for the humans, and eleven for the Z. I'd taken out two with the now bloody blades embedded in my left arm. With zombies though, I couldn't count on all my team-mates to stay on my side, if you get what I'm say-ing. Z Ball players covered any spare inch of their bodies with padding and extensive weaponry, but the zombies were resilient. Already this season, I'd lost four linemen, three wide receivers, and a run-ning back.

I needed to pass the ball. Yancey Hall was wide open about twenty yards down the right sideline, but putrefied flesh hung off my arm, covering some of the ball. A pigskin I could handle just fine, but not a zombieskin. I shucked off the blade along with the excess flesh and chucked the ball with a tight spiral towards Yancey. I didn't see him make the catch; I had another chaser on my tail and was forced to take the axe from the harness across my back to deal with it. I had to chuckle a little at the irony; my chaser had been a woman in her 20's when she'd turned. One of the few times a woman would have been able to play on the gridiron hap-pened only after her death.

I glanced up at the jumbotron to see the replay of Yancey's catch.

Good news, bad news. He caught the pigskin, but Yancey also caught a face-full of zombie teeth on his right forearm.

Nuts.

Yancey had been the best receiver I'd had since I lost Lawson Smith back in Week 1. I made a mental note to take him out on one of the next few plays. I didn't want to, but survival was certainly something I wanted more than friendship with a Z.

I was still staring at the jumbotron when they flashed a picture of me up there. "Vince Lager, QB," it read with a few of my stats from the game. I had to admit, I was a little impressed with myself. Then, I almost made the fatal mistake of scoreboard gazing. I turned around just in time to see a Z shambling towards me.

Just as quickly, I tried my forearm blades; I was all out. Last resort—I reached inside my uniform and found the clip of my shoulder pads. I popped a small compartment open and pulled out what was inside. I hadn't retreated—I never do—and the walker kept on advancing towards my position. Steady and purposefully, I took aim with my emergency armament and put a small caliber bullet right between the eyes of the Z. Less than five yards away, he stumbled and fell, his poisoned blood turning the green turf a dark brown.

The clock was winding down on the game anyway. I glanced from the jumbotron to the scoreboard. Los Angeles had put up 35 points against their horde, edging Detroit who had just 20 points (they showed the replay on the monitors at halftime at our game of Detroit's kicker getting mauled by a particularly gruesome walker).

Meanwhile, in our stadium, we were scalding Atlanta. In Z Ball, it was a combination of the old style American football, along with Arena Football, and a host of undead zombies. We had one side of the 50-yard line, and the other team—Atlanta today—had the other half. Simultaneously, we each took shots at the end zone, maneuvering through the zombies who got in our way. In spite of the debilitating injury Yancey just suffered (RIP Yancey), we'd put up 49 points on the day while Atlanta had just 14 points over on the other side. That's the breaks when the quarterback gets infected in the first quarter.

If we could hold on here without losing anyone else, it would be the first time in the ZFL championship for Chicago.

I gotta admit, I was pretty excited to play in the Brain Bowl.

Of course, that wasn't the official name, but that's what everyone called it. This year would be Brain Bowl VI, adopting the same Roman numeral system the NFL used for decades. The NFL still exists, so for copyright purposes, we'll call the final game of their season the "League Championship Game." The ZFL Brain Bowl leapfrogged that game its first year in existence and hasn't looked back.

The sponsorships are crazy for the winners— which, to be fair, are pretty few and far between. Even if you end up on the winning team, there's no guarantee of walking out of the stadium alive or uninfected.

Last year, Atlanta took the title, but only four players were left standing. Even then, after postgame blood tests, their quarterback Ernie Pilson, showed the beginnings of the Z virus. When I was in college, I quarterbacked for Arizona State. Pilson was just across the desert at University of Arizona. Really gave the sportscasters something to talk about—Pilson vs. Lager. Dubbed the Beer Bowl whenever the Wildcats played the Sun Devils. A heated rivalry, yes, but we got to know each other and I considered him a friend.

Too bad. No one ever saw him again. That is…until the first game of the season when Pilson's walking corpse took the field against his former squad.

Brutal.

That's how the ZFL Commissioner likes it. Really drives up the ratings, they say. Like we needed a ratings spike.

It wasn't that long ago when zombies were a fictional thing. Made up to show our humanity—in the face of death personified, what would we do? Books, TV shows, movies, video games—all devoted to it. The scare was there, but in the end people felt comfortable in their own homes because zombies weren't real.

But then somebody figured it out. A "walking death" of a sort. No one was really sure who did it. They're probably dead now, but a few years back the newly dead in the New York City morgues started coming back to life. And if that wasn't bad enough, it spread.

To New Jersey.

I'm not kidding. A few dozen ports throughout New York and New Jersey allowed those few mindless undead to have unfettered access to global grey matter. Soon, zombies threatened every continent on earth, save Antarctica. But, unlike in all those TV shows or movies, the hordes were contained. Most countries were actually more competent than people wanted to give them credit for, and those that weren't...well we don't call them countries anymore.

All told, it was estimated about twenty percent of the earth's population had succumbed to the plague. But, it wasn't over. The zombies still were a major factor in the remote areas of Africa, South America, Asia, and even a few parts of North America. Many of the governments had employed their military to contain the scourge, but in some parts of the world, private contractors were called in. Many had previous experience as military contractors in the Middle East, but a few newcomers cropped up.

Soon, one of the top contractors in the field of zombie containment was a company which became the ZFL.

* * *

The outbreak was in full swing when I was finishing up my senior year at ASU. Of course, there was a general isolation as a student athlete at an NCAA Division I school, but I heard things here and there. We weren't affected much until the season was mostly over.

Ironically, it was when I was away from the team that I not only learned about the outbreak in full detail, but when I also cemented my place in the future of the ZFL. The jail cell was cold and dank, but in hindsight, it was the wake-up call I needed. I stewed for a couple days until my roommate came down to the station.

"Vince, what are you doing to yourself?" Cal asked.

Cal Ervin, 6'6", 334 pounds. My roommate the past two years and the best left tackle in the Pac 12. He'd dealt with the best defensive linemen from schools like USC and UCLA, but perhaps his biggest challenge was corralling me.

I imagine my own scouting report read something like: "Vince Lager. 6'4" 230 lbs. First round arm. Fourth round legs. Questionable decision making. Highly questionable character. Not a leader. DO NOT DRAFT."

Even before the zombie outbreak, I was what you might call "self-destructive". Of course, what landed me in the Tempe City Jail was not self-destructive, but actually bar destructive. I'd heard sports analysts before the outbreak say nothing good ever happened between one and six in the morning. That axiom certainly proved to be true on an early December morning during my senior season. In my defense, those bar stools were really shabbily made.

I looked up from my cot in the jail cell. Cal was on the outside, holding the bars as if his paws were enough to bend them and free me. His expression was pained. We both knew I would have been out within hours if it had been my first offense. By the time you stop counting on one hand, people are less willing to give you chances.

"I don't know. I don't remember what happened," I said.

"That's bull, and you know it."

"Honest!" I said, sitting up. "I remember going to the bar and having a drink or two, but then the next thing I know, I'm laying in my own puke, my hands cuffed behind my back."

"Fine. But you know as well as me that you have a problem. If you can't control yourself, you have to stay away from the bars. Shoot, just last week, the Jags were talking about taking you with a flier in the first round. Now? You'd be lucky to get a walk-on audition with any team in the league."

I looked back to the bare concrete floor.

"That bad, huh?"

"You haven't seen the video."

Of course, the video from inside the bar was irrefutable. It showed me drinking a few boilermakers and then absolutely losing it when a random bar patron bumped my barstool. I found out the patron's name was Rick Welch, famous for making the Top 12 on America's Next Top Singer back in its heyday. Apparently he had quite the YouTube following. The stool was the first act of destruction, cracking down on Welch, immediately knocking him down and unconscious.

When I watched the video later, I was amazed at my own actions. I honestly didn't remember what I'd done, and wouldn't have believed it if not for the security video.

When the stool shattered, I grabbed one of the legs, and took out each and every bottle behind the bar, like an amateur baseball player. When the bartender came at me, I jumped up on the bar—pretty impressive for someone so wasted—and continued to hold off the employees and patrons with a mixture of bar stool parts and movie kung fu until the police showed up and tazed me.

Cal walked back out of the jail, but came back a few days later to check on me again. He was my rock on the football field and he was my rock off the field as well. My family had given up on me a long time ago, but for some reason, Cal Ervin thought I was redeemable.

The longer I sat in the jail, the worse the zombie outbreak got. I was mostly forgotten, and eventually the District Attorney just dropped the charges. Cal showed up with his Jeep the day I was released and we went back to our apartment, no words spoken between us. Cal had everything ahead of him in the NFL. My future hinged on a miracle.

For me, the zombie outbreak was that miracle.

What a miracle, right?

It took a couple years for the U.S. to get its zombie problem mostly contained, but once it did, people wanted to get back to "normal" — you know, apple pie, reality TV, football. It all returned (including reality TV, the malignant cancer on the underbelly of society), but football wasn't the same anymore.

Cal had gotten drafted, but had barely played thanks to shortened seasons in the NFL the past few years. I was happy for him, but the NFL wanted no part of Vince Lager. I got a courtesy call from the team that drafted Cal. They offered a practice squad spot, but it was too soon; pride held me in check. I got a job as a physical trainer for college players at a local gym, provided I do one thing — not talk to them.

But America had seen and suffered too much. After people lost loved ones to the zombies, the tame violence of American football no longer held their interest. In fact, it was a typical professional football game on a calm Sunday afternoon where everything changed.

If you can imagine Cowboy Stadium (of course you can — it's a Texas-sized shrine to football), then picture it on game day against the Eagles. The game was all tied up, 21-21, heading into the 4th quarter. A fan seated in the mezzanine (later identified as one Rafael Myers), had been bitten by his four year old son before he headed to the game with his buddies. Unfortunately for Rafael, his son, and a significant portion of the crowd that day, the bite transferred the Z virus. By the time the fourth quarter was beginning, Rafael was gone, replaced by a Z that only looked like him.

Rafael went berserk, eviscerating his drinking buddies in just a few seconds, and moving on to the rest of the crowd. With the crowd noise, people didn't catch on to what was happening in the stands, but poor Rafael found his way to the gridiron soon enough. There, he tackled and tore into the neck of the Eagles' punter. Just a few bites was all it took for the poor punter's head to be free of his body. Then, Rafael used the punter's thin helmet as a bowl for the head and brains of the cheapest player on the team.

Horror set in on the field and everyone ran. Everyone except one Jerry "Jellyroll" Parks. Jellyroll hadn't earned his nickname at the salad bar. The defensive lineman clocked in at 6'7" and a svelte 367 pounds. All the other players ran for their sidelines. The smart ones sprinted to the locker rooms.

Only Jellyroll stayed on the field. He alone would face Rafael the zombie. Jellyroll rushed the attacker, putting him on his back quickly and knocking the punter's helmeted head for a 20-yard loss. The abandoned TV cameras caught Rafael attempting to go after Jellyroll's skull instead. Thankfully, the lineman hadn't taken off his helmet. Rafael's teeth just bounced off the fiberglass. Jellyroll pushed him down and stood back up.

At this point, the crowd had either begun to stream out of the stadium as fast as they could, or they were transfixed by Jellyroll and his one-man stand against a Z. Reports put the number trampled to death at thirty-three, and the injured at over a hundred.

The clips of what happened next were replayed on YouTube over a billion times, and were essentially the inspiration for what ZFL could be. Just a few yards away sat a lone football. Jellyroll picked up the pigskin and gripped it in his right hand. His massive paw could hold it by itself, and he used it as a weapon of sorts. He didn't have any protection on his hands, so the football was insulation against any potential bites. Jellyroll used it over and over to pound on Rafael's face.

Apparently though, Jellyroll also considered himself to be an amateur wrestler. After a half-minute of toying around with Rafael, Jellyroll swiveled around the Z and put his hands and arms around the engorged neck of Rafael Myers. Jellyroll put him in a chinlock and pulled. Being so freshly converted, Rafael hadn't suffered decay like so many other zombies had; it wasn't easy, but Jellyroll grunted and twisted, eventually ripping Rafael's head off his already dead body.

Unfortunately, a second later, the still animated head of Rafael Myers was able to move its jaw enough to chew into Jerry "Jellyroll" Parks' very fleshy arm. Rafael was no longer a threat, but Jellyroll now had a sliver of the virus coursing through his bloodstream.

RIP Jellyroll.

It was clear Jellyroll would be joining the *other* team soon.

The Cowboys missed the playoffs that season, and had to respond to dozens of lawsuits. People were mad. They wanted vengeance, and the ZFL found a way to tap into that. The public *zeitgeist*, it was called.

Thus, the Zombie Football League was born. They recruited from recent college graduates, and I got a call on one of their first days open for business. They'd seen me play in college and loved my arm. They didn't say they loved me. Just my arm.

But they'd also seen the bar tape. That was also a plus in my favor for the ZFL. They wanted players who could handle their own on the field against zombies. I fit the bill in more than one way.

* * *

The question caught me off guard at the postgame press conference. Not only the question, but the one asking it.

"Vince Lager, what is your response to the allegations?"

The one posing the question was Kat Ellison, a national sports reporter assigned to the ZFL. I was more than familiar with her questions in the past, but this one was unexpected because I had no idea what she was talking about. It had been years since I'd been arrested for anything, and as far as I could remember, I hadn't done anything illegal in a while. Still, it sent my heart pounding.

"I'm sorry. What did you say?"

"The allegations about the ZFL. That they are illegally harvesting zombies? Surely you've heard the reports," Kat pressed.

"In case you hadn't noticed, I had a few things on my mind over the past few hours. Namely, trying to keep a few Z's out of mine."

That line sent most of the press corps into laughter. I was good at that. In spite of the blood and gore covering the field, you could always count on good ol' Vince Lager for a laugh. Scanning the room, I noticed one not laughing: Kat Ellison.

When the laughter died down a few notches, she interjected, "You didn't answer my question."

"Kat, I'd love to, but to be honest, I have no idea what you're talking about. I'll watch your report on the news later, I'm sure, but all I'm going to worry about this week is the Brain Bowl. After that, whatever the ZFL is doing, or not doing—that's between them and the Department of Defense. It doesn't have anything to do with me. Now, who wants to ask me about the decapitation in the second quarter? The touchdown on the switchblade sweep in the third?"

I was peppered with questions about the game, the zombies, my teammates—past and present—for the next twenty minutes, but all I could focus on was Kat's question. It was a source of pain, and one that had troubled me before. I knew the question would be asked of me again later that night.

* * *

This is a ZFL Special Report. Since its inception, the ZFL has provided the world with two services: a method of collecting zombies, and entertainment. What we have uncovered in an unprecedented in-depth investigation, is that the ZFL is not just collecting and keeping the world's zombies for use in the barbaric game called Z Ball, but that the Z population has dwindled so much that the league has resorted to the unthinkable.

As one eyewitness — who refuses to divulge their identity — says, the ZFL can no longer meet the needs of the ever-expanding league. With an average of twenty to thirty Z-infected people used in game play every Sunday afternoon and Monday night, the need is exceeding the supply.

"I've been to the zombie stables. There are just a few left. Each week the ZFL has to scrape the bottom of the barrel, plus some, to fill their rosters."

On screen, a blurred out face was seen in a darkened room talking to Kat Ellison. After a moment, images flashed across the screen from a few of this season's games. Eviscerations, limbs cut off, ligaments and tendons severed — from zombie and human alike.

"So what does that mean?"

"In the short term? It means the quality of play goes down. Think about it — in the first games of the year, what'd you see? A lot of violence, especially from the Z

side of the ball. But over the first month of the season, the best — the most fit — zombies all got what was coming to them. After that — especially in the last few games, what have we seen? Overweight, even obese...women, kids, the elderly — those who wouldn't even have been chosen for a backyard football game," the anonymous source said.

Kat was clearly annoyed by the comment, looking for something different, and she said so.

"Okay, fine. Forget the games for a moment. What else? What have you seen?"

"I've...I don't know if I can really talk about it."

Mr. Anonymous was getting agitated. It was obvious he would rather talk football than the serious issues Kat Ellison was confronting him with. For her part, though, Kat was empathetic. She reached over and patted the man's hand.

"Sure you can. Just tell me what you told me earlier."

He took a deep breath and launched in. What he said would be replayed over and over from that night until the kickoff two weeks later for Brain Bowl.

"People. Regular, ordinary people. They are taking them and converting into zombies. Ever since Week 6 of the season, the freshest zombies on the field are just that. Freshly turned. Gathered...harvested...taken off the streets just a week or two beforehand. I've seen the rooms where they were drugged. One by one, the zombies were allowed in, and allowed to...feed. Allowed to take normal people and make them zombies. All for...football. The greatest game on earth is now the greatest murder machine on earth."

* * *

For a half hour, Kat continued to probe and dig into the Zombie Football League. She and the network brought in experts from a number of fields, including the fairly new area of Zombie Ambulatory Sciences to discuss how "fresh" the latest zombies were and the likelihood of them being humans just days earlier.

I was transfixed in front of the television, horrified and somewhat justified at the same time. Of course, Kat gave ZFL Commissioner Rod Parnell a chance to respond as well. Surely she hadn't shown him the entirety of her investigation. There was no way Parnell would have let all that footage air without some sort of rebuttal, I thought. But at the end of the piece, the station noted Parnell was given a chance to reply to the allegations and declined.

Even though our victory earlier in the day to send us to the Brain Bowl should have led the news, Kat's investigative journalism sunk that. I couldn't escape the footage — it was on nearly every channel, it dominated the net, and Twitter was just beside itself. The spotlight had left the game itself and was now focused off the field. I dreaded going to the training facility the next day...and every day after for that matter.

Brain Bowl VI couldn't come soon enough, and after that, the offseason.

I switched off the television and sunk into my couch. My apartment was quiet, but only for a few seconds until a knock echoed throughout the small space.

I grabbed my hunting knife from the side table and went to the door. Everyone had some kind of weapon when they went out these days. Maybe it was a gun, maybe a knife, maybe a portable flamethrower. America — and the rest of the world — was armed to the teeth. You never knew what was behind the door, so preparedness was the word of the century.

I looked through the peephole. I couldn't believe it.

Kat Ellison.

I pulled my face back from the door and blinked. Just hours before I'd answered her question at the press conference and I just finished watching her report. According to her report, I was just a cog in a machine of death. Why was she here now?

Curiosity won me over. I bit the side of my mouth and opened the door. I didn't realize at the time I still had my knife in hand.

"Vince, are you planning to stab me? I mean, my report was bad for you, but I hoped it wasn't *that* bad..." Kat said when I swung the door open.

I stared down at my hand. I stuck the knife into the leather sheath at my side and turned my attention back to the TV reporter at my door. "What do you want, Kat?"

She leaned against the doorframe and gave me that smile. I hated that smile. Just like I hated donuts or bacon or beer. "Aren't you going to invite me in?"

"The one person trying to destroy my career?"

"That's debatable. Let me in so we can talk," Kat said.

Against my better judgment, I turned to let her in. She swept past me, her scent momentarily sending me back to college. Sending me back to when both Kat and I were nobodies. Yet, for a time, she was my everything.

In a way, my apartment probably looked a lot like I was still in college. Beer cans and pizza boxes littered the kitchen and coffee table. The only thing different was the blades, guns, and other small types of weaponry scattered around. My ZFL uniform was unique to me, constantly being upgraded, mostly at my discretion. I was always on the lookout for the newest, latest, sleekest way of killing a zombie. And finding a way to conceal it inside a football uniform.

"Geez, Vince. If we hadn't already gone through one apocalypse, I'd swear your apartment was the scene of one," Kat said.

"Very funny," I said. I was still standing by the door. She didn't indicate at all the visit would be short, so I slinked away and perched myself on a bar stool by the kitchen. I found a half-full beer still cold enough and took a swig.

Kat didn't sit, but leaned against the wall just next to the balcony door. I could tell she was just as nervous as me at being in the same space together.

"I'm sure you're wondering why I'm here."

A statement. No question. She was a pro, honing her skills the past half-decade since she'd left journalism school.

"Yup."

I'd also learned how to answer questions in the furnace of a ZFL locker room. The less said, the better.

"Did you watch my report?"

"Just finished, as a matter of fact."

"I'd hoped you would. Figured you couldn't help yourself. And that's why I'm here."

I put the beer down. I had a bad taste in my mouth, but it wasn't the alcohol. I glared at Kat, hoping she would feel the rage beginning to boil up in me.

"To gloat? To watch my career go down in flames, just like you watched when I nearly destroyed my own chances at success in college?"

She shook her head, but I wasn't having it.

I stood up and motioned to the TV. "You know what I saw when I watched your report? I saw that bar video on a loop. Over and over. Vince Lager is the superstar quarterback of the ZFL and you can't bear to watch your former boyfriend have success, so you find a way to sabotage it. I don't go to bars anymore, so what can you do? A fine job of killing my career, if you ask me."

I might've been a little angry. I stopped and took a deep breath. Kat didn't flinch.

"Running in head-first, and not using it for the brain inside. That's always been your problem, Vince," Kat said. "Can we just talk for a few minutes?"

I chewed on my lip a little and nodded. If there was anyone in the world who could bring me down, it was Kat Ellison. It was true when we were co-eds and it's still true now.

"Vince, I came here tonight because I still care about you. We...we lost what we had in college, but I can't lose you. And I'm afraid if you play in the Brain Bowl, I will."

"Kat, we both know Z Ball isn't the safest sport, but you know me. I can handle it. Whatever gets thrown at me will be easy, even in the Brain Bowl."

"The safest sport? Safe? There is *nothing* safe about Z Ball. How many fatalities last year?" Kat demanded.

"I don't know," I mumbled. Which was a lie. I knew. Forty-three players from eight teams. Dead or turned — which may as well be death.

"Whatever. If you don't know, you're an ignorant fool. If you're lying to me, you're lying to yourself as well. Those knives and guns are only going to work for so long. And even if you beat them all, you still haven't won. Commissioner Parnell won't let you."

She turned her head towards the clear glass door. I saw her reflection and thought I might've glimpsed tears streaking down her cheeks. Impossible. She'd shelved those feelings for me a long time ago.

"Parnell? What are you talking about?"

She turned back to me. I saw a glint in her eyes. Must've been a trick of the light. "Look Vince, just keep your head down for now. I need to do a little more research, but all I'm saying is there is more to my report than what you saw on TV."

Before I could respond, she marched across the room, her perfume once again wafting across my nostrils, a pleasant memory of a former life. She opened the door, gave me one last look, and walked out.

* * *

A few days went by. I didn't hear from Kat again, although her face was plastered all over the TV. Almost every time I turned on Sports Intel, there she was, talking about the apparent scandal, about how Commissioner Parnell and the ZFL were hiding their real actions from the public. Every time I saw her, I wanted to believe her, but I also wanted to keep my job.

After the team made the trip to Dallas for the prep week before Brain Bowl VI, (after what Jellyroll Parks did, Parnell made sure to get the Brain Bowl in Dallas every year) I got a phone call while sitting in my hotel room, just after I'd watched one such Sports Intel report from Kat.

"Hello?"

"Vince?"

I sat up straight, and turned off the TV. "Cal? What's up, man?"

A moment of hesitation on his end. "Not much. Just watching a lot of film. You know how it is."

I did. Even though our brand of football in the ZFL was totally different than the NFL, we still prepped for each game. We didn't play other teams exactly, but the league did provide film on the prospective Z defenders each week. The line-up was subject to change of course—accidents happened—but we had a line-up on which we based our plays and weaponry.

"Yeah, I got you."

"Hey—I'm sorry I didn't call earlier, but congrats on the Brain Bowl. I know you must've been pumped to get there. I mean, it isn't the NFL..."

"The NFL? What a joke, Cal. The ZFL is at the top of the world right now. You can't even compare the two," I interjected.

Another small moment of quiet from Cal. Yeah, I was a jerk.

"Vince?"

"Yeah Cal?"

"You're a prick."

We both laughed for a moment, and when silence fell again, I told him what happened.

"Cal, she came to see me."

"Kat? I saw the press conference. That what you mean?"

Now the pause was on my end. Since Cal had essentially been my on-field bodyguard in college, and Kat my off-field bodyguard, they were more than familiar with each other. The three of us traveled as a small pack for a while around Tempe. Even after Kat and I had broken up, Cal and Kat had remained friends. They had tried to hide it, but I knew.

"Nope. I mean *after* the presser. I went back to my place, watched her on the tube, and then bam — she was at my door, wanting to talk."

"And did you?" Cal asked.

"We did. A little," I admitted. "She claimed to have more dirt on Parnell than she put up in her initial report, but then left before she would tell me much else."

I could almost sense Cal nodding his head on the other end of the line. "Did she say anything else?"

"Like why she walked out of my life back at college? That the one day — the one *freaking* day I needed her, she was gone? Like how the next time I saw her I was fielding questions at a press conference like we'd never met each other a day in our lives?"

"Vince," Cal began.

"Nope. Not at all."

Another pause. Cal was hiding something, but before I could say anything, he dropped this on me — "Dude, you are an idiot. She never gave up on you. You gave up on yourself. You need to call her. See what she really has to say before you go and kill yourself on Sunday."

My mouth opened, ready to reply, but Cal had already hung up.

* * *

After Cal dismissed me, I spent the rest of the night with my thumb hovering over the SEND button on my phone. I convinced myself if my fingers twitched and my thumb landed on the green button, it was fate and I had been destined to call Kat. Okay, I was a jerk and a coward.

Somewhere along the way, though, I fell asleep, my mind replaying what happened between Kat and me. It was the bar brawl that did us in. I lost my temper and Kat all at once. We'd been stupid in love. Turned out, I was just stupid. She wouldn't talk to me when I got out of jail, and I was determined to not go crawling back. I felt really low and then her absence just about did me in completely. I never thought I would forgive her. It was hard enough to see her on Sundays after games. But, when Cal told me she felt like she did after nearly a decade...I was blown away.

My dreams were empty, just like my hotel room. I guess I'd hoped Kat would be running through my head while I slept, but instead it was me running from a pack of Z's. Kat didn't show, but she hadn't been in my dreams for a long time. It was no surprise.

When I woke, my right arm was numb, the nerves asleep from the unnatural sleeping position, but I still had my phone clutched in my grip. It took a moment to register, but my phone was ringing. Was Kat feeling the same way I did? Had she decided to call me first?

I quickly reached over with my left arm and swiped the home screen. With a half-dead arm, I clumsily held the phone to my ear.

"Hello?"

"Vince Lager?"

I shook my head to try to clear my mind. The voice on the other end of the line was definitely *not* Kat Ellison. It was a male voice, authoritative, yet familiar.

"Yes, you got him. Who's this?"

"This is ZFL Commissioner Rod Parnell," the voice on the other end announced. Even though he wasn't in the room, I sat up a little straighter.

"Yes sir. What can I do for you?"

"I'd like to see you in my office this afternoon. You know how to get there, I assume?"

I had never been there myself, but everyone knew where the ZFL was headquartered. I'd find it, one way or another.

"Yeah...I mean, yes. I'll find it. I've got a walk-through practice this morning with the team. How about 2 o'clock?"

"See you then."

By the time I put the phone down, the feeling in my arm had begun to come back. Sharp, stabbing needles prickling from the inside out, reminding me I had fallen asleep holding the phone. I mentally kicked myself for pining away for Kat. She obviously had it in for me and the league. I guess Parnell must've figured out our connection from ASU.

I slid down into the pile of pillows at the end of my hotel bed. I tossed my phone away from me, and tried to collect my thoughts. This whole Kat Ellison thing was getting to me. She...dammit. She was the best thing to ever happen to me, Z Ball or not. But there wasn't a choice to be had right now. Z Ball paid the bills and Kat wanted nothing to do with me. In fact, after her report, it was clear she had a vendetta against me.

A blinking light brought my attention back to my phone. I had a voicemail. How did that happen? Whoever it was must've dialed in during Parnell's call. I entered my passcode and sat up once I heard Kat's voice.

"Vince? Um...I got your call. But you didn't say anything. I just wanted to check to make sure you're okay. So...if you get this, um...shoot me a text or something. Okay?"

My thumb must've had a mind of its own after I'd fallen asleep. I had dialed Kat after all, somehow allowing my unconscious and subconscious to rule over my waking mind.

The next few hours were a blur. Of course, you still want to be on top of your game at practice. There have been incidents in Z Ball practice before. The league supplies the teams with a few Z for use in practice—the older, and slower ones. Usually missing a few limbs or having a pre-cracked skull or something like that. Practice came and went. I anni-hilated a few Z, but it was all muscle memory. When you've been playing Z Ball as long as I have, you can just about play in your sleep.

Just about.

Once practice ended, I readied myself for a trip to see Commissioner Parnell. I'd met him before, of course, but mostly just for photo ops.

Being commissioner of a professional sports league where some of the players occasionally had their throats violently ripped out on national televi-sion required a certain lack of a soul. For Rod Par-nell—a trial lawyer before the Z event—that re-quirement was no problem at all.

I arrived at the league offices early for my ap-pointment and was directed towards Parnell's office on the top floor. I cracked the door, and heard Par-nell inside call me in. The office was large, almost half of the entire top floor by itself. I was immedi-ately taken aback by what I encountered just past the door. There was a small hallway before the proper office space, but the sides of the hall were actually fiberglass enclosures, each side containing one of the undead, almost like trophies for Parnell.

On one side, a woman, still dressed in business attire, like she had stepped out of the office next door and had been infected. To my left was a man, wearing jeans and a flannel shirt, complete with a thick leather belt—almost like a handyman or plumber. They both were still at first, but as soon as I set foot past the doorframe, they screamed and lunged at me, slamming into the barrier separating me from them. Instinctively, my knife came out, but there would have been no way for me to protect myself against two that close, that fast. Eventually my heart found its way back into my chest and I heard Parnell calling to me.

"Vince? Hey, come on in, my star quarterback!"

I didn't make a show of it, but I hurried past the small hallway and into the office. Parnell motioned for me to sit, and I did in a chair across from his desk. The commissioner had a fairly sparse office for someone as powerful as he was. I didn't even get a chance to say anything before he launched in.

"Vince, my man. Let me get right to the point. You and Kat Ellison."

No question there. He proved he knew about me and her. Maybe he'd always known, but our history hadn't been an issue until now.

"Me and Kat," I repeated.

"As you can imagine, her little...report...has ruffled some feathers around the league," Parnell said.

He didn't ask a question. I didn't respond.

"So how close are you two?"

I sighed. "We used to be inseparable. Then...I got in the way of us. Really haven't had much contact since college until last week," I said.

"Yet, since then, she visited your apartment and then you called her last night," he said. Parnell leaned back, trying to gauge my reaction.

Should I have been surprised? I suppose, but after everything Kat said about the league, I figured at least a certain percentage had to be true. If they were bold enough to take people off the streets, what would stop them from invading every inch of the privacy of the star quarterback?

"To answer your question—we aren't close. She's vindictive and wants to ruin me. I called her, but I never reached her. She just came by my apartment to gloat. I finally make the Brain Bowl, and all she wants to do is destroy my life," I said.

"Really?"

"Really."

I could see Parnell was conflicted. There was no way he was comfortable with his star QB hanging out with the very journalist who was trying to sabotage his league before the biggest game of the year. But I wasn't giving him the pleasure of admonishing me for my relationship.

"Then here's what I'd like you to do: I want you to get closer and to find out what else she knows. If I go down, you go down. Say goodbye to football, forever. She clearly hates you, but the line between love and hate is thin. I want to use her feelings against her."

* * *

I left the meeting with the commissioner—walking right down the middle of the hallway to avoid the Zoo of the Undead I'd encountered on my entrance—and immediately called Kat again. I figured she wouldn't even pick up. She answered on the first ring.

"Hey you," Kat answered.

"Hey. We should talk," I said. I was reminded by the fact she said the same thing to me just a few days earlier.

It was almost as if I could see her look to her left and her right.

"Are you ready for the truth, Vince?" Kat asked.

"Isn't that what you've been giving everyone on TV this week? The truth?"

"Yeah...well, I'm going to blow this story wide open. We all know words aren't enough to convince the public. They need to *see* the truth. It's taken a lot of work, but I'm almost ready to give it to them."

Her words reminded me of the girl I fell for back in college. So sure of herself. So sure of her future. So sure of the truth—what was right and wrong. I was scared of what she had found.

"I want to see it, too. I'm ready."

"Okay. Meet me Friday night. I'll text you details an hour before we meet. I'm looking forward to it, Vince."

The way she said it almost convinced me she was serious. That there was some spark left after all these years. Perhaps there was something left. Or perhaps I was imagining everything after all.

I'd told Commissioner Parnell I would spy on Kat for him because I was sure she was dead set on my failure. With just days to go before the Brain Bowl, I hoped I figured it out soon.

* * *

Practice was relatively calm. By this point in the season, the league was down to the bottom of the barrel with their Z supply, especially for practices. On Friday morning, they sent us one without half of its rib cage. Seriously. I couldn't believe my working conditions sometimes.

But between the practices and the media sessions, I only had half a brain on the game. My other half was already with Kat Friday night. I didn't know what she wanted me to see, but whatever it was might destroy my career, so I was understandably a little apprehensive.

The text came in and I was to meet Kat at an industrial park on the outskirts of Dallas. "Come alone," the message said, "and be ready for anything."

"Be ready" in the post-Z world meant come with a weapon strapped to your body or be prepared to have your body ripped limb from limb. But with Kat...I wasn't so sure. I grabbed a couple of my favorite blades and a pistol just in case. Even if I wasn't meeting my ex-girlfriend, I would have brought lethal weapons with me. Her presence just meant I needed more.

The cab dropped me off in the old meatpacking district, just south of the Trinity River. I had no idea where I was, but the cabbie who dropped me off had no trouble filling me in.

Once on the sidewalk, I was immediately greet-ed by two hands on my back. Gut reactions took over and I reached into my jacket, fully prepared to go to battle with whatever was behind me.

"Whoa, whoa. Hold on there."

I recognized the voice, but it wasn't Kat.

"Cal?" I turned around and found my old col-lege buddy next to me. He had his hands up, slight-ly defensive, but ready to move should the situation turn. "What are you doing here?"

"He's with me," Kat said. She stepped out of the shadows and under a street lamp.

"But...Cal, you're married," I said.

"Not that like, you dope," Cal muttered. "I'm her...protection. I was...am her source."

I squinted at him. "What do you mean?"

"My job," he began.

"...is being an offensive lineman in the NFL," I finished.

He shook his head. "It is during the season, but the sport doesn't pay like it used to. Not since Z Ball took over the country. I had to take an offseason gig."

I looked from Cal to Kat and back again. Neither were smiling. "What do you mean? Like working as a trainer?"

He pursed his lips. "Something like that. Come on, follow me."

Kat immediately zipped up the dark hoodie she had on, and pulled the hood down over her golden hair. A pair of thick-framed glasses concealed her appearance; if I came across her on the street, I wouldn't have spotted her. She handed me a ball cap. "Put it on," she said. I did, sliding it down just above my eyes and ears. Cal didn't seem to care about altering his look.

"Where are we going?" I asked.

Cal didn't look back, but answered me nonetheless.

"Hell."

The closest building was a large steel-frame structure. Nothing different from a dozen other buildings within walking distance, but Cal headed straight for a set of stairs affixed to the outer skin of the warehouse. He paused at the bottom of the stairs, his head down.

"Come on, Cal. You've got to show him. Show him what his sport does," Kat said from behind me. I looked back at her. Her eyes were partially hidden by the glasses, but I could see fear and apprehension on her face. But there was more. There was determination. I knew that Kat.

"Okay. Please, remember the man who protected you in college, not one who protects...this," Cal said. He swiftly took the stairs two by two, not waiting for me or Kat. He pulled out a key to unlock the facility and ushered us inside.

Once inside, I realized the building itself was insulated. The noise inside was almost deafening, a cacophony of guttural voices, slamming against walls and every surface on the interior. It was dark, though, so I couldn't immediately see what Cal was bringing me to see. The open door to the outside was shut, spreading darkness everywhere until Cal slammed his hand against a switch on the wall, unleashing dawn inside the building.

The sight before me took my breath away. Almost as if she anticipated it, Kat reached out and gripped my hand in hers. Her skin was so soft and warm, a stark contrast against the death surrounding us. For an instant, if I closed my eyes I could have almost pictured the two of us back in college, untouched by the loss of the Z apocalypse.

But the Z apocalypse wasn't over. Proof was locked up in cages on the warehouse floor beneath us. Z everywhere, mostly milling about, but some were definitely more aggressive than others. Those berserkers rapidly strafed around the room, searching for an out, searching for blood, searching for brains.

"What...?" I managed to eek out. I managed to deal with maybe a dozen or so each week at games and a couple during practice, but there were hundreds below my feet. Maybe even thousands.

"Shh, quiet," Kat whispered. She nodded to Cal, who grabbed my arm and led me to a small alcove, shrouded in shadows. We could still see out, but no one could see in.

Just as quickly as we'd snuck into the warehouse, we heard another group enter from a different second story entrance on the opposite side of the building. I heard muffled voices, talking, even laughing with each other. I was able to get a good look at the group—a few men with large boxes. Wooden crates the size of refrigerator boxes. I asked myself what was in the boxes, but somewhere deep down, I knew. Kat had been right about everything.

I tried to turn my head, and Cal shoved me in the back with his elbow. "You don't get to pretend this isn't happening anymore. Watch."

So I watched. I watched the men load the boxes on a pulley system and lower them into the pit below. It was an area free of Z. With the flip of a switch, an electronic sound chirped and the boxes swung open. A group of men and women—mostly homeless from the look of their clothing—slowly emerged, dazed, but very much uninfected by the Z virus.

Once they were all free, the boxes were closed and raised again and the men hauled them outside. The people huddled together, seeing what was in the cages on every side. There was no exit for the Z, which meant there was no exit for those pinned between the cages, either.

Another chirp, and the doors to the Z cages swung open. I felt my stomach drop as a feeding frenzy began. Blood splattered on the floors and walls, and the sound of bones cracking and crunching made me want to vomit. I felt lightheaded, but once again Kat took my hand.

"This is the truth. This is what the league does. Commissioner Parnell has approved every bit of this. They pick up people—people who won't be missed—and they turn them. Just so they can line their pockets with TV revenue. Just so you can get paid."

I regretted everything. I had made a huge mistake, the last of which was texting Parnell before I had taken the taxi to the meatpacking district. I wanted to run—to be the coward I knew I was, but I ached to hold Kat's hand for as long as I could. I knew once we were found, she wouldn't ever agree to be near me again.

"Aha!" a voice shouted. A couple of large men just out of sight pulled us out of the alcove. Apparently our location was not as much of a secret as Cal had thought. The last thing I saw was a boot getting ready to slam into my head.

* * *

My mind was a fog. I tried to shake it out, but found myself weighed down. I almost couldn't move, but then noticed I was wearing my uniform. Helmet, pads, and all. I glanced down and saw bright green with white chalk lines.

I was on the field. At Cowboy Stadium.

I'd woken up in the middle of the Brain Bowl. I gave myself one more second to clear my head, and then I got to my feet. If I was already on the field, it meant...the Z were coming soon.

"And your starting QB for Chicago—Vince Lager!"

The public address announcer's voice echoed throughout the stadium, and thousands of fans cheered and jeered. Normally I would soak up the attention, but I'd lost over a day of my life. The last memory I had was in the warehouse with Cal and Kat. I looked over my arms and legs quickly and didn't see any bite marks. Whatever had happened, it hadn't involved the Z that had been swarming in the warehouse below us.

I looked around, and didn't see anything out of the ordinary for a Z Ball game. My teammates were on the sideline with me, waving to the crowd. The team from L.A. was lined up on the other side of the plexiglass partition, getting ready for the opening whistle.

Once again, muscle memory took hold and I went through the motions. My body was here, but my mind was elsewhere — back at that warehouse with Kat. I tried to put it out of my thoughts. I tried to focus on the game. If I could just get through the Brain Bowl, then I could get out of here and figure out what happened to my friends.

As I lined up on my 40-yard line, I heard a voice inside my helmet. Usually, I had the speaker turned off. Coach Foster liked to talk to us, but let us focus on the game while the clock was ticking. This voice was not Coach Foster's though. It was Commissioner Rod Parnell.

"Hello, Vince. No need to talk back, there's no microphone on your end. All you need to do is listen."

I looked around and found Parnell's skybox. It was almost directly on the 50-yard line, where he could see both teams equally. But he wasn't watching L.A., he was looking down at me.

"Here's the thing, Vince. You're a good quarterback, don't get me wrong. But I've learned something running this league the past few years. Everyone is replaceable. Even you. What about your buddy Pilson? He was going to be the next big thing, but then he got himself bit and played for the other side first chance he got."

I had a terrible feeling in my stomach. I'd faced down scores of the undead, but the most frightening thing in my life was the voice of Parnell in my ear at that very moment.

"So we followed you last night. Even if you hadn't agreed to help us out, we were going to find Kat and Cal. I knew about your relationship to both of them a long time ago, but with Cal, he insisted he wouldn't involve you. He was in breach of contract, so we had to terminate him, unfortunately. As for Kat..."

As for Kat, I didn't even hear his response. I saw her. At least, what used to be her. After the player introductions, the Z combatants were released from their containment area, and Kat was shambling out with the rest of them. I barely noticed the hulking form of Cal behind her. In that moment, I didn't care about my teammates. I didn't care about the other half-dozen Z. I didn't even care about myself.

The game hadn't started yet, but I ran towards the horde. For once I figured I would try to be brave. I was going to put whatever was left of Kat and Cal out of their misery. I was going to try to make up in some small way for everything I'd done. I would take care of all of them and spill the league's secrets after the game. Kat and Cal deserved that much. I reached for the sword latched to the back of my uniform.

But...my sword wasn't there. I pawed at my arms and found no knives. I reached for my hip pads, hoping for the back-up pistol I'd always kept there.

Nothing.

They'd drugged me and left me with nothing. Parnell's voice interrupted my thoughts.

"Thanks for a great career, Vince. You were and will always be one of the greats of Z Ball," Parnell said.

The fight wasn't over. I remembered Jellyroll's last stand, and fought and clawed my way through the undead. Even without weapons, the uniform protected me for a long time. I grabbed a nearby helmet and used it like a baseball bat against a few of the heads of the Z before me.

Parnell knew what he'd done. He knew who I was. I was the same, scared man who had gotten into a bar fight and lost a chance to have everything in the NFL. I had a chance to tell the world about the ZFL, and I charged, without thinking, into a full squad of fresh undead players.

I was a coward and a failure.

Cal, Kat, and the other Z slammed into me. I had a few more seconds of consciousness, and Parnell confirmed what I already knew.

"Long live Z Ball," Parnell seemed to whisper in my ear.

Within seconds, my own blood clouded my vision. Parnell had won, and I had lost. I knew I had failed for the final time.

Parnell's voice echoed in my ears.

"Long live Z Ball!"

A Word from Will Swardstrom

So often with zombies, we think of apocalyptic events and the end of the world. A ragtag group of survivors on the run, living day to day. We think of massive hordes that are too overpowering for the world's civilizations.

I'd like to think that even if zombies were to over-run the earth, our trained military forces would eventually gain the upper hand. We'd might even contain the threat. That was part of the idea behind "Z Ball". What if we not only contained the zombies, but also put them to work for us?

Back in 2008, the big banks in New York caused a huge financial crisis. Millions of people were affected between losing jobs, pensions, and their homes. Yet, nothing of consequence has happened to the bank executives. In fact, when the banks should have been bankrupted by their unethical practices, the government bailed them out with billions of dollars.

When a government that refuses to acknowledge when corporate corruption and crime exists, what happens when zombies enter the picture?

Then, in 2014, when Baltimore Ravens running back Ray Rice was caught on camera knocking out his then-fiancee, the power of the NFL commissioner was on full display. Again, a multi-millionaire CEO essentially was able to do what he wanted without many repercussions.

In a previous life, I worked as a sports reporter, so the football side of the story came naturally to me. I thought "Z Ball" could be an out-of-the-box take on the zombie genre, and I hope you enjoyed it.

Huge thanks to my brother Paul Swardstrom, Thomas Robins, Chris Fried, David Walters, Christy Winemiller, and Chris Pourteau for beta reading this story and helping it along. I'd also like to thank Samuel Peralta for his creation of *The Future Chronicles* and his invitation to be in *The Z Chronicles* and to Ellen Campbell for her excellent editing.

I'd love to hear from you, the reader. You can follow my adventures on my blog at https://willswardstrom.wordpress.com/, or my Amazon page at http://www.amazon.com/Will-Swardstrom/e/B00DJK9W02/where you can also find all my other books.

RIP Jellyroll

Gloria
by Hugh Howey

1

IT SOUNDED LIKE HANDS digging in buckets of popcorn, like Velcro pressed together and ripped back apart, all those fingernails gouging and scrambling against the bark of the tree. Gloria jostled with the pack beneath the limb. Mother and daughter sat above, quietly crying and whispering false hopes, cornered like cats by a pack of dogs.

There was no escape, Gloria saw. For the past few hours, she had studied the predicament of the two women, and there was no escape. Not for any of them. This was what frightened her the most: the left-behind souls scrambling at the trunk were just as trapped as the starving couple in the tree. And a steady trickle of the blood-crusted meat-eaters were shambling through the woods to cluster beneath that limb. It was like ants spilling down a slippery funnel they couldn't get back out of. They were all trapped, every one. They would be, until those women on that limb starved to death or lost their balance, until they were either consumed or their meat rotted in death and stopped smelling like sweet succor.

This was not a problem Gloria had foreseen. The living simply did not do this, they didn't hover almost within reach, neither running nor dying. They survived or they were consumed. They got away or they passed through the guts of the damned. One side or the other won, never a stalemate.

Not a stalemate, Gloria thought. Purgatory. Trapped in the in-between. They were a lot like Gloria in that way, and she wondered what they had done to deserve this. Something, obviously. The Lord was just, all sins accounted for. They had all done something to be trapped there.

Hours went by, thinking such circular thoughts. Gloria circled that tree, which she thought was an oak. She bumped into the others and took her turn scratching the rough bark. She clawed at the air and groaned at the nothing, secretly privy to the voiced fears and panicked whispers that drifted down from above.

And Gloria prayed for deliverance. She thought of that shoreline she had walked down hours before and wondered if turning toward the water, toward the thing she feared in that moment, may not have been the better choice. Wasn't this her lot? Her life? Was this the lesson God was attempting to hammer home?

Gloria kicked through the dry leaves and mulled over the times she'd felt both trapped and safe. Trapped in marriage, even after the baby was taken from her, even after her husband was locked away. The sin of divorce was that frigid lake, and so she circled Carl for years and years, pawing at the empty space around her.

A job she hated, turning over rooms, making bed after bed, picking up scattered towels and restocking stolen toiletries. Every day, tiptoeing through wrecks that looked more like robberies than a night's stay, dealing with creepy men who put signs out for service, but were still in there, sometimes a towel around their waists, pretending to be startled, sometimes wearing nothing at all. Men sent by the devil to harass her, to tell her she was pretty when she knew better, offer her money for unspeakable things.

A job she hated, but change was the other way. Applications and learning something new were the icy deep.

The city was a funnel. Gloria looked around her, something she secretly did on the subway. All different colors, different backgrounds, all the accents. Ants drawn to honey, but they can't get away from the city. They land with their parents or bring their own children, get that first job, learn to drive a cab or flip a room, and never leave.

This was her sin, Gloria thought. God had given her command of her feet and had set her on the shore of life, and she had chosen to live the least. She had always chosen to avoid her fears, had shrunk from the daunting and the risky. And what had her Savior done? Had he walked away from the challenge, or had he strolled across the water knowing he would not sink?

Gloria let out a frustrated gurgle, a prayer to Saint Anthony, the liberator of prisoners:

Tear down my prison walls. Break the chains that hold me captive. Make me free with the freedom Christ has won for me. Amen.

She prayed to Saint Leonard, the patron Saint of captives, slaves, and all those held against their will:

Pray for those like me in prison, Saint Leonard. For those forgotten in prison, pray for them. Amen.

Gloria prayed for herself, for her own plights. She prayed for someone to grant her the courage. She prayed for deliverance, for rescue, for something to break her free of the cycle in which she'd long been trapped. She prayed that she could do it all over again, that she might head west and live in a small town, find a different job, a good man, try once more to start a family, to have a child or two or four. She prayed and prayed the same prayers, her words running out, forming small loops, memorized verse, begging and begging for release as she circled that tree, bumping into so many others, but giving little thought to them at all.

2

Morning came, and birdsong filled the air around all the trees but one. Unlike the squirrels, which would burrow through the leaves by undead feet, the birds chirped warily and from a distance. When they did swoop in, it was only briefly to pick maggots from a cheek or eye socket. They would perch on a shoulder and pluck a morsel or scrap of rotten flesh, maybe a torn bit of fabric for their nest, and then flap away to a far branch. While they preened and ate and squawked at the world, another leaf would lose its precarious grip and drift down around Gloria and the others.

It had been an especially cold night for all of them. Frost lay in patches, the browning leaves looking as if dusted in sugar, the uncut grass and tall weeds adorned with frozen crystals. Gloria wasn't sure how the mother and child in the tree had survived the bitter cold, but they were already moving about on the broad limb. The mom directed her child into a patch of sunlight that managed to lance through the distant buildings and silent trees to warm a spot of air. Their whispers leaked through chattering teeth.

Gloria had spent much of the night drifting in and out. She remembered coming to and hearing the sobs, which she assumed at first to be from the child, but it was the mother crying. She also saw the pack had grown in number. The tree was one of those crab pots the poor animals could crawl into but never get out of. Gloria and the rest would be there until the couple starved and rotted, until the appetite was gone, the scent dissipating.

It was bitingly cold, and the evidence formed in puffs of false breath, the undead groaning in hungry frustration, the woman and young girl above adding their own shivering clouds to the air.

Gloria circled beneath them. She watched as the mother seemed to succumb to the stress and cold, as she lost her mind. It took a moment to realize what she was doing, that she was stripping herself bare in the morning chill. With her chin lifted toward the promise of a meal, Gloria followed, curious and confused, as the woman tore her thin shirt into strips and began twisting them together. She was talking to her daughter as she worked, explaining something, some kind of plan.

Whispers of a plan made Gloria feel torn. There was the thrill of maybe witnessing an escape, perhaps a dash down the creaking and frost-slick limbs, a daring swing or jump to a neighboring tree. Some plan that relied on racing naked ahead of the stumbling pack, running through the woods still dappled in darkness, hoping to avoid the promise of a roaming bite.

Gloria felt the allure of such daring and guile. She also dreaded the loss of a meal, no end to her infernal hunger, and all those days wasted following their scents.

Strips of clothing were tied together. A belt. Torn and threadbare jeans, much too large. The mother worked in her underwear fifteen feet above Gloria's head. It was the daughter's turn to cry. While she sobbed, her mother looped the knotted fabric around the limb on which they crouched. They were both sobbing. The mother stroked the girl's hair, caressed her cheek. Gloria could see them shivering. Maybe she imagined the blue cast to the woman's naked skin. Perhaps it was real. How they survived the night, she couldn't understand. With her clothes off, Gloria felt she could see every bone in her emaciated body.

"Shhh," she said, consoling her child. "It's okay."

She arranged the improvised rope around her daughter's neck, adjusting it as if getting her ready for school. The girl's thin arms held her mother's wrists. Bits of bark rained down from their movement on the limb.

"I love you," the mother said. The words were interspersed with sobs.

And before Gloria could process what was happening, before she could fully wake, there was a final kiss on the forehead, a scrambling of thin arms as the child realized what plans her mother had for their escape, and then a painful shove out into the open air, the crunch of rope on bark, the yank and pop of a young neck, and then bare feet swinging in the frosty air, the last of the leaves from that great bough leaping to their deaths, shaken off by this disturbance in the tree.

Gloria circled beneath the girl, horrified. A police officer waved at the air, the flesh hanging just out of reach, the child slowly spinning as the twisted rope settled.

There were curses above, the mad screech of a woman at the end of a more figurative rope, the yell of anger at the world that Gloria secretly longed to erupt with, that sort of anger with a silent, invisible, and cruel God that bubbles up with every injustice, every heartbreaking loss, every turn of bad luck. Screams instead of whispered prayer. A woman's throat working and yelling all that needed saying.

Gloria's gaze was lifted to the heavens, to this brave mother, and she saw that the curses and screeches were not directed at any God, but rather at the demons below, the hellspawn she had joined.

More leaves fluttered from their weakening stems as the mother pushed off. And with a great leap, she threw herself out of her misery, not enough rope for the both of them, and Gloria, unable to resist, horrified, dove in with the others and claimed her share. And as she fell on the brave soul, something snapped. Some sinew or thread in her brain, whatever it was that anchored her to sanity, she felt it snap and knew, with righteous surety, that God made no mistakes. He had left her there for her sins, for not being perfect enough. This was her damnation, her eternal reward.

She fought her way through the feeding pack and lowered her face toward the mother's screams. Her first bite was of gaunt and trembling cheek, flesh tearing away. She chewed the mouth of this fallen woman, the rubbery lips, hungry for the mind inside. Hungry for it, even as she lost her own. Even though she was, as ever, unaware that anyone resided there. Unaware that anyone other than her suffered at all.

A Word from Hugh Howey

Being a zombie is not at all what we've thought all these long years. It turns out that zombies know exactly what they are doing, they just can't stop themselves. Not only is this just as sound scientifically (there are disorders where motor control is subverted or lost while mental faculties remain intact), it's also much, much more interesting. This is the premise behind "Gloria", one of the souls from *I, Zombie*.

Hugh Howey is the author of the award-winning Molly Fyde Saga *and the New York Times and USA Today bestselling* WOOL *series. The* WOOL OMNIBUS *won Kindle Book Review's 2012 Indie Book of the Year Award -- it has been as high as #1 in the Kindle store -- and 17 countries have picked up the work for translation.* WOOL *is in hardback from Random House UK and keep your fingers crossed that Ridley Scott and Steve Zaillian will do something exciting with the film rights!*

Hugh lives in Jupiter, FL with his wife Amber and their dog Bella. When he isn't writing, he's reading or taking a photograph.

www.hughhowey.com

Her
by David Adams

*You know, gay, lesbian, bisexual, transgender –
people are people.*

- Judith Light

DIANE

WHEN I WAS ALIVE, I used to wonder: can a
ghost and a zombie come from the same person?
The question made sense, I suppose, based on what
I knew at the time. A zombie was the reanimation of
flesh without a soul in it; a ghost was a soul without
flesh.

It turns out that zombies are real.

I don't think ghosts are real. I think this because,
when you're bitten by a zombie, and turn into a
zombie, your consciousness is still in there. Trapped
inside. A spectator to your own life, watching every
horrible thing that you do to those you love.

Canada's gone now. And I don't mean gone as
in a giant smoking crater — that would be a welcome
development at this point. I mean it's mostly overrun with the living dead. The undead. The walking

dead. Whatever we are; shambling corpses staggering around, running, biting, chewing.

The physics of it defy me. My limbs have severed tendons yet still manage to move. My muscles have mostly rotten away but I'm stronger than ever. I eat, even though the meat falls out the empty side of my jaw, and yet I don't die.

When you're a corpse you have a lot of time to think. Almost all of my day is spent wandering the frozen streets of Vancouver, trying to find the living. There aren't many of them left these days. Sometimes we find them.

They don't last long.

My wanderings took me all over town. Into people's houses. Climbing up disused stairs, past debris and ruin and rubble. The city was rotting just like its inhabitants were; falling apart. One day I wandered past a train station. I don't know why my body went that way; when I was alive I rarely took the train. I had my own car. Not a nice car, but it beat riding the train.

Trains were dangerous for girls like me. Yet, in my undeath, I was drawn to the tracks. Further evidence of the gulf between my living and dead self.

Even though there were no living there, my body decided it liked the train station. Up and down the platforms. The doors to the place where the tickets were sold — I don't know if it had a proper name — were locked. There were bodies inside. Dead ones. Proper dead. People had hid there to escape the zombies, I suppose, and finally shot themselves when they realised escape was hopeless. I could see the gun they passed around; the last of them had used it on herself.

The audio recording at the platform was stuck in a loop.

"We are sorry — We are sorry — We are sorry — "

Canada, eh.

I reached the end of the platform and turned, walking back. Sometimes I would pass by the windows of the ticket stand — that was it, the ticket stand! — and, although the glass was caked with dust and snow, sometimes I would see myself in it. A rotting, shambling corpse, still wearing that dark green dress, now stained a rusty brown colour because of all the dirt and blood.

I liked seeing myself like this. I couldn't imagine many others of my kind would; all rot-ten, flesh falling off, almost unrecognisable except for our secondary characteristics. My green dress. Broken glasses, still on my face. Long hair.

Truth is, for the first time, I looked like a real woman.

I was born a boy named Brian.

Being trans affects everything. How you look. How you walk. How you talk. Dating. Masturbation. Sex. Even beyond that sphere; work, travel, family. My family disowned me which, in some ways, made the transition a lot easier. Having a supporting family is excellent for trans people, but if people don't support you, they can't be a part of your life.

Canada is a very safe, very accepting place for trans people, but even the safest place on Earth's still far from perfect. Even if most of my fear was irrational, it was still real; present, like a sour taste in your mouth you can't get rid of, just kind of learn to ignore.

Sometimes people ask me what this fear is like.

Imagine, for a moment, you just got the following text from your parents:

Call us now, urgent.

Picture your phone with that message on it. That feeling you're feeling—the tightening of your chest, the ache in your body, those flashes of almost-memories as you try to imagine why they might send something like this and what it could mean—that's how I felt walking down the street on an average day.

These days, though, I didn't feel anything like that at all. And it was good.

I reached the end of the platform and my body turned to do another endless lap. And then it stopped.

I could hear a train coming.

There hadn't been trains since…whatever had caused the zombies to come. Yet there it was; a whistle in the distance, so faint I thought I was imagining it. The faint clatter of wheels on tracks. The faintest change in air pressure.

The smell of living humans.

Then it came. The front of it was covered in bloody spikes; bodies, some still moving, were impaled upon it. A grisly machine tearing down the tracks, faster than any train I'd ever seen. I could sense my body wanted to go to it, to leap upon the metal cage, tear it open and devour the people inside. There must have been dozens. Hundreds.

Yet, my body just watched the train thunder by. It was full of people, a cacophony of steel and flesh. Going where, I didn't know. Further down the lines. How the humans aboard had managed to get that thing to work, I had no idea.

The scent of human flesh was ambrosia to me...or whatever part of me controlled my body. It turned, following the metal carriage as it passed, looking at all their faces. Their horrified, disgusted faces.

At least, this time, they looked that way for an entirely justified reason.

The train disappeared down the tracks, its cargo of flesh taken with it, and I followed.

* * *

As I followed the train tracks, drawn by the scent of the living, my body did so on autopilot—even more than usual. I barely noticed the changing scenery. The train's arrival, and the loathing on those people's faces, had got me thinking.

My parents hated me for becoming a woman. But, you know, I didn't hate them.

It's hard to avoid meeting hate with hate, even if you try not to. Everyone wants to be good; everyone wants to feel that they're right, justified, correct. They want to feel that anyone they hate deserves it and anyone they love is worthy of their affection. This can work in reverse; for some, there is a feeling that everyone you love *must* be good, and everyone you hate must be bad. Good people don't hate good people.

When it doesn't work out this way, cognitive dissidence occurs; that uncomfortable feeling of knowing your beliefs are wrong but trying, as hard as you can, to justify them.

Parents are probably the most extreme version of this. They get a picture in their head of what their child should be, and will try as hard as they can to make sure that said child becomes that vision. A parent might want a football player or the opposite of a football player, they might want them to love or hate Dungeons and Dragons; a thin daughter, an outgoing daughter, an A student…an image is painted before the child is even born.

My parents wanted a son. A strong, lacrosse playing, frat-boy son, and for a time, I really tried to be that for them. It never felt right; it was a mask, a lie, a painting over another painting. Children pick up on these. They know, consciously or subconsciously, when they're not meeting their parents expectations. Eventually, when I went to college, I had to be me. The real me. I shed Brian like an old skin, and I became Diane.

Parents may not stab their children, but they wound them with a thousand tiny cuts whenever we say, "Your brother always got A's," or "Why don't you have more kids over?" or "Maybe cheerleading just isn't for you."

So many people are so in love with the imaginary kid in their heads, they miss the kid right in front of them.

Mine sure did.

The scent of the living grew stronger, carried on the wind, along with oil and metal. The train was up ahead; it had stopped. At first I suspected mechanical failure, but as my body drew near — drawn by the scent of flesh, I could only assume — I saw something else was afoot.

They were offloading the people into an area surrounded by high walls topped by barbed wire. It looked like some kind of safe zone. Men stood at the top, weapons in their hands.

This was a dangerous place for me to be. Those weapons weren't just for show.

They hadn't seen me yet. I pleaded with whoever — whatever — controlled my body to take a different route. That walking down the tracks, in clear view, was suicide; I would be gunned down. There was no cover, and even if there was, the single minded, animalistic "me" didn't seem to care; it walked, casually as you like, towards the tall wall. A shout from the wall alerted everyone to my presence; they sighted me in.

As a living corpse, could I even die?

They didn't shoot. I didn't quite know why, at first. They just let me slowly walk to-wards them. There were no other zombies around; for some rea-son, only I had caught the train's scent.

"Hey," called some woman through a mega-phone. "You, on the train tracks. Are you alive?"

I said nothing, of course. Just lumbered towards them. I could feel their eyes on me; see the glint in their scopes. At least it would be quick.

One of them fired some huge gun with a barrel opening the size of my fist. Instead of a bullet, how-ever, the projectile blossomed into a net on a rope. It enveloped me, entangling my hands and feet and blasting me back onto the railroad tracks.

I thrashed. Kicked. Hissed inhumanly at them as they pulled me in, dragging me toward the safe compound. My dead flesh fell apart as the gravel scraped it away. A part of the wall opened, reveal-ing a cage. I was dragged inside, a woman inside a zombie inside a dress inside a net inside metal bars.

"Nice shot, Sally," said one of the men. A tat-tooed woman wearing a blue cap stood on top of the cage, peering down at me with indifferent eyes, cropped blonde hair peaking out from the edges of her hat. This woman was a hunter. A fighter. She disliked seeing me alive.

My body hissed and thrashed at her. My mind asked all kinds of questions: why did she have a net? Why had they gone to all this trouble?

Then I saw it. Around me, beakers, machines, diesel generators pumping life into computers. Everything here was assembled by hand; cobbled together from scrap. No consistency, a DIY job in the middle of dead Vancouver. The people I'd seen were wearing a mixture of military uniforms and lab coats.

This wasn't a sanctuary.

It was a laboratory.

"Get to work," said the woman, jumping down off the cage. She walked away without looking back.

* * *

The first thing they did was feed in catchpoles and hook me with them. They were the kind of thing one would use to catch dogs; hollow poles with thick wire. They got my arms, legs, and neck, holding me securely.

Then they injected me with green stuff.

It was a huge syringe that seemed too big for a human. As it pierced my rotten abdomen—why could I still feel that pain?—one of the people in lab coats said something to one of the people wearing the army uniforms. It was a horse needle. 14 gauge apparently; I didn't know what that meant. It was a big one, though.

Some fluid was squeezed into my dead flesh. Every human face was hopeful, excited even; as though I was a lucky break, the pinnacle of some great achievement.

My skin swelled with the amount they injected. It felt like pressure; not really pain, although it was uncomfortable. As the minutes went down the swelling likewise abated. I had no circulatory system anymore so I had no idea how this happened.

My body, of course, reacted violently; it lashed out, thrashing against its bonds, trying to break free. The catch-poles held me tightly, the net and the cage all containing me.

The humans around me waited. Nothing happened.

"It's not working," said the warrior woman, looking at me instead of the person she was talking to. Frustration tainted every word. For a brief moment our eyes met — I don't know why my body made that happen but it did — and I sensed her anger, her frustration, the growing sense that she was wasting her time. "The injection doesn't work, Frank."

"Don't worry," said a short, balding, middle-aged man I could only assume to be the person in charge of this operation. They spoke without care that I could hear. "It might take some time to take effect. Simone, you know as well as I do that we don't truly understand what drives the former human's biology."

Simone folded her arms. "What's the next step?"

Frank smiled nervously. I could sense he liked this warrior woman; and who wouldn't? She was fit, strong, and pretty. "We have several options," he said, folding his hands in front of him. "We can try a larger dose; we can try localising it to areas of the flesh less damaged, or we can try an injection directly into the brain."

"Will any of those work?"

He clicked his tongue. "Only one way to find out," he said. "I suggest perseverance. This one is perfect for our aims; whole enough to still be alive, if the rejuvenation is successful, smart enough not to run in front of the train, but alert enough to follow it to the destination. We couldn't ask for any better."

It wasn't intelligence that prevented my body from leaping in front of the spikes in front of the train. I didn't know what it was, truly, but I truly had no control over my body. I didn't know why I was different.

"Right," Simone said. "Frank, make it happen."

"Of course," said Frank. "Of course."

Frank and the other people in lab coats went away. They couldn't have gone far—the compound was not that big—and my body and I were left in the care of the military personnel.

They didn't like me being here. They looked at me with distain, fingers on their weapons, especially Simone.

The sun began to set. Frank returned, with three syringes, all the same size as the first.

He inspected my body through the bars, disappointment palpable. He prodded my side where the needle had gone in; the flesh seemed almost pink, almost alive, but it weeped the same black ichor all the other zombies did.

"A stronger dose, perhaps," he said to himself, and injected the first of the syringes into me.

Nothing. The flesh pinkened slightly — or perhaps it was a combination of wishful thinking and the dying of the light — and then nothing.

Frank's nervousness returned. I could smell the sweat on his oily skin; see the slight tremble in his hands as he slid the next needle deep into my chest, at least four or five inches in. The plunger was depressed, and more green fluid pushed into me.

The slightest tingle, like pins and needles, and then a warm sensation moved from my feet to the top of my head. It was brief — fleeting, almost — but it remained, as heat clings to coals.

"Fuck," said Frank. He seemed so mild mannered to me; his foulness came suddenly, as though some built up emotion had seemed through the cracks of the emotional dam he'd built to keep them in.

The last syringe. He slid it into my ear.

A most disturbing sensation. I could feel the metal scraping against the inner ear canal, feel it ever so gently rupture the eardrum, poking a hole. That ear went silent. The needle felt its way into my head, scraping past the bone, and then into softer stuff. I felt, rather than saw, Frank inject it.

This time I felt something more; shock coursing all up and down my spine. My body jerked as though it were alive, howling. Frank jumped back.

He watched, eagerly, excitedly, as the warm feeling spread from my hands to my fingers, from my feet to my toes, and I felt heat — so much *heat* — inside, as though I might suddenly burn alive.

I clenched my fist. *I* clenched it, not whatever had controlled me for the last age. It was me. I was in control again.

And then the feeling faded and the zombie returned.

Feet came running. Booted feet. It was Simone, flanked by two soldiers.

"What happened?" she asked. "Did that sound come from…?"

Frank nodded, the smile on his face almost consuming it. "Yes," he said. "Yes, yes, yes!"

Simone, however, seemed less impressed. My body hissed at her, at Frank, at the world.

"It still didn't work," she said.

"It's a reaction," Frank said, his voice gilded with hope. "Much stronger with the third dose, straight into the brain."

Simone smiled, the first genuine reaction I had seen out of her yet. "Look at the skin," she said. "Look."

My skin was pinkening all over, as though blood was returning. The warmth a fire within me, growing stronger once more, and my dead flesh started to take on some vague semblance of life.

And then, with the sound of rain soaked shoes splashing through a puddle, the flesh on my abdomen liquified and dropped off.

My entrails flopped onto the ground, limp worms and lumpy hunks of meat. The flesh—what was left of it—turned blistery, fiery red and inflamed, bubbling as it turned to goop.

"Looks like your formula requires some work," said Simone, the ambivalent scowl on her face returning. "I'm guessing *that* will be happening to the brain soon enough."

"Soon enough," conceded Frank, gritting his teeth in frustration. "Still, we might be able to study the—"

Simone's tone was firm. "Enough, Frank. We'll collect another sample. This one's no use to us any more."

For a moment he seemed like he might fight the issue, and then he sighed, running his hand through the rest of his hair. "Put her down then," he said, practically spitting the words.

The woman drew her pistol and lined up my head.

Put her down.

These people had no reason to like me and every reason to hate me; whatever exper-iment they were running had failed, and they didn't seem happy. Every living human had every reason to say I was worthless…enough reason to throw aside the pretence of politeness and say what they really thought.

It's a freak, a man in a woman's dress, a fake girl, a pervert. Just like other people whispered behind my back but didn't have the guts to say to my face.

Maybe they knew I still had a penis, but I felt these two recognised, in some way, what I was trying to be and respected that. Respecting the living person I had been and that person's wishes.

Simone fired and I died my second death, happy.

A Word from David Adams

This story is designed to challenge you. More than just a book about the dead, "Her", and its companion book *Eh, Zombie*—just like Hugh Howey's *I, Zombie* before it—is a look into the minds of the living.

Some of what you will find there is disturbing. Shocking. Challenging. You should, at some point, be offended.

Being offended is good. It means you have principles. It means you have beliefs and they are worth defending. The scenes in this book are a fiction, but there is realness too; *Her* is a story spun from the threads of reality. We are peeking inside the hearts of fictitious undead. Genuine horrors don't gnaw on brains in post-apocalyptic Canada.

The real monsters are inside us.

Read more stories from Hugh Howey's world of *I, Zombie* in my novella length work, *Eh, Zombie!*

Thank you for reading! If you got this far, please consider leaving an honest review at the place where you purchased this book. Reviews help us out a lot. :)

Want more information about new releases?

Sign up for my "new releases" newsletter here:
http://eepurl.com/toBf9

Like my Facebook page here:
http://www.facebook.com/lacunaverse

Check out my webpage here:
www.lacunaverse.com

Or email me here:
dave@lacunaverse.com

Special thanks to Hugh Howey, who lets me play in his worlds.

The Soulless:
A History of Zombieism
in Chiitai and Mihari Culture
by Lesley Smith

Monsters exist in all cultures but the zombie – a Terran designation referring to re-animated corpses popularised in local media towards the end of the pre-Contact period – is a prevalent one. The Union has its monsters and medical science is often to blame, as is the case with the Soulless.

What began as an attempt to end a terrible war decimating the Chiitai Conglomeration would ultimately be used by the Mihari Empire in its own machinations for power across the known galaxy, the ripples still affecting both Union and non-Union worlds alike.

- From *A Medical Examination of Genetically-Manipulated Drones in Chiitai and Mihari Caste Structure (Doctoral Thesis)*, Sandis Mythreia, School of Medicine, Arcadia.

SANDIS WAS ONE OF THE FIRST to stumble into the classroom. The last day of the spring term wasn't known for high turnouts, not with the Festival of the Revealed Trinity the following day. Most skipped class and blamed clan or religious obligations for their absence.

Their teacher, a visiting professor from Sandis's own homeworld, was a lot more tolerant of the honest ones who simply wanted a chance to lie in or over-indulge. The festival was simply another day, albeit one where the three stars of the Sirian system revealed themselves together in all their glory. But born on a planet of eternal twilight where the entire horizon was a net of stars, Sandis wasn't easily impressed by three of them.

Sandis liked the chance to have a day off like any other student but today was *Ask Anything Day*, a tradition among the staff where they would talk about whatever their students wanted to know.

"Morning Sandis!" Rheia called. "A little eager, aren't we?"

"Oh I've been waiting for this for months. After all, I get to ask you anything."

"Within boundaries, you do." She sounded intrigued, intentionally not reading Sandis's mind to find out what he wanted to ask about. "It should be good way to spend a morning, then."

Rather than teaching from the podium in an amphitheatre, Rheia had chosen one of the smaller rooms for the day. She descended to the floor and indicated the students, wandering singly or small groups, should join her. They pulled cushions and low chairs into a circle. Today they were not teacher and students, physician and trainees, today they were people, and most of those who had turned up had been trying to word their questions like you might a genie's offer of three wishes.

Rheia was dressed in purple skin and goat ears, *soirei* tattoos flowing under the summer dress she'd chosen instead of her normal red physician's uniform or teacher's garb. Appearances could be deceptive and most of the students knew that was just an outfit she wore, that Rheia of the Ashterai was born on another planet a long time ago, one that had just been contacted by the Union.

Some people asked about life and the cessation of it ("Not my area but you'll find out when you die, you've done it before, after all."). Others wondered about space-time ("It's a river, you can see the whole thing but if you get too close it pulls you under.") and one girl even asked what the answers to next term's examination questions would be.

Rheia had laughed at that one: "I'm not telling you that! It'll get me fired. You'll have to wait, be patient and revise. Now then. Sandis, you mentioned having a question for me. Care to surprise me?"

"Is there any scientific basis to the human belief in zombies?" Sandis asked.

She stared. "Zombies? *Really*?"

"Yes. It's a valid question, right?"

He'd said the world in English, *zombie*. Contact with the planet, known locally as Terra or Earth, had only happened a year previously, and while Rheia understood the interest in a new world, Sandis was sure it baffled her that someone would be so curious about a creature that didn't actually exist.

"Have you been reading Wikipedia again?" she asked, unable to hide her surprise. "Because if I find you using that or any other source not supported by the medical faculty's peer review panel, I *will* fail you."

"It was in a book I read, a horror novel I found in the archives." The others looked at him. "What? I like medical fiction. It was a book about autopsying a zombie with long and complicated medical notes at the back. Oh, and pictures, anatomical drawings. I thought it was a real record for the first hour or so."

"What's a zombie?" Malani asked.

"It's an Earth legend," Rheia said. "Originally, zombies were supposed to be the dead who had returned to life, animated by people who said they had magical powers, abilities to control the dead like mindless slaves. Then popular culture embraced the idea, but re-cast zombies as caused by a plague. You die, you turn into a zombie. They bite you, you die, you turn. The only way to kill a zombie is to sever the spinal column or destroy the brain."

"So it's caused by an infection? A virus?" Sandis asked

"Sometimes, but not always." Rheia was speaking carefully, as if she couldn't believe she was entertaining a discussion on zombies in the same way she might the Arcadian plague. "Traditional zombies were slow, but popular culture began talking about slow and fast zombies. Faster zombies usually means they haven't been dead long."

"So a fast one was bitten more recently?"

"Generally yes. Some sources suggest that the reason most zombies are slow is that their brains are functioning at the lowest power setting: no emotion, no memory or conscious thought, just the core brain. All they have to motivate them is the need to feed on living flesh and, by extension, to infect other people with their condition."

Sandis saw that Rheia continued to treat this as if it was a disease, a scientific discussion, and not a random trope from an alien civilisation. The young men, woman and others sitting around her were all destined to be doctors, nurses and members of the School of Medicine and so she was hell bent on treating even the most outlandish conversation in a clinical manner.

"Are they real?" another young man, Gaavi, asked.

"Real…" Rheia murmured.

Sandis clarified, not just for his own benefit but for his classmates as well: "Do they actually exist?"

Belief was personal and many humans—he knew from his reading—believed zombies not only could exist but that their appearance would herald an apocalypse. Some humans even stocked up on supplies: food, water, and basic survival tools in anticipation of the end of things, and bought weapons that would offer protection from a zombie horde.

"There are visual narratives, movies and television shows produced for entertainment purposes focusing around their existence, or around a world overrun by zombies. Of the various apocalyptic scenarios for Earth, it's one of the less far-fetched, especially if you add in human scientists tinkering with viruses they didn't quite understand."

"That's insane," Tahi muttered.

"That's sensible," Sandis retorted. "Everyone should have an emergency kit."

"There's a difference between flooding or winter storms and a plague of mindless aliens who want to eat you. Cannibalism? Mindless monsters? Really, Sandis?"

"Before you start judging, Tahi, remember other races' histories." Rheia said. "The Mihari, for example. Half their society is held in place by a subjugated underclass—"

"Yes but the Helot talk, they have minds and feelings, they're just subjugated by the aristocracy," Tahi interjected. "There's a difference between soulless and mindless. Plus the Helot, they're not cannibals."

"I didn't mean the Helot, the lowest caste. I was referring to the Sankai, specifically the Rulani, the Mihari's engineered clone army. In fact, a bit of history for you, who's heard of the Chiitai Conglomeration?" Rheia asked. "Come on, some of you must have. Malani, you're from the outer rim of Union space, you must have heard tales of the Great Hiveworld? They were the ones who first realised how to control another being so completely that they are, effectively, zombies."

"Deep space trader talk. Legend, nothing more than that. Hives of sugar and coloured glass...mothers and daughters left while the clans warred. Black creatures that descended like locusts."

"What about the Sankai?" Rheia asked. Not giving them the answers, but instead prompting them to start asking the right questions, as anyone wanting to go into the medical sphere should.

"Clones?" Tahi asked. "I saw one once, one of the free-range ones before the Mihari took over their maturation-farms."

"They didn't start that way," she replied. "And sometimes, once a generation or so, the process doesn't work."

The chimes signifying the start of lunch rang, melodic and calming. Rheia rose and the students waited a moment before following. For most, the discussion had just been a fantastical one, a thought experiment. Sandis headed to the library and went looking for answers in the archives.

* * *

Sandis sat at one of the booths by the reading windows, with a view of the gardens and enough of a breeze to rival even the carefully temperature-controlled stacks. He had books and a terminal linked to the medical, historical and general archives, as well as records dating back to An'she and Elys, one of the first to swim deep into the star-filled sea.

Even amongst the Union, whose territory is the smallest but most stable of the carved up Milky Way galaxy, knowledge regarding the Chiitai Conglomeration was scarce.

The Chiitai kept to their own worlds for a reason; initially it was because of their culture and the order of their hives. At one time they had apparently wandered the universe but at some point decided to keep to their own worlds. However, it was known that, before the Union's formation, they became embroiled in a territorial dispute recorded as 'the War of Bloodied Fields'. Though that conflict was now, by all accounts, concluded, the Chiitai retained their isolationist stance—to rebuild their worlds, too focused on that to pay attention to anything other than their own affairs.

The records didn't go into specifics about the cause or the ending of the war. Sandis checked scholars' accounts, rumours jotted down by passing ships, annotated musical maps of the explored universe—but for naught.

Sandis laid out a sketch done based on An'she and Elys' recollections, of a glorious city of spun sugar and domes of glass hives which caught and channeled the sunlight, of rooftop gardens and arching foundation vines. The city had survived for a single reason, the same one which gave the war its name: because it was fought in the endless fields of the Chiitai homeworld, in trenches and pits so that the highest caste of queens needn't see the violence or hear the cries of the dying, the fallen gutted in their names.

Were they still out there? Why did Rheia mention them in class? What did their feud have to do with zombies anyway?

* * *

The rains battered the triage tent where Muzzac, warrior of the Gefaia Hive, lay resting after his brush with death on the front lines. His mandible had been crushed and it still pained him, even bound and splinted up. The scurrying nurses and medics had more seriously wounded to worry about, and so he bore his pain stoically.

The injury meant his days on the battlefield were over and he was almost glad. While lying injured on the field, surrounded by the dead and dying, he had had an epiphany: If this war did not end, then the Conglomeration and every Chiitai within would be consumed. Their species would fight until no one was left. Such an ignominious end for such an old and mighty civilisation.

The females, the Jiha Queens would live on. Warmaking was for the warrior classes, the drones. He imagined hives of spun sugar and sweetglass on other worlds after all the lower rungs had been trampled in the mud. For a moment he almost saw a new empire, not a conglomeration but something different, a place where the Queens ruled with impunity, controlling a select number of worlds and billions, be they Chiitai, mammal or others entirely.

Their burden would be the fallout from this endless, bitter war.

"Ah, you live!" Velok, second-in-command, slipped under the tent flap, exo-armour scraping together as he ducked in, the scent of ash, blood and smoke washing in behind him as he searched for his commander and old friend.

"Velok! Come, and let us talk strategy." Muzzac beckoned him over, his chittering notes and pheromones garbled slightly by the weather and by the lingering scents of pain and death.

"We must finish this." Muzzac said, his remaining mandibles translating a mournful song, not only his thoughts but the depth behind them. "Or this entire quadrant of space, our territory and those of the others will all suffer for it."

"You mean the Demons' Empire and the mammals, that biped Queen's coalition of worlds?"

"I do." He propped himself up, comfort still eluding him. "This war, it has no end, not unless we finish it. We need to take control."

"And how do you suggest we do that?" Velok asked, entertaining his commander in what he was sure must be the trauma of his injury.

"We alter a batch of drones and then we seize power."

The movements, the noise Velok made betrayed his shock. "A coup d'etat against the Jiha Queens? Against the Conglomeration itself?"

"A necessary evil. If we take their minds, control them, we control the hives and the Conglomeration."

"For what?"

"To end this war."

"And afterwards?"

"We bury this and move on. Drones have short lifespans; we send them in, we take control, they die off and we begin writing a new chapter in our history. Once we put this stupid war behind us, we can move and grow." Muzzac was suddenly reflective. "Do you even remember how it started, old friend? Who exactly stepped over the lines and into another's land?"

"Only the stories, and those feel more like myths than fact. Did nearly dying do this to you?"

"It clarified things somewhat, yes. We only get one life, after all."

"Almost dying will do that," he agreed. "The Queens…if they knew, they would unite against us."

"We do this amongst ourselves, the warrior caste. The Jiha are figureheads. They control the hives but the power has always lain with us, the defenders of the hives. The drones are the foot soldiers and we are the strategists, the brute force."

It was another year, five seasons and much healing, before Muzzac could put his plan into action, but war can be a slow thing, and warriors the most patient souls ever born.

The time away from the front line allowed Muzzac to prepare: drones came with the winter moons, destined to die before the same moons rose again the following year. They would steal a generation and win the war.

Altering the drones was simple. A change in the genome, modifying the chemistry of the jelly used to mature them. Rather than a Jiha Queen's genome, Muzzac in-

stead replaced it with a substitute based on his own. Drones would be born loyal to him, not to the Hive Queen.

And so the end of the War of the Bloodied Fields began.

The Jiha's attention was normally focused on birthing and grooming their heirs, that one embryonic Chiitai in a billion who was literally born to lead. Rather than a golden daughter with wings the colour of the sky and the shifting green seas, a Jiha Queen was born to Muzzac's own Gefaia hive with a body black as the warrior's own. She was his daughter and the Jiha realised too late that control had fallen from their grasp.

The civil war was easier in some ways, less bloody and quicker. It was over in days rather than generations, with a minimum of causalities. The drones died quickly but the Black Queen remained and a new hive, the Hedrim, was created to ensure that the War of Bloodied Fields would never be repeated. The Chiitai would learn to police themselves with a hive that was part mediator, part peacekeeper, with a queen who did not sit with the Jiha but instead watched from the sidelines.

Muzzac met his end as he had lived, and died a hero, his name remembered and his remains preserved.

But he had only ended one war. Another much more deadly one would take its place...and it was for something none of them, not the warriors, the drones or the Jiha had ever suspected: the Demons had arrived.

* * *

Sandis went to the refectory, his stomach growling, to get a late lunch and then returned to the blissful silence of the near-deserted library. The Academy had cancelled afternoon classes for the festival. With another load of source material, more terminal-based than books this time, Sandis turned his attention closer to home.

The Mihari were a part of his history, their expansion having been the driving force behind the Union's formation. The Mihari — referred to by some races simply as the Demons — were the sea monsters who would devour unwary wanderers of deep space, races who were beginning to explore the galaxies. The Union had formed to combat the Mihari Empire, based on the idea that together the races were stronger than they ever could be alone. That one idea had allowed for eight millennia of peace within their borders.

He knew from his childhood history lessons that the Mihari Empire held the least stable but largest span of stars. They ruled with an iron fist, headed by an Emperor who demanded the very souls of his subjects to feed a creature that gave him near-immortality, a creature they named their Shadow God. The wraith, more a parasite than a deity, gave the leaders of the ruling dynasty long life and then jumped from father to son at the moment of death. Each generation was forced to offer their most precious commodity — their souls and the souls of their children — to ensure the continuity of the Empire.

Like the Chiitai, they had also gone through a period of expansion, but the Mihari continued, descending on weaker worlds not protected under the Union banner. That was how Earth, a world Sandis found oddly curious, came to be Contacted years ahead of schedule, because the Mihari's watchdogs, the Rulani, had been snooping around the Sol system for decades, trying to decide if the planet was worth their interest.

Mihari Prime orbited an old sun, one in the last vestiges of its life cycle and it was a given that, if the Mihari Empire was to continue, it would need to search for another homeworld. They seeded planets in a particularly brutal and irreversible way, wiping out all other life with nuclear weapons, and returning eons later to reclaim the planet. Others they mined for resources and a few they just subjugated because they found the natives useful.

That was how they had stumbled across the Chiitai Conglomeration and stolen the race's greatest secret.

* * *

On Mihari Prime, a dust storm had blanketed the city for five long days, the air so thick you couldn't see more than a footstep ahead. The Helot would die in droves, then more of them would have to go out and dump the bodies in the magma river that encircled the capital like a moat of fire.

Death came, even here: the Slow Drowning. The dust mixing with the air and moisture in their lungs and killing them slowly. Sticky mud that would drown them even as they breathed, lungs gasping for air. Anyone forced to roam the streets was a walking victim to the sickness. Sometimes it took weeks to die, sometimes months or even years, but all Helot succumbed eventually. Such was their lot.

The Emperor and the aristocracy had no such problems. Current incumbent to the Shadow God and aging Emperor of the Mihari, Arokae's only concerns were focused on the survival of his Empire and for the sons who would come after him; the hosts for their god.

Their sun was burning up and that meant they had, perhaps, a half millennia left before Mihari Prime became uninhabitable. The star would expand and burn their world to a crisp, but even before that happened, they would all be dead. The heat was already rising, too hot for even the Mihari, the dust storms becoming more violent, more frequent as the planet convulsed around them.

Darak was the Emperor's emissary and one of many warriors given leave and ships to search the stars for a new home. His task was grave and of the utmost importance, but it also proved that all was not well on Mihari Prime, despite the facade.

He stood watching from the shadows of the Emperor's court and it hit him: the Shadow God living inside their ancient emperor didn't want to die, and Darak could understand that desire. He believed the Shadow God would survive the supernova, but over the aeons since it had found its way to Mihari Prime, it had grown used to corporeal hosts and physical forms, perhaps even comfortable with them. So this problem of the dying sun and what it was doing to its hosts was what Darak had been tasked to solve.

Face covered to protect from the Slow Drowning, Darak left the Emperor's audience chamber with his orders – to go as far out as it was possible, to seek out promising systems for a new homeworld. There were old star charts from the period of expansion long ago, worlds ready and waiting if they could only find them. Every Mihari, be they Helot or aristocrat, knew there were a myriad of places in the universe that could sustain life, if you knew where to look.

But he had not expected to find the insects' world or that they would fight back.

After three years journeying, of diving into unknown space, they found the planet almost by accident. It had too much water, too much green for his liking, this jewel in the starry void of heaven that they stumbled on outside the rim of known space. There were minerals though, mountains of them that could be refined into fuel even if the world was too harsh for their liking. To the Mihari, this world was the equivalent of an icy tundra and certainly not suitable for habitation.

They landed their craft outside the main city, making no attempt to hide. The city was made of sugar spun into buildings, delicate in appearance, but strong. Light filtered through coloured glass and tall structures, and creatures flittered from high gardens, the air almost vibrating with the noise.

Darak found the whole thing repugnant, the light, the smell, the alien vista. Black creatures with exo-skeletons like armour began to land, standing between the Mihari and their precious city. The Mihari were outnumbered, but the creatures looked fragile enough. As their wings beat and their legs moved, sound transmitted and the translation matrix turned sound into words they could understand.

"Who are you?"

"We are the Mihari, servants of Emperor Arokae. We claim this world in the name of the Shadow God and our Empire!"

"This is our land," the aliens responded. "We have fought hard for our peace, and we will not yield to invaders!"

Darak didn't know of the Chiitai's history, of how the War of Bloodied Fields had begun and ended. Had he, his strategy might have been different. Instead, blinded by lust for the resources, he raced into battle and the aliens decimated the Mihari until the remainder were forced back to their remaining ships.

But not before Darak discovered their secret.

While his troops were being slaughtered, he watched with a veteran's eyes and quick mind. The black soldiers were the main fighting force, joined sometimes by a caste of what seemed to be strategists or more experienced commanders.

But if their commanding officer was killed, these soldier-drones were useless, almost like the Helot of his own world, the ones the Emperor summoned to his palace so the Shadow God might devour their essence. The pesky alien insects were left blank-eyed and incapable of movement until another commander took the place of the one who had fallen.

Darak saw a resource more valuable than even the planet, so he led a mission into the black hive, the one set apart from the city, and stole the matriarch, their Jiha Queen, and a half dozen incapacitated drones. Then they ran across the alien fields and the familiar stars, heading home with a prize that Darak was sure would ensure the Empire's continuing strength for millennia.

It took them nearly five generations to crack the genetic code linking the Black Queen with her warrior drones. But once they found the key, it was the moment the Mihari Empire truly became a force to be reckoned with. They took a single iceberg of a planet and turned its inhabitants into a perpetually-renewable army.

The Sankai were one of their earliest discoveries, a race of identical mammals who reproduced via cloning and communicated purely on a non-verbal level. Their reliance on cloning made them the perfect choice for enslavement, especially as they had already achieved a high level of technology which saw them beginning to travel to the stars.

Their world was an iceberg; their star of origin a speck on the horizon, but on this one occasion, the Mihari had endured their hatred of the cold in pursuit of a larger goal. Their combined forces swamped the tiny unprotected planet and took control of the cloning centres. Within a year the first Rulani—the name the few remaining Sankai-in-exile, the ones who ran and hid, gave to their successors—began to make noise across Mihari and Union space.

* * *

Sandis turned to his terminal where a black and white movie was playing, dialogue and sound piped through his wireless connection. The neural rig he used to understand alien languages was proving useful when it came to digesting Terran media. The humans might not have heard of the Mihari or the Chiitai but they knew the Rulani.

Known on Terra as Greys—and their place cemented by a much-publicised crash in 1947 in Roswell, New Mexico—these creatures were in truth the Rulani, the Mihari-enslaved foot soldiers. Through sheer numbers, these mindless clones and soulless abominations turned the Mihari Empire from a civilisation on the edge of collapse into the most feared force in the Universe.

Rumours preceded them but it was sometimes a generation between the first reports of abductions and the ships descending with Rulani pawns and Mihari overseers that overran their chosen targets. In the last half century alone, the Rulani had been responsible for subjugating fifty worlds.

* * *

The maturation chambers on an iceberg-asteroid on the edge of the Zeta Reticuli system were a sight, rows stretching as far as the eye could see and still further, a sea of artificial wombs that would birth generation after generation of clones.

Once they had been the Sankai, scholars and scientists, advocates and artists, but since the forced occupa-

tion of the system all the chambers now decanted were soldiers. The Rulani were born loyal, decanted with a single purpose: to conquer and die for the Mihari Empire.

On the edge of the forest of chambers, two overseers stood and surveyed the latest batch, their eyes settling on a single individual.

"It's defective."

Clone 873e, decanted a month previously, stood silently as one of the overseers looked it over. Functionally identical to its batch mates, the only difference was a marker tattoo, a barcode-like sequence that identified it. It was naked, unblinking, and the Mihari treated it as if it were a stupid animal, even as they tried to place the nature of its defect. Behind those black eyes, however, a mind was listening, comprehending their words even as they decided its fate.

Behind the grey skin and eyes deeper and darker than a black hole was a mind stripped out by genetic manipulation. 873e was different—but no one could quite explain what it was that made it stand out amongst its hundred identical siblings, born on the same day from the same genetic sample.

To recognise a soul, you must first possess one yourself. It had been generations since the Sankai's own enslavement, and the Mihari guards had long ago surrendered their own to their Emperor. No one remembered what a soul was anymore.

"It doesn't look defective," the other overseer said. "Physically it looks just fine. It's obedient, it follows commands. Aside from that blip after decantation, it seems just like the rest of the batch."

"And the mental interface?"

"It seems to have settled down. The neural readings are certainly more active than its brethren, but they're within normal parameters for a clone."

The superior nodded. "Keep an eye on it then. As long as it remains docile and obedient there's no problem. Where is it assigned?"

"The next world on the list."

"What was the local name? Saruvoi?"

"Yes, sir. Apparently the radiation killed off the mammals but it also pushed the reptiles to the top of the food chain; they have a basic level society."

"Well they won't for much longer. This planet is top of our list for resettlement, it's the most viable candidate."

"Sir? Is he…does that mean the Emperor is going there?"

"That information is above our grade. Get that clone to where it's supposed to be and let's move on. We've got a new batch due for decantation in two hours."

873e let itself be guided, or herded more like, to the waiting pods. It and thousands like it were about to be dropped on a hostile world as shock troops, trained to subjugate the native population and assert control within a few days.

873e was disturbed by this knowledge, although it wasn't aware of the name for the emotion it was experiencing. The blip the overseers had mentioned hadn't really been a blip, but a suppressed panic attack that had almost broken its sanity. 873e was defective, but not in the way they assumed. 873e was self-aware.

It had woken to self-awareness moments after decanting. The neural link between it and its siblings was silent; they were blank slates and it was not. It had been like standing in a cavern and shouting, only the sound of its mental voice echoing back. If any of the others heard, they didn't have the capacity to answer. It was alone in a sea of identical faces and blank minds.

Stasis forced 873e to contemplate, its mind never quite switched off as the others were. Through the link, 873e had access to a million other minds and senses. It felt the cold of its home-world, saw a nebula spinning in deep space, watched a family cowering as they were taken so the Mihari might know their potential enemies better, understand the weaknesses to be exploited when they landed on that world's doorstep and decided to move in.

It understood it was alone but as long as it kept silent, 873e would live. There was no one else like it, not amongst the Rulani or the Mihari. The latter might be sentient but they were still under the thumb of a higher power; 873e had free will and the knowledge that it could disobey at any time, even if that moment would be its last.

So 873e kept silent.

Saruvoi was a hot world, dusty and parched from residual nuclear radiation dropped so long ago than no one remembered why or who had been responsible. There was water, and from all other standpoints this planet was similar to Mihari Prime–but without the peril of a dying star.

It would make a suitable home, once the natives learnt their place. That was where 873e and its brethren came in.

When the invasion began, the Rulani moved in formation, quickly, killing what lay before them. 873e kept back, knowing what death was.

"Search the dwellings!" the Mihari overseers ordered. "Find the stragglers, kill anyone who resists."

The city was ordered, built in the caldera of a dead volcano and offering protection from dust storms. The Rulani fanned out, moving like ants down streets, and 873e found itself forcing its way into a house, the door hastily barricaded.

As it entered, words came to him, the tone making the inhabitant's threat obvious: "Come one step closer and I will kill you."

873e stopped.

The native was protecting a female, her legs obviously defective as she used a staff to walk. They were trying to escape the house through a tunnel bored into the bedrock, likely an escape route out of the city. The male was a boy, anger and terror in his eyes, his scales the calm blue of childhood.

These two weren't like the rest of their race. The natives of Saruvoi might be sentient but what 873e saw in his eyes was deeper, memory that went beyond existence. Worse, they saw the same in it, understanding that behind the blank expression there was a conscious mind screaming for release.

873e stepped back and lowered its weapon. Then it focused and projected a thought, hoping the native would hear.

"Go."

The boy cocked his head, then realised this wasn't a time for questions, rather it was a chance to run, and mo-

tioned his companion further into the bolthole. "Alia, quickly."

There was no time for questions. 873e watched them go as the male sealed the entrance behind them and it returned outside. Its superiors knew there had been people in the house and it realised retribution would come, swift and unforgiving. Had it been worth it?

"There it is! You two, follow the two who escaped! Find that hobbled girl, she's what passes for royalty here, and we'll need her if the rest of the populace are to be tamed!"

The overseers sounded angry and advanced on 873e, their spittle landing on its skin as the Mihari vented their rage with kicks and blows. 873e was grabbed; it dropped its weapon and made no attempt to fight back. There was no point. They forced it to its knees, then a weapon was pressed to its temple and fired. Its body slumped into the dust but, in the microsecond before its death, 873e realised that its batch number wasn't just a designation, it was more than that.

It was a name.

* * *

The hologram of the Rulani, one of the engineered Mihari zombies, rotated on an invisible axis, spinning slowly a few inches above the library floor. Sandis sat looking at the creature, transfixed as he mulled over an afternoon's worth of research.

They were drones, shock troops, and yet once they'd been a vibrant society with their own customs and technology. Most people thought of the

Rulani, not of the Sankai, their precursors, the ancient culture the Mihari had almost completely wiped out. Did they even exist anymore? Were they hiding on some distant moon, some forgotten asteroid waiting for the Empire to burn itself out?

Rheia would know; there wasn't much she didn't. He wondered if anyone had asked her that. Disabling the emitter, Sandis collected his things and decided, as it wasn't too late, to see if she was still in her office. He had a few more questions to ask that only she, he suspected, could answer. It was, after all, still Ask Anything Day, even if classes were done.

A Word from Lesley Smith

Zombies are one of the few things which terrify me (another thing is Sadako from the Ring series). They're voracious, they never tire, they don't stop, they can't be reasoned with and they'll eat you. That said, they've been done to death in so many ways that finding a new angle is a delicious challenge.

For the past couple of decades, I've been immersed in a very unique multiverse and this seemed like the perfect opportunity to explore a very alien concept of 'traditional' zombies.

In my Ashteraiverse, I primarily set my stories on worlds belonging to the Union, a peaceful collective of planets not unlike the Federation (except that Earth is a new member, not a founder, and a lot of people do not want us to be a part of it). However they're not the only force in this universe, two other empires share control of the galaxy and this story allowed me to focus on them for a change: the isolationist Chiitai Conglomeration and the malevolent, power-hungry Mihari Empire.

I got interested in the idea of insects, of drones and how they work together as a unit to achieve things. This idea translated nicely into the concept of a mindless drone controlled by an outside source to achieve aims, some honest, even heartfelt and others much more nefarious. What if it starts with actual drones? In this case a Chiitai caste of foot soldiers much like worker bees and the knowledge stolen to be abused by another race, the Mihari.

I'm a big fan of mythology and know a lot about the roots of supernatural creatures. I might live in a world of *28 Days Later* and *The Walking Dead* but I grew up with the classic stories of men raised from the dead by nefarious means, mindless, to do the work of their masters. That idea stuck with me and lingered. What if the zombies aren't just mindless but soulless as well and then, what if one drone in a billion was decanted from an artificial womb, miraculously self-aware and able to fight that control?

This story was the result.

In a former life Lesley Smith was a freelance journalist, but now writes fiction fulltime. Her debut novel, The Changing of the Sun, *is out now and she is hard at work at other instalments of the* Ashteraiverse, *including a sequel called* The Parting of the Waters *and a short novel called* A Star Filled Sea, *both funded via Kickstarter and due out this summer.*

Lesley's hobbies include baking, archery, and binge-watching box sets on Netflix. She lives in a small English market town with three cats and her guide dog, Unis.

She blogs at www.lesley-smith.co.uk and lives on Twitter as @LesleySmith. You can also find out more about the Ashteraiverse on the official Facebook group: www.facebook.com/groups/1607302972847560

Hybrid
by Geoffrey Wakeling

CHAPTER 1

"SHUT THAT BLOODY DOOR, FREYA."
His cry rushed down the corridor towards her as if a dam had just been overcome by torrential flood-water. The sound echoed, bouncing along the un-furnished walls, before spilling over the lip of the laboratory doorway and intermingling with the tragic tones of Joni Mitchell that accompanied her working day.

"Freya! Shut. The. Door."

His cry was increasingly urgent and breathless as he clutched the end of a frayed and stained bench, the branching crimson etchings on his shirt steadily becoming overcome by a blanket of red. She tore her eyes from him for a moment, as if attempting to lift her white knuckled hands to the override button with a forced stare. It didn't work, and her fingers remained tightly clenched on the thin metal surround of the security quarantine door.

He can make it. He has to make it. I can't do this by myself. Run. Run.

"RUN!" Freya finally screamed, her call coming only seconds before she glimpsed the dark shapes over his shoulder. Her plea was even greater now, though she saw it was fruitless, for her mentor was wilting towards the floor.

"Save yourself. Protect the subjects. Don't let it all be in vain. There's a place for Pacifier, you know it. You're the brightest kid I've ever known. Pacifier 6 is yours."

The words still rang through her head hours later. *Pacifier 6 is yours.*

"I can't do this alone," Freya mumbled, trying to shake away the image of his slumped body as it was overrun with Frothers. The rancid foam splattered from their decaying mouths to his twitching body. Limbs convulsed and muscles were torn as their teeth sank into the blood-drained flesh, devouring every morsel with their unquenchable appetite. They'd not yet set eyes upon the seventeen year old girl who sat slumped and sobbing on the other side of the two inch thick, quarantine lock door.

"What was that? Speak up, Freya?"

"I can't do this alone."

"My dear girl, whenever have you been alone?" Mrs Gilbert offered an arthritically gnarled hand towards Freya and helped pull her from the floor. Those feasting upon her mentor's flesh had left the hallway now, and she sat alone in the laboratory as the songstress' dulcet musing continued. "Now, where's Professor Baidlin?"

Tears pricked in Freya's eyes again; hot and salty. They only aggravated the stinging, and she blinked them away quickly, though not fast enough to elude Mrs Gibert's keen eye.

"Well, I suppose it's not to be unexpected with the work you two are doing. Pacifier 6 will be yours now."

There it was again. Why did she have to bear this responsibility? What made them all think she was their saviour?

"Now I know what you're thinking," the middle-aged woman carried on, pulling Freya with her as she swept out of the room, right by the quarantine door and through the halls. "That you can't do it alone, that it's an impossible task. But you can't think that way. You mustn't think that way. You're but a young girl, and the future will be bright for one that can cure the world's problems."

"Maybe I don't want to cure the world," Freya said through gritted teeth as she attempted to wrench her arm from the claw-like fingers.

"Don't take that tone with me. You might be a genius, but God knows, Baidlin gave you a long leash. You need to toe the line now. You need to set an example. It's a fraught place we live in…death is expected, not pushed to the back of one's mind and forgotten about as once was. You can change that. You can save humanity."

They reached an intersection, and Mrs Gilbert led Freya towards an open door.

"Now, get yourself cleaned up and shake off those doubts." She reached inside and clicked on the light. "And, Freya…mourn for him later. Your uncle was a good man, a compassionate man, but most of all, hugely ambitious. You're his legacy. You need to save us."

The door was closed behind her without another word.

Her uncle's bed was unmade in the corner, his belongings still scattered from where, each morning, he'd crawl from the cot, his eyes bloodshot and dark, and knock his meagre possessions over the floor. Whilst he grumbled, cursed and swept them back towards his bed, she'd dutifully fluff her own pillow and fold the thin duvet as best she could.

Only hours had passed since she'd conducted this daily ritual, and she gazed at her own bed — it felt like days.

What the hell am I going to do?

She surveyed the room, heavy with the insurmountable burden now placed upon her. She'd been his aide, his technician. She was not, and never had been, the innovator.

Freya moved across to the thin mirror that hung above the badly plumbed sink that dripped constantly and haunted her dreams, before studying in her reflection. She'd never been the classic beauty, but some said her awkward and unbalanced features were quite striking. That hadn't stopped the bullying, particularly from the stereotyped bombshells of the class. They were all dead now, she supposed.

There was blood in her hair which, in her attempts to escape, had been whipped across her face in great red streaks. She turned the tap and began to massage away the crusty marks. A small clean patch appeared, and she drenched herself with increasing ferocity as she realised just how far the dirt had crept in. Tears swam in her eyes again, and this time she allowed them to fall as she pawed at her scalp, pulling brown matted hair away from her eyes. Her nails dragged across her face, uncovering the pale skin but inadvertently replacing dirt with fresh, pink scratches. Freya noticed blood on her hands and wrists too, and she began desperately scrabbling at the stains, sobbing and allowing her heart to break; both for the past and for what was to come. Bright crimson appeared below her fingertips, mingling with the water and spreading a red film across her skin. More followed, and her tears dried as she scrutinised the area, reaching out for a piece of tissue paper to dry the spot. Her stomach sank as her hope wasn't realised and, for the second time that day, her heart began to race with fear.

There it was — small and unnoticeable, but a scratch nonetheless. The more she rubbed it, the more the blood flowed. She was almost certain the break wasn't fresh, but several hours old. She began to panic, and attempted to recall her day's movements, trying to identify exactly when the tiny but significant tear had occurred. No wound was insignificant now. Every injury had to be documented and treated with the utmost caution.

She couldn't let them see it. They couldn't find her like this.

Rushing across the room she threw her belongings to the floor, ripped the duvet from her bed and pulled on her long-sleeved nightshirt, grabbing the material with her fingers so it was held over both wrists. Her mourning was over. If she spared him her thoughts, she'd see him again. He'd be there, waiting for her in the dark gateway that led to death...waiting as she passed him by and began a far worse fate than his.

CHAPTER 2

"Take out their teeth," Freya demanded, arriving in the skills lab with a sense of determination. She'd focused her mind on the short walk through the dingy, dirt and occasionally blood-smeared hallways of their community; there was no time for hysteria.

"What?"

"Are you sure?

"How do we do that?"

The voices rang out across the room; various sitters manning each station where their '*tamed*' Frother sat conducting its work.

"I don't know how," Freya continued. "Just do it."

"Where's Baidlin?"

"Dead. Because of those things. Now do as I say."

They eyed her suspiciously, and she suspected it was not for the fact they were being ordered around by a seventeen year old, but more her sudden onset of leadership. Even she was slightly alarmed as to where the authority came from.

"And do it one at a time in a different room," she added. "I don't want panic spreading. These are the last ones we have, we can't afford any accidents."

Freya marched amongst the benches and avoided the stares. She pressed her hands onto the workstation that was fixed to the opposite wall to steady herself, glancing momentarily at the thin red tear on her wrist. She turned back to the room quickly, pulling her sleeve down once again to hide the noticeable mark.

They had eight left; eight pieces of hope. When the end had begun, as rabid Frothers tore across the land leaving little alive, there had been nothing to do but run. Yet, amongst that tide of death, there'd been reason to live. As far as she was aware, any promise of returning the ravaged to their former selves was gone — the disease, the virus, was unrelenting in its control. But, in the process of attempting to find a cure, her uncle had found Pacifier; a drug that eliminated the dead's lust for flesh and reduced them to walking slaves. Only, it didn't work...not for any reliable, consistent length of time.

The majority of the dead were useless husks once treated, reverting back to crazed beasts as the drug wore off. However, about 22per cent — by her own statistical findings, no less — retained former skills. Those who'd once been bricklayers, cooks, tailors and gardeners could still be put to work. It took some training to get the expertise to remerge, and it was limited to manual trades; she'd found no computing genius yet, though the current state of the world no longer demanded such skills. To re-build, they needed workers. And, if she could hone Pacifier down to the perfect drug, they'd have all the labourers they needed.

"Leave that one. I'll do her myself."

The last of the eight was being led from the room. The Frother's sitter looked relieved as Freya took hold of the reins and led the creature to the iso-lation chamber, taking care to slide the door to a close behind her.

"You really are a disgusting thing," she mum-bled.

She flicked the chain around the Frother's neck so that it converted into a strengthened baton, be-fore pushing the creature towards the shackles on the wall. There was nothing but a small groan as it stumbled backwards and the wall clamp automati-cally sprung around its neck. Freya let the chain go slack again, before carefully tying each arm and leg into the bindings.

The thing wasn't much older than herself, Freya saw, as she stood back and eyed her prisoner with distaste. Once a youthful girl, its skin had become leathery and cracked. The muscle and fat had disintegrated away, leaving an anorexic profile of rubbery sinews and gaunt features. It had hair; thick, wiry and dark that formed a matted cloud of black above her dead eyes.

"I don't know why we even bother," Freya said, wrinkling her nose. Even Pacifier couldn't remove the stench. It was hard to think that the rancid thing before her was capable of causing such terror, such death. Now, constrained in shackles and under the influence of mind-calming drugs, it was nothing but a pathetic laboratory rat.

Freya turned her attention to the bench behind her, casting her eye across the rusty and blood-stained tools. It didn't matter; there was no fear of infection to these things. Teeth. *What would get teeth out?* A pair of particularly gruesome pliers lay abandoned towards the end of the bench, the handles clean, but the grooved vices congealed with blood and hair. She picked them up, scrutinising the horror that was plastered across the tool. *These would do. These were perfect.*

She turned, device in hand, and looked to where her victim was snared against the wall. Those young eyes had been so pretty once, that skin mostly likely unblemished and supple. But no longer. Now, death had overcame the girl inside, had stripped away sentience and compassion. Now, there was nothing more than a loathsome beast reminding Freya of everything and everyone she'd lost.

Stepping forward, Freya snapped open the pliers and pushed them against the Frother's thin, rubbery lips. Its mouth was open, unaware of what was to come, so she wasted no time in snapping the tool shut and wrenching with all the force she could muster. A gargled scream came from the creature as Freya staggered backwards. Fragments of bone shattered to the floor as the pliers whipped upwards, and Freya looked to see dark, viscous liquid seeping from the creature's mouth.

Three down.

She sighed heavily at the task in hand. *What had her life become?*

Stepping back towards her subject, she pushed the pliers forwards. This time, however, the lips remained closed. She probed the skin harshly with the end of the metal but to no avail, the Frother had its mouth clamped shut.

"Hmmmm. Think you can get around me that way, do you?" Freya said, her lip curled, and thoughts of her uncle swimming across her vision. The anger she fought so hard to hide, that she locked away deep inside, began to bubble as if it were molten lava being released from a volcano. It only took moments for it to explode; there was no stopping it now.

"I'll teach you."

She dropped the pliers to the floor with a clatter and turned back to the bench. Scalpels, scissors, razorblades; all useful, but not what she wanted. She lifted the claw hammer slowly, allowing the elation to fill her, balancing the tool in her hand and feeling the weight shifting through her fingers. She smiled. The claw had lost its sheen and sharpness; to her benefit.

"You know, we could have done this the easy way," she said aloud, turning slowly on the spot.

The creature remained silent on the wall, its limbs splayed out like a starfish, its eyes unfocussed, and its body utterly vulnerable to attack. Yet its mouth was firm and determinedly shut; it wasn't as vacant as it made out to be.

"If you won't let me have your teeth, I'll just have to take your jaw," Freya screamed, allowing her emotions to get the better of her before lunging towards the girl and smashing the hammer down on her face. There was a splintering sound as the blunt weapon met with the leathery skin, before a horrifying moan filled the air. Beneath the flesh something snapped, bone moved, desiccated flesh stretched like thick elastic. She swung the weapon and attacked a second time, unable to tear her eyes away as the creature writhed in its restraints, powerless to escape and unable to attack. She couldn't stop now, and Freya brought the hammer down time and time again, allowing the rage to overtake her.

They'd done this. These creatures. They'd pay.

The splintering sounds began to subside and the noises turn to squelching as the hammer caught in the skin and tore the thickened hide from its place. Brown, sticky ooze sprayed across the wall and filled Freya's eyes as the hammer bore down unceasingly upon its victim.

Her family. Her friends. Her uncle. Even those unrelenting bullies. All gone because of this thing.

There was a hand beside her, clawing and pulling, and she wrenched herself away thinking it was the creature's long, bony fingers. It wasn't, and soon she was on the floor as her instrument of torture was ripped from her. There were knees on her chest, hands on her neck, and she cried out at her confinement.

"What are you doing?" Mrs Gilbert screamed, "She's our best seamstress."

Freya roared in rage, fighting off the hands that dragged her away from her prey. There were too many of them. They gripped, wrangled and snaked their way around her until she was forced to relinquish everything but her screams of hatred for the beast.

It hung there, a shackled menace, twitching and jerking with disgusting animation amidst the gore of treacly body fluids that were spattered across the room. *How did it live when her Baidlin was gone? How would she ever learn to accept this horrific new world?*

CHAPTER 3

The room seeped into her consciousness gradually — three bright lights in the blurry darkness.

What the hell happened?

Freya squinted, before quickly blinking in an attempt to clear the fogginess from her eyes. She cracked her neck from side to side, instantly feeling the pang of an ache running down her back.

Where am I?

She leant forwards and felt the restriction; the neck brace prevented her from moving more than six inches from where she sat. She flung a hand towards her face, and found they were both restrained to the wall.

"Oh no," she cried out as the ball of panic inside grew exponentially. She knew where she was now. The three lights, the dark interior, the rusty fixtures on the wall; this was the place people were put to die.

"Help," Freya screamed as her skin flushed with icy terror. "It's me, Freya. I'm fine. I'm not hurt. Please, listen to me. Help!"

Her senses were alert now, and she looked towards where her hands were individually strapped into straps on either side of her. They'd neglected to tie her feet, but they weren't of any aid to her. She'd seen this before, this process. 'The Chamber', that's what they called it. It was the room where the infected transitioned. These walls were the last things they ever saw before human eyes and consciousness were eroded by viral death. It was the first step on the passage to hell.

"HELP!" Freya screamed again, writhing around in the straps in a bid to loosen them. She was unable to prevent the panic rising to her throat, and could do nothing as tears pricked in her eyes.

Why am I here? This was not the place of those temporarily losing control. This was the...

Freya stopped, before slowly and fearfully looking down at her wrist in the dull light. There was no longer a small and insignificant scratch, but a larger and deeper tear.

"No. Please, I don't deserve this," she said, before beginning to sob. She didn't know how it had happened, whether it had been the Frother itself or if, in her own rage, she'd inflicted the damage upon herself. But that didn't matter now. It was almost a certainty she'd infected herself in the attack.

"Freya?"

The whisper through the crack under the door was almost inaudible, and she missed it the first time.

"Freya?"

"Darshna?"

"Are you okay?"

"No," Freya replied, watching the shadow of her friend's head moving in the strip of light emanating from the hall. "Why did they put me in here?"

"You know why," her friend's sad reply came.

"But there's still work to do. Maybe I can fix this..."

"Like you fixed that Frother's face?"

"I, I — "

"I don't blame you," Darshna added quietly. "Give me another hammer and I could've done the other side."

Freya began to sob again, unable to stop the tears from rolling down her face.

"I've ruined everything. Uncle Baidlin, everyone here…they had such faith in me and I've just…" Tears continued to stream from her eyes as she choked up.

There was movement behind the door, and within the second it took for the click, Darshna was inside. She ran across the room and engulfed Freya in a hug, the familiar smell of the rose-scented moisturiser in her hair helping to calm Freya's terror.

"I need you to help me," Freya whispered into Darshna's ear. She wondered whether she'd said it loud enough, for her friend continued with the vice-like grip and showed no acknowledgment of the words.

"I need you — "

"What do you need?" Darshna asked, pulling away and allowing Freya to see there were tears in her eyes too. "I can't let you out," she said fearfully. "I would, but I — "

"No, I don't want that. I need you to get me some Pacifier 5 from the cold storage locker in the lab."

"W-why do you need that? H-how would I get it?" Freya saw she was startled by the request.

"Trust me, Darsh. Please. You're not releasing me, not putting others in danger. You're just getting me a few syringes of Pacifier."

"Okay," Darshna said, though seeming unconvinced. She pulled away from the embrace, repeating her words as if willing herself to act on them.

"The phials are in the backroom. The lab should be empty. I need them — urgently," Freya stressed.

Darshna nodded. She stood in the room as she thought, clenching her jaw as the request turned over in her mind.

"Darsh?"

"I'm going. I can do this for you," she said, scooting in for another hug. She smiled and wiped a tear from Freya's cheek before leaving the room. As soon as the door was closed and Darshna's footsteps were heard echoing down the corridor, Freya unfurled her fingers to reveal the wooden hairpin she'd managed to pluck from her friend's long, thick hair.

The restraints around her wrist were simple leather ties; not the chains and handcuffs they used for Frothers. The Chamber was for those who were much more alive. She looked at each restraint. Her captor's knots were a half-hearted attempt — a single knot with a bow. They were far from secure.

With extreme caution, for if she dropped the pin then her escape attempt would be less than brief, Freya shimmied the tool between her fingers and flipped it into a vertical position. It was excruciating work, made worse by the fact her hands had become clammy with nerves.

Don't drop it, don't drop it, don't drop it.

With the point facing towards the floor, she jabbed the pin down gently, attempting to catch it in the leather. But the knot was harder and more drawn than she'd first thought, and her limited flexibility became increasingly aggravating. She caught the pin in one of the bow loops and managed to unravel the strap from its fixture, but it did nothing to loosen the knot that held her in place.

Just one bloody hand, that's all I ask.

Freya sighed heavily and attempted to extinguish the nausea in her stomach. Determined focus was what she needed. She continued gently jabbing, occasionally catching the point in the knot, but never managing to push it all the way through. However, her repeated attempts were making a difference and, though it was painfully slow, the single knot was becoming looser.

Her gaze fell upon the injury on her wrist and she wondered, with hope, if the reason for her furious attack could be blamed on infection. Whether it wasn't fear or hatred that had spurred her on, but a biological imbalance to which she had no power over. The mouth frothing always came first. It was the first sign. She licked her lips tentatively and was relieved to find them dry.

"Shit, YES," she gasped as the needle point finally lodged in the leather knot.

She worked carefully for several minutes, first loosening the tie with the pin before shaking her wrist back and forth to enlarge the hole. At long last, her tiny hand popped through the stretched hole and within seconds she'd freed the other. Her fingers were at the neck bolt now, carefully tracing their way around the metal ring to where the locking mechanism still ensnared her. It was nothing more than a bolt lock; Frothers weren't logical or intelligent enough to think about such escape, even though many had the dexterity to make such a feat relatively easy. Once free, Freya crept over to the door and took up position.

Despite the urgency she'd conveyed, Darshna showed no immediate signs of returning. *Perhaps she hadn't been able to get into the lab. Perhaps she's decided not to help!* But, just as the questions began to gnaw at Freya's mind, she heard quiet footsteps coming towards her.

"Freya?"

"Still alive," she replied in a whisper.

"Sorry it took me so long, Mrs Gilbert's getting her nose into everyone's business."

Freya heard the door lock slide back, and she inched further into the shadowed recess. Then, as the door gradually opened, she grabbed the handle and threw open the doorway in a single movement. There was time with Darshna's surprise to pull the box of phials from her friend's arms and shove the girl forcefully into the room.

"I'm sorry," Freya apologised, pulling the door shut behind her as the girl began to yell. "But I'm not about to die in that hole without even trying."

CHAPTER 4

Once the door was securely locked from the outside, Freya looked at the Styrofoam package in her hand. If she was going to do it, it had to be now...it should've been yesterday, when the infection started.

She removed the lid and looked down at the bundle of bright green phials. Baidlin had a sense of fun, she thought as she smiled to herself; the vivid colour that seemed to almost glow was food colouring, nothing more. Every morning, she'd arrive to the lab and he'd have changed the colour again. It became a game; drawing her out of slumber to see if she could guess which lurid tones his newest concoction would have before she reached the lab.

The cold was escaping, and she pulled out a syringe and quickly replaced the lid.

"Here goes nothing."

Popping the plastic cap and letting it fall to the floor, she plunged the long needle into her wrist and pushed. It didn't need a blood vessel; just the leathery, desiccated flesh of a Frother was enough. Once in, the drug gradually seeped through the system, overriding those powerful urges to kill. But the speed of treatment was one of their failings — it took too long for Pacifier's effects to surface.

Freya watched as the mixture pumped into her body, awaiting the agony, the pain, the convulsions that were to come. Nothing.

Hmmm, well that's a good start.

Without time to lose, Freya left The Chamber behind her. It wouldn't be long before Darshna was missed and her screams heard. Then they'd be after her, and with the infection risk so high, no chances would be taken.

The halls were unusually deserted, and she found it quick going as she wound her way through the labyrinth of tunnels. The subterranean level of the former shopping centre relied upon an old and very rusty generator for light, and the few lighting strips that had survived were dim and flickering. She knew her home well enough though, and she made her way easily.

Where is everyone?

Ahead, she saw the closed quarantine door of the lab and felt a pang of sickness at what was ahead. There was no choice but to go on, to skirt his viciously torn and eviscerated body. If there was any hope of achieving her goal, she had to face that fear.

She reached the door and paused. *Should she look? Or could she save herself the heartache and avoid adding him to her collection of horror-scarred memories?*

She pressed the locking mechanism, keeping her eyes averted from the scene ahead.

No. Her Baidlin, unlike the others, would be a pre-served and cherished memory for now.

She stepped over the threshold and quickly closed the door behind her as her heart began to race. The lights flickered overhead as her ears reached for the slightest sound. The others wouldn't follow her, not here, not now infection was at the door seeking to destroy everything they'd built.

But where were they?

She banished the thoughts as one of the lights whirred and flickered above, causing a sudden rush of panic.

You're fine, she commanded herself. Get to the lab.

With extreme care, she began moving along the hallway, keeping her eyes on the corner ahead and determinedly away from where her uncle lay. She could smell him, even after the few hours he'd lain there. The putrid smell wrinkled her nose, and she couldn't stop the tears from welling up again. There was bloody splatter on the walls, a sign of his death she couldn't avoid, but she tried as she'd done with all the others, not to let the reality in.

Above her, the lights flickered suddenly, and she gulped away her nausea and fear, maintaining constant step by quiet step as she crept along. Her heart was racing, and she could feel her left leg beginning to tremble.

They were here somewhere. Around that corner, perhaps. Awaiting more flesh. Wanting to feel skin, and muscle, and gristle snap and tear beneath their teeth.

She was by him now, focussing on her path but unable to put the smell, that awful smell, from her mind. The ground was sticky, and her silent steps squelched as she circled him, trying, as quickly as possible, to get away. There was no movement from the floor, no sign that he'd been taken down the same hellish route that she'd begun. Infection had skipped him. He was lucky. Though perhaps there wasn't enough of him left to animate. She grimaced at the thought and wiped the tears from her eyes.

Pull yourself together.

Freya put a hand out to steady herself, and felt the cold concrete wall beneath her fingers. It seemed icier than normal, as if the winter had crept in. She smeared the last tears from her eyes and felt the frost on her skin. It wasn't her surroundings; it was her that was different. Her tears were gone but the faint blurriness remained, her rising temperature continued to burn. Infection was coming.

Freya stepped around the corner without waiting and stared down the corridor, expecting a sea of Frothers and certain death. Instead, the continued cold and barren landscape met her, the sparse hallway showing no signs of life or movement other than the whirring strip lights above. She quickened her pace as a result, needing to get the lab quickly, realising that her time was wanting. She licked her lips again. *Still dry. No froth. That was a good sign at least.*

There was a click behind her and she froze.

Fuck.

Freya couldn't help but look back. The empty hall was vacant no longer. Three Frothers ambled from a side room and sniffed the air, the yellow froth of decay bubbling over their lips like sea foam.

They can open doors now?

She stood, transfixed with the thought, and wondering if they'd see her. But it didn't matter; they smelt her all right, for their noses twitched and pulled at the air, until all three horrific faces swivelled on their decaying and sinewy necks to stare her down.

There was no choice but to run, and Freya, the phials of Pacifier gripped tightly in her hand, turned and raced away. She could hear them behind her, snarls and growls echoing through the otherwise empty corridors. She could outrun them, of that she was sure. There was no way they'd catch her.

Another Frother appeared ahead, lumbering around a bend and instantly devouring her with its eyes. *Three behind, one in front. She could do this.* Another Frother appeared ahead to the join the other, and then another. *Shit.*

Freya was tearing towards the newly appeared beasts with speed. She slowed a little, trying to clear her blurry eyes and focus. The chasers were catching up now, their grunts wrenching her stomach with fear. Just those three behind and it was a breeze; an adrenaline filled game, even. *But caught in the middle?* Freya felt fear like a needle through the heart.

She hesitated momentarily, before regaining both her focus and her speed. Charging ahead, she left the Frothers behind and hurtled towards the increasing mass of creatures in her way. She reached the first and struck it with her arm, screaming aloud as gnashing teeth came in her direction. The beast flew towards the wall at her strike, its limbs thrown into the air as if a rag doll had been smashed with a baseball bat. The next she bludgeoned with her fist, bringing her curled hand down upon its shoulder and watching as the bones shattered beneath the force, the blow moving through its body with a domino effect.

What the — ?

She'd been slowed by the attack, and though still bleary-eyed, Freya could tell there were now far more Frothers than the original six. Those behind were almost on her, and she readied herself to feel their bony fingers upon her skin. An arm lashed through the air, whipping her across her face. She ducked just in time to avoid the razor-sharp fingernails clawing her skin, before kicking out and watching the Frother crumple to the floor.

Well…this was strange.

Freya's newly acquired strength, despite her increasing nausea and temperature, came as quite the surprise. She toyed with it for a minute, stopping in her tracks and turning to face those who sought to destroy her. Lashing out time and time again, she watched the beasts repelled by this newfound force. They were unceasing, returning time and time again to try for flesh, but her speed, heightened sense of awareness and manoeuvring kept them at bay.

There were arms around her neck, fingers clawing her back and she screamed as she felt something sharp puncture her skin and stab into her spine. The Frother in front of her received a blow to the face in response, and she saw its leathery nose snap so that it hung from the face by a dry piece of skin. She whirled around, wrenching away the jaw that was clamped to her back and pushing its owner to the floor. There was blood and fresh flesh on its froth-smeared lips, and she gave a well determined stamp to its skull, feeling a sense of justice as she heard splintering bones.

Caught in a sea of flailing, tearing, blood-seeking limbs, Freya relinquished the need for revenge as the box of phials was almost snatched from her hand. The Frothers seemed endless, and though she was sure she could fight off each and every one, she didn't have time. Infection was spreading, flooding through her veins as her ferociously pounding heart pushed it. It seeped into her muscles, her cells. She didn't have long.

Kicking the last grappling hand away, Freya began to clear a path forwards, punching and elbowing the gnashing jaws aside. She began to run, hoping to clear the creatures and leave them far behind. She could hear them at her heels, moaning and grunting as they attempted to pull her over and feast. She sped even faster, panting as she stretched her legs into a sprint, her arms swinging back and forth like pistons and propelling her forwards.

Almost there.

She could see it in the distance; the broken neon lights of the sign glinting above the pharmacy. It was in that dilapidated shop that this had all begun. Where she and Baidlin had first begun the process. It wasn't quarantined, it wasn't secure, but it was the birthplace of their lab and she and her mentor had determinedly stuck to it, despite the debate and fierce objections from the others.

Keep. On. Going.

She was beginning to get tired, her muscles began to burn, her eyes swam and became blurrier by the second. There was something ahead, and she panicked as another Frother loomed into view. She couldn't do this again. Her momentary heroism was gone. She was jaded, tired. Infection was coming.

She raised an arm and prepared to strike. *She'd take this last one down and make it. She had to. She couldn't come this far and fail.*

It was within reaching distance now; its warped and vicious face visible through her bleary and tear-strewn eyes. She drew on her hatred, the pit in her stomach, the vision of Baidlin telling her to save herself. It was all the fuel she needed. She felt flesh under her knuckles as she brought her fist down upon the lumbering beast. But instead of the piteous moan she expected, a human cry rang out as the body was thrown to the floor.

CHAPTER 5

"I'm sorry," Freya repeated as she looked across the room. Jorge still had the ice pack to his head, and was using bandaging to try and repair his buckled glasses.

"Couldn't you see it was me? I was hollering as soon as you began racing down the promenade."

"I don't know. I was just —,"

"Scared, I know. It's okay."

"No, that's not it. Jorge, something happened out there, to me I mean. I was fighting those things off with super strength. They were coming, and coming, and I could've stood there all day knocking them back like skittles."

"Adrenaline's a funny thing," Jorge said, testing his glasses, before using additional plasters to correct the bent metal.

"It's more than that. I feel like crap. Fever, blurred vision, aching muscles…nausea. This god damn infection isn – "

"You're infected?"

"Of course I'm bloody infected. Why would you be here otherwise? They didn't tell you what happened? How they threw me The Chamber to rot?" Freya's eyes narrowed with suspicion. "Why are you here? Nobody comes to this lab."

"They said you were dead, that I needed to take over you and Baidlin's work."

"You were told I was dead, yet you've sat there worrying about infection?"

She eyed him carefully, looking for his nervous twitch. It was there; that noticeable chewing at the insides of his mouth. "Jorge, straight up...what's going on?"

"Nothing, I promise. I've been sitting in here for hours, totally freaking out. Fix Pacifier...me? I'm a first year biology student...how the hell am I supposed to know what to do? Baidlin's dead. You're dead. I'm supposed to save the world? How the hell is that even possible? And then everyone goes off grid, I can't get a line down to home base and the next thing I know you come screaming down through the mall in a sea of Frothers." He fell silent, sliding off the metal stool he was on and moving to the window to stare down to where the Frothers were pounding on the pharmacy's thickened glass windows below. They were on a mezzanine; a one-time stockroom that she and Baidlin had converted into a makeshift laboratory. "We're screwed, aren't we?" he said quietly, staring down at the undead below.

"Not necessarily," Freya replied, moving across the room and standing beside him. She'd known him long enough to see the honesty in his words. She didn't need fear him. "Jorge. I need your help. I'm going to survive infection."

"How?"

"With these."

She drew out the box of phials from the Styrofoam container and looked at the bright green mixture.

"I should be dead by now. I have almost all the symptoms and, okay, I feel like shite, but I'm fine otherwise...I gave myself a dose," she continued, revealing her wrist and the dark bruise that had begun to emerge around the syringe's puncture mark.

"Why doesn't that surprise me?" Jorge said, taking hold of her wrist and scrutinising first the injury and then the dark welt. There were faint green streaks under the skin as if the lurid Pacifier drug had caused permanent staining.

"Will you help me?"

He glanced out the window towards where the Frothers showed no sign that their interest was waning.

"Do I have a choice?"

Freya stared down at the needle protruding from her arm. If she lost much more blood, it wouldn't be transitioning that killed her. She was feeling faint, and for the past four hours Jorge had been steadily winding digestive biscuits into her in an attempt to maintain blood sugar level; *like that was her main concern*. But, though she dared not hope too much, the nausea had subsided a little. Her eyes were clearer too, though overriding tiredness was making it harder to focus on the task in hand.

"I just want to confirm it," Jorge said as he removed the needle and passed her yet another cotton ball to push upon the site.

"We can't confirm anything until we test it," Freya said as she swooned.

"You need to rest."

She didn't need to voice her reply, and threw him a deadpan expression instead, easily conveying her thoughts on the matter.

"Okay," he added quickly. "But do me a favour and stay there. I can't have you falling over and ruining everything we've been working on."

She nodded her head and watched him as he moved across the room to the array of laboratory instruments. As he'd already done numerous times, Jorge transferred the withdrawn blood into a separation tube, opened the lid of the centrifuge and placed the sample inside. As he closed the machine and it began to whir, Freya allowed herself to relax. It was only a matter of time till they knew for sure.

"How are you bearing up?" Jorge asked as he returned to the seat next to her.

"Aching, tired, but, you know, I'm not trying to gnaw your face off, so that's a plus."

He smirked. "I should've known that if anyone could do it, it'd be you. Though, I don't think I realised it would be quite so literally."

His words resonated with her. She'd never imagined this would happen, that her Pacifier, Pacifier 6, the finalisation of Baidlin's work, would come about because of infection. They'd never tested it on people before; only Frothers. Only the monsters they wished to calm. They'd always waited for someone to transition before they stabbed the syringe and began to pump the green syrup in.

Why hadn't it ever occurred to her?

But it didn't matter now. She'd found it eventually. It was a virus; of that she was sure. It was vicious and rapid in its attack and replication. There was no eradicating it, no overcoming its fatal effects. It killed indiscriminately, taking every living creature that a single, self-replicating bastard cell got into, not matter how strong someone was, regardless of their immune system's determination to hold the invader at bay. Eventually, all humans succumbed.

It was the toxicity levels of the virus that brought about the rabid, vicious characteristics of the dead. Pacifier had always sought to target this feature, to thin those invading cells. But humanity's very core — *uniqueness* — was also their flaw. No matter how much Baidlin and Freya had tried, they'd never managed to reduce viral load consistently. They'd never been able to establish regular downtime during which they could guarantee the pacification of an otherwise ravaged monster. But this, this seemed to work.

"Freya."

She was roused by Jorge's gentle hands as they shook her awake.

"Freya, it's ready."

"Already?" she murmured, wiping drool from her chin. She panicked momentarily, questioning whether it was foam and feeling sick to her stomach at the thought of it. Jorge's reassurance that it wasn't calmed her, and she breathed a sigh of relief before getting to her feet and stumbling across the room to the microscope.

"Is this it?" she asked, looking towards the blood-smeared slide that awaited her. Jorge nodded, and she pressed her eye to the lens and stared down with hope. It was apparent right away that her predictions were correct. The blood cells before her weren't the misshapen, ruptured husks of the infected that she was so used to seeing. The virus hadn't broken cell membranes as before, hadn't decimated the body, not only of its immune defence system, but those vital oxygen carriers. Here, the cells were engorged. They looked, at first glance, to be completely healthy.

Freya shifted the microscope's focus, targeting the fluffy edges of the cells. To the undiscerning eye there was nothing wrong, but on closer inspection, each cell's surround was not the smooth surface it should be, but was covered in tiny nodules.

"The bastards! There they are," she gasped, focusing in further to see that the virus had become stuck to the cells in tiny clusters, like iron filings attracted and caught by a giant magnet.

"It's not a cure," Jorge said quietly over her shoulder.

"I can tell that," Freya said quickly, having already realised her mortality was still very much in question. Being so smothered, there was no way the blood cells could continue to function properly.

"But we don't need our subjects alive. We just need a way to thin the virus density. This is it, this works."

It was crude; of that there was no denying. But whatever the reason, Baidlin's Pacifier and her blood worked together. The virus was clustered in the blood stream and, if she guessed correctly, drawn back out of the tissues and muscles. Its density was thinned, reducing its host's hostile characteristics. It wasn't even deforming and breaking down the cell membranes any longer.

"Have you heard from the others yet?" Freya asked, withdrawing her gaze from the blood sample and turning to look at Jorge's grave face. He shook his head slowly.

"Take more of my blood," Freya said, moving towards the window and staring out across the dozen Frothers that ambled below.

"You can't handle it."

"Jorge, take my blood. We're going back to get them out."

CHAPTER 6

They erupted from the pharmacy without warning, smashing their way through a window and rounding on the Frothers before the grotesque beings knew what was happening. Coupled with staggering faintness and vicious tiredness, Freya's vanquished symptoms had begun to return, but she hid it from Jorge as she struck down the first beast with her boot, knelt on its neck and thrust a bright green syringe into its skin. They were armed with a new weapon now, something far more deadly to their enemies than knives, baseball bats and brute force. A drug that sapped the strength and bloodlust from the dead: Pacifier 6. It was hers. She was *in* it. Though no one else but Jorge would ever know that fact.

She saw him struggling with a Frother as she took out another two, jabbing each with their new armaments. She was surprised how fast it worked, how quickly those on the receiving end of her assault became quieter and placated.

Freya looked again to where Jorge was being backed towards a glass plate window, the knife in his hand outstretched but inadequately brandished. *She knew what had to be done. It was the only way to guarantee her safety.*

He called out for her, and she relinquished the thought, immediately jumping to his aid, unable to let infection take another. *There would be a way. There had to be a way to trust him, to safeguard her secret.*

If she'd had her earlier vigour, Freya would have stayed and laid waste to those before her, but the faintness ate at her determination. Instead, she simply felled the dozen or so Frothers and pacified them, still shocked at the speed with which her medicinal concoction worked. They could deal with them later.

Once free from the horde, they moved on, retracing her steps back towards the safe zone. She felt odd, different somehow. Not in physicality, but in character. Infection was there, filtering through her veins, pumping around her body but being held at bay, for now, by Baidlin's work.

They entered the corridor that led to the quarantine door, noting the flickering and whirring lights above. Each step took her closer to his body, to the smell of death and decay. It was only then that she realised what was wrong. Fear. There was none, it was gone.

"Come on," she called back to Jorge as he sidestepped the mass of crushed limbs and discarded body parts from her earlier rampage. In the midst of the fight, she hadn't quite realised the extent of her damage. The walls were splattered with dark ooze, the occasional piece of dried flesh and skin, some still with hair, stuck to the place it had landed. The floor was littered with those she'd despatched, the force at which she'd hit them having eventually rendered most completely inanimate. She saw Jorge wince as he stepped over the crushed skull, and she squinted to see her flesh still between its teeth. Freya stretched her back, expecting to feel a vicious sting from the wound those teeth had inflicted. There was nothing.

No pain either?

She ached, that was true, but now that she sought any twinge or throb, there was none to be found.

"I'm going ahead," she called out as Jorge continued to stumble through the dim hall.

"No, wait for me," he replied, but she ignored him and moved forwards without a second's thought.

She turned the corner and, this time, looked down. He lay there, quiet and still; the blood that pooled around him was beginning to turn brown. She took a step forwards, noting his body fluids were starting to dry and become a viscous, sticky syrup.

"We did it," she said, leaning over and attempting to find an ear on his mutilated head. There were no discernable features left, and so she simply stared at the torn flesh instead, trying to place her memory of the man onto the remains. She couldn't find his face in her mind, however hard she tried. It had vanished, evaporated as if it had never been there.

But he was gone, and she was not. She shrugged. That's what mattered now.

Before she drew away from his corpse, she hesitated. The browning blood paste was beneath her face. It was so close; the stench of it drew her in. *Should she?* The thought repulsed her, yet she reached out anyway, drawing her fingers through the thick, congealing blood. Freya put the hand to her lips and tasted him. She shrugged again; it wasn't as good as she'd expected.

"What are you doing?" She heard Jorge's quivering voice over her shoulder, and quickly wiped the blood on her trousers.

"Nothing," Freya replied, leaving her uncle on the floor and moving on. "I know why there wasn't a response from home base."

She drew to one side and allowed Jorge to look past her. The quarantine door from which she'd escaped earlier was wide open. A body lay on the threshold, its legs quivering and convulsing inhumanly.

"They must've tried to come after me," she said. "They're dead."

"Oh God."

"But it started before that. It was quiet before I got out," Freya continued as she stepped over the corpse and looked down. She'd known him, though only by sight. He snarled at her, unable to move. "Someone's fighting back," she added, noting the lacerations that had sliced his limbs away and left him defenceless. Jorge pulled out a syringe and bent down.

"No," Freya said, pulling his hand away. "It's a waste."

He paused as he saw her face and took in her meaning. Their supply was limited. Only those deemed a threat needed dosing.

"Y-y-you have blo-od on your lip," Jorge stammered as their eyes met.

"I must haven bitten myself," she replied, turning quickly away and moving deeper into her home. *He knew. He'd seen her.*

The body was the first of many. They littered the halls as she and Jorge inched their way closer to the cafeteria, the core of their community. Each and every one was eviscerated and heavily sliced, allowing the duo safe passage.

"Hello?" Freya called out as she pushed a pair of double metal doors open. The café was strewn with furniture, its regimentally ordered benches thrown on their sides, smashed plates and tins of rations scattered across the floor. Body parts were everywhere, most deathly still, torn from bodies before infection was able to set in and rot. A few, like the others they'd passed, twitched, unable to move but stuck in perpetual animation.

"Over there," Jorge whispered, nodding his head towards the utilities cupboard. The door was firmly shut, but was covered in smear marks and scratches. A trail of bodies snaked towards the room; a sign they'd been struck down as their attacker had retreated.

Freya put a finger to her lips and pointed, guiding Jorge around the room so they took up position on either side of the doorway. Then, without warning, Freya wrenched it open and jumped aside to evade the unknown.

"You're alive?!"

Freya peered into the darkened room and saw Mrs Gilbert hunched in the corner amidst the mops, buckets and jars of cleaning fluids.

"No thanks to you," Freya scowled.

"Jorge! Well I never." Mrs Gilbert beamed as she scuttled from her hiding place, ignored Freya and placed her arms around the young man's neck. "How on earth did you — "

"Freya," he replied, throwing praise in her direction. "If it wasn't for her, I either be dead or locked in that lab."

"If it wasn't for her we'd all still be alive," Mrs Gilbert said as her voice quivered in rage. "It was that Frother you attacked that started all of this! Thought she was Pacified, didn't we? Thought she could be patched up and put to work. But you —" She turned and jabbed a finger towards Freya. "You had to steal the limelight with your self-centred 'I'm a little genius' ways, didn't you? First you ruin our seamstress, then you manipulate poor Darshna…oh yes, I know all about that," Mrs Gilbert continued without taking a breath. "Poor mite's still locked up in The Chamber, though no doubt to her advantage in light of what's happened. I wouldn't wonder if she's tried to claw her way ou — "

Mrs Gilbert's voice turned to a scream as the teeth sank into her throat and ripped a chunk of flesh away. Freya had seen it coming, creeping from behind the discarded furniture, attracted by the woman's tirade. The seamstress, despite the smashed jaw and missing teeth, still carried a bite,

Freya saw, as the Frother got a taste of blood. Mrs Gilbert choked and pulled away as blood flooded in a torrent across her chest and to the floor. With a new meal in its sights, the beast showed no interest in Jorge or Freya. Primal instincts drove it to devour the prey in its grip. Freya smirked slightly; there was enough there to keep her going for a while.

"Shouldn't we Pacifier it?" Jorge asked as Freya took his arm and pulled him away.

"Leave it. It's satisfied…for now."

They left Mrs Gilbert writhing on the floor, picking their way back across the room and moving back into the hallway.

"Jorge, we couldn't have done anything," Freya said, realising her comrade's loyalty was waning. "It's just you and I…and Darsh. We have to stick together. We know how to stop them. We have a real chance now."

He was quiet, but she saw the horror on his face fade a little as he quickened his step and walked alongside her instead of traipsing behind. They arrived at the stairwell and hurried down the steps, descending to the parking garage where the place of torment lay. Here too, the lights flickered back and forth, whirring above their heads and threatening to go out at any point. But it didn't matter, they were just two now. There was nothing to fear.

The Chamber was ahead. It seemed so recently that she'd awoken there and realised her fate. How quickly things change.

"Darsh?" Freya called out. "Darsh, are you there?"

"Oh my god, Freya?"

As soon as she heard her friend's voice, she knew she was no longer alone. Turning towards Jorge, she plunged the knife into his chest and watched as the blood drained from his face and began to pump across his shirt.

"I'm sorry," Freya gasped, dismayed at how different it felt to sink a blade into flesh instead of a leathery corpse. She'd thought it would be easier, that he'd just become another number. But the way in which it slid so easily took her by surprise. "You know too much," she said, holding his body as he sank to the floor. Jorge gasped for air, unable to say a word, his eyes rolling upwards as the blood drained away. Freya left him where he lay, closing his eyes before she stood and walked to walked to the door.

"It's just you and me now, Darsh. I have Pacifier 6. We can tame them, all of them. I hope you're ready for a new world."

A Word from Geoffrey Wakeling

Horror has always been a fascinating genre to me; a genre that I both love to read and watch. I remember vividly attempting to find a film that truly scared me when I was university. I sat through countless hours of spine-tingling terrors, slasher-esc blood fests and psychological thrillers. My love for all things science fiction naturally led me to one of the best horror films ever created – *Alien*. Zombie flicks, though not necessarily scary, became a firm favourite, and I could quite happily sit for many an hour enjoying this niche.

"Hybrid" is a very different story than first imagined. Having written *Pacifier 6* a couple of years ago, I was keen to follow up on this novella in some respect...not necessarily with the same characters, but with the same premise of a world where zombies were being viewed as a potential labour force.

In an original concept, Freya was a young teen, stranded by a zombie apocalypse and fighting alongside her uncle to find a cure. As you've now read, things took a darker route for her; it's somewhat strange to see this innocent girl become something I'd never planned. Though, it does compel me rather to see what she gets up to next!

If you'd like to learn more about the *Pacifier* world, please feel free to visit geoffwakeling.com to read the first chapters of my novels, check out my book blogs, sign-up for my newsletter, and more. In addition, you can follow me on Twitter (@GWakelingWriter) or join me on Facebook.

www.geoffreywakeling.com

Free Fall
by Peter Cawdron

CHAPTER 1 - HOME

STARS PEPPER THE INKY BLACK DARKNESS. Little more than an inch of reinforced clear plexiglass surrounded by insulated sheet metal separates Jackson from the cold, empty vacuum of space.

"Hi Honey, I'm home," he says, his fingers resting on a computer screen, touching lightly at a pale blue dot in the electronic distance.

Physically, Earth is still too distant to be resolved by the human eye. Besides, with both the engines and the shielding on the Phaethon facing in the direction of travel, there are no windows facing Earth. This is the closest Jackson will get to seeing Earth until the Phaethon passes the Moon.

Phaethon, Faith on, Fave on, Rave on—on any given day Jackson can pronounce the name of his spacecraft half a dozen different ways depending on how tired he is and how lazy his tongue feels. He isn't supposed to talk to himself. Mission psychologists say it isn't healthy, but fuck 'em. They aren't the ones strapping themselves to a spacecraft powered by a daisy chain of thermonuclear explosions.

They aren't the ones risking their lives to test the viability of interstellar travel.

Fame? Is that really his motivation? His wife said he was selfish during the divorce, but she was hardly an impartial observer. She said he never cared about anyone and never could. Part of him hates to think she might be right. No, curiosity, exploration—this is what drives him on. Of course he cares about others. He's human, not a machine.

"Houston. This is Phaethon. Do you copy?"

That there is no reply isn't too alarming. At the speed the Phaethon has been traveling over the past two months, the shields have produced a ridiculous amount of radiation as everything from fine specks of dust down to individual atoms adrift in interplanetary space collided with her.

Named after the mythical son of Helios, the mighty sun and giver of light, Phaethon has propelled itself up to 97% of the speed of light relative to Earth. Between the glowing outer shield and the electromagnetic pulses produced by the engine, communication with Earth isn't possible until the Phaethon's speed drops back below 10%.

Jackson should be right on the cusp of reestablishing comms, but there is no reply.

"Houston. You should have seen her. She was beautiful. She did everything that was asked of her. Not more than a 2% deviation from the flight path. Outbound arc north was nominal, as was the southern return.

"We had a little tremor at the halfway point while orienting for the decel burn. For a while there, I was a little worried the engines wouldn't align with the shields and I'd sail off into space like Major Tom, but the old girl didn't let me down.

"Oh, and hey, onboard tracking detected another fourteen trans-Neptunian dwarf planets. Yes, you heard that right, fourteen of the suckers, and that's just what we could observe on the fringe of the Oort Cloud. The largest is slightly smaller than Pluto, but what a beauty. In the UV, she shines like an opal."

Jackson runs his hands over his face, cleaning out the grit in his eyes as he says, "For the record, I don't recommend 1.4G constant acceleration. It's OK at first, but after vacillating between that and zero over dozens of alignment burns, I feel like shit. I cannot wait to get back to a constant one gee."

His mind wanders. If someone could see him — if there was some cosmic eye watching him, what a sight they would behold. Rather than floating around like the Apollo astronauts or those in the Shuttle or onboard the Orion, Jackson is stuck to the wall. For him, the leading face of the spacecraft feels like a floor, but that is the illusion of deceleration.

"I want pizza and beer," he says, wondering if Houston can hear him, hoping someone down there is taking notes. "Seriously, pizza and beer. Nothing fancy. Just a pepperoni pizza and some cheap, nasty beer. Hell, it could be warm for all I care. And football. I have got to sit my ass on a couch and mindlessly watch men charging at each other like mountain goats. Hey, who's looking good for the Super Bowl next year?"

Silence is the only reply, but Jackson doesn't care.

"Okay, Houston. I'm entering a sleep phase. Wake me on approach, will yah? Goddamn decel is screwing with my vision. Eyeballs must be deformed by pressure or something. Hell, I can concentrate and push through it, but I'd rather not bring on another migraine. I'm going to get some sleep. You get that pizza and beer ready, you hear?"

Jackson rests his headset on the command console and dims the lights in the cramped confines of the Phaethon.

"Two months here, almost four months back there," he mumbles to himself as he climbs into his sleeping bag and curls up on the pseudo floor of the craft. "That relativity shit does my head in." He laughs, adding, "Better goddamn pay me for four!"

He is asleep within seconds; his worn, tired body shuts down his mind.

An eerie blue light shines in through the windows of the Phaethon.

Jackson squints, wondering how long he slept. He's surprised by the light. For him, it seems as though just a few seconds have passed, not the almost ten hours displayed on the inflight clock. After months of darkness, the brilliance outside is baffling. He tries to get up only to find there is no up. He is floating weightless in free fall. There is nothing to push off of to get up as he's drifting almost a foot from the floor.

Spasms electrify his body. In that split second, it is as though he's in a dream, falling from a cliff. His body shakes, wanting to wake him before he hits the rocks, only in space there's no escape from free fall. Instead of waking to find the comfort of his bed holding him firm, he wakes violently to the nightmare of falling forever down a rabbit hole. It takes a couple of seconds for his mind to reorient itself and embrace the weightless experience without fear.

Wriggling with the floppy sleeping bag, Jackson works his legs out of the bag, summersaulting slowly around the cabin of the Phaethon.

Home.

"Good morning, Houston," he says, picking up his wireless headpiece and slipping it over his ear. "Looks like a beautiful day down there."

There's no reply, but Jackson doesn't care. He's excited to see the emerald greens and azure blues of the Bahamas drifting so calm and serene beneath his window. Fluffy white clouds pepper the sky hundreds of miles below him.

"I know you get this all the time from us astronuts, and I know it's kinda cruel pointing it out, but damn, you haven't seen Earth until you've seen her from orbit!"

The sleeping bag drifts lazily beside him. He bundles it up, scrunching it into a ball and stuffing it into a cupboard, loving the way that action slowly pushes him away from the wall. Free fall is a lot like swimming, only without any resistance from the water.

Jackson is expecting mission control to begin talking to him about reentry. As exciting as it is to be home, he's going to miss space. Like most astronauts, Jackson spent his first few days feeling seasick. NASA likes to call it space sick, but for Jackson, motion sickness in free fall felt all too similar to a deep sea fishing expedition he once did off the Florida Keys. He could have died on that boat and he wouldn't have cared as long as he could stop vomiting and dry-heaving. Once he acclimatized to space though, free fall was like living on a roller coaster.

He loves it.

"Free fall," he says, distracting himself and feeling as giddy as a child at the sight of Earth rushing by so close below. "It's like playing in the ball pit at McDonalds. You know you'll never get us kiddies to leave of our own accord. It's just too much fun."

Still there's no reply.

The Phaethon has automatically brought Jackson into a slightly elliptical orbit roughly five hundred miles above the Earth's surface. Although his formal title is pilot, Jackson understands the reality of the mission. He's a guinea pig. He's along for the ride. NASA humors him with a handful of tasks and objectives along the way, but for the most part he's an observer. He's trained in how to repair critical systems, but the term 'repair' is a misnomer. Swapping parts is something a robot could do. Jackson's on board so the brains at NASA can evaluate how well his body copes traveling at almost the speed of light, but he doesn't care. It's his name in the history books, not theirs.

Dozens of contingency plans have been preprogrammed into the Phaethon, covering every possible emergency. Flying the Phaethon is like choosing menu items at a restaurant. All the hard work has been done by someone else. Jackson follows his training and starts bringing up the various options for reentry on his computer terminal. There's no internet connection, but that's not surprising as it tends to be flaky at the best of times.

"Houston?"

The silence is unnerving, but Jackson shrugs it off.

"What's the plan? Do we have confirmation of a recovery ship in the Pacific drop zone? What's the weather like down there? I'm picturing clear skies over Waikiki... Please don't tell me I need to come down in the Atlantic."

He pauses. This time, rather than waiting a few seconds to avoid talking over the top of mission control, Jackson waits a full minute.

"Houston?"

Nothing.

"Ah, mission control?"

Instinctively, he looks out the window, watching as Texas drifts by beneath him. Towns and cities are visible as little more than grey smudges on an otherwise sandy colored desert. Pockets of forest dot the landscape. Farms are scattered like patchwork quilts, with multicolored squares breaking up the harsh, barren landscape.

"Houston, why am I in a retrograde orbit?"

He laughs, adding, "What? You guys didn't think I had enough to deal with up here? You decided I should play dodgeball with space junk?"

The silence is eerie and unnerving.

"Okay, Houston. Assuming it's not April 1st I'm activating a dead comms protocol. Switching to auxiliary systems. Outbound transmission looks good. Inbound looks fine, but if you're transmitting, I'm not reading you."

Jackson busies himself, checking technical manuals, not noticing as the Continental U.S. slides silently beneath him and his tiny craft.

Dark clouds hide the West Coast as the Phaethon races across the vast, lonely Pacific. Night falls abruptly somewhere over the ocean. With each orbit taking ninety minutes, he knows he'll be back over Texas well before the sun sets on the Lone Star state, having passed through a night and a day in a surreal hour and a half.

"I hope you can hear this," Jackson says, unscrewing a panel on the bulkhead as he drifts helplessly within the Phaethon. "I know you can hear this. I know you're doing everything you can to reestablish comms, but I've got to tell you, this is freaking me out a little. So close but so far, you know."

He's chatty. After two months, he might have become somewhat introverted, but Jackson finds solace in talking, even if he's talking to an empty ship and a silent radio.

"Professionalism, right? Keep your cool. Solutions present themselves to a calm mind. The anxious miss the obvious. Well, all that advice seems a little patronizing when you've got an entire planet set firmly beneath your feet. When you find yourself hurtling around Earth faster than Superman and his proverbial speeding bullet, reality is a little different. Little things can freak you out."

Screws float carelessly beside Jackson as he pulls a panel away beneath the main flight controls. With a flashlight between his teeth and a computer tablet in one hand, he begins checking fuses. Although he's floating upside down relative to the seat on the command deck he feels as though he's climbed up inside a simulator. Memories of his training come flooding back.

"Okay," he says, letting the flashlight drift from his lips now he's had a good look at the wiring. "Dead comms, let's do this by the book. Fuses — check. Main bus switch — check. Auxiliary bypass — check. Redundant back up — check. Circuit board — check. There's no sign of any discoloration, no burnt smell, nothing. But, hell, who knows what's going on inside those circuits. They could have been slowly roasting over the past few months and I'd never know it."

Frustrated, he slips the cover back on and screws the panel in place.

"I'm going to check the radio in the reentry pod."

As he drifts past the window, Jackson gets a glimpse of the dark Earth below. A typhoon is forming out at sea, with brilliant white clouds spiraling in toward a tight, tiny center. In the distance, the coast of Asia is visible in the moonlight.

"Huh," he says to himself, wondering why there are no lights. Although Jackson isn't sure which part of Asia he's flying toward, he's aware Asia is the most densely populated landmass on Earth. But with electrical infrastructure from the last century, blackouts are probably common during the storm season.

Jackson moves hand over hand through the Phaethon, making his way to the reentry pod.

It takes a few minutes to power up the pod. Backlit controls glow in green and red.

"Houston, I'm broadcasting on the emergency band, using the reentry pod. Do you read me? Over."

Silence.

By now, he figures he must be somewhere over the Middle East. There should be relay stations or satellites automatically routing his signal around Earth and into the control room in Houston.

"For good measure, I'm activating the emergency beacon. Just trying to make some noise up here and get some attention. Banging pots and pans, as it were. Don't freak out on me now. I'm doing a good enough job of that myself."

He turns up the radio.

Static hisses in the air.

"Great," he says sarcastically. "I can pick up the remnants of the Big Bang some 13.8 billion years ago, but I can't get a message from five hundred miles away."

Jackson fiddles with the settings on the radio, setting the tuner to search through the kilohertz and the megahertz bands used by commercial radio.

"Can I at least get me some Country and Western? At this point, I'll settle for a foreign language service."

The radio fails to lock on to a signal so he returns it to the NASA broadcast band and settles for static.

Back in the cabin of the Phaethon, Jackson watches as the Mediterranean slides quietly beneath his spacecraft. Cyprus, Turkey, Greece, Malta and the familiar shape of Italy are visible through the spotted cloud cover.

"No lights?"

The south of France and the Spanish peninsula are dark as dawn breaks over Europe.

"I don't get it," he says, slipping his headset over his ear and hoping he's talking to someone on Earth. "What's happening down there? Houston, what the hell is going on?"

For the first time, Jackson considers the possibility his radio is working fine. Even if no one is listening down on Earth, he knows his flight recorder will retain two week's worth of voice and data metrics. Whatever happens, someday someone will examine the black box so he is deliberate, documenting his thinking, reasoning, and subsequent actions.

"Okay. I have no knowledge of what has happened on Earth other than that the planet is quiet in both in radio and light emission. The lack of light pollution might be a boon for astronomers, but it's probably not that desirable for the rest of the population.

"I'm trying to stay objective and not stress about family and friends, but it seems some kind of global calamity has occurred, something that has taken out electronics, maybe?

"What could do that? Nuclear war? What would the remnants of a nuclear blast look like from space?

"Approaching the U.S. West Coast, I can see long, thin tendrils of smoke from fires, but that could be anything. An explosion at a chemical plant, a forest fire."

Talking himself through the details he can see helps him to be objective.

"I have enough oxygen and water to stay up here almost indefinitely, but food is going to become an issue within about a week."

Jackson doesn't like where this is leading.

"I can't stay up here forever," he says. "I'd rather not be forced down. I'd rather come down on my own terms, so I've got a week to figure out what the hell I'm going to do and how I'm going to do it."

Steeling himself, he speaks clearly for the benefit of the flight recorder.

"This isn't suicide. It's survival."

The Phaethon passes over Florida and into the Gulf of Mexico. Jackson looks for the wake of boats on the sea, but clouds obscure the gulf.

"I am shifting my search to commercial and private radio channels in an effort to contact someone, anyone."

Using his computer, Jackson conducts a burst transmission across the major frequencies.

"This is Captain Dan Jackson of the U.S. Phaethon. Is anyone receiving? Over."

Jackson uses a computer macro to record his outbound transmission and sets it to repeat every two minutes. It takes a bit of savvy, but he figures out how to lock on to any reply and switch exclusively to that frequency, but there's no response.

Dejected, Jackson sips on a bottle of water.

It doesn't take long for the monotonous repetition of, "This is Captain Dan Jackson," to become a point of despair.

Jackson stares out the window as he crosses the coastline. Somewhere down there is his home just north of Corpus Christi. He's sad.

Static flares and the crackle of a young voice asks, "Hello? Is there someone out there?"

Jackson feels his heart race.

He grabs at the console, pulling his weightless body closer to the controls and yells. It's as though close proximity and the strength of his voice are somehow going to make his transmission clearer.

"Hello! This is Captain Daniel Jackson. Who am I speaking to?"

His heart pounds in his chest. The voice coming through on the radio is weak, breaking up and crackling.

"This is Daisy."

"Daisy," Jackson replies. "Boy, am I glad to hear your voice!"

"Can you help me?" Daisy asks. "My daddy said I should get help over the radio."

Jackson's blood runs cold.

"How old are you, Daisy?"

"Seven. I need help. Can you help me? Please? I'm scared. I'm really scared."

Fuck!

Jackson wants to swear aloud but he holds himself back. Just when he thought there was hope, his lifeline with Earth seems hopeless. Initially, Jackson ignores her plea.

"Where is your daddy? Can you put him on the radio?"

There's no reply and Jackson panics, wondering if he's said something to upset the young girl or if he's moved out of range. His heart pounds in his chest.

"Daisy? Daisy, are you still there?"

"Yes."

"Where are you?"

"In the police station."

"Which police station?" Jackson asks.

The silence is painful.

"I can't help you, if you can't tell me where you are," Jackson says, appealing to the young girl.

"Pasadena," comes in soft reply.

"Pasadena? Out in California?"

"In Texas," Daisy replies and Jackson gets excited.

"Texas? I know where you are, Daisy! You're in the southern suburbs of Houston, right?"

There's no answer.

"Listen carefully, Daisy. I'm an astronaut. I'm above you right now, somewhere up in the wild blue yonder above the clouds. I'm soaring high overhead, do you understand?

"I can't talk to you for long. I'm moving too fast. I'm going to sail over the horizon. Daisy? Can you still hear me?"

Jackson slows himself down, realizing he's rushing. The poor girl is scared. She's asking for help. He needs information, but he's got to slow down and be considerate. Her silence isn't helping. He's not sure if she's agreeing with him and nodding, not knowing he can't see her, or if she's too freaked out to talk. She knows how to use a radio. She's been using it for a while. Daisy and her father must have made contact with others over the radio or she wouldn't be using it now.

"Daisy?" Jackson says, slowing his speech.

"Yes."

That one word sounds so sweet. Just to be in contact with someone, anyone gives him hope.

"Daisy. I want to help you, but I need help too. Is there a police officer down there? Or your mom? Or another adult? Can I speak to them?"

Jackson pulls at a railing beside the window, pulling himself closer and peering out at the brilliant splashes of ochre and sandy browns breaking up the Texan wilderness. The coast slips away. Already, the radio signal is breaking up. He has seconds, not minutes.

"Daisy?"

"They're monsters!" she yells. "Don't you get it? They're all monsters! They lied! They said they'd never leave me, but they did. And now there's just me. I'm the only one left!"

"What happened, Daisy?" Jackson asks, panic rattling his voice. "Can you tell me what happened to everyone down there?"

"I've got to go. I can hear them. They're coming. They're coming for me!"

"Daisy!" Jackson yells within his empty spaceship.

Daisy screams. She must have locked the transmit button because Jackson hears the microphone being dropped. Furniture is knocked over. Someone scrambles away, bumping into a chair, causing it to scrape across the ground. There's yelling, screaming, growling and groaning.

"DAISY!" Jackson yells again.

The radio signal breaks up as the Phaethon moves out of range, sailing on at five miles a second, several hundreds of miles above Earth.

"Noooo!" Jackson cries, slapping his hand against the window and peering back at Texas. The gulf coastline disappears over the horizon. "Goddamn it, no!"

Jackson doesn't understand what's happening on Earth, but what was a vague, general crisis is suddenly personal.

"I'm coming, Daisy. Hold on. I'm coming for you!"

Static dominates the radio waves.

"Hold on, Daisy," Jackson repeats, feeling helpless, knowing she can't hear him. With the radio conversation over, the automated scanning routine kicks in again, racing through thousands of frequencies, but there's no one else down there listening. No one that can talk back to him and explain what has happened.

Jackson brings up a map of Houston on his computer. When it seems no one is alive down there, one solitary voice is enough to stir something deep within him. Self-preservation is suddenly subordinate to the survival of humanity as a whole.

"What are you doing?" he asks himself. "What the hell do you think you're doing, you dumb fuck!"

He zooms in on southern Houston, looking for the Pasadena police station.

"This is stupid," he says, berating himself. "You can't come down over land."

His finger runs over three airports on the outskirts of Pasadena: La Porte, William Holly and Ellington Air Force Base. Lots of clear land. Nice, long, flat runways.

"What else can I do?" he asks himself. "Sit up here waiting for a call that will never come? And then what? Splash down in the Pacific and paddle like crazy?"

On the map, it all looks so simple. There are no houses, no buildings, and no topographical markings, making the land beyond the various airports look flat. For Jackson, the deception holds a certain appeal, helping him to justify the lunacy of his plan. If there was anyone at mission control in Houston, they would say he's crazy, and they'd be right, but it's Houston. Jackson's been to Houston enough times to know the lay of the land. If there's anywhere to come down, it might as well be somewhere he knows. If mission control won't talk to him, he'll go to them!

"I-45 cuts right through there," he says in one breath, followed by, "You can't be serious. Your landing ellipse is at least eight miles in length and a mile or two wide, depending on winds. You could hit goddamn power lines, skyscrapers, trees.

"No, there's three airports. It's going to be wide and open. Nothing above two stories. No high power lines."

His finger picks out several parks and a golf course on the map.

"You can't do this," his rational mind says. "Touchdown speed is 30 miles an hour. You'll break your stupid back!"

No sooner has he spoken than he grabs his toolkit and unscrews a panel on the bulkhead beside the reentry pod.

"I'm not leaving her," he says softly, knowing his voice is being picked up by the flight recorder. "I don't know what the fuck has happened on Earth, but Daisy's alive. I can't pretend I never spoke to her. Judge me if you want, but I can't live with myself if I don't try something. I can't turn my back on the only person I can reach down there... I can't abandon a child."

The aluminum panel drifts to one side, turning freely through the air as abandoned screws summersault slowly around the cabin.

"I'm not crazy."

Jackson pulls at the thermal foam lining the inside of his spaceship, tearing out a long sheet and cutting it off with a box knife. He leaves the foam floating beside him as he pulls off another two panels and tears at more foam.

"I'm coming down sooner or later. Why delay the inevitable? And why risk drowning? I can do this. Get down in one piece. Figure out what's happened."

In the back of his mind, one word leaves him unsettled.

Monsters.

What did she mean? What awaits him on Earth?

Is he unduly panicked? Has he taken things too far? Jackson doubts himself.

What the hell are the air traffic controllers at Ellington going to make of a reentry vehicle coming down on three massive parachutes, landing in the middle of a restricted military base? If he's got this all wrong, he's going to be on the evening news for months to come as the astronaut who freaked out.

"Houston?"

Jackson doesn't expect a reply. That none is forthcoming is almost a relief.

Sweat beads on his forehead as he works with the foam, anchoring his feet beneath a railing so he can get some leverage. He stuffs both sheets of foam into his sleeping bag and drags it into the cramped confines of the reentry pod.

"You're a goddamn idiot. A fool," he says, loosening the straps on his couch and laying the stuffed sleeping bag on the seat.

"Duct tape," he mutters, giving both himself and whoever may one day listen to the flight recorder a running commentary of his actions. "Don't leave orbit without a Texan toolkit-in-one!"

Jackson uses the tape to fasten the sleeping bag to the couch, ensuring the padding covers the headrest, torso and hip area but not bothering with the lower legs.

"This is either the dumbest idea in history or the stupidest. I'm struggling to figure out which. Who put a goddam redneck Texan on this mission anyway? Hah. What else did you expect?"

Jackson laughs as he programs the coordinates for reentry into the onboard computer, centering the landing ellipse on Ellington Air Force base.

"With a little luck," he says, knowing his comment is a gross understatement.

Static hisses around him.

"I'm coming, Daisy," he says softly for no one other than himself.

Back in the main cabin of the Phaethon, Jackson suits up, slipping into his day-glow orange recovery suit and white helmet. He programs the Phaethon to move into a higher orbit some fifteen hundred miles above Earth roughly an hour after he departs. As far as he's concerned, five trillion dollars worth of space hardware deserves more than a deteriorating orbit, the damage to the internal insulation notwithstanding.

Outside the Phaethon, night has fallen yet again. Already, he's somewhere over a darkened China or perhaps Vietnam.

"Goodbye, old girl," he says, slipping into the reentry pod and taking one last look at his home for the past two months before closing the hatch.

As crazy as his plan is, Jackson feels positive. To be doing something rather than waiting and reacting is a psychological relief if nothing else.

"Hang in there, Daisy," he says, finishing his prep before punching the release. A soft shudder announces the separation of the pod. One spacecraft has become two.

"I'm christening her the Odyssey," he says somewhat proudly before settling into his professional routine.

"Okay, Houston. We have separation. All systems online. Radar is good. Fuel cells good. I'm heating the chutes. De-orbit burn and heat shield alignment are preprogrammed. All metrics are nominal. Switching to internal oxygen."

Jackson closes his visor, feeling the clip catch. He turns a valve on the side of his suit. Oxygen flows into his suit as a contingency against any loss of cabin pressure during reentry.

"Houston, I am good to go. Repeat—good to go."

There's no answer, but Jackson barely notices. He's too busy checking the subsystems and double checking the landing sequence.

"It would be really nice to get a weather report on the target area," he says. "I'm assuming light cloud cover and a gentle south-westerly this time of year."

The reentry pod is barely larger than the old Gemini capsules, intended only for transit or emergency. Comfort isn't a consideration in space flight.

"Rolling."

The capsule turns slowly and Earth comes into view through the tiny, triangular windows.

"I've got a great view of Miami. Nice day to be at the beach."

His thick, gloved hands work with a variety of toggle switches.

"Initiating pitch. I'll see you soon."

Jackson is surprisingly calm. Most of his reentries have been conducted in the Orion with crews of anywhere from three to six other astronauts, but the principle is the same in the Odyssey.

Slowly, the reentry pod tumbles backwards in response to a soft burst from the forward thrusters. Another burst causes the pod to pause with Jackson facing backwards. Looking overhead, he can see blue ocean and white clouds passing by.

"Houston. This is Odyssey."

He pauses.

"We are GO for reentry burn."

Those were supposed to be the words spoken by mission control, but Jackson uttered them habitually.

A gentle rumble passes through the Odyssey as the spacecraft begins slowing, dropping deeper into the thin, outer layers of the atmosphere.

"Picking up some hull ionization. Angle of entry is good. Shield aligned."

A slight shimmy grips the Odyssey and Jackson tightens his five-point harness, pulling himself hard against the insulation padding his seat. He breathes deeply. From here on out, there is nothing to do but enjoy the ride. Enjoy? That brings a smile to his face, and he shakes his head at his own stupidity.

Strands of plasma flicker past the windows like streamers, fine glowing ribbons of fire.

Some astronauts hate reentry as there's a sense of inevitability and helplessness about the procedure, but not Jackson. The laws of physics test the engineering prowess of humanity in a fiery display of raw power.

For Jackson, there are worse ways of dying in space than being flash boiled at 7800 Kelvin, a temperature hotter than the surface of the Sun. The tiniest crack in his heat shield and plasma will cut through the Odyssey like a chainsaw. Death will come in microseconds, but that doesn't bother Jackson.

The superheated plasma building up in front of the shield begins buffeting the Odyssey, causing the craft to shake as though it were about to spin out of control, but the weighted center of gravity ensures the pod remains aligned like a cork in the ocean. For all the talk about rocket science, reentry requires no more math than throwing a rock into a pond.

Jackson watches both the altimeter and his airspeed continue to plummet. Slowly, the flames subside and the darkness of space softens, becoming a radiant light blue—a terrestrial welcome home.

"We're pulling six gees," he says, as his cheeks sag under the intense deceleration. "Slightly more than expected. Adjusting the glide angle to compensate."

The capsule rotates slightly, catching the atmosphere at a different angle and changing the rate of fall.

After almost a minute, the capsule jerks to one side.

"Drogue shoot deployed," he says, not that anyone else cares.

Jackson knows what's coming next. He's careful to position his head and arms so they're not touching any metal or likely to fling into the console when the three vast primary parachutes deploy.

Thirty seconds later, the capsule is yanked violently into the sky. In reality, he's still falling, plummeting to the Earth, but the sensation of rapid deceleration in that moment gives the illusion of being dragged upwards for a split second. His seatbelt bites into his shoulders, holding him firmly in place.

"Main chutes deployed."

Jackson is jerked to one side in his seat as the parachutes unravel, unfurling over almost ten seconds.

"External camera confirms three canopies. Looking good at 25,000 feet, Houston. I've got to say, it's nice to be home. Not sure what the welcoming committee is going to be like, but for now, it's a smooth ride."

Smooth by his standards. Most normal, everyday people would be terrified by the sense of helplessness in descent, but for Jackson a few bumps along the way keeps things interesting.

Jackson tries to sound confident. In reality, he's nervous as hell, but not about the flight or the landing. He's worried about what he's going to find when he opens the hatch.

Monsters.

As the minutes pass, Jackson busies himself looking at the projected landing zone. The lower he descends, the smaller the landing ellipse becomes, slowly zeroing in on a region north of Ellington Air Force Base.

"Yeah, this isn't looking good, Houston. There's a few housing developments down there. Looks like I'm about to drop in on someone for dinner.

"Depending on the wind at ground level, I may come down on the edge of a residential area near what appears to be a football stadium."

Still there's no reply.

"Houston, if this doesn't get some attention from someone down there on the ground, I'm not sure what will. There's got to be someone alive down there other than a seven year old girl, right? Houston? Do you read me?"

Jackson brings up the Pasadena Police Department and looks at the distance. Drifting north is good, bringing him closer to the station.

"I'm using the chute camera to survey the ground," he says, using a joystick to control the onboard computer and shift the gaze of the camera tasked with monitoring the parachutes. The camera view swivels, pointing down to one side. The leading edge of the Odyssey takes up almost a third of the screen. Jackson adjusts the orientation of the camera so only a thin sliver of his craft runs down one side of the screen, giving him a bird's eye view of his descent.

"Passing through 10,000 feet. I can see houses, cars, trucks, but nothing's moving down there."

Jackson shuts off his internal oxygen and opens the faceplate on his helmet.

As he descends lower he notes, "There're a few fires down there. Smoke is billowing north by northeast."

For almost a minute, he watches details on the ground slowly come into view in mesmerizing clarity.

"Coming down to two thousand feet. I got a glimpse of the stadium a moment ago as the Odyssey drifted to one side. The stadium is west of me. The playing field looks cultivated? Are there gardens in there? Plowed rows? I'm not sure. At a guess, it must be five or six in the afternoon down there. I'm seeing long shadows, so I could me mistaken."

He's nervous.

"A thousand feet. I've got a good view of the ground now. There are people wandering in the streets. I can see cars and buses, but they're not moving. There are lots of people! Hundreds, maybe thousands of them out on the streets watching the Odyssey descend.

"I can see the headlines now: *Astronaut freaks out and lands in suburbs*—a single faulty fuse on his radio and he junks a multimillion dollar spacecraft in a backyard swimming pool.

"I've got to tell you, Houston. I'm feeling pretty damn stupid right about now."

Jackson stiffens in his seat, waiting for the inevitable thud that will mark his landing.

"Hundred feet... Fifty feet... I'm drifting. Have visibility of a mall, a parking lot, a main road. There are so many people. They're running toward the Odyssey. Get them back! Tell them to stay back!"

The Odyssey swings wildly to one side.

"I've clipped a tree. No, I think it was a street light."

He braces.

The Odyssey thunders down on top of a vehicle, crushing metal and breaking glass. Even within the confines of his reentry capsule, Jackson can hear metal twisting and breaking beneath two and a half tons of spacecraft returning from orbit.

Jackson is thrown violently to one side. His body jerks, fighting against his seat restraints and the extra padding on his couch.

He shouts.

"Houston, I'm down! Odyssey is down! Over."

The Odyssey doesn't come to a complete stop. The parachutes drag the spacecraft a few feet across the crumpled metal. On the monitor, Jackson catches a glimpse of crushed bodies lying in the street, but the capsule twists beneath the parachutes and the image shifts to a shot of a radiant sunset.

"Oh dear God. I think I've hit someone! What the hell are they doing out there? Get them away, Houston. Get everyone away from the capsule."

The capsule comes to a rest at an angle, making it difficult to unbuckle. Jackson climbs out of his seat. His muscles complain at the exertion of moving under gravity, but he forces himself on. He grabs his emergency survival kit including a first aid pouch.

A bloody hand reaches up from below the capsule and slaps at the glass on the hatch. Dark fingermarks streak the glass as the hand falls away.

"Houston, we're going to need paramedics. I'm okay, but there's at least six or seven injured people out there. I'll help as much as I can, but I've only got a one major trauma kit. This is Odyssey signing off."

Jackson unlocks the hatch, pulling at a lever that causes the hatch to swing in and to one side. Almost immediately, he's overwhelmed by the stench of rotten meat in the stifling humidity outside. He steps forward, his legs feeling unsteady.

Hands reach up from below, grabbing at the hatch. Dozens of people are clamoring to get into the Odyssey, which is confusing.

Standing in the hatchway, Jackson gets his first good look outside. The Odyssey has come down on the back of a bus, crushing the rear roof. A large crowd has gathered, numbering in the hundreds, perhaps thousands. They're all trying to get on top of the bus. And it is then, Jackson realizes what has happened on Earth.

Zombies.

CHAPTER 2 - RUN

"Houston?" Jackson mumbles into the microphone on his helmet even though he's disconnected from the comms unit. No one can hear him. No one ever could.

The zombies immediately below the capsule tear at each other, clambering to reach him and pull him into the horde. Their hands grab at the shattered frame of the bus and slap at the bottom of the heat shield on the Odyssey.

He's surrounded by a sea of arms grasping at the air, pressing to get closer. There's nowhere to run to. No escape.

Mindless groans fill the air along with snarling. Teeth snap at the breeze. Jackson starts to back into the capsule, but there's nothing back there for him. There's no hiding from these monsters. To retreat is to wait to be overrun. Already, several zombies have climbed on top of the bus. They're on the far side of the Odyssey, but not for long.

A dark shadow blocks the setting sun.

The last of the three massive parachutes that slowed his descent from the Phaethon drifts slowly to the ground, landing some thirty feet away, blanketing the zombies to his right. Jackson realizes this is his only chance. He slings the survival pack over his shoulder and runs down the length of the bus. The edge of the parachute flutters as it drapes over dozens of zombies tearing at the fabric. There's still a mass of zombies between him and the canopy, but he doesn't hesitate.

Jackson doesn't slow his pace. He thunders along the roof of the bus with his boots slamming on the thin sheet metal. Bloody hands reach up on all sides, beckoning to him. A ghostly wail calls out as sunlight fades.

He launches himself off the roof of the bus, still pumping with his legs, and lands heavily on the shoulder of a rabid zombie.

Jackson falls face first into the horde, sinking into the sea of undead animated corpses.

Hands grab at him, tearing at his clothes. Teeth bite into his day-glow orange flight suit, but no sooner has he hit the concrete than he's up again, pushing through the press of zombies.

"Goddamn it," he yells, reaching with his arms and pushing zombies aside as he wrenches himself free and runs through the crowd.

He reaches the parachute and launches himself up and on top of the thick material, scrambling on hands and knees over the undulating mass of zombies trapped beneath the parachute. He tries to run but it's impossible, and he finds himself peg-legging through the horde as though he were running through waist deep snow. Several zombies follow him, but they can't make headway, snarling and growling as they flop around on the vast parachute.

Jackson is breathing hard, pushing off of trapped zombies with his gloved hands. He lifts his knees high as he runs, trying to get on top of the swell. It feels as though he's sprinting up a steep mountain. His heart is going to explode, but he pushes on.

The zombies thin out and Jackson finds he can pick his way through the last of them as he bounds over the parachute. His boots are like lead weights strapped to his feet.

As he clears the flapping edge of the chute, he looks back and sees dozens of zombies swarming over the bus, fighting with each other to see who will climb into the Odyssey. They're like a pack of wild dogs fighting over a bone.

Jackson jogs on, but he's exhausted. He stops by a sapling tree on the edge of a park. He has to. He can't keep running. His heart feels as though it is about to explode out of his chest. His lungs scream for oxygen. It's all he can to not to collapse. He leans forward resting his hands on his knees, sucking in air.

With his head down, his helmet blocks his peripheral vision. He wrestles with the locking ring around his neck and pulls the helmet off, holding it by the collar.

"Should have stayed up there," he manages between breaths. "Should have died in orbit."

A dog growls and snarls behind him, and he turns to see an overweight middle-aged man in an immaculate pinstriped business suit staggering toward him. At first, Jackson is confused. He could have sworn he heard a dog. The banker bares his rotten teeth and the realization that his clean white shirt and paisley blue tie is meaningless becomes all too clear.

"Hey, Mr. Space Man," a voice calls out. "Over here!"

A woman waves at him from an alley, not daring to expose herself to the horde but trying to get his attention.

Jackson jogs over. His lungs hurt.

Another zombie lunges at him. Jackson swings his helmet, hurling it at the monster's head as though it were a discus but keeping a firm grip on the chin guard. The back of the helmet connects with the zombie's jaw, sending the creature tumbling backwards to the ground. In that split second, Jackson learns something. His helmet gives him both added reach and leverage, making it an effective weapon. He runs on, not looking back at the zombie writhing in a pool of blood on the ground.

The woman in the alley cuts a slight figure. She's wearing a tank top and jeans. Her arms are gaunt, bordering on anorexic. Long dark strands of matted hair hide her face.

Jackson slows his jog as he reaches her. He starts to say something when she slams him into an open door and he finds himself sprawled out on the floor of a department store. The door slams and locks behind him.

He again tries to say something when a hand grips his mouth.

"Shhh," the woman says, pointing as a zombie ambles past the glass window toward the alley. She whispers, "Smell, sound, sight—in that order."

The zombie disappears around the corner and Jackson can hear it bumping into the fire door, trying to follow them into the store.

"This way," the woman whispers.

She runs through the store as graceful and silent as a cat, barely making any noise as she springs over fallen clothes racks and scattered dresses. Jackson follows her, running on the balls of his feet to reduce the noise from his boots.

"Wait," he calls out in a whisper, but the woman disappears into the shadows. She leaves by the rear of the building. Jackson follows her out into a back street. Glass breaks somewhere behind him. The zombies have busted into the store. Out on the narrow back street, the woman pauses beside the alley, looking down at the door they passed through just moments before. A small band of zombies pounds on the metal door. Beyond them, one of the parachutes from the Odyssey lies draped over a tree.

"Always against the flow," she says, darting across the alleyway. Jackson follows her. "They go this way, you go that way. Yes. That's the way to go every time. Every time. Yes?"

"Yes," he replies, trying to keep up as she runs on.

Her speech is as erratic as her motion.

"You were spam in a can—man," she says as she stops behind a strip mall. "Oh, they were looking for a good feasting. They thought you were a gift from the gods. They saw those red parachutes and thought they were lollipops. You're crazy, man. Crazy! They say, I'm crazy, but not me. You, man. You're the crazy one."

She leads him up an external staircase to a roof-top, chatting incessantly.

"You're a madman. What made you come down here? You should have stayed up there. You're insane. Certifiable. I mean, like straightjacket and leg restraints insane, you know?"

And Jackson gets a glimpse of who's lost their marbles. He nods as she leads him onto an open rooftop connected to various other buildings by a waist-high walls. A sleeping bag lies crumpled in one corner. Flies buzz around empty cans piled up against an air vent, but Jackson can see why she lives up here. She can range over almost an entire block on the shop roofs. There must be dozens of entry and exit points, and they're all highly visible.

Severed zombie heads sit skewered on poles mounted by the edge of the building. Their eyes follow him as their teeth grind.

"What the?"

"Oh, you like my little darlings? My scarecrows?"

"I—ah."

"What? You think I'm too petite to handle an ax? I haven't survived this long by being Ms. Congeniality."

And she laughs, but her laugh is unsettling.

"What's your name?" Jackson asks, trying to shift the subject.

"Jennifer. And what do they call you? Mr. Buzz Lightyear?"

Jackson fakes a smile. "Dan."

"So what have ya got for us, Dan?" she asks, gesturing toward his backpack.

"Ah, it's a survival kit," he replies, feeling uneasy about the reference to 'us.'

"You got ray guns?"

"No," Jackson says. "No ray guns."

Not that anyone sane would need to be assured of such a thing.

"Just water purification tablets, a flare gun, first aid kit, thermal blanket, matches, things like that."

"Can I see?"

See? In Jackson's mind, anything Jennifer sees is going to become a point of contention so he ignores her, saying, "I'm looking for someone. A young girl. Daisy. She's trapped in the local police station."

"Daisy's dead," Jennifer snaps, never taking her eyes off his backpack. She twists her head to one side, intensely curious about his pack with its NASA logo displayed proudly on the side.

The sun is setting. He's running out of time. From the rooftop, he gets his bearings. Knowing the sun is to the west, he faces north looking at the sprawling suburb before him. The stadium is behind him and to his right. Mentally, he triangulates his location against his memory of the map on the

Phaethon, and figures he's no more than two blocks away from the police station.

"I have to go," he says.

"So you're a knight in shining armor, is that it? You think you'll last out there? You won't last five minutes in prison clothing. They'll see you coming a mile away."

It takes Jackson a moment to realize what she's referring to, but his flight suit does look like something from the county jail. He loosens the locking cuff on his gloves and strips down to his t-shirt and shorts.

As he changes out of his flight suit, he asks, "What happened here?"

His boots are bulky, but given all the broken glass he's seen on the streets, Jackson doesn't want to go barefoot so he puts them back on and fastens them tight.

"It's the Book of Revelation, man. Judgement has been cast. We have been weighed and found wanting. It's the apocalypse. The end of the world. Hell has been emptied of her demons. The devil has come to Earth."

"But how did it happen?" he asks.

"Who knows?" she asks, "Does it matter?"

"It matters," Jackson replies, rummaging around in his pack and pulling out a protein bar. He tosses the bar to Jennifer and she tears it open, stuffing it in her mouth in one go. He tucks the flare gun into the small of his back and picks up his helmet. It might not be as effective as a baseball bat or a machete, but it will crush a skull.

"Come with me," he says.

"Oh, no," Jennifer replies with her mouth full. She waves her finger at him, saying, "You're crazy."

Jackson says, "You should come."

She shakes her head as though she's a dog shaking itself dry. Her matted hair whips around her face and he gets the message.

With the sun dipping behind the distant buildings and shadows burying the land, Jackson starts jogging across the rooftops, climbing over the low separating walls.

"Scent, sound, sight," Jennifer calls out after him. "Remember!"

He doesn't turn back, but not because he's rude. She's wrong about Daisy. He spoke to Daisy not more than two hours ago. But two hours is an eternity in the zombie apocalypse. Jackson buries that thought.

He's not thinking straight. As an astronaut, he's mission focused. The mission is everything. The mission demands precision, dedication. He has to find her. There are no other considerations.

At the end of the block, Jackson climbs down a fire escape and drops the last few feet to the ground. No sooner have his boots touched the concrete than a growl comes from the shadows.

Jackson jogs down a broad avenue, staying in the middle of the road. He's running into a breeze which gives him a slight advantage as his scent trails behind him, allowing him to run past unsus-pecting zombies before they realize he's there. They snarl and growl as he passes by, but he's able to give them a wide berth. Behind him, though, a swarm of zombies builds, following in his wake.

"Hang on, Daisy," he says between breaths. "I'm coming."

Although he kept up an aerobic exercise regime on the Phaethon, nothing could condition him for the jarring blow of each thud of his boots against the concrete street. His knees are sore, but he keeps go-ing.

The police station looks like the Alamo. Cars and trucks have been rolled over on their sides to form barricades. Zombies hang twitching from razor wire stretched over the hood of a burned out SWAT van. The tires have been shot out, lowering the truck's profile, but that hasn't stopped zombies from crawl-ing beneath the chassis. Dead legs stick out onto the road.

Bullet holes pockmark the vehicles. Black scorch-marks stretch upwards above the windows in the police station, testifying to an inferno. It's a war zone.

Jackson doesn't have long to weigh his options. He needs to get in and out of the station quickly as he's got his own party in tow.

A zombie staggers up to him wearing a police uniform. Jackson doesn't hesitate, swinging with his helmet and connecting with the undead officer on the side of the head and sending him tumbling to the road.

Bodies lie in the street. Some of them are still moving, crawling slowly forward. One of the police cars has been dragged out of place, allowing Jackson to jog through and up the steps of the police station.

"Daisy!" he yells, stepping through the broken front doors.

Glass crunches under his boots.

An overturned desk has crushed a police officer. Even in death, the officer's right hand grips a semi-automatic Glock.

Jackson puts his helmet down. He reaches out slowly, peeling the gun from a cold, dead hand only to have the hand suddenly grab at his wrist. He springs backwards, almost dropping the gun. The zombie growls, trying to pull itself out from beneath the desk.

Jackson retrieves a flashlight from a side-pouch on his backpack. He shines the light on the rabid zombie and steadies his aim. A single shot rings out and the side of the zombie's head explodes.

In the stunned silence following the crack of gunfire, Jackson hears the police station slowly coming to life.

"Not smart," he whispers, recalling the crazy woman's warning about scent, sound and sight. He picks up a few spare magazines lying on the floor. They're different weights. He keeps the heaviest two magazines, hoping they're full as he stuffs them in his pocket.

A door creaks.

Feet pound along a hallway upstairs.

In the basement, there's the banging of steel bars, someone's shaking a cell door, but are they undead or alive?

Glass crunches underfoot, but Jackson isn't moving. He turns and sees the outline of a police officer wearing riot gear. A deep snarl tells him the officer is not here to help, and Jackson fires again, aiming for the head. Blood, brains and bone explode from the back of the zombie's head and he collapses in a heap.

"Not good," he says, knowing how ill-prepared he is and realizing that if trained professionals could be overrun when they had strength of numbers on their side, he doesn't stand a chance alone.

Goosebumps rise on his skin, but he's come too far to back down. Although the decisions he makes over the next few minutes could be the death of him, he cannot flee. Daisy is here somewhere. He can still hear her cries over the radio and the terror in her voice. Something deep inside him will not allow him to run for his life like a coward, and so he creeps forward.

His flashlight is pathetic, having been designed for map reading, not exploring a burned out police station. Smoke drifts from the glowing embers of a doorframe. Shell casings lie scattered on the floor.

Free fall.

Life was simple with an entire planet swinging by beneath his feet every ninety minutes. Oh, what he'd give to be in free fall. His heart sinks at the re-alization he'll never leave Earth again. The police station is a tomb, a desecrated crypt. One that may bury him.

Jackson steps into the darkness.

"Daisy?" he whispers, climbing an interior stair-case, stepping over bodies, praying they don't move. His boots squelch in the fresh blood on the landing. Slowly, he turns up the next flight of stairs, expecting a zombie to burst from the shadows at any moment.

The body of a woman lies jammed in the door-way at the top of the stairs, allowing moonlight to enter the stairwell.

Glass shatters in the darkness.

Wood splinters and breaks.

Zombies rage on the floor below, overturning furniture and smashing windows, but they haven't followed him into the stairwell.

Yet.

Jackson steps over the dead woman and out into a darkened hallway. His flashlight dances between her outstretched arms, looking for the faintest tell-tale twitch. Behind him, a growl announces the swarm of zombies moving into the stairwell.

He's about to drag the body of the woman out of the doorway to close the fire door and buy himself some time when he sees a young child standing in front of a window at the end of the hall. Her slight frame is silhouetted against the dark sky.

"Daisy?"

The child growls, and his blood runs cold.

He drops the arms of the woman, turning to face Daisy. His flashlight flickers across the young girl's face.

Dark eyes stare back. Blood drips from her mouth.

"Please. No."

Daisy runs at him, lowering her head and charging through the darkness.

Zombies pound up the stairs, swarming from below, but Jackson cannot take his eyes off Daisy. He raises his gun, aiming squarely at her forehead, but he cannot bring himself to fire. His finger squeezes the trigger, but he cannot pull it tight. He can't bring enough pressure to bear on the slender steel trigger. If this is all that's left of humanity, Jackson cannot go on. It's no wonder Jennifer's crazy. Is there any other way to survive in the apocalypse? His hands tremble. His knees begin to buckle.

Daisy snarls, baring her teeth as she runs at him, more animal than human.

Zombies crash into the wall of the stairwell, pushing and shoving each other in their mad desire to savor his flesh.

The cover of an air conditioning duct collapses on top of Daisy, knocking her over. She tumbles to the slick floor as a head appears in the duct, crying, "Quick!"

Jackson's eyes cast up.

"Daisy?" he yells as a young girl in the vent reaches out a hand for him, beckoning for him to follow.

The young zombie on the ground is dazed, trying to figure out what has happened. Jackson runs and jumps, grabbing at the edge of the duct. He tosses the gun and flashlight into the vent as a zombie grabs at his legs, pulling him backwards. Jackson fights, kicking with his boots as his hands slip on the slick sides of the duct. He shoves his boots against the chest of the zombie and pushes himself up into the vent.

Below him, zombies snarl. Hands reach for the duct, but Jackson scrambles into the confined space. He's so big he barely fits. He grabs his flashlight and looks back, shining the light on young Daisy. Her face is filthy, but she smiles.

"Keep going," she says. "It's steep ahead, but this goes to the roof."

Jackson wriggles out of his backpack, giving himself a bit more room in the duct. He tucks the gun beneath his belt and holds the flashlight between his teeth, pushing his backpack ahead of him as he works his way through the duct. The stainless steel flexes with each motion, making an almighty racket. The zombies hear them but they cannot reach them.

"You came," Daisy says, following behind him. "I can't believe you came for me."

"I told you I would," Jackson replies, reaching a vertical section of ducting and making his way toward the roof.

"You're crazy," Daisy says.

"You're the second person that's told me that."

Looking through a vent cover, he catches a glimpse of a radio in an adjacent room. A row of car batteries line one wall. A zombie ambles through the door sniffing at the air.

"I saw you," Daisy says in a soft voice, but one full of excitement. "I saw your spaceship and the parachutes. I think everyone saw you."

"I think everyone did," he agrees, removing a grate and pulling himself out on to the roof of the police station.

Jackson is exhausted. He sits with his back against the low stone wall surrounding the roof, watching as Daisy climbs out of the duct. No sooner have her feet hit the ground than she bolts over to him and throws her arms around his neck.

"Hey," he says, patting her back. "It's nice to meet you too."

She sits next to him, saying, "You're so silly coming here alone."

She won't let go of him, and wraps her arm beneath his, which brings a smile to his face. It's been a long time since Jackson spent time with anyone and already she's melting his heart.

"Some might say crazy," he says, and she smiles. "Are you hungry?"

Daisy nods. He hands her a protein bar from his pack.

"What now?" she asks, still leaning up against him in the cool evening air. "Can we fly away in your spaceship?"

Jackson laughs, saying, "Oh, I wish we could."

He points at a dull glow on the horizon, saying, "You see that?"

"The football field?"

"Yes," he replies. "I got a glimpse in there on the way down. There are people there. Survivors just like you and me. Tomorrow, we'll go there."

"Tomorrow," she says, snuggling up to him for warmth, and Jackson realizes what he's been missing after so long in space.

Touch.

For the first time, Jackson feels as though home is somewhere other than being lost in free fall.

"Tomorrow," Jackson repeats, putting his arm around her.

The Beginning

A Word from Peter Cawdron

Zombie stories are about people. They ask the question, how do we survive in the most vicious of circumstances? Will zombies bring out the best or the worst in us?

When ordinary, everyday decisions can spiral out of control and end in death, how do we respond? Do we give up on our humanity? Or do we decide humanity is the only thing worth fighting for? "Free Fall" explores the social connections that make us human.

If you've enjoyed this story, you'll love my zombie novel *What We Left Behind* available exclusively on Amazon.

My thanks to Samuel Peralta and Ellen Campbell for their work on *The Z Chronicles*. It's a privilege to work with them and so many other great authors on this unique anthology.

Thank you for supporting independent science fiction.

Peter Cawdron is an independent science fiction writer from Brisbane, Australia.

You can find more of his writing on Amazon, and you can catch up with him on Facebook and Twitter. Sign up for his email newsletter (http://goo.gl/KLlggE) if you'd like to hear about new releases.

Girl, Running
by Kris Holt

TWO MILES TO THE COAST, Elie says. Two miles. Four thousand steps. It's nothing, Elie says. It isn't the distance, though Little Shrew isn't used to travelling on foot and certainly isn't built to run all the way to the harbour. The horde is circling at the end of the street, moaning. It won't be easy to sneak past them unnoticed.

Elie is her usual self, stretching, preparing, perfectly composed. You need to get yourself a weapon, she tells Little Shrew. Something heavy you can use to bash their heads in if they get too close. A baseball bat would do. If only we had guns...

'No guns,' Little Shrew says.

Everyone who knows her calls her Little Shrew. Like Nottingham's Little John, she has a name steeped in irony. She stands over six feet tall in her bare feet, and towers over Elie. When they first got together, Little Shrew was bewildered as to what Elie saw in her. I love how big and powerful you are, Elie said. With you there, I'll never need a windbreak.

There's that moment she has with Elie where the girl is deadpan, but Little Shrew takes her seriously.

Then Elie will smile that smile, the one where snow-white incisors brush against her lips like the cutest Manga fangs, and Little Shrew is lost. So a wind-break she is, and more. This is a task she's well-suited for, after all. Little Shrew is as wide as she is tall, but it is her tiny elfin lover who has the looks, and enough presence for two. Despite her size, people often look right through Little Shrew. It is Elie who commands their attention, with natural gifts of her own.

Her pre-cardio routine complete, Elie retreats to a cupboard under the stairs and reappears in a tracksuit and baseball cap, carrying a golf club. 'My dad isn't going to miss these now. There's more in there. You should grab one.'

'I'm not sure I'll be able to hit anyone.'

'They told us that we need to be ready to defend ourselves.'

'Still,' Little Shrew says.

Elie takes her hand and holds it tenderly for a moment, a gesture that Little Shrew appreciates.

'Dorothy, we're not in Kansas any more.' Elie's own tiny fingers uncurl and leave the handle of her father's five-iron behind. Little Shrew looks at it sadly, remembering a time only hours before when life was safe and simple.

'You know that's not the proper quote, right?' she says.

* * *

Last night, the pair had just been teenage girls. They'd been lying together in their pajamas and watching films when the sirens went off in the distance.

'I don't really mind the whole alien thing,' Elie said. 'But the idea that you can avoid a nuclear blast by hiding in a fridge is just dumb.'

'I'm not sure,' Little Shrew said. 'I don't really know much about the science.'

'Back in the '50s, kids all over America were climbing into fridges and suffocating. They had latches back then so you couldn't open them from inside.'

'That's a pretty sad way to die.'

Elie ignored the comment and surveyed a shining set of fingernails. 'I'm not sure how I feel about this colour. It looks okay now, but I guess I'd have to see what it looks like in daylight.'

Little Shrew leaned to one side and opened the curtain a crack. The air was cold close to the window. In the distance, at the far end of the road, a lot of people seemed to be milling around.

'I might take it off and try something else.' Elie put the pot down and reached into a drawer for some cotton buds. 'What's going on out there, anyway?'

'A lot of people are out in the street just standing around.'

'People are weird.'

'I think there's like a protest going on or something. Police are there.'

'Oh, hey. Did you see there was a protest down at the farmer's market on Saturday?' Elie was suddenly animated. 'It was all about GMO food. They had these people dressed as Frankenstein, except they had carrots through their heads instead of bolts.'

'That sounds bizarre.'

'You had to be there,' Elie said, reaching for the remote. At that moment, there was a series of loud bangs outside and her eyes opened wide.

'Oh my god. Is that gunfire? Quick! Pass me my phone.'

Little Shrew did as she was told. 'What are you going to do?'

'I'm going to video what's happening outside and put it on YouTube. We're going to be famous!'

Little Shrew looked doubtful. 'I don't know. It sounds dangerous.'

'It's exciting,' Elie said.

Behind them, the TV announced, 'We interrupt this broadcast for an important public service bulletin...'

* * *

Little Shrew, on her first day of college, had to duck to fit through the art room doorway. She apologised for being late, except no one could understand her mumbling, and she left the class without having spoken another word to anyone.

She thought that it was maybe the way that she looked. Little Shrew had curly, fair hair and a little piggy nose that was too small for her face. Her glasses framed her eyes too well, becoming an extension of the natural edges and giving her a permanently startled expression.

No one greeted her. For Little Shrew, art was a solitary activity anyway, and she gave up on her fellow students quickly. Instead, she toyed with the idea of taking up a sport. This was an awkward undertaking, though. Women didn't play football. Little Shrew had the height for basketball, the raw power for softball, but no talent for either. Dejected, she wandered out towards the track. She hadn't even made it as far as the bleachers before a number of girls were giving her openly hostile stares. What would a blubbery mess like her add to a track team? She turned and began to walk away.

It was only then that someone new caught her eye. A tiny girl in an all-grey tracksuit was doing stretches on the sidelines ahead of her track practise. When she saw Little Shrew, she smiled. It was the gentlest, most genuine smile Little Shrew had ever seen.

'Hi,' Elie said.

* * *

Elie clicked the remote and the TV faded to black.
'No way,' she said. 'No fucking way.'

There was a long pause, broken only by Little Shrew, who couldn't stand silence. 'Great. I guess they're probably not going to put the film back on now.'

'Fuck. Who cares about the film? Really. This is actually happening. Fuck.' Elie's phone slipped out of her fingers and was lost among the duvet. Little Shrew looked through the curtains. In the distance, she could see smoke and flames. The aimless, groaning crowd seemed to be growing by the minute.

'What are we going to do?' she said.

'You heard what they said,' Elie shrugged. 'We have to move. They can't guarantee our safety here. Heading to the harbour makes sense. The military are there, and they can get us to a safe location.'

'Whatever's happened, it's turned people into crazy, flesh-eating freaks. Where in hell is going to be safe?'

'The military will have it covered,' Elie said, and Little Shrew thought back to all the times that she had watched Elie saluting the flag at track meets. 'We just have to get to them.'

Little Shrew watched as Elie orbited her, transferring a variety of foodstuffs, sentimental objects and improvised weapons into two backpacks.

'I think a backpack will really slow me down,' she ventured.

'I don't feel well,' Elie replied. 'I feel bloated. I should have left those yoghurts in the fridge.'

'People are dying,' Little Shrew said gently. 'I don't think yoghurt should be top of our list of things to worry about.'

'I knew I should have done a kickboxing class. Or Tae-Kwon-do.'

'It's kind of late to be thinking about that now.'

Elie beamed at her. 'It's a good thing I have you to keep me grounded. You always were the practical one.' And then, while Little Shrew was still trying to work out whether she was really the practical one, or indeed if being practical was a good thing, Elie hugged her.

'I'm glad I have you with me,' Elie said.

Something inside Little Shrew curled up and mewled.

* * *

Before Elie, Little Shrew hadn't much thought about what or who she liked. Nobody had really paid much attention to her, let alone asked her out on dates, and she was used to being on her own. That evening, she found herself watching Elie run four hundred metres with less effort and more grace than a cougar. In no time at all, the other girl had stepped out of the shower room with the steam still rising off her shoulders and invited Little Shrew out for malts.

As the weeks passed, the girls bonded easily over TV tropes, internet memes and music remixes. Even though Elie was stunning and immaculate and

Little Shrew habitually looked like a haystack had fallen on her, she always asked Little Shrew's opinion on hair, clothing and makeup. As well as competing on the track team, Elie volunteered at the local homeless shelter and made her own clothes. If someone had asked Little Shrew what kind of hobbies she thought Elie might have before she knew her, they weren't the kind of activities she would have gone for.

They'd been to the cinema on the day it happened. After the film (including staying to the very end of the credits to ensure they saw the blooper reel and the thirty-nine seconds of bonus footage tagged on the end), the girls had planned to go back to Elie's parents' house for a sleepover. With her father working abroad and her mother sleeping deep Xanax dreams, Elie raided the liquor cabinet and in no time at all, the pair had worked their way through two bottles of Californian red.

'So, there I am,' Elie was slurring, her face flushed with cheer. 'Got myself up on the roof, and I'm telling everyone, I'm going to do it, gonna jump down into the pool. I'm gonna do it!'

Little Shrew giggled, imagining the scene.

'And it's not enough that I'm up there, I have to have an audience, you know? So I'm calling everyone over, my friends, my brother, my brother's friends, these guys from the town who called in just because they heard the noise. Everyone there.'

'Crazy,' Little Shrew said.

'I'm on the roof, I have my audience, and I decide I'll dance a little, throw in the entertainment.' Elie swayed a cobra-like stomach around in an eye-catching circle as evidence of her moves. 'And then I think, wait a minute, I still have all my clothes on. Can't jump in fully clothed, and there's no way I'm walking away with everyone watching. So I decide to strip down to my underwear, right there.'

'Man,' Little Shrew said admiringly. 'You must have been wasted.'

'Society kid in her underwear on a roof! Let the neighbours talk, right? Except it doesn't happen. I get my top off easily enough, but I got my foot stuck in my jeans. The guys are shouting up at me to take care, my brother is telling me to get my ass down before I hurt myself. And then I fell.'

'Off the roof?'

'To the side, where Julio the gardener had been piling up compost for the rose beds for weeks.' Elie touched her arm. 'I never did make it in the pool. Instead, I landed in the compost with my jeans round my ankles, and now I can never look at the roses without thinking about it.'

Little Shrew marvelled at how easily Elie could tell this story. If it had happened to her, Little Shrew would never have gotten over the shame. Then, of course, it never would have happened to Little Shrew, because she avoided risk-taking of any kind.

'You could have been badly hurt,' she said.

Elie smiled that smile, the one with the manga fangs. 'My ankle still kinda hurts. But I got one hell of a story out of it.'

She reached over, trying to clink their glasses together, but she only managed to slosh her Pinot noir into Little Shrew's lap. 'Oh, my god! I'm so sorry.'

'Oh, don't worry,' Little Shrew said. She reached out her hand with a tissue to mop up the wine, but in her own muggy fog, slipped into Elie. Their faces met, and Little Shrew was amazed at how warm Elie was. Then the girl brought her eyes up to Little Shrew's, holding her there with her gaze before descending upon her.

It was a kiss. The kiss. Little Shrew's first, and the first of many. And all the while they were kissing, Little Shrew was aware of this light-headed feeling, like something inside her was stirring.

* * *

Elie was the happiest person that Little Shrew had ever known. Even when she had no idea that anyone was looking, she would sit in a lazy, comfortable position and spontaneously break into song. She couldn't sing for dimes, but her ecstatic, crazy randomness made others laugh. It made Little Shrew laugh, and she needed to laugh just then.

'Are you just going to sing all day?'

Elie added a perfect pirouette to her cabaret routine and said in a faux-royal voice, 'I believe I shall.

The post apocalyptic world will need someone to remind them what Katy Perry sounded like.'

Little Shrew grinned. 'You don't sound like Katy Perry.'

'A girl can dream.'

The pair stood close together for a moment, and Little Shrew sensed that Elie might move to embrace her. Instead, she smiled shyly, and led the way to the garage.

'We can't take the minivan,' Elie said. 'I know you're not keen on travelling on foot, but we'll draw less attention if we go on foot.'

As ever, Little Shrew knew that she'd lost the argument. Still, she made a half-hearted attempt to resist. 'I still think we could just barricade the door and stay.'

'Sweetie, you heard what they said. They can't guarantee our safety here, so we're going to the harbour. We can't ride out the apocalypse by sleeping for days and watching Cumberbatch shows on mute.'

'What makes you think the place we're going to is any safer than here? And anyway, I don't just watch Cumberbatch shows.' Little Shrew was affronted.

Elie smiled goofily, and Little Shrew's frost melted. 'I can take or leave the shows. But that accent...'

'It's a good accent.'

Elie had already turned away and begun to practise some wide, measured sweeps with the golf club. Automatically, Little Shrew's eyes drifted to her favourite part of Elie's body — her thighs and calves. She stretched beautifully, with such measured ease. She was an artisan's creation, one that didn't so much break the mould as utterly defy it. Little Shrew wanted to protect her, take her hand and guide her to safety, but she knew that if she took Elie by the hand, it would be her that got pulled along. Defiant to the last, Little Shrew placed her hands in her pockets. Oblivious as ever, Elie continued to practise her swing.

For a full minute, the only sound was the swipe as the metal shaft cut through the air again and again. It was as though each of them was waiting for the other to make a decision. The silence lengthened until Little Shrew couldn't stand it any more.

'Okay, so maybe a lot of Cumberbatch shows,' she whispered.

* * *

'Don't worry,' Elie said later. 'Of course they like you.'

'I don't know. I just get the impression that they don't, that's all.'

'They're just self-involved,' Elie said. 'Dad lives for his work and Mom is on all of these charity committees, the neighbourhood group, church committee. She likes to stay busy.'

Little Shrew was used to making an indifferent first impression, but the memory of her first meeting with Elie's parents left her with a unique sense of disappointment. Both tanned to the colour of overcooked biscuits, their words were warm enough, but their smiles didn't reach their eyes. Elie's father blinked too much, like looking at her was painful. Elie's mother wrinkled her nose. Little Shrew approached them to shake hands, but they just stared at her palm like they might catch something from her.

'I'll just...uh...go upstairs, then,' Little Shrew had said.

She got to the first landing and turned out of sight, but she could still hear the barely-disguised whispering below her. 'I know. But don't say anything. I'm sure it's just a phase she's going through...'

It got no better with time. Elie's parents never spoke to her unless she spoke to them first. Even Julio the gardener, with his tenuous grasp of the English language, seemed to sense her lowly position in the pecking order. He would give Little Shrew wary glances when her walk along the garden path took her too close to the rosebushes.

Elie's college friends were all sylph-like and came from the same moneyed background as her. It didn't take Little Shrew long to realise that their honeyed appearances hid a veritable host of sharp edges, emotional problems and temper tantrums. Even so, Elie allowed herself to be ferried around at the centre of their group, as though she was the President and they were the Secret Service. When Little Shrew approached, they withdrew into a phalanx of sarcasm and cutting remarks, and if she persisted, they shooed her away in squawking voices.

Ultimately though, it made no difference. To a casual observer, Elie may have seemed as fragile as a leaf on the breeze, but she was used to getting what she wanted. What she apparently wanted was Little Shrew, and no one's disapproval was going to make the slightest bit of difference.

Elie's was a rare determination, one that was intense to the point of being sensual, or scary, or sometimes both. Each Friday evening, Little Shrew would stay behind after class and watch Elie run from the bleachers. In the months since meeting Little Shrew, Elie had gone from being a decent junior to an elite in the making. In the last track meet of the season, she romped home a full second ahead of the rest of the field, the quickest time recorded in the whole county that year.

As always, when the race was done, Little Shrew made her way down to trackside and smiled bashfully at Elie. Elie winked at her and emptied a bottle of water over her own hair, shoulders and chest.

When she met Little Shrew's eyes again, she looked positively devilish. Little Shrew could have fallen to her knees and thanked her then and there for the mere fact of her existence.

Instead, she fought back her desire and said, 'That's your personal best. Congratulations!'

'That's what you do,' Elie replied between breaths. 'That's what you do for me.'

Little Shrew didn't know what to say, but her heart felt like it might burst. She's just a girl, she told herself. Just a girl, running.

* * *

'You should run.'

'I can't run,' Little Shrew said.

'Everyone has to start somewhere.'

Little Shrew knew that she was going to run. In a world in which she was constantly being told what not to do, Elie was all about what she should. Even so, it would not be an easy process. The running shorts Little Shrew bought were comically wide, her thighs rubbed painfully together with every step and the earth felt heavy beneath her feet.

The track stretched out before her. It might as well have been a thousand miles long. With Elie's words of poisonous encouragement burning in her ears, Little Shrew's vision narrowed until she could only see directly ahead. Her heart was beating in her ears. She could feel a hundred eyes upon her as she lumbered maladroitly across the finish line.

She hated every second of it with the exception of the one directly after it was over. Elie placed a hand upon her shoulder and said, 'You did it, Little Shrew!'

* * *

Little Shrew's vision is clouding at the sides again, like it always does when she is under pressure. Like it does when she is forced into things she doesn't want to be a part of. Everything else is hazy around the edges, like the things that have happened in the last twenty-four hours are all products of a disordered mind.

There are no memories from today that she wishes to recall, so she goes back to something else, anything else, to distract her. The last time that they had sex. Saturday, two weeks ago. Or maybe three.

'Hold me down, hold me down,' Elie moaned. She likes Little Shrew's weight pressing down on her, pinning her to the bed. Little Shrew doesn't know why hearing this upset her so much — she has heard Elie say it a hundred other times, after all — but right there, at that time, it infuriated her. It's a reminder that Elie isn't with her because she's smart, or funny, or beautiful. She keeps Little Shrew around because she likes her weight, the power it implies.

That was when Little Shrew decided to exercise that power. She stopped, lifted her body upwards.

'No...no, don't,' Elie said.

Little Shrew balanced herself on her elbows. 'How do you actually feel about me?'

'Carry on, please,' Elie begged.

'Tell me.'

'Really? Really? Do we have to do this now?' Elie's tiny fists punched at the bed and she rolled out from beneath Little Shrew.

'You didn't have to do that,' Little Shrew said.

'It couldn't have waited?'

'Why should I have to wait?'

Elie rolled her eyes and put her dressing gown on.

Little Shrew sank downwards onto the bed. She felt small and sad and humiliated.

Elie sat for a long time, hands over her mouth, looking out the window. Finally, without turning round, she whispered, 'You should probably go.'

* * *

Little Shrew fiddled with the locker door in front of her. The mechanism was simple enough, but when she stared at it, it turned in on itself like an Escher drawing and gained extra dimensions that punished her eyes.

'Why don't you ever hang out with me at college?' Little Shrew said.

'Sorry?' Elie said. She was fresh out of the shower, towel wrapped around her waist, steam still rising off her hair. Her ankle was heavily strapped, and she was walking with a slight limp.

Little Shrew was sure that Elie had heard her and was hoping that she wouldn't pose the question again. But she wasn't in the mood to let this go.

'You heard me. Your friends are really mean to me, and you never challenge them.'

'You're just imagining it.'

'No, I'm not.' Little Shrew persisted. She figured that since the noose was around her neck, she may as well jump off the horse. 'And anyway...it's not just your friends. Your parents never even talk to me, and you never call them out for it.'

Elie looked away and busied herself with her kit bag. 'Do you really care what they think?' she asked.

'I don't care what they think,' Little Shrew said, carefully emphasising each word. 'I care what you think.'

A few seconds passed in silence, and Little Shrew found herself wondering if she actually imagined the whole conversation. Over her shoulder, Elie fired up her hairdryer.

* * *

Little Shrew has driven down the harbour road any number of times, and it's only now that she notices the colossal gap that has formed somehow in her memory. She remembers the way that the verge slopes downhill towards the soupy brown water. She remembers the blooming yellow fungal tufts that threaten to overwhelm the corrugated iron of the harbour building walls. What she hasn't remembered, until now, is the great chain link fence that cuts the water off from the harbourside completely.

The pair stop behind a wall at the edge of the car park.

'We'll have to go through the harbour building itself,' Elie says. 'Quickly, before they see us.'

Little Shrew follows Elie's pointing finger to a swarm of limbs and fury that is leaning into the fence, creating a bulge and threatening to tear it down. Behind the fence, Little Shrew can see a tiny military cordon in front of a transport ship. The soldiers are eyeing up the bulge as it swells, but they seem reluctant to shoot.

Little Shrew is still calculating in her mind — speed versus distance versus pain in joints — when Elie says, 'Okay, in five seconds, we're going to run for the Harbour building.'

'Elie, no. I'm in a lot of pain.'

'Sweetie, we can't wait, you know that, right? The soldiers aren't going to shoot because the sound will bring even more of these...people...over. There's not enough of them there to hold the place as it is. If the fence comes down, the military are going to close the doors and sail away.'

Little Shrew is incensed by Elie's steely calm observations. She's not sure whether the pain she is in is stopping her from thinking straight, or her inability to think is somehow contributing to the pain.

Elie slaps her on the back and practically pulls a salute. 'Time to shine, Little Shrew. This is where that time on the track is going to pay off.'

'Two more minutes,' Little Shrew pleads.

Elie vaults the wall in a single movement, graceful as a cat. One of the shamblers nearby is more alert than the others, and takes a three-iron to the temple for its trouble.

'Damn it, Elie!' Little Shrew follows way behind, taking precious seconds to negotiate the wall and get back into her stride. Pounding across the concrete, she soon has the attention of every shambler within earshot. A large group of them leaves the fence as one, sweeping round in a wide crescent that meets her at the tip. Little Shrew has the momentum, and pushes the leader into the rest. What follows is a stumbling of domino limbs as the ones at the front fall, and the ones behind lurch over them. Only one threads a way through, and as it opens its mouth to chomp down on the hapless Little Shrew, Elie strikes it a blow across the skull that leaves the golf club bent like a brace drill.

'Got your back,' Elie says.

With barely a pause, she bounces away in the direction of the harbour building. Little Shrew follows behind. Only when she reaches the doorway does she pause to wipe the terror foam from her chin and spit on the floor.

* * *

They creep through the office areas, staying low behind desks and avoiding the windows.

'We need to get out of the offices and into the warehouse,' Elie says.

'How come you know so much about this place?' Little Shrew asks.

Elie keeps moving forward. 'My dad does a lot of his shipping through here.'

'So?'

'He brought me here to see how it all works.'

Little Shrew is nonplussed. 'Why would he do that? You never seemed to care before how he makes his money.'

Elie leads them through to a small door into the darkened warehouse. 'He was going to offer me a role in the company. Give me a chance to travel, make some money, see a bit more of the world.'

'Oh.' Little Shrew shuffles along behind, taking small footsteps in the darkness.

'What?'

'What?'

'What did you mean by that?' Elie says.

'I didn't mean anything.'

'That's not how it sounded.'

Little Shrew, in pain and miserable from having been a passenger throughout the journey, says, 'Well...you know, if you were taking a new job or going travelling, I just wondered when you were going to tell me. That's all.'

'We hadn't really sorted any of the details. I was going to tell you as soon as I knew.'

'Oh. Well, okay.'

Little Shrew sees Elie's head cock in the shadows. 'Are you sure? You don't sound okay.'

'It's just that it's pretty damn dark in here.' She knows that Elie won't buy it, but maybe she'll pick up on Little Shrew's desire to drop it and move on. It's not like it matters anyway, not now.

'The lights are somewhere on this wall.' There's a click, and the room floods with a dirty yellow haze that makes Little Shrew blink. Even as her pupils contract, she takes in the figures all around them. The straggling gait, the wild eyes.

There are a lot of them.

'Oh my fucking god,' Elie says.

Little Shrew grabs her around the waist with a single beefy arm and bundles the pair of them through a door next to the lighting panel. Elie twists in her grip. 'No, that's a box room!'

The door opens and closes again behind them, which to Little Shrew is all that matters just now. There's no lock, so she leans her weight against it. It's the best that she can do.

Their new real estate consists of a dusty four-foot-by-four-foot cupboard with a tiny window up above their heads. They could probably reach it, but it's way too narrow even for Elie to climb through.

The scratching begins at the door. To Little Shrew's ear, it sounds almost apologetic.

Beneath her, Elie pulls an awkward smile. 'At least we have natural light.'

* * *

Elie starts singing again.

'Can you stop with the singing?' Little Shrew has never asked for this before. Elie lapses into silence. Still the pair are locked together, mutual memories of happier times causing them to feel a closeness they cannot take from one another.

'We're going to die in here,' Little Shrew says.

'No, we're not.'

'In case you haven't noticed, we're trapped.'

'We'll find a way out,' Elie says. 'We're not trapped.'

'We're stuck in here,' Little Shrew says, 'and they're out there. In what way are we not trapped?'

Elie looks down and scrapes the toe of her shoe against the floor. 'We should be thinking about how we can get out, not wasting our time being pissy with one another.'

Little Shrew is so angry that her fists become tight, fleshy balls. 'Seriously? You're going to call me pissy? Here, now?'

Elie flinches. 'It's what you're being.'

'Okay. Okay. So you want to see pissy. Fine. I'll show you pissy.'

Elie visibly shrinks as Little Shrew tells her the truth — that she came over last night to kick Elie to the kerb. And yes, she knows how unlikely it sounds that she is choosing to dump someone who is blatantly out of her league, but why shouldn't she get a choice in the matter? She has agency, damn it. It's not as if she even asks for that much. Can't Elie just listen to her from time to time? Maybe take her side, just once? Would that be so hard? Why does she keep pushing Little Shrew to do things, like the running, that she clearly doesn't want to do? AND NO, SHE DOESN'T CARE THAT THE GODDAMN ZOMBIES CAN HEAR HER. If they're going to die anyway, Little Shrew isn't going till she's got this off her chest.

'Why are you doing this?' Elie asks.

'Doing what?'

'Why are you trying to make me feel bad?'

'Oh, I don't know, let me think. You drag me here at top speed, even though you know I can't keep up with you. You force me to take a weapon, even though I told you I didn't want one. You lead me straight into two hordes. You even club one to the ground in front of me and act like I should be grateful.'

'I was just trying to protect you.'

'Well, maybe I don't need your protection. Maybe I can do things for myself.'

Elie pushes herself upright and takes a deep breath. She will not meet Little Shrew's eye. Finally, she says, 'We're gonna make it through that door. I swear. We'll find a way through if it kills us.'

'That's a really crappy choice of words,' Little Shrew snaps.

She is only sorry when she realises that Elie is crying.

* * *

The pair have been standing a long time in silence. Little Shrew is glad. She's long since run out of words.

'The scratching has stopped,' Elie whispers.

'Really.' Little Shrew is only really half-listening. She is staring out of the tiny box room window at the impossibly blue sky, watching a seagull as it trails lazily overhead. To have wings, she thinks. To fly away from this, leave it all behind.

'You're not even listening.' Elie taps her foot. The sadness in her voice is something Little Shrew has never heard before, and it shakes her from her reverie.

'I'm sorry,' she says.

Just like that, Elie is in her determined place again. 'This is our chance. We're going out there.'

'Right.'

'Did you get a good look at the warehouse?' Pouting, Elie describes what she saw before Little Shrew bundled her through the door. The shamblers were mostly on one side of the room — the side with the exit that they're heading for. In the centre of the warehouse, there is a large stack of crates that forms a natural island in the space.

'I'll head away from them, towards the door we came in by. Once they're all following me, you go out to the left. Head for the bay doors — the military cordon we saw earlier is just beyond. I'll double back round the crates in the middle, and catch you up.'

Little Shrew can see, clear as day, that this is a suicide mission. 'You'll never make it.'

'Watch me.' Elie pushes her aside and steps through the doorway. Little Shrew watches in amazement as she tags the arms of the nearest shamblers, causing them to stagger into others. The horde looks up as one, sees her; pursues. In seconds, as promised, Little Shrew's way is open.

She should run, but she can't. Her legs are lead, her chest on fire. And she is sitting on the bleachers, watching in agony as Elie's graceful strides carry her forward. Elie is elite; she will succeed where others would fail.

Little Shrew remembers what she told herself at the track meet the year before. Elie is just a girl. But she is so, so much more than that, and Little Shrew knows it.

Elie gets clear of the crowd, rounds the crates and turns back on herself, exactly as planned. But there is a yelp. It's that ankle. Little Shrew would have rested it, but Elie carried on running, because owning up to pain of any kind was just too hard for her to do.

In slow motion, Little Shrew watches as Elie's leg gives way underneath her. She watches the girl fall and land heavily. Dozens of the hissing denizens descend upon her, pinning her down.

Little Shrew knows that she's calling Elie's name, but she can't hear her own voice.

* * *

She reaches for the wall to hold herself up. A tear rolls down her cheek.

'I'm sorry at the way things have turned out,' Elie says. 'I'd hoped this would go differently. You must know that.'

Little Shrew can't reply. Everything hurts too much, and she leans her head against the hollow wooden door. The surface is cool to the touch, and maybe cool is enough.

'No,' Elie says. 'C'mon now. Get up.'

'Why should I? I don't deserve to get out of here.'

Elie wrinkles her nose, reminding Little Shrew of the exact face that Elie's mother pulled when she met her. 'Self-pity isn't an attractive trait.'

By now, Little Shrew is a sobbing, wretched mess. 'I don't care.'

Elie might have been small, but her heart was huge. You could have poured the world inside and never filled her up.

'I just did what I had to do,' Elie said.

'You didn't have to do that. We would have found a way.'

Elie's eyes were dull. 'No, we wouldn't. You said that yourself.'

'I didn't mean it! Why did you have to pick today of all days to listen to me?'

The celebratory roaring from the creatures in the room next door sickens Little Shrew to her stomach and beyond. Elie pulls her around and stares into her eyes, the way that she did the first time that they kissed.

'Little Shrew, listen to me. You need to focus. There's still time, but the window is closing. You know the way.'

'I don't.'

'Out of here, turn to the left, run to the bay doors. The cordon is just ahead. But you're going to have to move like lightning.'

Little Shrew feels the strength return to her legs and pushes herself upright. She knows that she can't look back without breaking the spell.

'There's something I have to tell you,' she says.

For a moment, Elie's voice breaks. 'Do we have to do this now?'

'When I said earlier that I was going to break up with you, I was just going to do it. Like you tear off a plaster quickly so the pain is there and then it's gone, you know? I was just going to say what I had to say and go. But when I got there, you were funny and you were kind, and it was like old times, like the arguments had never happened. So I couldn't go through with it. I knew it had to be done...but you were always so good. Too good for me. You were just...you, and I couldn't go through with it.'

Elie is upon her then, her tiny arms snaking around Little Shrew's hips and shoulders. Little Shrew's eyes are closed, but tears are still streaming down her cheeks. The touch is so real, so undeniable, that she can almost fool herself that the arms are not her own.

Just a girl. A girl who did a brave thing.

'And now you've gone and sacrificed your life for me,' Little Shrew says, 'and I can never forgive you for that.'

Elie's last smile is thin and sad, like sunshine in a lonely place. 'You should probably go,' she whispers.

A moment later, the track stretches out before Little Shrew. It may as well be a thousand miles long. As she runs, she can feel the other competitors behind her, clawing at her, trying to drag her down.

Her vision narrows as the horde descends. She hits the bay doors with all her weight and keeps going. Her heart is beating in her ears. She can feel a hundred eyes upon her as she stretches towards the finish line.

And then, it's over, and Elie's hand is on her shoulder.

'You did it, Little Shrew!'

Just a girl, running.

A Word from Kris Holt

We all have a plan, those of us who love George Romero and *Resident Evil*. We all keep a sword under our bed, or a chainsaw in our garage. We know the quickest way to the mall, and we practise our stealthy moves when no-one else around is watching. We know where we'll get food, water and gasoline, and where we'll stay until society gets back on its feet.

We know the zombies are coming.

Lovecraft was arguably the first to raise the dead in *Herbert West – Reanimator*. Richard Matheson's *I Am Legend* raised the bar. What followed was inevitable. *Pride and Prejudice and Zombies* saw walking corpses in the world of Jane Austen. By the time that *Warm Bodies* became a movie, we were literally falling in love with the *Living Dead*.

So what's left to still fascinate us, to fire our imaginations when another wall of flesh crashes off our barricades? We may have explored every possible facet of the creatures themselves, but we'll never stop wondering how we'll cope on the day the dead rise – our friends, our family, our loved ones. Which of us will fall? Which of us will thrive?

"Girl, Running" is about just that – two ordinary girls who run, because that's all that's left for them to do. They're our friends, our family, our loved ones, and they're the ones we'll look to when the world crashes down.

For more about my work, please my my website (www.4thousandwords.blogspot.com) or catch me on Twitter (@KrisHolt1).

The Sin Eater
by Stacy Ericson

HEAT FROM A LONG AFTERNOON hung in the air and the cottonwood branches carved the simmering light into tight beams sliding through the trees. Dark sedans already lined the street. The girl fixed her eyes on the plate of deviled eggs she carried. Their concentric circles created gentle humps under the white dishcloth.

Near the picket gate she placed her feet carefully, taking care not to catch the spiked heel of her pumps in the broken places where the pavement heaved, fractured by tree roots in the previous century. She blew gently on a piece of drifting cottonwood fluff before it could settle on the pristine towel.

A gentleman unlatched the gate for his wife and the girl knew well enough to step back, allowing the couple to pass first. Despite the heat of the day, his wife wore a black sateen jacket and the girl could see pebbles of sweat rising beneath the powder on her face. A swift passage of lilac and then the woman stopped to shoot a sharp glance at her husband, still holding the gate. He didn't look at his wife, but nodded to the girl and waited for her to pass be-fore carefully latching the gate behind her.

Inside, guests already crowded both front rooms. A mahogany coffin squatted in the bay windows of the library. The girl snaked between murmuring couples, moving toward the kitchen where she could lay her burden down.

"Why, honey, you brought those lovely deviled eggs? Why look at you in that pretty little dress. Bless your heart, I remember your mama wearing that very dress. She always did love a flower pattern." The Widow's sister dug thin fingers into her arm, pressing the girl toward a sideboard already laden with specialties from every kitchen in the township. An enormous arrangement of white carnations loomed over celadon green punch, crisscrossed pies, and cut-glass pickle dishes.

"Let me take that for you, child." Someone removed the plate from her hands, one neighbor plucking the cloth from the platter as if it were fly-specked and not bleached to an almost transparent veil.

"I'm so sorry for your loss," the girl said.

"Who would have guessed." The Widow's sister leaned in, her city accent hard and clear. "Everyone says he was in his prime. Cut down like that, his heart giving out, and right there on Main Street. Sister's just beside herself. I can't imagine what she'll do now. This house is just too much for her." She wedged the platter of deviled eggs between a macaroni mold and a pinkly gelatinous beet ring.

"Your mama was famous for these," said the sister, and plucked up an egg, leaving a gap in the circling pattern. The girl shifted the platter slightly to the right to hide a chip in the porcelain.

"What's your secret?" The other women leaned in.

The girl glanced toward the kitchen, trapped by a wall of matrons in navy and black. "My secret?" She ran damp hands down the front of her dress. "You can't keep a secret in a town this small."

"Isn't that the truth. But your Mama sure kept to herself, didn't she?" For a moment no one said anything, the silence as empty as Main Street on Sunday morning. Then the sister spoke again, "I don't think she ever told a soul what she used to devil those eggs. That little bite at the end? What is it? Cayenne?"

The girl closed her eyes, seeing suits and trouser legs. "Well, there is a little Cayenne."

"But you are just not telling, are you? Something else? That secret ingredient... I can't put my finger on it." The sister slid her tongue along the side of the glistening egg white, then turned to the others, "Can ya'll figure it out?"

"Surely, I can," one neighbor said, taking a judicious sample. "After all, there's only one store in town, and I doubt her Mama went all the way into Newtonburg, just for one secret ingredient." The women looked at each other as their friend chewed and swallowed. They looked at the egg as if it were their sworn enemy. At last it was decided. "Chili sauce, I'd stake my reputation on it. *Heinz* Chili Sauce."

The Widow approached and conversation stopped as she asked, "Can someone get me a drink?" Everyone moved at once. In seconds a punch glass appeared. The Widow looked at the girl. She blinked slowly, waved the punch glass aside. "Lime sherbet won't do right now," she said. A little island of pale foam slid dangerously close to the edge of the glass. "Too sticky."

An old woman came out of the kitchen. She carried a bottle of beer and the mourners parted before her.

"Why you don't want that, Sister. That beer is warm. Honey, if you want a beer let me get you a cold one..." The city accent hung harsh in the silent room. The Widow stepped toward the girl and there was silence.

The old woman stood in the kitchen door and waited until all eyes were on her, then spoke into the silence. "Neither in the streets nor in the meadows will he walk again, nor in his own hall," she said and handed the beer bottle to one of the men.

Each man passed the brown bottle to another, who passed it on.

The girl cleared her throat. She coughed. For a moment it seemed that she might be choking. "Dry mustard," she said. "The secret ingredient. A pinch of dry mustard changes everything."

The Widow picked up a napkin and a tiny plate. "So that's the family secret is it? Something you and your Mama shared." she said. "I always wondered."

She looked at the iridescent plate in her hand. "This china, I forgot how delicate it is. See?"

She held one small plate up. "You know these plates, I forget how delicate they are. See, they're like little shells. It's a wonder they never get broken at these funerals. But they don't. They never seem to break no matter how many times we use them. Sure enough they just...they just show up at the next one."

In the silence the mourners watched as the Widow chose food from the side-board. Corn bread, a chunk of salt ham, one cherry tomato, one slice of canned pineapple.

"Have you paid your respects?" the Widow said to the girl, holding the beer bottle now in one hand and the little plate in the other.

The Widow and the girl passed easily through the crowd. They walked from the dining room, through the entry and into the library without touching another soul.

The girl clasped her hands before her, but she raised her head. As she passed the stair, she smiled at the little boys on the second step. The blonde one smiled back and waggled his fingers at her as if they had just met outside the library.

They stopped by the coffin. The satin was the same pearly color as the dead man's face. He wore his blue suit, a new tie tied up tight beneath his chin, but no one had replaced that one missing button and its tiny thread curled up in a question mark at the bottom of his vest, where the jacket parted just above his belt. She thought of it, that one dark button, tucked away in the powder box on her dresser at home. The shirt she had not seen before. Pale blue. Forget-me-not blue, they called it this year. His hands were no longer so large, but tucked in at his sides, as if they had never been his.

The Widow passed behind the coffin to stand in front of the bay windows. With the light at her back, the girl couldn't see the woman's face. She was just a shadow or a hole in the brightness coming in from outside.

"Does anyone have a coin?" The Widow said.

One of the little boys stepped off the stair. "I got a nickel. My grandpa gave to me this morning."

"Well then, put it in her pocket, would you please?"

The child, dark-haired as his uncle had been, took a step down from the stairs. He looked at the nickel in his hand. His fingers curled around it. "Why should I?"

"Go on now."

The boy walked over to them. It only took a second to find the decorative pocket on the skirt of the girl's print dress. A second or two to undo the little pearl button that held it closed. The nickel slid into her pocket and she could feel the weight of it. The boy turned away, not looking at anyone, and went back to his place with the others on the stairs.

The Widow stretched her arm out over the coffin to pass the tiny iridescent plate across the belly of her husband.

The girl had to use both hands to hold the plate and keep it from tilting in that passage. Only the crowd breathing together sounded in the room.

The girl began to eat. She ate the meat first, sweet and salty. Then the cornbread, which she took in small dainty bites to keep it from crumbling onto the carpet. Then the tomato, with its scent of bitter stem. Last came the pineapple, slick and sweet. She set the plate on a table beside her and waited.

The Widow passed the beer to the girl, passed it across the white satin and the mahogany and the empty flesh.

The girl looked at the bottle, the familiar brown glass, the foil sticker, the scarlet printing and the black. She wondered if someone had set it out in the sun all morning.

As if she had never used a glass, she raised the bottle, tipped her head back and drank. She refused to hurry. After a moment she paused. She wiped her mouth with the tips of her white fingers. Three times she stopped, using the time to breathe, before raising the bottle to her lips again.

Someone took the bottle and the plate from her hands. Outside the light fell into a reclining angle. Outdoors there would be the evening sweetness and the scent of Russian Olives on the breeze. The girl turned away.

"I'm sorry for your loss," she said, moving by the line of men standing near the door. They smelled of cigarettes, and Old Spice and bourbon and the taste of salt and hops lay on her tongue. A man in work clothes stepped forward to open the heavy front door. She reached toward the worn green paint of the screen door and saw that her hand would leave a grease mark there.

Pushing the door open, she looked out onto the dusty street and felt a man's hand lying heavy on the small of her back. She stepped out into the cool of the evening where the sky went lavender and nighthawks called to each other and dove across the sun.

A Word from Stacy Ericson

I have always been fascinated by the tradition of the Sin Eater since I first read Elizabeth Goudge's *Child of the Sea*.

The role of the Sin Eater was traditional in English villages until the late 19th century. A designated local outcast, usually a man volunteered to take on the sins of the dead. The Sin Eater, a role often passed down through the generations, consumed a ritual meal of bread and beer standing over the corpse of the deceased. After receiving a coin it was believed that he would bear those sins and lighten the burden of the departing soul. In "The Sin Eater" I asked myself the question: who serves the role of Sin Eater today and imagined what it would be like the first time she moves into society in this new role.

Twenty-first-century zombie imagery reflects today's cultural anxieties about invasive diseases, but in the previous two centuries zombie themes had more to do with cross-cultural mysteries. It is interesting that both veins of zombie-related narrative reflect tensions and consequences of colonial occupation. Recent speculation about neurotoxins, Taino shamanism, and early zombie traditions aside, these themes have one thing in common — issues of honor and shame, contagion and purity, good and evil, and the uneasy relationship between the living and the dead.

Early anthropologist Zora Neale Hurston interviewed an elderly Jamaican man who addressed succinctly a basic fear found in most cultures: "Everyone has evil in them," he said, "and when a man is alive, the heart and the brain control him and he will not abandon himself to many evil things, but when the duppie leaves the body it no longer has anything to restrain it and it will do more terrible things than any man has dreamed of so it is not good for the duppie to remain among living folk."

This idea was as prevalent in European culture as any other and the Celtic tradition of the Sin Eater reflects one attempt to neutralize that unleashed, unrestrained evil using a classic "scape-goat."

In my story "Sin Eater" I asked myself, who today are the outcasts in society? Who carries our sins and to what extent does that contagion define all of us? To me these are a few of the themes that make zombie stories continually compelling.

Stacy Ericson is a writer, playwright, and photographer living in Boise, Idaho. She now travels primarily in the border colonies of historical and speculative fiction, far away from her origins editing anthropological papers and studying ancient history and religion. She is currently working on a mermaid novella, tentatively titled Sea Legs. *For more information on her work, visit her website (www.stacyericsonauthor.info) and join an info list to receive a free story.*

The World After
by Angela Cavanaugh

CHAPTER ONE

ELLA AND MARK ate their printed breakfast in silence, waiting for the door to signal that they were allowed to leave. Once the workday started, they had only about a minute to exit the apartment before the solar panel windows would switch from transparent to opaque and plunge the apartment into darkness.

Ella sharpened her knife between forkfuls of carefully balanced cloned-cell protein and fresh vegetables. She liked to keep her weapon ready because she never knew when she'd need to use it. The zombies that worked inside the wall presented little threat. They were kept under constant sedation and feed just enough lab-grown brains to keep them animated. Yet every so often, she'd come across a wild one or someone who had recently turned.

The door emitted a soft beep and a green glow. She folded the blade into its handle and slipped the knife into her boot. A moment later, the door opened automatically and they hurried out into the city.

Their footsteps fell loudly on the travertine paved streets. The entire city was constructed with the strong, fire-resistant stone that could stand for hundreds of years. The stark white of the cityscape and empty streets felt sterile to Ella. Strict curfew and constant monitoring ensured that everyone was either at home or work, without any loitering in between. But despite these precautions, people still went missing and got bit. Every time it happened, the reins tightened. Ella knew it was for their protection, but it felt intrusive.

Sensing her mood, Mark held her hand and squeezed it to remind her she wasn't really alone. Her disposition was more common in older generations, those who had lived through the war. But even born into this city, Ella had the sensation that humans weren't meant to be kept inside of fences. She had never seen further than she could see from the watchtowers, but she was certain the world expanded far beyond the horizon. It had to. She had been taught that once the Earth held billions of people, a number so large that she could hardly wrap her head around it. Her city, the last city on Earth, held a steady population of only about ten thousand.

They crossed through the city center. It was a large, square common ground that hardly got use these days. Ella heard a faint thump. She stopped in place and tugged on Mark.

"What is it?" he asked.

"Listen."

They waited for the noise to come again. The silence was pure at first. Birds and bugs, as well as other species, had an adverse reaction to the Necrovirus. Instead of turning them into flesh hungry killers, they became suicide bombers, and made themselves extinct.

"I don't hear anything," Mark said.

"Guess I was wrong."

They began to walk, when a loud thud came from far behind them.

"Then again, maybe not," Mark said.

Another bang sounded, followed by softer thump. They followed the noise and found the source a block away. The city had public restrooms scattered through it. This t-shaped cluster had one-stall rooms facing four directions and all but the doors were made of stone.

The thudding had grown softer, but persisted. They identified the stall and Ella tapped on the door.

"Hello? Is anyone in there? Do you need help?" she asked.

A howl of moans and the sound of fingers scratching against the door came from inside.

She took a step back, readied her knife, and motioned to Mark to open the door. He turned the handle and jerked it open, hopping backwards out of the way as he did. As she expected, there was a zombie inside. It tripped as the door flew open and fell to the ground.

Ella sized it up. The zombie was a middle aged man and about two hundred pounds, or would have been if its leg wasn't missing. Its shirt was torn at the collar, and she could see teeth marks by a patch of dried blood. Judging by the decomposition, she expected that it'd been turned less than two days. The hot day wasn't doing any favors for its smell. She took out a pair of one-panel glasses and put them on. The transparent eye-plate spanned the width of her head. The device was useful for a number of things. Currently, she was looking for a tracking device.

She scanned the body and found the information she was looking for. A readout popped up in her display space.

"Darren Gibbs, reported missing almost two weeks ago," she said.

"Two weeks? Where has he been all this time? No way he's been a zombie that long."

The zombie pushed against the ground but couldn't right itself. Ella knelt next to it to study it closer. The zombie lazily bit at her.

"Looks like he hasn't fed in a few days. But he ate something, someone, at some point. But that still gives him almost two weeks of living with the virus before eating. No. He'd have died by then."

Her visor performed a blood analysis. A medical report appeared.

"He had cancer," she said.

"Do you think he did this to himself? Either a suicide by zombie or some messed up attempt to stave off death?"

"Maybe. Could explain why he went missing. He could have been seeking out an opportunity to find a zombie. But his tracking chip is still active. He never should have been missing at all."

"Given his condition, maybe no one was looking for him? Maybe the family knew?"

"I don't know. But I don't like it. We'll need to request an investigation when we file the report."

The zombie rolled onto his back and pawed pathetically at the air.

Ella pressed on the sub-dermal implant on her collarbone and spoke.

"This is Agent Lane. I've got a drifter in section alpha."

"Copy that," The voice came through a speaker implanted just behind her ear. "Threat level?"

"We're not in danger of this one eating anyone and he's damaged."

"Any viability?"

"Total scrap job."

"That's a shame. We need more drifters."

"Seems like we need everything these days," Ella said. "Okay to put him down?"

"Go ahead. We'll send a clean-up crew. But make it quick. You two are needed for your shift at the wall."

The call ended.

Ella pulled the visor onto her head and gripped the five inch blade.

"Sorry, Darren," she said and plunged the knife through its skull.

It didn't even twitch.

"Let's move him out of the way," Mark said.

They each grabbed an arm and dragged the body out of the doorway. Ella turned as the door was closing, and noticed that the zombie's missing leg was in the bathroom. They dropped the body, and Mark went in to retrieve the leg.

"Ella, come here," he called from inside the stall.

She went in, wondering what he could need, and stopped when she saw that the leg was half wedged under a tile.

"What is that?" Ella asked.

Mark didn't answer. He pulled the panel fully open. There was a hole ten feet deep. He jumped in.

"Mark," she said, but he didn't respond.

He disappeared down the tunnel. She wondered if she should go after him, but waited. A few minutes later he returned, wearing his visor and out of breath.

"Were you running?" she asked.

"Yeah, I wanted to see how far it went."

"And?"

"I didn't come close to reaching the end. It gets dark, but I used the light on my visor."

He climbed out of the hole and placed his hand over his collarbone.

"Why are you doing that?" she asked.

He placed his other hand over hers.

"So they can't hear us."

"They can't hear us if we don't press the button."

"As far as we know. I just don't want to take the risk."

"What risk?"

"I think this tunnel goes outside the city," he said.

"You can't know that."

"How else could Darren, a drifter level zombie, disappear for two weeks and wind up in the center of town, in this bathroom, half trapped in this tunnel?"

Ella thought about it.

"Let's say you're right. We have to call this in."

"This tunnel wasn't put here by accident. My guess is that somebody already knows about it. And I don't think we're supposed to."

Ella was about to speak, but a call interrupted her.

"Why are you two still in sector alpha? Are you having trouble with the drifter?"

"No. We found," she paused to think of what to say.

Mark shook her head at her. She wasn't used to withholding information from her bosses at the Center for Zombie Control, but she did as her husband asked.

"We found his leg in the bathroom. We were just moving it. But we're done now, and are on our way."

"Hurry up," the voice said and hung up the call.

Mark covered their implants once more.

"Thank you. Let's just keep this between us for now."

"Okay," she said.

They closed the panel, took the leg outside, and headed to work. They were quiet on the walk there. Ella wondered if Mark was right, and if he was, what else the leader of the CZC might be hiding.

CHAPTER TWO

Ella and Mark stood on the covered platform that was Watchtower Two. The square floor was flush with the top of the fifty foot wall. As Ella scanned the horizon, she braced herself by carefully holding onto the rounded side of one of the spikes that lined the top of the wall.

In the distance, young trees grew along deserted roadsides. Once tall buildings were burned out, collapsed, and long abandoned. Everywhere she looked, the infrastructure that once existed was being reclaimed by nature. The world outside the wall was eerily still, but she hadn't come to expect much else.

She dropped the glasses back over her eyes. The transparent surface would alert her to any distant movement, to the unlikely presence of a heat signature, and enhance her vision if needed. She tried to imagine the ruins as they once were. She suspected that at least a few of those buildings must have dwarfed their wall.

A flashing red light went off in the corner of her display, disrupting her contemplation. She turned her head to look directly at it. The motion sensor showed two bodies moving slowly through the trees. As the figures came closer, a faint heat signature showed. Not warm enough to be a living body, but not cold enough to be a zombie, either. She zoomed in on the figures. They were far away and still blurry. One of the figures had only one arm. The other walked with a bad limp. She pushed the visor to zoom more. The fuzzy images had the coloration of dead men.

"You seeing them?" she asked.

"Yep," Mark said.

"Think they're the same ones from the other day?"

"Most likely."

"They're carrying something," she said.

Mark could just make out the curved outline of something. One zombie handed it to the other, who then slung it over its back.

"Is that a bow?" he asked.

"I think so."

"Why would a zombie have a weapon?"

"They must be someone's zombies. Do you think that there's someone alive out there, domesticating zombies like we do?"

"No one living could survive out there. Maybe they're ours."

"No tracking signature. Makes sense for the one missing the arm, but if they were ours, they would have given him another. And look at your heat sensor. They're warmer then the surrounding area. And since when to zombies work together? In proximity to each other, sure, but they're usually oblivious of it."

Trying to get a better look, she leaned over the wall, holding the spike but being careful not to touch the tip of it. As she did, a gust of wind kicked up, pushing her towards the pointed edge. She dropped her other hand to the side of another spike and held fast to both, catching herself. The motion forced her to face down. A wild flurry of red lights went off in her visor as it looked directly below. A zombie ran over the decades of bones that lined the base of the wall.

Ella couldn't tell how many bodies lay forgotten there, but her guess was thousands. The bones were mostly from the zombies that had starved to permanent death after running out of humans to feed on. They didn't decay like normal bones, bacteria wouldn't touch them, and there weren't any animals around to scavenge. Below the zombie bones was a layer of dust that had once been the human remains of people trying to gain access to the city to escape the zombies.

Ella steadied herself and stood upright.

"Are you okay?" Mark asked.

"Fine," she said. "We've got a sprinter below us."

"Two zombies in one day? It's like Founder's Day with presents."

"You have a strange gift list," she joked. "Check the book. Should we salvage or put it down?"

Mark looked at a tablet. The computer displayed the orders.

"Looks like we need him."

Mark grabbed a rope. He tied a slipknot and lowered the rope over the edge, spinning it so the loop stayed open. The zombie raised its hands as it jumped in an impossible attempt to reach them. Mark used the zombie's movements to his advantage and slipped the rope around the zombie's torso. He pulled, and the rope went tight under the zombie's arms. It seemed not to notice. Together, Mark and Ella pulled the zombie up.

It came to the top of the wall with its arms still up, which made its hands easy to restrain. The chomping mouth was another matter. It was also tricky to maneuver the thrashing zombie over the spikes without damaging it. Ella held the part of the rope that bound its hands while Mark worked the zombie over the edge. The zombie was nearly over when the tattered remains of its pants caught on a spike.

Ella pulled the zombie's top half away from Mark as he lifted its feet and tried to free its leg. The zombie bucked and pulled. As its leg came free it kicked out, pulling Ella off balance and letting the rope slip just enough for the zombie to turn back to Mark. The zombie bared its teeth and Mark tried his best to drop out of the way. He held his arm up to shield his face as he kicked at the zombie, but wound up catching a forearm full of teeth.

Ella rushed over, grabbed the zombie by a small patch of its remaining hair, and pushed its head down onto a spike. The sharpened metal went through one temple, and poked out the other. It stopped moving. Ella let go and was careful to avoid the blood.

Mark sat on the watchtower, stunned.

Ella ran to a box mounted to the wall. She pressed her thumb to the sensor, and after a moment, the box opened. She grabbed a first aid kit out of it and ran back to Mark.

Mark was still seated. He held his arm close to body. Ella sat down next to him. She tore off her visor and reached for his arm. He pulled it away.

"Let me see," she said.

Reluctantly, he offered her his arm. Two rows of dental impressions were visible near the elbow. A sob burst from Ella, but she quickly choked it back and began to bandage his arm.

"I was hoping it didn't break the skin," she said.

"Me, too."

She reached into the case and took out a pill. Mark opened his mouth and she placed it inside. The pill dissolved in seconds. She removed a tube of medical sealant and spread the liquid bandage over his wound. It stopped bleeding.

The two sat there in silence, considering the situation.

"Mark, I'm so sorry."

"Don't be. It wasn't your fault. Maybe the antiviral will work. Or who knows, maybe I'm one of the luckies and I'll be naturally resistant."

A voice spoke in Ella's ear.

"Agent Lane, we received an alert that Agent Mark Lane was bitten by a zombie. We have a team headed to your position. I know that he's your husband, but you need to secure him until they arrive. Understood?"

"Yes," she said.

The call disconnected.

"The CZC is on their way," she said.

Mark rubbed his fingers over the raised indention of the tracking device in his arm.

"They're fast. Must mean that it's already in my blood."

"We don't know that. Someone could have heard the commotion and called it in."

"Doesn't matter," he said. "They know I'm bit, and now, they're going to come and collect me."

He reached for her and held her close. She put her head on his chest. His heart sounded steady and calm. Hers was racing. He held her tighter and tears rolled down her face.

"Maybe it's not so bad," he said.

She glanced at the impaled zombie.

"How can you think that?" she asked.

"There has to be something inside of them. Some echo of who they were. And this isn't our grandparents' generation. It's not a death sentence to be a zombie."

She pushed back from him.

"Seems pretty close to me."

"Please, Ella, I need to believe that being a zombie is preferable to death. If you don't think it is, then you should just end me right now."

"You're right," she said, nodding unconvincingly. "Maybe it'll be okay. Maybe we'll even still get to work together."

"Human, well, zombie shield, reporting for duty."

They both gave a small chuckle, more out of discomfort than any real amusement at the joke.

"What do we do now?" she asked.

"We wait."

CHAPTER THREE

Ella heard the distant roar of a truck engine. Vehicles were rarely used, and almost exclusively for collection of the infected. The sound echoed through the city and grew louder, until it was almost deafening.

The truck pulled to a stop and men with automatic guns jumped out. The roar of the truck was replaced by the rattling click of guns bouncing against bodies and boots as the soldiers ran up the stone staircase.

As they rounded the last flight, they pulled their guns up to eye level, ready to fire if needed. Ella recognized many of the faces that were half hidden by rifles.

"Put those down," she said.

"Sorry Ella, we have orders," one of the men said.

They formed a semi-circle around Mark and Ella.

"Turn around, hands behind your backs."

Ella watched as Mark turned around.

"You too," he said.

"What?" Ella asked. "I wasn't bitten."

"Orders are to bring you both in. Turn around. I won't tell you again."

Ella could hardly believe what she was hearing. Stunned, she turned slowly and was pushed forward against the wall. She tried to glance behind her, but caught an arm to the face for her trouble. A tone sounded inside of her head as pain blossomed across her face. She felt dazed and numb. She shook her head and clicked her jaw, trying to rid herself of the sensation. She managed to regain enough wits to look ahead, over the wall as her arms were bound tight.

They placed a gag in her mouth. She tried to protest again, remind them that she hadn't been bitten, but all that came out was a muffled, panicked noise.

Next, they bound her feet. She wondered how they expected her to get down the stairs, until two men picked her up, one by the arms, the other by the legs. They carried her down the stairs. She dared crane her next to try to look behind her, and saw three men carrying Mark in much the same fashion.

At the bottom of the stairs, they were loaded into the canvas-covered truck. Inside, there was a metal cage. Ella struggled as they pushed her into it. Despite her objection, they managed to shove both her and Mark in and locked it.

The soldiers piled in behind the cage. Ella pounded on the metal in frustration. The soldiers mistook the action for violence. One of the men produced a dart gun. A pop sounded, followed by a whistle. Ella felt the sting of the dart as it pierced her chest. She looked down to see the fuzzy, black back of it protruding from her chest.

She heard another pop and whistle. Her vision began to blur. She looked at Mark, and saw that he had a matching dart in his chest. She kicked at the cage again, but with much less vigor. Soon she found that she couldn't hold herself up.

The truck started. The sound seemed muted inside the vehicle. The vibrations of the engine aided the sedative as it tried to coax her to sleep. Unable to fight the drug, she laid down in Mark's arms. He was much more awake than she was. He held her. As she lay against him, she noticed that Mark wasn't his usual space-heater self.

She squeezed into him, holding his arms tight against her. As the sedative won and she began to fall asleep, she wondered if this would be the last time he'd ever hold her.

CHAPTER FOUR

Ella awoke alone in a dark room. She had been propped up in a chair with her hands secured to the table by tight metal shackles with magnetic locks. The gag was still in her mouth. She shifted her foot in her boot. Her knife was gone.

She felt woozy from the sedative, but fought against it. She tried to call out into the darkness, but only a muted sound emerged. She worried that her cries would go unheard, but a moment later, the lights came on and Dr. Bell walked into the room.

Dr. Bell was the head and founding member of the Center for Zombie Control, as well as their city. Everyone worked under her, but Ella had never met her before. Still, she knew who this woman was. Bell was in her mid-sixties, but could have passed for being in her forties if not for her shoulder length gray hair. Her posture projected confidence. As always, she wore a long white coat, with the words: *Dr. Bell* stitched in red just below the left shoulder. The words sat above an embroidered, red bio-hazard symbol.

Two soldiers entered behind the doctor. Bell instructed them to remove Ella's gag and release her hands. The soldiers did as instructed and left the room, closing the door behind them. Ella wondered if she were being let go. And if so, then why was she still in this room?

"Dr. Bell," Ella said, her voice equal parts raspy and concerned.

"Hello Ella. Sorry about all the trouble. We had to make certain that you were not infected. You understand that every precaution must be taken when someone is bitten, right?"

Ella nodded. She wanted to scream at Bell for the way she'd been treated and remind her that she was never bitten. She knew that all anger would do was get her in trouble, so she kept it to herself.

"How's Mark?"

Bell took a seat across the table from Ella.

"He's been bitten, Ella. You know what that means."

Ella knew. A practically eternal life of mindless servitude if he's viable. Certain death if he isn't.

"Isn't there any chance that the anti-virals will work?" Ella asked.

"It doesn't look good. He's already taken to eating."

Ella was surprised.

"You fed him before you even knew?"

The Necrovirus worked by preventing cells from replicating. The virus allowed for only the most basic functions to be left intact to ensure the host's survival. However, it was far from a perfect system. The virus had to replenish itself and its host with fresh cells. The more cells, the more virus. This was what compelled the zombies to eat, and why the virus spread so quickly. By feeding Mark one of her lab-grown brains, Bell had quickened his transformation.

"It's better to not waste time in these situations," Bell said. "I hope that you will find some comfort in the knowledge that he shows a lot of promise. We think he could be valuable. Perhaps the two of you will still be able to work together."

An image of Mark as a mindless, decaying shell of his former self flashed in her mind. She cringed and held back sobs.

"I want to go outside of the wall," Ella said.

"There are better ways to commit suicide."

"I'm not talking about suicide. Dr. Bell, I have reason to believe that there is a cure beyond the wall."

"That's absurd."

Ella shifted in her chair and straightened up, trying to project a confidence to match Bell's.

"It's not," Ella said. "I've observed strange behavior in some of the zombies out there. They're working together, not just alongside each other. I think that there is someone out there controlling them. And as you pointed out, no one can survive outside the wall, let alone well enough to control zombies. He must have a cure. Or at least some sort of partial cure to make those zombies more alive than ours."

"You're upset. It's understandable. But you're misinterpreting what you've seen."

"Please, just let me go outside and look. I don't need anyone to go with me. I'll go alone."

Bell stood.

"The answer is no, Ella. Let's forget for a moment that there's no way to get outside of the wall, other than climbing down the wall and dangling like zombie bait. If anyone saw you outside, then they'd all want to go out. And if that happens, you can say goodbye to our society. You can say goodbye to the human race. So again, Ella, the answer is no. And if you try to go outside, you will be shot."

Bell didn't wait for Ella to reply. She began towards the door, certain that the conversation was over.

"What if I took the tunnels?" Ella asked.

Bell stopped mid-step, but didn't turn around.

"What tunnels?" she asked.

"Mark and I, we found tunnels that appear to lead outside of the city. It must let out farther than we can see, or we'd have known about them. I can take it and no one will have to know."

Bell hung her head and shook it.

"Oh, Ella."

382

Bell left the room. Ella was about to follow when the soldiers returned. She stood, but they rushed to her and pushed her back in her seat. They re-secured her hands to the table.

"What are you doing?" she shouted.

The soldiers paid her no attention and left the room.

Bell returned with a zombie behind her. Ella didn't recognize the drifter. It followed behind Bell as she came further into the room, dazed and dumb.

"What's going on?" Ella asked.

"No one is supposed to know about the tunnels. I can't allow that information to leave this room."

She led the zombie closer. Ella jumped from her seat. Her body was snapped forward by her bound hands. She pulled, dragging the table until she ran into the far wall. She dropped to the floor, trying to hide under the table.

But there was no escaping. Bell led the drifter to her, pushed its head down, and guided its remaining teeth into her arm. Ella cried out at the pain of her tearing flesh. Bell pulled the zombie back. The taste of real flesh made it feistier than before, but it was still drugged, and so Bell handled it easily. She pushed the drifter toward the door. It lazily protested, flailing its arms in the direction of Ella.

"It's a shame," Bell said. "We need a bigger zombie work force, but I was hoping to spare the females, what with breeding season coming up. Oh well."

With that, she left the room with the drifter ahead of her.

Ella lay under the table, trembling and afraid that in trying to save Mark, she'd been sentenced to a fate far worse than death.

CHAPTER FIVE

It had been more than a day since Bell infected Ella. Ella felt tired, yet restless, and her muscles were stiff. She knew that the virus was taking hold of her.

More than almost anything, Ella wanted to eat the brain that sat on a plate on the table in front of her. At its first presentation, just hours after she had been bit, it repulsed her. The soldier took it away and two hours later, brought her a new one. Each time a fresh one arrived it looked better. She tried not to look at it, not to smell it, and not to let on that she was salivating. A force inside her told her to eat it. But she resisted. Eating the brain was giving up.

"This is your last chance," a solider said.

He had delivered the brain. Every time, the soldier dropped it at the table, stood in the corner until the brain was no longer fresh and therefore would no longer be desirable, and then removed it. This would be his last delivery.

The soldier checked his watch and determined that she was out of time.

Ella refusal to eat would mean that she would be judged as unviable. Next would be real death for her, either by the virus or the hands of the CZC.

The soldier came to her. Rather than collecting the brain, this time, he unfastened her hands from the table, though they remained bound. He pulled Ella to a standing position. She resisted.

"Wait," she said. "I'll do it. I'll eat it. Please."

The solider released her arm. She turned to pick up the plate with the brain on it. She brought it close to her face and opened her mouth. The soldier watched intently. She was just about to take a bite, when she swung around, plate in hand, and bashed it into the soldier's head. He fell down on one knee and looked at her with rage in his eyes. She brought her arms up, and slammed the metal shackles down hard on his head before he could react. He fell flat on the ground.

Ella was stunned by her own violence. She hadn't fought a human before. She knelt over the body and removed the gun from the soldier's hip holster. She searched his pockets for a release for the shackles. She couldn't find one. While she was close, she could see that his chest still rose and fell. She was relieved that she hadn't killed him.

A pang of hunger struck her. The smell of fresh blood, of real, living flesh was almost overwhelming. Her heart pounded so hard that it ached. She closed her eyes and tried to refocus. She thought of Mark. The urge to eat passed. Once she had collected herself, she grabbed the guard's key card and stood up.

She held the badge in one hand, and the gun awkwardly in the other. She wouldn't be able to effectively wield either with her hands bound. She went to the door, angled her body, and clumsily swiped the key card over the electronic lock. It beeped and pressed in. She waited a second to see if any reinforcements were waiting to burst into the room. No one came. She carefully put the key card and the gun in her pocket. She placed one hand on the doorframe and pulled the other as far out of the way as she could. She took a deep breath. Then, with her leg, kicked the door closed as hard as she could.

It landed on her hand with a crunch. There was pain, but it felt muted, and far less than it should have been. The magnetic door locks tried to pull the door the rest of the way, threatening to cut off her hand. She slipped her foot, and then her leg, into the gap and forced it back open. The lock made a low tone and relented.

Ella's hand was mangled. It slipped through the shackle, untethering her hands. Now, with her good hand, she could grip the gun effectively. She found that she still had a little mobility in her damaged hand. Her thumb and pointer finger could still grasp. She held the key card with them. There was a grinding feeling, but the pain had almost disappeared.

She poked her head out the door and confirmed that the way was clear. She left the room and closed the door behind her. The building was shaped like a honeycomb with long stretches of corridors that spanned out in hexagonal loops that connected with new junctions at the points. She knew her way through most of the building. To her right, there were offices and labs. To her left, there was a practice area for field training zombies before letting them out into the work force.

She hurriedly navigated the maze. She was almost to a side exit when an office worker walked by and noticed her hand and the gun. Before the woman could run, Ella grabbed her. The woman struggled but couldn't get free. She pressed the implant on her chest and screamed into it.

Ella eyed the exit and considered the pros and cons of having a hostage. It could buy her time, but she'd be slowed down. She could use her as a shield, but the soldiers would be experts in headshots. And after what Bell had done, Ella couldn't discount the possibility that she'd go through an innocent civilian to stop her.

Ella stopped struggling with the woman and let her go. Her escape was now known. She dropped all pretense and sprinted for the door. She scanned the key card. The door opened just as the alarms began to sound. The door tried to close as Ella was exiting. She twisted and contorted, and managed to slip through before the door could cut her in half.

She ran from the CZC and didn't look back. Her muscles ached more than her broken hand. Still, she pushed on, dashing the few blocks to the public restrooms where she had found the tunnel. Stunned pedestrians looked at her as she ran through the city center, but they stayed clear.

She found the correct stall, went in, and locked the door. She placed the gun on the counter and tried to catch her breath. She rested her hands on the counter, and caught a glimpse of herself in the mirror. She had lost at least ten pounds. Her muscles were beginning to atrophy and she had dark circles under her eyes.

She looked at her hand. The bones hadn't broken through the skin. She turned her attention to her other arm, and the bite mark. She began to curse Bell in her mind. The wound hadn't begun to heal and it never would. She began to dig in the wound with her thumb and finger. The bite wasn't far from her tracking device. She prodded and twisted her flesh, seeking it out. She could feel the pressure from her fingers, but there wasn't any pain.

She found what she was looking for and grabbed for the implant. Her fingers fumbled, but she got purchase and yanked. With a tear, the implant gave and came out in her hand. She reached for a towel to stop the bleeding, but realized there was no bleeding.

She dropped the tracker down the sink and wiped her hands again. She figured that Bell wouldn't hunt her down outside the wall, or even into the tunnel, but she couldn't risk it. She opened the door to the tunnel and dropped down into it. She closed the door and darkness filled the corridor. Slowly, she followed the tunnel as it led her out of the city. She was terrified and exhilarated. She had never been outside of the city. No one living had.

CHAPTER SIX

Ella emerged from the tunnel three miles from the city. She could see the wall towering over the trees, but was confident that any standing guard on top would be unable to identify her. She did her best to suppress the fear she felt about being outdoors. She surveyed the area and noticed a set of two foot-prints headed in the same direction.

She followed the tracks through the trees until their end. She stood at the edge of a ruined city. Grass and vine had crawled over much of it, but the bones of what it had been still showed through. She walked down the cracked and overgrown street. Old traffic signals hung in the air, long dead and screeching in the wind.

She came to a part of the road where the grass had been completely rubbed away and lost the tracks. She searched the area, but couldn't find a new lead.

A scent caught her attention. It smelled familiar and like death. She looked up, and saw two zombies. One was missing an arm, the other had a badly broken leg. She was face to face with the zombies that she had been tracking. Some instinct told her that she'd be fine. Zombies didn't eat zombies. But these two were different, so she kept on guard.

"Hey," she said.

They both stopped and turned to her.

Concerned, she raised her gun and pointed it at them. Mockingly, the bigger zombie raised his one arm and pointed a gun back at her. She dropped hers to her side.

"What are you?" she asked.

The zombie dropped its weapon, too, and gestured with its one arm that she should follow.

It led her into a nearby abandoned building that she suspected used to be a church. At the altar, a man sat in an ornate and over-sized wooden chair. Candles dimly lit the space. He was leaning over someone in front of him who was being held up by two other zombies.

As Ella moved closer, she realized that the person on the throne wasn't a man. He still looked half human, but with ash gray skin color and sunken features. He was a zombie. And he wasn't just leaning over the person in front of him, he was eating the brains out of the still-writhing body.

She gasped, fearing that the man being eaten was still alive.

The zombie on the throne looked up from his meal.

"I assure you, dear," he said, "he's been dead for at least ten minutes now. I can hardly stand to finish eating, it's been so long. But the human nervous system does some interesting things even after death, especially when the brain is being fiddled with."

The zombie took another bite, then pushed the body away like an empty plate. His men were about to take it, when he stayed them with a motion of his hand.

"Where are my manners?" he asked, flashing a crooked, yellow grin, "Would you like some? He's still warm."

Ella's stomach growled at the thought. She swallowed and tried to deny her conflicted feelings.

"No, thank you," she said.

"Suit yourself."

He waved his hands and the zombies holding the man dragged his body to the corner, and began feeding on his flesh in a frenzied manner.

"We caught her trying to sneak in, boss," said the one armed lackey.

His speech was far less eloquent and came out like a caveman's.

"I wasn't trying to sneak in," she said.

"Of course not. Come now, Stumps, where's your hospitality? It's so rare that we receive unexpected guests. Especially not ones as lovely as Ella"

"How do you know my name?"

"You have a lot to learn about being a zombie," he said. "There is more to eating brains then mere nutrition. First off, it's better than any other flesh because it cuts down on the competition. So often a hungry zombie will bite someone in the arm or leg, and all they wind up with is an empty stomach and another zombie. You simply must eat the brains. No brain, no zombie. Beyond that, you get a glimpse at a person's life when you eat their brain. You get some memories, information, even the occasional visual. I ate someone not long ago who knew you. Funny, I can't remember his name, but I knew yours."

"And what should I call you?"

"The boys like to call me the boss. It's as good a name as any. But you should be far more concerned with yourself. You're living on borrowed time. It won't be long until you die, unless you start eating."

She looked back at the feeding zombies. Her stomach rumbled as they tore the last bits of flesh from his bones. She shuttered and turned back.

"I'm not eating any living, or recently living flesh," she said.

"Fine, have it your way. Starve to real death."

"I'm hoping that I won't have to. I'm here to find a cure."

"Aren't you supposed to be a zombie expert? I don't have the cure. Clearly, I'm still a zombie."

"But you're not like any kind of zombie I've ever seen. You at least know how to keep the rot away. You must have some sort of partial cure. You say you're a zombie, I think you're something else."

"I am a zombie. One of the founding fathers of the zombie apocalypse, actually."

"So, what then, are you just some sort of special zombie? An older model?"

"I'd like to think that I'm special. But I was like the rest of them, in the beginning. Mindless, running around eating whoever I saw. Taking two bites then deciding I was full. And next thing you know, there was competition."

"So what happened? How are you what you are now?"

"Being one of the zombie forefathers put me in the position of being a perfect lab rat."

"Then someone is trying to make a cure?"

He laughed and reclined in his seat.

"Not trying to. Just because I don't have the cure doesn't mean there isn't one."

Ella was getting tired of the run around. She just wanted a straight answer.

"Where can I find the cure?"

"At the CZC of course."

Ella scoffed.

"If the CZC had the cure, they'd have used it by now."

"You poor, naive girl. Tell me, how'd you get that bite? I know it wasn't one of my boys. The CZC wants there to be zombies. They need there to be zombies."

"I don't believe you."

He leaned forward. His eyes were stern, and his voice deepened to a gravelly tone.

"Then you'll die. Listen, girly, I was test patient number one. They experimented on me. Gave me variations of the cure to get a viable zombie work force. They determined that they had gone too far with me. That I was too smart to be of much use to them in your city. Same with my lackeys, only they weren't advanced quite as far as I was. I struck a deal with your Dr. Bell. I'd occasionally supply them with new zombies whenever the population grew too large or they had a slave shortage. In return, they let me live free out here, and look the other way when a person goes missing."

"That's why the tunnels exist."

"Exactly."

"But how could that be? The city was built to protect us. The CZC wouldn't just give you free access. It'd be too dangerous."

"Honey, who do you think started the zombie plague? The CZC is all too comfortable with danger."

Ella thought about his words and it struck her that her whole life was a lie. The anti-virals didn't work because they weren't meant to. The luckies just made it look like the meds worked. Her home had never been a safe haven for survivors. It was a base of operations for the people who wanted to thin out and control humanity.

"I need you to help me," she said.

"And just why would I do that, dearie?"

"Because I think you're planning something. I've seen your 'boys' as you call them. They've been stockpiling weapons. You're planning to make a move against Dr. Bell, aren't you? Are you after the cure?"

He snickered, then turned serious.

"You're quite right. I do want Bell, and I want her alive. I can't trust my boys not to eat her. And I'm not going to step foot back into the CZC. But maybe you are the one who can bring her to me. Given your vegan diet and all."

"Why do you want her?"

"I'll be honest with you, dear, I'm going to eat her. If I consume her brain, I'll know how to make the cure. Then I can create it."

Ella's fingers traced the open wound on her arm.

"Okay," she said.

"Good," he said with a smile. "My men and I will get armed. We can take the tunnels."

"There's more than one?"

"Oh yes, dear, and we're going to use them all."

CHAPTER SEVEN

Ella marched through the tunnels with an army of zombies at her side. The tunnels were lit by candles. Ella could see now that the tunnels were square and built from the same stone as her city. If she had any doubts about Bell being connected to the tunnels, they were gone now.

They reached a three-way fork in the path and the boss stopped the company.

"Well, my dear, here is where we part ways. Continue straight and the tunnel will let you into the labs of the CZC."

"I guess I'm going in alone."

"Me and the boys have other matters to attend to. We'll create a distraction in town and lure out the soldiers in order to buy you time. If we're successful in securing the city, you'll find us in the town center. Bring Bell to me there. If we've had to retreat, it'll be harder, and you'll have to take her to the church. Understand?"

"Got it."

He instructed his men to split up and cover both tunnels. Ella was hesitant to allow a few dozen zombies loose in the city without trying to stop them. But she believed that they would succeed. She would get the cure, and any bites would be reversed.

She followed the tunnel to its end. Above her she could hear a flurry of alarms, as well as the sound of frantic boots. She waited until the footfalls stopped, then pushed up the door. As promised, she found herself in one of the labs.

Inside the lab she found a zombie strapped to the bed. From her experience, she could tell by looking that it had turned long ago. The zombie wasn't conscious. Ella knew that zombies were regularly sedated, but she'd never known one to be knocked out. Two IVs had been inserted into each arm.

Ella heard activity in the hallway. She crouched beside the bed to hide. As she did, her hand brushed the zombie. It was warmer than she was. She stepped back, and almost ran into a heart rate monitor attached to it. The machine showed a pulse. It appeared that Bell was still experimenting.

Ella scanned her stolen key card and opened the door. The halls were empty. The boss's diversion was working.

Ella hurried down the hallway, not wanting to test her luck. She removed the gun she had stowed in her waistband. She hurried to Bell's lab, which was right where the boss had said it would be. She scanned her card, and the door opened. Bell stood behind a stainless steel table as she worked on a vertical tablet. Ella hurried into the room and closed the door behind her. Bell turned as she heard the door.

"You," Bell said as Ella entered. "All that going on out there, that's because of you?"

Ella pointed the gun at Bell.

"Hands in the air, step away from the computer."

Bell put her hands up and took a half step backwards.

"Farther. I don't want you to be able to touch the computer and alert anyone."

Bell stepped sideways from the keyboard.

"How do you know they haven't already been alerted?"

"This is where you keep your secrets. I have a feeling that this room is resistant to monitoring.

And as you pointed out, your soldiers have their hands full right now."

"I never pegged you as the type to turn against your own kind."

"The zombies are my kind," Ella said. "You made it that way. Now come on, we're going for a walk."

"I'm not going anywhere with you."

Ella closed the gap. Bell stiffened as she neared. Still, she held her ground.

"Yes, you are. Don't make me force you."

"I don't know what you think you know. Or what Jeffery, or the boss, whatever he calls himself these days, has told you. But I can promise you that he's using you."

"Nice try. I saw your experiment."

"You'll never understand what I was trying to do here."

Ella moved closer to Bell until she was almost talking into her left ear.

"You're right. I'm not the monster here."

Bell pressed in closer to Ella.

"You'll see the real monster soon. And he isn't getting my brain."

With that, Bell grabbed the hand that Ella held the gun in. In a flash, Bell placed the barrel to her temple. Before Ella could react, Bell pulled the trigger. The bullet ripped through Bell's brain, and tore through the skin of Ella's forehead. Bell had hoped to take them both out with the shot, but had missed. Brain and blood splattered on Ella and the wall.

Bell's body went limp against Ella, and they both fell to the floor.

"No," Ella yelled.

Breathing heavily, Ella turned from Bell's body and tried to figure out what she was going to do. She had failed in her mission. She hadn't gotten the cure.

The smell of bloody flesh made her stomach growl. She looked back at Bell's body and the mess it had made. She wondered if there'd be enough brain left to glimpse anything. She grabbed a small piece of brain that had fallen out, and brought it to her mouth. She felt that what she was about to do was wrong and she knew that eating it could make her turn. But there were bigger things at stake than just her life. She closed her eyes, opened her mouth, and tried to pretend she was eating something else.

The brain was still warm and was firm against her tongue. It tasted better than anything she had ever eaten. She needed more. She began shoveling handfuls of splattered matter into her mouth. She tried not to, but she couldn't help enjoying it. The tissue satisfied the hunger in her and gave her body what it craved. Before she knew it, she was licking the walls, desperate to get all she could.

She stopped mid-lick and looked curiously at the wall. It looked solid, but she had the feeling something was there. No, more than a feeling. Bell had known something was there. She dragged Bell's body by the arm, raised her hand, and placed it on the surface. After a moment, the outline of her hand glowed bright blue, and a seam appeared in the wall. Ella dropped the limp arm and a drawer opened with a whoosh. Ella moved closer and saw that there was a glass vial in the drawer. She reached in and pulled the vial out. A pale green liquid suspension halfway filled the glass tube.

Ella had found the cure.

She put the vial in her pocket and wiped the blood from her mouth on Bell's coat. She picked up the gun and placed it at the small of her back, and went into the hall. She felt drunk. She stumbled at first, and had to brace herself on the wall. The lights felt too bright.

She began having visions. She saw Bell as a young woman, talking, no, flirting, with a living version of the boss. Jeffery, as she had called him. Before he, or anyone else was infected. He was a scientist. They had created the Necrovirus together. He had also created the cure, not Bell. She had it stolen it from him, and knew how it worked, but she didn't know how to make it. Didn't care to. She was trying to create something else when she purposefully infected the boss and experimented on him. She wanted to create something close to what he was now, only more human. So far, she had failed.

Ella saw the city being built. She saw top minds being recruited and plans for the perfect civilization. She saw that they miscalculated. That they needed a larger work force. That was when they decided to train the zombies.

Ella saw Mark. She was observing him, no, Bell was. He had been shoved full of synthetic brains to turn him faster. They were grown in a lab, pumped with sedatives, and programmed with task memories. She observed Mark in the field. It was a mock-city. He stood on a street and a figure popped up feet from him. It was shaped like a person, and was covered with lab-grown tissue and brain.

The lab-grown brains provided just enough sustenance to sustain a zombie and ensured they stayed hungry enough to eat the drugged brains. It took training to teach the zombies not to eat humans. Mark hadn't learned this yet and he rushed at the dummy. Ella wanted to yell at him to stop, but it was just a memory, and would do no good. As soon as he touched the figure, a course of electricity shot through him. He let go and fell to the ground in convulsions.

She had to find him and free him.

She searched Bell's memory, but she couldn't find his location. She pulled herself together, determined to seek him out. She scanned the guard's badge and opened the door to the training field, hoping that he might be inside. As soon as the door opened, he was there, as if he'd known she was coming. He reached out and took Ella's mangled hand. She couldn't feel pain, only love. If Bell had experimented on him chemically, those memories were lost to the bullet. Ella chose to believe that he knew she was there because they were connected.

Physically, Mark was hardly the person she had left. His cheeks sunk in, his skin was pale, and he breathed, if in fact he was breathing, through his open mouth. Still, she loved him, and couldn't have been happier to see him.

She pulled the vial from her pocket.

"Might as well do this now," she said.

She titled Mark's head backwards. His mouth still hung open. She took the cap from the vial and carefully poured it into his mouth. He gagged, but drank it.

Ella led him through the automated training field. There were other zombies loose in the field, but they paid them no attention. They found an exit on the back wall. Ella tried to scan the guard's badge, but fumbled with it. She was feeling stiff and tired. She tried again. This time it worked. By time she left the CZC, she felt like she was sleep-walking. They continued, shuffling toward the city square. She felt dazed. So much so that she hardly heard a voice coming from behind her.

"Ella?" Mark asked, coming out of his own fog.

She turned to see him looking into her eyes. He was really back. She wanted to express her joy, cry, hug him, but she couldn't. She felt trapped inside her own body.

"Ella?" he tried again.

He took her by the shoulders and shook her gently. When she didn't respond, he looked her over, and saw the bite on her arm. Tears streamed down his face.

"No, Ella. How?" he asked.

He hugged her tightly. Ella wanted to return the embrace, but her arms remained limply at her side. He pulled back, pointed her face towards his, and sobbing, kissed her. She wanted to yell at him. He could have reinfected himself after she had gone through so much to save him. She felt an anger rise inside. The world was coming back into focus. She could feel herself breathing and she felt as though she might burst.

"Idiot!" she screamed.

"Ella?"

She realized the words had come out. She began to weep tears of happiness and held Mark tight.

She felt drunk again, but this time, it was with hope and love.

Hand in hand, they ran to the city center. They had just arrived when Ella heard a boom behind them. She looked back to see that an explosion had destroyed the CZC.

CHAPTER EIGHT

Ella parted ways with Mark, instructing him to quietly cure as many zombies as he could.

She found the boss in the city center. His boys had over taken the soldiers.

"Where is Bell?" he asked.

"Bell is dead. She took her own life."

The boss seemed to ease at this.

"I didn't think she'd have it in her. Well, what's done is done."

"I thought you'd be more upset. You did want her for the cure, didn't you?"

"Of course. But what can you do? Bell is dead. And I assume that the boys destroyed the building?"

"Yeah. Thanks for the heads up on that."

Bell laughed and flashed his crooked, yellow grin.

"A man has to keep some secrets."

"You're no man. And I doubt that was your only secret."

"Skepticism. That's good. I warned you about being naive."

Ella put her hand behind her back and gripped the gun, but waited to pull it.

"You used me," she said.

"Yes. And you did a wonderful job. The cure, and all knowledge of it, has been destroyed. And as a bonus, we control the city. All these humans, perfect for farming."

"You might control the city for now, but not all knowledge of the cure is gone. It was quite an ingenious cure you created, Jeffery. A benign virus that was stronger than the Necrovirus. The competing viruses fight for the cells, and the Necrovirus loses, which restores the cells to their former active, splitting selves. To put it another way, it makes the zombies human again. But of course, you knew that."

The boss looked surprised.

"You ate her? And I thought you kept a strict diet."

"I cheated."

"But if you ate her," he said, piecing things together, "you should be turned. You found the cure."

He began to back away from her.

"I only ever wanted immortality," he said.

"Don't worry, Jeffery, I wouldn't cure you."

She pulled the gun from her belt, raised it, and shot him square in the forehead.

The recoil hurt her arm and she had to drop the gun. She looked at the limb, and saw that her wound had begun to bleed for the first time. She put pressure on her arm and smiled.

She was human again.

A Word from Angela Cavanaugh

This story was one that challenged me. I didn't want to write the typical zombie horror story. I love those stories, but I wanted to push myself and try to create something that I hadn't seen before. I wanted to explore what happens to the world after the zombie apocalypse. What happens when the remaining humans come back together and rebuild?

My answer to this was a technologically advanced, dystopian city with dark secrets. They've managed to neutralize the zombie threat, and even domesticate them. But their lifestyle comes at a cost, and the most powerful, and dangerous, people have hidden agendas. I don't always write happy endings, but I was pleased that this story had one. But in some ways, I think their ending was really just the beginning. I'd like to think that Ella and Mark, as well as others from the city, will find happiness outside of the wall since they no longer need to fear the zombies and have the freedom to explore.

I hope that you enjoyed this story. If you'd like more stories, including free ones and opportunities to review free advanced copies, please join my newsletter: Angela's Newsletter

For weekly content, please follow my blog: www.angelacavanaugh.com

And check out my other works on Amazon: *Otherworlders*, *Dauntless*, *Human Network*, un *The A.I. Chronicles*, and *22 Short Scifi Stories*.

Lastly, I'd like to invite you to post honest reviews, as they are always appreciated. Thank you for reading.

Curing Khang Yeo
by Deirdre Gould

KHANG'S NOSE WAS BADLY BROKEN. But judging from the strength of the rancid meat smell that still reached him, he considered it a small mercy. What distressed him was the fact that he had finally realized it was broken. It meant he was either better or dead. He kept his eyes tightly closed so that he wouldn't have to find out which. He didn't remember dying. All around him he could hear other people weeping or screaming in misery. What *did* he remember? He remembered being hungry. He was still hungry. Hollow even. There had been a boy. A boy in the woods. The boy had shot him and Khang had chased him, not caring. Just hungry. He'd chased the boy to a field and Khang had fallen, still reaching out for the boy's thick leg. He'd been so close that Khang had blacked out imagining the salty sweat of the boy's skin, the stringy toughness of his calf muscle between Khang's broken teeth.

It made him want to retch now, remembering that. He almost did, but he remembered he'd have to sit up and look around if he did. He clenched his mouth shut and willed his empty stomach to relax. The people around him were fading away, leaving. He lay there still. Before the boy... before the boy was a jumble. A long, hot streak of rage. How long had he been that way? Days? Weeks? His skin was stiff with filth and his mouth tasted rotten. He probed at a tooth with his tongue. It was jagged where it had been broken and a sliver crumbled away as he touched it. He shuddered. He could hear the wind in the grass now, rustling around him. The smell was almost gone. If this was hell, it wasn't as terrible as he'd expected. He tried not to dredge up any more memories. He had a feeling they'd be even worse.

"Think we've got another one, Doctor," said a voice above him. Khang felt a heavy jab to his side and groaned involuntarily. He opened his eyes at last. A man with a gun towered over him, but Khang had frightened him. He jumped back. "Christ," he swore, "Are you alive or not?" He pointed the gun at Khang's chest. "Are you still Infected?"

"I don't know," croaked Khang, his voice weak and uneven, as if he'd been shouting for a long time.

The man shook his head. "You're Cured. And you aren't dead. C'mon, get up if you can." The man nudged Khang again with his boot. He sat up and looked around himself at last. He was in the field where he had chased the boy. A massive tent rippled and flapped above him. Around him, the long grass was pressed down where dozens — maybe hundreds of bodies had lain. The crushed hollow bowls reminded Khang of empty graves. He got slowly to his feet.

"Go on," said the man, waving toward another mass of white tents on the horizon, "go get some chow and clean up. Christ knows you need it."

Khang looked back at the man. He could see now that he was a soldier. Uniformed. Normal. "Well?" said the soldier, "I can't babysit you all day, I got bodies still to move. Not everyone was as lucky as you. The Cure doesn't work on all of you."

Khang walked slowly toward the tents. He could see other soldiers now, all in the same dark uniform, dragging bodies past him toward a large truck. He shut his eyes for a moment to try to erase the image. A hand on his arm made him open them again. It was a small woman in light green doctor's clothes.

"I'll lead you," she offered, "You don't have to look if you don't want to."

"Where am I? Who are you people?"

The woman began pulling his arm gently. He followed her without resistance. "You're in a Cure camp. I don't know how much you remember, probably not much yet. That's how it seems to go. But you were sick. So were a lot of other people. The soldiers, doctors and nurses who are here are spreading the Cure as best we can."

"So the bodies..."

"The Cure takes a few days. Some of the Infected are in very bad shape. They haven't eaten in a long time or they have secondary infections. We do all we can, but sometimes they don't make it. You would have seen the nurses working and the dozens of IV stands, but you were a late riser." She gave him a smile.

Khang raised his hand and stared at the plastic tube taped to his hand.

"We'll take the needle out and get you cleaned up and fed in a few minutes."

He nodded but he didn't really register what she was saying. He kept staring at the large ovals of crushed grass where people had lain. There were so many. How many people had been sick?

The sound of people talking and weeping grew into a soft roar as they approached the edge of the other tents. He could see shadows of dozens of people sitting or walking and the smell of warm bread thickened the air. The smell of rot was gone, except for on Khang himself. He realized how filthy he was and was ashamed to walk into a place with so many other people.

"Is there somewhere to clean up?" he asked, forgetting she had just said that there was.

She didn't remind him or scold him. "There is a shower room, just ahead. We need to do a short interview first."

"Interview?"

"We just need to find out who you are so we can see if you have relatives looking for you."

"Yes! My daughter and son—" but he trailed off, something in his mind strobed a warning not to look for them just yet.

The woman led him to a small desk in a corner of the tent. She pulled a curtain around them. He knew he must smell terrible to her, especially in that confined space, but he was grateful for the privacy. He sat down in a folding chair. The metal felt especially cold and hard. He looked down at himself. There was no fat to cushion him against the world anymore. Just bones that poked painfully out of his skin. He had no clothes except a few shreds of cloth that still clung to his wrist and collar. He was too confused to be embarrassed and the woman didn't even seem to notice. She sat down across from him and pulled out a folder from the desk.

"This won't take long," she said, "but if you need to stop, just let me know."

Khang nodded.

"Let's start with your name."

"Khang Yeo. What's yours?"

The woman looked up, startled. "Oh, sorry, I'm Nella Rider. I should have said that."

Khang nodded again. Dr. Rider wrote his name across the top of the folder.

"What's your age?"

Khang thought for a moment. "I don't know. I remember it being snowy. It's not snowy now. I don't know how long I was sick."

"How old were you when it was snowy?"

"Fifty-three."

"And do you remember hearing reports of the December Plague anywhere? On the news or radio maybe? Or the power going out? Military arriving in your neighborhood?"

413

Khang shook his head. "No, none of that. Dr. Rider, what's happened?"

She put the pen down and folded her hands on the desk. "Mr. Yeo, you've been ill for a long time. Perhaps as long as two years." She waited while the weight of the news plowed into him.

After a few seconds he said, "And those other things— the military in the street? The power being out? You don't even know where I'm from. Which must mean..." he trailed off.

"That they happened everywhere," she finished for him. "The Plague was very bad. I'm afraid it was worldwide. Things— aren't the same. I'm sorry to have to be the one to tell you. You can ask me anything you like, but I think it's for the best if you take your reentry into the world as slowly as possible. There will be time to absorb what has happened, and our staff will be here the whole time to help you if we can."

"I have to find my family," said Khang, half standing. Dr. Rider watched him as he realized he had no idea where he was. He sat back down.

"Maybe I can help," she said calmly, "We have lists of people looking for each other. Even if they haven't registered, they might be looking for you. Who would you like to start with? A spouse?"

Khang shook his head. "No, my wife passed away years ago. My children though— I have a daughter and a son."

"What are their names?"

"Jia and Lee."

She pulled a large pile of printed paper from a desk drawer and flipped to the back, scanning names as she went. When she reached the end, she wrote the names carefully in. She looked up at him. "And where was the last place you remember seeing them? It will help us know where to start looking."

Khang sat back on the cold chair and shut his eyes, trying to focus. That day had been a bad one. He had been off-balance. Not dizzy really, but slow, clumsy. He'd had a minor accident at work when his bus had hit a hydrant. Luckily no one had been hurt, but dispatch had made him take a few days off. He was supposed to have an appointment to check his inner ear. He remembered that. Jia had stopped by to check on him with food from the restaurant. He'd been asleep on the couch. He could still feel the cool cloth she pressed against his head to wake him.

"You have a fever, Dad," she said, "You should go to the doctor."

"This afternoon," he'd mumbled.

"I brought you some lunch." She set the styrofoam box on the coffee table with a plastic fork. She opened it for him and he watched little droplets of condensation slither down the inside of the box. "I'll heat up the soup," she said, grabbing a small plastic cup. She rattled around in the kitchen behind him as he slowly sat up and picked at the food.

"Lee's coming to check on you in a little bit. He said you had an accident at work?"

Khang scowled. "It was nothing. Some idiot placed a fire hydrant too close to the curb on Winslow Street."

She came back to the living room carrying the hot cup carefully. "He's just worried about you."

Khang waved off his daughter's worry. She sat down beside him and handed him the cup. The cup wobbled when Khang took it and soup scalded his hand. He hissed with pain.

"Oh jeez, sorry Dad," said Jia, grabbing a towel from the nearby laundry basket and wiping off the soup.

"'Sokay. Forget it," he said grumpily, shaking his hand.

She turned back to the laundry basket and started folding the contents. He hated when she did that. She straightened the newspaper he'd left on the coffee table and then plugged in the vacuum.

"Don't Jia," he said.

"It's okay Dad, it'll only take a sec."

"Don't—" he said again, but she flipped the machine on anyway. She treated him like he belonged in a home. They both did. He was only in his fifties, for Christ's sake. He knew Lee would come over and try to convince him to stop working so much. Stop driving so much. Khang slammed down the cup, splattering soup everywhere. The vacuum was too loud for Jia to notice. Her back was to him. She never *listened*. He leapt onto the coffee table, scattering food and papers. He reached over and yanked on her long hair. Her silky straight hair. He could still feel it wrapped around his fingers two years later in the Cure camp. She'd shrieked and flung her slender arms up. He yanked harder, a deep rumbling roar rattling out of his chest and smothering her scream. They stood there like that, him roaring down at her as her eyes filled with tears, her head bent back, thirty seconds? A minute? And then he bent down and clamped his teeth around her soft throat. His lips vibrated with the scream that gurgled out of her torn throat and he twisted her head, once, with a hard yank on her hair, snapping her neck. She was gone.

Lee had been next, breaking down Khang's door when he didn't answer. The vacuum had still been running and his son had thought that Khang had injured himself, was lying helpless on the floor. Instead he found his father crouched over the body of his sister. Lee had run to help Khang, to find out what had happened. In his shock he never even registered what his father was doing until Khang sprang on top of him.

Khang used his fists. Lee struggled to get free, never hitting him back.

"Dad, stop, please," he'd cried. "It wasn't me, I didn't hurt her!" thinking Khang had mistaken him for Jia's murderer. But Khang hadn't stopped. Couldn't. His son's cries had become weaker and farther apart and had finally ceased.

Khang opened his eyes in the bright light of the Cure tent and wailed, having said nothing to Dr. Rider. He didn't need to. She placed a warm hand on his back as he wept, wrapping a thin blanket over his shoulders. She didn't interrupt him or even speak, but gently pulled his arm out and injected the IV port with a mild sedative. Then she sat beside him for a long while until he cried himself out and looked up at last.

"Both?" she said.

He nodded.

"I'm sorry," was her only response.

"You've seen this before?" he asked.

"Yes. You aren't alone."

"Why? Why did I do this? I'm not a bad man. I never hurt my kids. Never even spanked them."

"The Plague. It makes your own body fight your brain. It makes infected people aggressive, clumsy, have pica — that's a craving for something that's not food."

"You mean — for people?"

"In this case, yes. Well, meat of any kind it seems. And since the Plague itself isn't deadly, the infection persists. Until now, until it was cured."

Khang clutched his head as if he could force the memory out. "My own children," he muttered, "I can remember every day of their lives. They were my entire purpose. How could I? This must be hell. Anywhere else and I would have been struck dead on the spot. This must be hell. I must be dead."

She let him talk, watching him as he rocked on the cold metal chair. The curtain swung open and a man peered in. "Sorry to disturb you, Dr. Rider, but your assistance is needed."

She frowned and looked hesitantly at Khang. The she nodded at the other man. "I'll be right there. Could you take Mr. Yeo to the shower room when he's feeling up to it?" She gently placed a hand on Khang's shoulder. "I'll be back soon, Mr. Yeo. I've given you a sedative, so you should feel a little calmer in a bit. I know it's an impossible thing to ask, but try not to think beyond the present for now. Try and concentrate on filling your physical needs for now. I hear it makes this transition less difficult. I'll check in with you in a little while."

Khang barely noticed that she'd left. When he finally raised his head, a man sat across from him.

"Let's get you into the shower. And after, you can get some lunch. I promise it will make you feel ten times better," said the man.

Khang doubted it, but he followed the man numbly, too exhausted and depressed to argue. The man handed him a toothbrush and a small tube of paste, a bar of soap, a towel and a bland set of mismatched clothing from a long table.

"It's not high fashion, but we don't have much choice these days. What size shoe are you?"

"Nine," Khang said blankly. They walked into a long trailer that smelled like fresh soap and was still filled with steam.

"Looks like everyone else is done. Don't know how much hot water you'll have left, but at least you'll get some privacy. I'm going to get you some shoes."

Khang placed everything but the soap onto a damp counter. The other man turned around. "Look, I'm supposed to watch you. Cured people — they try to overdo it on the cleaning. You can't clean it up, all right? You can't rub it out with a bar of soap, no matter how much we all wish you could. I think you've been through enough. You deserve some time to yourself after all this. So I'm going to go get shoes, right? And you're going to relax in the shower and not do anything stupid. 'Cause you're just going to hurt yourself worse if you do."

Khang stared at him and then nodded. He waited until the man disappeared into the steam of the long trailer and then pulled off the shards of stiff cloth that still clung to him. They were stiff, like cardboard, and just tiny patches of what they had been. His work shirt was almost gone, just the buttoned collar and a shred of cloth with his name embroidered on it. He yanked on the button, pulling it from the cloth. It had come loose a few days before the accident and Jia had sewn it back on. Here it was, surviving whatever he'd done. Surviving her. Khang kissed the button and folded it carefully into the pocket of his new pants. He stepped into the shower stall and the struggling tank managed some lukewarm water. He let it roll over him, his mind a blackening, directionless bruise. The soap slipped from his hand and he looked down in surprise. He didn't recognize his legs as he leaned past them to pick up the bar. They were stilts, sun-beaten driftwood. He rubbed one with his hand to be sure it was real. They were crisscrossed with thin scars where he had run through brambles or knocked into fence wires. He held his arms out in front of him. They were just as deteriorated. One of them had broken at some point. It wouldn't straighten all the way. He wondered about his face. Khang leaned out of the stall only to realize there were no mirrors here. He thought of the hundreds of others discovering their bodies weren't as they recalled and guessed it was probably a good thing they couldn't see themselves.

He hoped he looked like a stranger. He didn't want to see what his children must have. He didn't want to know how frightened they must have been to see the face they'd trusted their whole lives twist into a monster. Khang sobbed and shook his head. *Try to concentrate on now, she said*. He watched the drain suck thick scales of dirt and sticky, melting blood clots away, back into the dark where they belonged. Was it his blood? He'd never know. *How many people have I killed?* He squeezed the dissolving bar of soap furiously. *Not now*. The soap slid over his skin, trying to clean away the questions as it broke up the filth. His caretaker came back, holding up a pair of sneakers.

"You almost done man?"

Khang nodded.

"You brush your teeth yet? You do that and we'll see about that nose and then food."

Khang turned the shower off. The man passed him a towel. "I'll go tell Dr. Taylor you're almost ready."

Khang waited until he had left to step out of the stall. He dressed almost frantically, because as soon as the man had mentioned his teeth, Khang could taste the foul, greasy film that coated his mouth. He wanted to vomit, even though seconds before the taste had barely even registered. He stumbled to a sink, the paste shaking onto the brush. He plunged it into his mouth and almost screamed as the brush touched the nerve inside one of his broken teeth. The taste was worse than the pain and he pressed on, roughly scrubbing the gritty slime that covered the interior of his mouth. He kept spitting and spitting, but still the taste lingered. The tube was empty and he kept scraping the brush over his tongue. The spit turned pink and his caretaker came back and stopped him.

"Shouldn't have left you alone for that bit. You all do that."

Khang swiped a hand over his mouth. The caretaker sighed and reached into a pocket.

"Here," he said, handing Khang a tiny silver-wrapped stick. "But don't tell anyone. Gum is hard to come by these days, especially with all the people who had to quit smoking."

Khang stared at the gift. "Thank you," he said, before unwrapping it and popping it into his mouth. The man nodded and led Khang out of the trailer. They stopped in a larger tent that still bustled with people. The man helped him up onto a gurney.

"You're lucky today." The man reddened and scratched his head. "I mean— aside from the obvious. Dr. Taylor is going to see you. Not often you get the head of the whole shebang to treat you, is it? He'll be by in a minute. I'll come back to take you to the mess hall when you're done."

Khang fumbled for the tiny button in his pocket. He pressed it between his thumb and forefinger hard enough to leave dents in his skin. The doctor walking toward him was pristine. His coat was ironed, he had a dress shirt and tie beneath. He sat down in a low chair across from Khang and stuck out a hand. Khang shook it in his own, bewildered.

"Hello Mr. Yeo, I'm Dr. Taylor. I'm going to give you an exam, just so we know the extent of any injuries you might have. I see your nose recently suffered a break. Do you remember when?"

Khang shook his head. "Maybe when I fell in the field out there," he guessed.

"And I see you have an old break in your right arm as well. Have you noticed any other serious injuries?"

Khang shook his head.

"Well, let's take a look then." Dr. Taylor stood up.

"I was told you run this place," Khang said abruptly.

"The Cure camp? Yes, I'm the administrator here."

"Did you invent it?"

"The Cure? Goodness no. This is just one camp. There's half a dozen scattered over the length of the Barrier— never mind, I'm sure this is all very confusing. You don't need to worry about that now. But Dr. Carton is the one who invented the Cure." He leaned in to look at Khang's nose but Khang leaned away.

"But you're the one who decides who gets cured, right?"

The doctor stood straight up with a frown. "It's not really a decision. If we find Infected, we bring them in for the Cure."

"Why?"

The doctor looked startled. "What do you mean?"

"Why are you curing us?"

"Well, if simple compassion isn't good enough for you, then I suppose it's because the Infected are killing the rest of us. I don't know what you've been told about how things are now, but without the Cure, we aren't going to make it. You haven't seen it yet because the camp is crowded and we have plenty of food and electricity for things like water and surgical instruments. What you don't know is that this camp, and the others like it, have all the resources the City can spare. We're monopolizing the electric plant, the manpower, even the food to *bring you back.*"

"And what are we meant to do in return? Are we meant to be slave labor? Breed new people? Why did you bring us back?"

Dr. Taylor stared at the wasted, skeletal man across from him. "We're *good* people. We don't enslave people. Sure, we need skilled people, I won't lie. I'm a psychiatrist, not a physician, but I have more medical training than most so I pick up the slack. I'd love to find a good physician among you. But I wouldn't force them into working. We have boys and girls manning our Barrier. Kids that should be going on first dates and worrying about prom, not holding a gun, because we don't have enough soldiers. But we're *good*. What did you do Before?"

"I drove a bus," Khang said flatly, "you want me to drive a bus?"

"If that's what you want."

"I killed my children. My neighbors maybe. I can't even remember who I've killed. The other people here— they did too. They slaughtered and ate their fellow man. You want us to go to your City and just what? Pick up where we left off? Pretend it didn't happen? Live with people whose loved ones we killed?"

"What alternative is there?" asked Dr. Taylor, folding his arms across his chest.

"There's dying. An end to this misery. Did you know, doctor, that when you cured us, we'd remember everything?"

"Not at first. We found out at the same time our first Cured patients did."

"But you knew before you cured this batch. If you were truly as good as you say you are, you would have killed us instead. It would have solved your war and been a mercy to us."

Dr. Taylor nodded. "That's a common reaction after the Cure, Mr. Yeo, but not everyone feels that way. And once you've moved through your initial shock, I think you, too, will change your mind about that."

Khang shook his head. "You don't know. You can't know. You've taken away one sort of madness and replaced it with another." He raked his hands across his cheeks.

Dr. Taylor stood up. "Please, Mr. Yeo, remain calm. Try and concentrate just on what's happening right now. Take a deep breath —"

"I can't concentrate on 'now'! Now is pointless. Now is a nightmare. Just let me —"He made a swipe for the tools on the table beside the gurney. Dr. Taylor shoved it aside before Khang's hand could close around the scalpel.

"Nurse!" called Dr. Taylor. He grabbed Khang's shoulders. The Cured man fought, but he was terribly weak and soon fell still. Dr. Taylor continued to inspect him as if the outburst hadn't happened, but the nurse stayed nearby. When he was done, Dr. Taylor looked up at the nurse. "Would you please show Mr. Yeo where he can get a meal?"

But Khang shook his head. "I'm not hungry. Just check me out and I'll be on my way."

The nurse and doctor exchanged a glance.

"Mr. Yeo, you have to eat," said Dr. Taylor, "you may not like it, but it's my job to keep you alive, to help you recover. For the time being, you are under my care and must remain in the Cure camp. I won't argue with you about it until you've had a chance to process what has happened. You just woke up. If I must, I will put in an IV in order to get you the proper nutrients, but I know you'd feel better if you just ate."

Khang glared at him. Dr. Taylor sighed. "We've gone to great trouble to bring you back. You might not appreciate it, but we've sacrificed to keep you alive. So have the people you — you consumed. Can you at least honor that sacrifice for the moment and let us help you? Can you put off dying just for a few days to recognize what's been given to you?"

The point hit home and Khang thought of Lee, begging Khang to stop hurting him, but never striking back to defend himself. He nodded at the doctor.

It was noisy in the large tent, even at night. They'd moved him in with the others after he'd eaten and he watched them dully from his cot. He had expected to see people of all ages and sizes around him, but time had whittled them all to the same genderless spike of bone and skin. They all looked around sixty to Khang, though he doubted many besides himself actually were. Some of them talked to him. They were all looking for someone. A brother, a spouse, children. No one had answers for them. He watched the person across from him crying. Too tired to sob, it just leaked at its eyes. It noticed Khang and shrugged with a half smile.

"I know it's stupid. There's so much that's so awful," a woman's voice came from the bony figure, "but I had the prettiest hair once. My mother used to brush it for me. Now the barber is coming to cut it." She raised her hand to point across the room where a man with blunt scissors and a bucket of trimmings made his way down the cots. Khang thought it would be a relief to be rid of the tangled, itchy filth on top of his head. But he remembered Jia and the dark stream of hair that fell over her shoulders. How beautiful it had been! Before he'd twisted it and torn it. He stopped a passing nurse.

"Excuse me," he said, already blushing, "is there a hair brush around anywhere?"

The nurse smiled and went to find one. Khang patted the cot. "Come here," he told the woman, "I used to brush my daughter's hair, after her mom passed away. She used to get the worst snarls."

"Oh," said the woman, "I know it's just silly. It will grow back. And I'm sure there's — stuff tangled in there. I don't think it will come out."

Khang shook his head. "It's not silly, if it will make you feel better. It will make me feel better, too. Do an old man a favor and let him remember his daughter in happier times."

The woman shrugged shyly and came over to sit on the cot. He stood up and gently picked at the strands of hair with the brush. It took all of his concentration to untangle the mess without hurting the woman, but it soothed him and he lost himself in it until the barber reached them. The woman started crying again and Khang looked up. The barber shook his head.

"It's okay, darlin' you don't have to snip it if you don't want to. I have something that might help." He pulled a small bottle out of his pocket and knelt down in front of the woman. "Now don't be saying anything about this. It might be the last bottle of conditioner there is for all I know. But most of you — well, most of you just want to chop it off. You take this into the shower while I tidy up this gent. Then, when you get out, we'll see what we can do. I promise you'll be the prettiest girl in the whole place."

"Thank you," she said, shakily taking the bottle. She gave Khang a smile that would have been bright if her cheeks hadn't been so hollow and walked off toward the shower.

"That's the kindest thing I've seen since I woke up," said Khang.

The barber ducked his head and shrugged. "She your kid?"

"No," said Khang, "I don't know her."

The man nodded and placed a stool down for Khang. "Yeah, well, it's a little creepy, isn't it, shearing all these people like sheep. Reminds me of those old concentration camp photos. Gives me the willies. Never been able to get past that. Makes me feel better to let someone keep it if they want to. Normally don't have enough time to do a nice job with it though, and it still ends up chopped a little. But she'll keep most of hers, thanks to you. And what about yourself? A little off the top?"

Khang sat on the stool, his back to the man. "Shear away," he said, "It'll be a relief."

When the lights went out for the night, the woman in the next cot whispered, "Thank you." Khang just smiled. "Good night," she said and he nodded. She turned away from him, relaxing into a light sleep. Her hair flowed down her thin back. Khang could still feel the tough strands biting into his skin as his fist tightened on a clump of his daughter's dark ponytail. *I'm so sorry Jia*, he thought, *If only I could give you my own life for yours*. He squeezed the thin button in his pocket. In his dreams that night, Khang was drowning in rivers of black hair.

He woke just before dawn, when gray light slicing through the tent seams slid over him. He opened his eyes and watched the small bundles of cloth around him. They were still now, not restless as they had been when he fell asleep. As if the nightmares shrank and fled away, leaving the Cured to rest for a few moments before they met the terrible visions again in their waking memory. The night nurses slipped away and the morning shift bustled in. People began stirring, the soft static of running showers became constant, and the smell of cooking filtered into the tent. Khang didn't move. He wasn't the only one. Here and there, other people lay in their cots. Some stared at the rippling canvas roof. Some closed their eyes. Some cried without sound, devastated to wake up again. Dr. Rider walked over to his cot and crouched down. She took his pulse and gently peeled a bandage off the back of his hand.

"Were they little?" she asked, "Your kids, I mean."

Khang shook his head. "No. All grown up. A chef and a police officer."

Dr. Rider nodded. "I know you're thinking that nothing can make up for hurting them, that no deed you do will ever erase it." She looked at him for a long moment but he didn't respond. "I've been doing this a little while now. You aren't the first to think it. Not even close. I don't know what you believe about what comes after this world, but it doesn't matter much. What I've seen are people struggling to fix this one. Not to erase what they've done, what they've endured, but to at least make life a little better for whoever comes after. I've also seen a lot of dead people. Dying doesn't erase what you've done either. Dead people don't atone. They don't make the world a better place. They just rot away and leave a stain on history."

Khang shut his eyes and released a shuddering sigh.

"Would you like some breakfast?" asked Dr. Rider gently.

Khang shook his head.

"Okay," she said, "I'll leave you be." She stood up and gave his hand a gentle squeeze before walking off.

A flash of Lee's small face hit Khang. They were standing in front of a coffin. Khang's wife lay inside. Lee had been eight, Jia just six. Khang was tired of crying. He was tired of talking about her death as if it were the entirety of her existence. He was tired of people trying clumsily to comfort him. He stood in front of the coffin, staring at its open lid instead of the thing that was no longer her. He didn't know what he was supposed to do, or to say, or to feel. But then Lee gently squeezed his hand. His little face looked up at Khang, calm and without tears. "Let's go home, Dad. Just us and Jia," he'd said.

Just us and Jia. Time to leave the rest behind. She's wrong, he thought, *There's one other thing that dead people do. They forget.*

It wasn't something he'd ever dreamed of doing before. He used to shake his head in disgust when Lee would tell him about a jumper or an overdose. There was nothing so bad it couldn't be turned around or fixed. People were too quick to give up for silly reasons. Money, romantic failure, job loss. So many replaceable things causing people to give up the irreplaceable. But that was Before.

Khang sat up in his cot. He looked around him for a nursing station, a sterilizing tray, anything.

"Do you ever actually talk them down?" he'd asked Lee once. He'd shook his head and peeled at the label around his beer bottle.

"Not usually. Not unless you can physically grab them before they do it." He glanced up at Khang who was sitting across from him in Khang's cramped kitchen. "I'm not *bad* at it Dad," he'd said, as if Khang could ever doubt him, "it's that any argument I could make, they've already had it in their own head. They've already thought about what they would miss. They've already agonized about how it will make their friends and family feel. They already know whatever their religion says. They've weighed it all and still found it wanting. The pain they are in eclipses all that completely. The just want it to end. They just want to forget there ever was such pain, even if it means forgetting everything else too. Even if it means somebody else has to feel it instead. What am I supposed to say in the face of all that?" He leaned in very close, as if someone else was listening.

"Sometimes," Lee said in a low voice, "when I hear what they've been through, sometimes I don't want to talk them down. Sometimes I think it's better if they *do* jump. Sometimes I want to help, give them the final push they're trying to build up the courage for." He had let go of the beer bottle and covered his face with one hand, ashamed to cry in front of his father. The other hand lay on the table. Khang reached out and gave it a gentle squeeze before getting up to let his son cry in private.

He had even less to stop him than the people Lee tried to talk down. The world had nothing and no one that he wanted. He had no one to grieve for him. And whatever he had believed in before the Plague had been swept away in the violence he had, himself, been allowed to commit. He wandered to the edge of the tent. The trucks carrying corpses were gone, but the grass had not sprung back yet from where the people had lain in it. Empty graves. He should have stayed in his. He wandered out into the field. A nurse tried to stop him.

"I just need some air," Khang gasped.

The nurse nodded and let him go. He stumbled out into the field. The matted grass had dried in long tangles of gold. The sky was covered by low, greasy smoke, but the heat of the day wasn't diminished. It pressed in on his chest, as if the air were trying to wring a few more drops of moisture from his withered, driftwood body.

He ignored his discomfort and sat down where the grass met the road. His gaze followed the stem of the smoke, twisting and narrowing to a faraway bonfire where they were burning the corpses from the day before.

How he envied them! They never realized what they'd done. If only Lee had shot him that first day. Khang shook his head. No, he couldn't wish his guilt onto Lee. His son had been a good man. Khang had believed himself to be a good man too. It had been his one constant comfort in the worst parts of his life. No matter what went wrong, how poor he was, how badly people treated him, he knew he had remained a good man.

And now when he most needed to believe that he was good, when it would have been his greatest consolation, he couldn't. Regardless of what he did, or how much longer he had to live, he knew he'd never be able to convince himself he was a good person again.

"Mr. Yeo, the staff tell me you haven't eaten this morning."

Khang looked around, squinting at the bright shards of unclouded sky behind him. Dr. Taylor stood there, frowning down at him. Khang shrugged.

"I'm not hungry," he said.

"I assure you, your body needs food. Your lack of hunger is just a symptom of long term deprivation—"

"I'm not hungry. My body doesn't need food because I don't need it to keep going."

Dr. Taylor shook his head. "If you refuse to eat, I'll have to force the issue."

"I forgive you for bringing me back. There's no way you could understand—"

"You *forgive* me?" sputtered Dr. Taylor, "You should be *thanking* me and my staff and the City for expending precious resources on your behalf. You should be falling over yourself trying to repay a massive debt to humanity—"

Khang stood up. "I *forgive* you, Dr. Taylor." His voice was calm but firm. "And I forgive your staff and I forgive the City. You cannot possibly understand the misery you create every time the Cure works. I wish your soldiers had shot me instead. But if you force more medicine upon me, *knowing* my wishes, then *you*, Dr. Taylor, will be responsible for my life and the misery it causes. You won't ever again be able to tell the Cured that you didn't know that the Cure would bring so much heartbreak. I will haunt you for the remainder of our lives, until a portion of my guilt and grief and horror has passed on to you."

"You ungrateful—" Dr. Taylor stopped and took a deep breath. "Mr. Yeo," he began calmly, "We can no longer afford to be selfish. We're at the very edge of extinction. We need every member of humanity to contribute, to help rebuild. Don't you feel some sense of obligation to help us survive? Don't you feel even a little of what you owe to the people whose lives you stole? To your children's lost potential?"

Khang shook his head. "Don't speak to me of my debts. You have no idea of their enormity. They can never be repaid, never even be lessened in the slightest. This debt you *think* that I owe? It was not my choice. I gained *nothing* from the devastation that I've caused. I didn't ask to become ill and I didn't ask for you to cure me. There is only one service you can do for me that would make me grateful. One thing that would prove you are good because you choose to be and not just by luck." Khang's fists knotted by his sides and his chest ached as his flesh stretched over his heaving ribs. His pale rage and the smoke from the corpse fires made him seem half-wraith to Dr. Taylor. The psychologist shook it off as nonsense.

"I suppose you're going to tell me you want me to let you die," he snapped.

"No. I was going to ask you to *help* me die," said Khang. "I don't need your permission. Everything has a right to die, doctor."

"Mr. Yeo, you've made clear what you want, but a physician has to consider more than just a patient's wants. I have to consider what is best for you and what is best for the society you live in. I cannot believe you or any of the Cured are so irredeemable that the only improvement is death." He waved an arm and a pair of large male nurses emerged from the tent. Khang tried to bolt away, but he was weak and slow and they soon caught him. He struggled and shouted but the men seemed oblivious or simply used to it. They calmly strapped him onto a gurney and started a nutrient IV under Dr. Taylor's orders. Then they left him alone in a mostly deserted corner of the camp.

Khang waited until shift change. He told the night nurse he knew he'd been irrational before, that he was calmer, that he just wanted to use the restroom. By himself. Like a grown human being with some dignity. She pitied him and unstrapped the restraints. He tottered meekly to the bathroom, gently rolling the IV stand over the uneven dirt floor. As soon as the door closed behind him, Khang carefully pulled the plastic tube from the casing on the back of his hand. The bag dribbled fluid onto the floor. He yanked the other end of the tube from the mouth of the bag and cool liquid splattered over everything. Khang ignored it, wrapping the tube around his hand, pulling at it to see how far it would stretch. He was looking around for a high fixture when the nurses began knocking. The showerhead might work. But he was out of time. He wrapped the plastic tube around his bony waist and covered it with his shirt. The door opened with a jingle as the spare key unlocked it.

"I'm sorry," muttered Khang while holding his hands out to indicate the mess. "My line came out. I was trying to clean up. I don't know what happened."

The nurse didn't buy it, but she also didn't notice the missing tube. She had him strapped down again and a new IV bag soon hung over his shoulder dripping life back into his shriveled veins. This time, she gave him a sedative and then ignored him. He lay there, staring at the flapping canvas above him, wriggling his hands desperately trying to get loose. He almost laughed as a violent twist of his wrist tore the needle from the back of his hand. The sheet was soaked in a mix of warm blood and saline by the time anyone noticed. Khang had become lightheaded and hopeful that he'd be able to bleed out before they found him. But the wound was too small and Dr. Taylor made his rounds too soon.

"If you force me to put a line in your foot, it will be quite painful," he said as he bandaged Khang's hand.

"Let me go," begged Khang, "It can't really matter to you what one man does. Pretend I died before. Pretend the Cure didn't work. Just let me go."

"Don't you understand? There are people out there who *hate* the Cure. My own subordinates question me every day whether it would be best to keep you ill and institutionalize you so you couldn't harm anyone. Some have even suggested rounding you all up and euthanizing you. *All of you.* Every suicide makes those options seem less and less insane.

"But some of you want to live. Some of you fight to prove yourselves equal to the faith we placed in the Cure. And some of us have been through hell to give you that chance. To see loved ones return to us. I have to consider all of these things. I can't allow you to die."

They added more straps to stop him from wiggling free. The nurse leaned over to adjust the strap across Khang's head.

"I'm sorry," the nurse whispered, "But you'll be released much faster if you just play along. And who knows? Maybe the world isn't as bad as you expect. Maybe you'll change your mind. And if not— well, you'll be free then, gone from here. You can do what you want."

"How long?" asked Khang.

The nurse shrugged. "A few weeks if you stop pulling stunts like the last one." The nurse stood up and walked away.

A few weeks. When every moment the memory of his daughter's skin prickled on his tongue. And his son's cries rattled around inside Khang's chest. They wanted him to wait weeks. He was starting to remember others now, other terrified faces, other friends running as he chased them down. They advanced on him in anger or grief when he was awake or retreated as he dozed, but they were never fully gone.

The nurses wheeled him into group therapy sessions where he watched the other Cured try to remember. As if the memories were a rotten tooth and they couldn't help poking it to see how rotten. He watched as what they began to remember was worse than even their imaginations had suggested, watched as they crumbled and collapsed, inconsolable, one after another. He and Dr. Taylor both watched. One was like some malevolent spirit of Christmas past, silent and judging, the other an increasingly nervous Ebenezer trying to deny the agony all around him. Khang could see enough of what the others remembered to know that he didn't want to. Still, the faces leaked in uninvited. And in his lonely corner of the camp, he wept himself to sleep night after night.

The woman whose hair he had brushed visited him every morning. Every morning he begged her to untie him. Every morning she cried and refused.

Until at last, she showed up beside his bed one night, her face a mirror of his misery. She unstrapped him without speaking and he knew she'd remembered something awful that day.

"Thank you," Khang whispered.

"Hurry," was all she said.

He pulled the plastic tube from his new IV and balled it up in his hand. He crept to the edge of the tent and looked out. A tree hovered over the long grass, its lower branches thick with leaves. He glanced around, but only the woman was watching. He sprinted to the tree and scrambled up it, the rough bark bruising him as he struggled out onto a heavy branch. He carefully unwound the long plastic tube he'd hidden under his shirt days before. It left a greasy red mark on his stomach. Knotting the two tubes together, he tied one end around the branch. The other he looped around his neck. He looked back at the tent and the woman stood in the doorway, watching him. He raised a hand in thanks. Then he jumped.

The branch bounced, the tube caught him up short but then stretched and slipped. He didn't notice. The world grew gray, then black. He let himself drain away into the dark. But the plastic tube gave out and snapped. He thudded to the ground. He was still coughing when the staff found him.

He was back on the gurney. No one visited him now. He didn't try to reason or beg any more. Just counted the hours down. The camp slowly emptied, became silent, as more and more of the Cured found relatives or were taken to the City. It was Dr. Rider who released him in the end. He let her tell him what to expect in the City, automatically lied when she went through her discharge questions, even accepted the small backpack of spare clothes she handed him, gently tucking Jia's button into a zippered pocket of the bag.

The soldiers were packing up the camp, moving it farther out, getting ready to devastate a whole new group of Infected by waking them up. Khang couldn't let it happen. He didn't care about the world. Didn't want to wake up inside it ever again. But the idea that there were hundreds like him, that Dr. Taylor would continue to make more people like him, disturbed Khang. It was as if those people would be *him*, that he'd be reincarnated every time. Never resting. Never released.

He followed the dull green trucks that headed farther and farther from the City. The trucks moved slowly, lumbering down the shattered tar of long abandoned roads. Khang was slower. He didn't find Dr. Taylor's new tent until evening. It faced the dusty track, its flaps gaping open. Dr. Taylor wasn't in it. He was setting up for the next batch of Infected.

Khang sat on his knees in front of the tent and waited. When Dr. Taylor saw him, he ordered the soldiers to remove him.

"I'm not your patient anymore," said Khang.

The doctor scowled, but the soldiers let Khang be. Dr. Taylor closed the tent flaps so he could no longer see the man dying outside. Khang just waited. Trucks full of soldiers armed with dart guns drove around him. Khang sat. A thunderstorm drenched him, but he didn't move.

In the morning, Dr. Taylor emerged from his tent and saw Khang still there, staring at him. He shook his head and walked away. Khang waited. The sun blazed on his head and shoulders. He was dizzy with thirst and heat. His lips cracked and his skin began to rise and bubble. Dr. Taylor came back and offered him a glass of cool water.

Khang gave him a pitying smile and shook his head. Dr. Taylor shrugged and placed it on the grass beside Khang's knee. The sun sank at last and the trucks returned, their rumble tipping the glass of water into the ground around Khang. He didn't move.

The camp grew loud and bright with electric light as the sleeping Infected were carried in to the tents, Cure darts still poking out of them. The doctors and nurses scuttled from patient to patient trying to stabilize those that needed it or putting in IV lines to keep them hydrated and fed while the Infected slept the disease away. The night chilled Khang's burned skin. He dozed anyway. It was early morning when he woke, still kneeling. His legs, which had pierced his calm with cramps the day before, were now completely numb. As if his death were creeping, toe upwards, to devour him. He smiled at the thought.

By the time the sun had fully risen and Dr. Taylor emerged from his tent, Khang had lost the feeling in his arms as well. His chest and throat still blazed with thirst. Again, Dr. Taylor set a full glass of water at Khang's side without speaking. Again, Khang ignored it. Dr. Taylor made his rounds, but the day was slow. All of the Infected still slept. The soldiers removed those who hadn't lasted through the night. Again the trucks rolled past Khang, this time filled with bodies, and again, he didn't turn to look.

Dr. Taylor returned to his tent. He stopped to stand over Khang for a moment. "What do you want?" he asked at last.

"You owe me my death. I'm waiting for you to give it to me," said Khang.

"I'm not going to kill you. I've fought to keep you alive and to restore your humanity. You can keep waiting, but my mind will not change."

Khang would have shrugged, but he could no longer move below his neck. "If you will not provide my death, the world surely will. I will be here to meet it when it comes."

Dr. Taylor was furious but said nothing, flinging himself into the shady interior of the tent instead. Khang's skin began to flake away where it had burned. His throat felt like sandpaper and his eyes stung and blurred. Gradually, as the sun began to set and the shade inside the tent met the evening gloom, Khang could see Dr. Taylor sitting still in his camp chair. He was watching Khang, maybe he had been all day. The two men stared at each other until the sun was gone.

"We were only trying to help," cried Dr. Taylor.

"There is no help for what I've done. There is no return. No matter what I do, it would never be enough. Especially not as a slave to your City."

"I told you, we don't enslave people."

"You do. You may not chain us or whip us, you do it with guilt and with a crippling sense of unworthiness and gratitude. How could the Cured ever be equal to others in your City? You go to bed every night satisfied, smug, convinced that you are good. That you are *better*. Yet every day you prolong the misery of people who were also good, once. As good as you. Better maybe. And you expect them to grovel before you, to thank you for making them finally realize what suffering they've caused and what evils they are truly capable of. Yet what separates us? You had the good fortune not to fall ill, that is all. It could have been you, sitting here in my place.

"Who could go on after all this? Who could even pretend to be normal? The world is scarred. No one can be happy in it, except those who enjoy making others suffer. The only people who will ever be glad to wake up and remember are the ones who were murderous animals before the Infection," Khang croaked.

Dr. Taylor scrubbed his cheeks with his hands. "I can't believe that. I can't believe that all these people died for no purpose, that there's no reason for their deaths."

Khang laughed. It was a dusty, toneless gasp. "You want to justify all this pain, all the slaughter of the past two years? *You* are the one who is mad. There is no purpose. No justice to this. No, what you really want to know, Dr. Taylor, is why you're still alive. How can you be *good* and still survive this when so many better people haven't. What is *your* point? What is *your* reason? That's why you can't let us go." Khang fell silent. Dr. Taylor watched him.

The moon rose behind Khang, his shadow stretching between them.

"I forgive you," he said out of the dark. He coughed and was quiet again.

Dr. Taylor watched until the trucks came back. The headlights of the final truck stopped on Khang's form. The truck door opened and then closed with a slam. A soldier walked up to Khang and prodded him with a booted foot. Khang didn't move. Dr. Taylor stood up, startling the soldier.

"Sorry Doc, didn't see you there. This one going to the pyre too?"

Dr. Taylor nodded. "Yeah, the Cure didn't work on him."

The soldier grabbed Khang's cold hand and began yanking him toward the back of the truck. Khang's body thumped sideways onto the ground. It made a soft hiss as it slid through the long grass. Dr. Taylor turned away. He found the box of bullets and his gun in the top drawer of his camp desk without turning on the light. He loaded it in the dark and stuffed the box of bullets into his lab coat pocket. The gun he hid in his waistband under his shirt.

"The Cure didn't work on him," he muttered to himself, "Doesn't work on any of them. It doesn't work."

He walked to the patient tent and dismissed the night nurses. He watched the dozens of sleeping people, already hearing the wails of despair they'd make when they woke in a few hours. That they'd be making for the rest of their lives.

"The only people who will ever be glad to wake up and remember are the ones who were murderous animals before the Infection," Khang had said. Dr. Taylor pulled out the gun.

"Everything has the right to die," he told himself.

A Word from Deirdre Gould

For me, the most terrifying part of the zombie story is the "turn." Mostly because it always makes me wonder if the person that was is still in there somewhere. The logical side of me (if such a thing as logic can apply to zombie lore) says, yes, there must be something of the person left, because they are driven to violence (or to seek brains or flesh or whatever the act may be). The drive must come from some sort of will, even if it's partially instinctual. And the idea that a person can somehow be transformed by a disease into something either so insane or so evil that they could harm even those closest to them, is horrifying. But biology is showing more and more how small changes in our brain chemistry and even our body's bacteriological content can cause wild swings in emotion, cognition and behavior. *Staphylococcus Pneumoniae*, the bacteria that the plague in Khang Yeo's world is a variant of, can even trigger an autoimmune response in children that presents as a series of behaviors and tics not dissimilar to classic "zombie" traits. The Plague, of course, causes highly exaggerated extremes of these behaviors.

But the idea of becoming so insane (and my heart says it's insanity, not evil) isn't as bad as realizing what has happened to you. If you are a survival story nut, like I am, you tend to ask yourself what you would be capable of doing in extreme situations. But what we tend not to ask ourselves is what happens when the extreme situation is over? What happens when survivors of truly dire circumstances return to normal civilization? What happens when you know for sure what you are capable of doing to another human being? Unlike shipwrecked sailors trying to cling to life or soldiers fighting in a desperate struggle to return home, Khang Yeo and the Infected don't have the comfort of excusing their actions in the name of survival. Is waking up to face your own deeds a fate worse than death?

That's not to say that I think Dr. Taylor is evil or bad-hearted. Or that the Infected shouldn't have been Cured. It's a natural impulse, to restore those who are ill to health, or those who have had a mental break to their old selves. He, along with the other Immunes in his world, also has to live with the consequences of the Plague. No doubt he and the others killed Infected to remain alive. No doubt he has his own reservations about whether the Cure is compassionate or just necessary. His expectations of the Cured going on to lead normal, productive lives is also not evil, it's just short sighted. Is he good by "default"? Is Khang Yeo evil because of his actions and despite his intentions?

If you'd like to read more about Khang Yeo's world (and a little bit more about Dr. Taylor) you can grab the first in the series, *After the Cure*, from my Amazon page: http://www.amazon.com/Deirdre-Gould/e/B00BSUFIIA

If you'd like to chat about Khang Yeo or Dr. Taylor or zombies, the apocalypse or happier things, catch me on Facebook or email me dk.gould@live.com I love meeting new people!

A Note to Readers

Thank you so much for reading *The Z Chronicles*. If you enjoyed these stories, please keep an eye out for other titles in *The Future Chronicles* collection, a series of short story anthologies in speculative fiction. Currently available titles in the *Chronicles* include:

The Z Chronicles
The Dragon Chronicles
The A.I. Chronicles
The Alien Chronicles
The Telepath Chronicles
The Robot Chronicles

Available later this year will be *The Immortality Chronicles*, *The Time Travel Chronicles,* and *The Galactic Chronicles*.

And, before you go, we'd like to ask you a very small favor, if you please: *Would you write a short review at the site where you purchased this book?*

Reviews are make-or-break for authors. A book with no reviews is, simply put, a book with no future sales. This is because a review is more than just a message to other potential buyers: it's also a key factor driving the book's visibility in the first place.

More reviews (and more positive reviews) make a book more likely to be featured in bookseller lists (such as Amazon's *also-viewed* and *also-bought* lists) and more likely to be featured in bookseller promotions. Reviews don't need to be long or eloquent; a single sentence is all it takes. In today's publishing world, the success (or failure) of a book is truly in the reader's hands.

So please, write a review.

Then tell a friend. Share a link to us on Facebook, or maybe even a Tweet—link to our books at *http://smarturl.it/future-chronicles*.You'd be doing us a great service.

Thank you.

Samuel Peralta
www.amazon.com/author/samuelperalta

Subscribe to *The Future Chronicles* newsletter for news of upcoming titles, and to be eligible for draws for paperbacks, e-books and more – *http://smarturl.it/chronicles-news*